A Past With No Future

Jonathan van Bilsen

Amr entered the temple through a small opening and stood surrounded by total darkness in what he believed to be a corridor. He stumbled his way into a larger room and saw a dim light coming from an opening at the far end. He sensed he had been walking downward and was probably underground by now. The light was coming from a torch in a connecting hallway leading into a second chamber. He carefully stepped in, allowing his gun to lead the way, and was relieved when he saw no signs of life. Again lit torches were suspended against the walls. Their flickering flames danced wildly, creating shadowy movements on the colourful wall paintings inside the room. He followed another hallway, leading to a third chamber which was smaller inside than the first two, and again found it to be empty. As he entered the passageway leading further underground, he began to hear faint voices. He crept slowly, forward his gun poised as he tried to make sense of the sounds that became more aural with every step.

"Enigmatic men, a compelling plot and exotic locales. What more could you ask for?"

"A tightly plotted espionage adventure in the tradition of Tom Clancy and Clive Cussler with danger in every shadow."

A Past With No Future

Canadian Cataloguing in Publication Program
van Bilsen, Jonathan, 1950-
        A Past With No Future

ISBN - 0-9680432-0-8

        1. Title.

PS8593.A53834P38 1996   C813'.54   C96-900062-6
PR9199.3.V354P38 1996

All rights reserved under International Copyright
Conventions. Published in Canada by
Shady Vale Publishing
527 Brunswick Avenue
Toronto, Ontario M5R 2Z6
(416) 709-1907

Mass Market:
First Edition: February 1996

Printed and bound in Canada

For Cookie and Junior

PROLOGUE

SUNDAY, May 2, 1982 - SOUTH ATLANTIC: The shivering, white-capped waves of the gelid, southern waters, spilled violently across the shiny decks of the Argentine cruiser General Belgrano. Dancing wildly, they caused the massive hull to sway back and forth in the choppy, uncontrollable seas.

On board the battle-ready ship, men were busily scurrying about, skilfully engaged in their daily activities as the massive, floating war vessel continued to be caressed by the icy waters. The dauntless garrison pursued their tasks with great determination as they briskly cleaned the salt-stained gun ports and carefully counted the explosive ammunition. They rearranged depth charges with the care and caution a mother would give to an ailing child. Most of the water-drenched, uniformed soldiers were merely boys, barely old enough to be released from the grasp of their mother's security. Although trained for battle on the play-field of an Argentine military compound, none had come close to facing the reality of the bloody battles that now lay before them. The wind howled fiercely throughout the ship's armour-plated cavities, causing the company to move swiftly as the polar air about them created a cold and dank atmosphere.

The lingering battle with Britain was far from over. There were silent, increasing fears the scattered fighting would unfold into an all out war. Argentina, the proud and noble land she was, refused to surrender. Britain, in her self-appointed role as master of the world's oceans, continually warned of an expansive increase in military pressure if Argentina refused to capitulate her armies in the Falklands.

The faithful officers of the mighty Belgrano scoffed at the self-righteous arrogance of their enemies. They watched proudly as their battleship summoned the terror from the sea about them and faced it with conquering fervour. They knew that their stalwart battleship was virtually indestructible. The fourteen ton cruiser was the second largest ship in the entire Argentine fleet.

Argentina's President, Leopoldo Galtieri, had assured his people earlier that day, in soothing comfort as only a leader of men could have done, that under no circumstances would their homeland raise a white flag in defeat. Like a passive flock mindlessly following its guardian shepherd, the people believed him.

The cold wind fulminated fiercely across the iron deck of the mighty Belgrano. Her sailors, a sublime breed, loved their ship as well as their country. Each of them would readily relinquish his life to keep enemies from capturing either.

With winter rapidly approaching the region, the South Atlantic was turning into a vicious, uncaring predator of anyone who dared wander within its grasp. Argentina knew she would be the benefactor of the harsh, frigid months. Already the Spanish speaking nation had over ten thousand troops in place on the Falkland Islands. The

British would encounter a challenge even the all-powerful English navy would find devastating.

The Captain of the General Belgrano stood exalted on the bridge. He received a message from his radio operator.

"We are very near the British blockade, sir."

The message had not yet been completed when another, a much more excited voice, echoed hurriedly from the little, round speaker in the nerve centre of the floating metropolis. The young radio operator's voice screamed a warning from somewhere deep within the confines of the floating tomb. It was a shearing, piercing sound shrieking loudly above the continual clashing of the dancing waves against the steel frame of the battleship. Suddenly, the ear shattering screech reverberated from the speaker, throughout the entire length of the fighting ship.

"British submarine within striking range!"

The warning message came too late. With a sudden gust of fury, a thundering torpedo ripped savagely through the hull of the massive, unsinkable Argentine battleship. The crippling blast was immediately followed by a second destructive projectile.

Fireballs were vaulting wildly from within the bowels of the solid battle destroyer. Flames were dancing upward, spreading recklessly as new, flammable objects came within their grasp. Thick, black clouds billowed in all directions as the icy wind carried the choking smoke skyward.

Every member of the thousand man crew was running heedlessly in all directions. Those more daring plummeted over the sides of the ship, only to be swallowed up by the unforgiving Atlantic waters. Others perished as the fiery flames from fierce explosions raced through countless areas of the once invulnerable giant of the Argentine navy.

SUNDAY, MAY 2, 1982, - LIMA, PERU: The clean, white

walls of the great meeting hall were lined with people supporting cameras, both still and video. Men and women of varying nationalities securely held microphones as they waited patiently, facing the large, wood-grained podium with the presidential seal affixed to its exterior. Several rows of chairs had been positioned to accommodate the multitude of reporters assembled in the great hall of the South American Presidential Palace. Thin-necked microphones dangled from the lead crystal chandeliers, suspended overhead by large, brass chains. The press conference was about to commence. Silence was requested by the uniformed officer at the front of the grand, brightly-lit conference room. The sixty or so newspaper and other reporters began to take their places. They had gathered for an important message from Fernando Belaundo Terry, the President of Peru.

The distinguished leader of the small yet respected South American neighbour of Argentina entered the press gallery with flair and determination. His black, double-breasted suit, offset by a thin, gray pinstripe, had been deftly tailored and moulded his body perfectly. A red-with-gray silk tie was flawlessly positioned against a crisp, white, well-starched shirt. A small, rose coloured carnation had been pinned to the lapel of his jacket, resulting in a striking figure of authority. All attending fell silent as he spoke of peace and an end to hostilities in the neighbouring country.

The frightful, shocking events of the past four days would be no more. He smiled as he spoke, having been well-trained in the art of public addressing. The words flowed freely and with conviction. The masses in the great hall were quiet, as the reputable leader of the stable country spoke. Negotiations were under way to ensure that peace was on the horizon. He calmly reassured all present of his confidence that Peru's neighbour, Argentina, and her recent temporary enemy, Britain, would come to mutually agreeable terms very shortly.

The correspondents in the huge, echo-filled chamber eagerly noted the important words of the famed, South American leader. They had not yet heard the news about Britain's attack on the General Belgrano.

WEDNESDAY, MAY 5, 1982 - LONDON, ENGLAND: Eric Coleman sat regally behind his bulky, walnut desk. The floor of his beautifully decorated office was covered with a velvet green carpet. Centred against one wall stood a meticulously-crafted, wooden bureau. Colourful, leather-bound editions of English literature filled its many shelves. The beige walls surrounding the desk were decorated with delicate paintings of Devonshire villages. Beyond the glass panes of the oak-framed windows, rain was heavily pouring from a dark, cloudy sky. The continuously inclement weather brought a gloomy atmosphere to the interior of the tastefully decorated office.

The authoritarian figure behind the desk was carefully opening his mail, probing each envelope with a gold-stemmed letter opener, using precision a surgeon would show during the most delicate of operations.

Eric Coleman had been responsible for many of his nation's strategies. The passing of time had favoured his appearance. Although he was in his early sixties, he maintained a distinguished image. His thick, silver gray hair slightly covered his ears and complimented a neatly trimmed moustache, giving a dash of elegance to his already imposing guise. The navy-blue suit he wore had been extremely well tailored and was expertly pressed. As he continued to pierce each envelope, he was mentally composing a memo to the spokesman of the Ministry. Suddenly a buzzing sound filled the quiet ambience of the stately office. Eric Coleman frowned and with agitation pressed the control on the small, wood-grained intercom unit, dwarfed on a corner of the impressive desk.

"What is it?" he snapped angrily, annoyed by the

interruption. It seemed his tolerance threshold was slowly decreasing with the continuous increase in pressure from his demanding position within the ministry. He became more agitated by the constant interruptions in his daily routine as his stress level increased.

"Mr. Olson is here to see you." His secretary spoke timidly, constantly aware of the intimidation reflected by her director. Even with the distance of separate offices between them, a simple change in his voice inflection caused her grave discomfort.

He softened his tone, realizing his appointment had arrived. He was anxious to meet with William Olson. The two men had worked together for many years and Olson was one of the few individuals Coleman respected. He was not a squeamish little follower; a quality so many members of his staff seemed to display in his presence. "Send him in please."

A moment later the solid-wood door opened and a short, bald, dignified gentleman gracefully entered the over-bearing office. He carried himself with propriety, despite his plump stature. Coleman smiled as he stood and walked around the desk to appreciatively greet his visitor.

"William, how good of you to come."

"I couldn't refuse your request. You sounded rather distressed."

"I am," Coleman said, returning to his chair. "Please, have a seat." He pointed to one of the two large wing chairs directly before his desk. "Would you care for some tea?"

"Yes, that would be lovely," Olson's feet barely touched the floor as he settled into the soft, oversized chair.

Coleman rang his secretary and asked her to bring them tea and biscuits.

"So what's troubling you?" Olson asked inquisitively.

"It's this damn thing with Argentina. I honestly think we've gotten ourselves into something that's running out of control." He stroked the pointed tips of his silver-haired moustache as he spoke.

"What do you mean? Surely you don't think that we are going to lose the conflict, do you?"

"No, no, of course not," Coleman quickly responded. "I know we'll win. It's just that we never anticipated such a challenge. We are, after all, talking of nothing more than a collection of rocks thousands of miles away from any living thing. Why in God's name would Argentina wish to retain them?"

"Why would we?" Olson interjected softly with diplomatic flair.

Eric Coleman did not answer. His silent gaze was fixed on his short, overweight ally, dwarfed by the massive chair across from the desk. He raised one eyebrow and slowly allowed his stern face to break into a smile.

"William," he began, "I must remind you that those islands are a part of our Commonwealth. We will not allow anyone to mock the British Empire."

"But we already have more troops there than inhabitants." William Olson paused before he continued. "Pride certainly motivates men in strange directions."

Both men smiled. Eric Coleman was the first to continue speaking. "The problem we're faced with is turning into a nightmare. It looks as if we could be engaged in this battle for quite some time. As you know, we've sunk one of their largest ships, the Belgrano."

"She was nearing the blockade," Olson said justifiably.

"Nevertheless she's been sunk. God knows how many of their men have been killed."

"Alright," Olson said. He shifted his weight in the chair, striving to find a more dignified position. "I know you didn't call me in here just to tell me that we're in a hopeless situation."

Coleman leaned forward in his brown, antique leather

chair. "What I need from you William, is a plan." He stood up slowly and paced back and forth before the large, velvety draped window behind his desk. "I am fully aware that you have a brilliant mind, especially when it comes to scheming."

Olson tugged on his waistcoat which was slowly creeping up as the short man sank deeper into the chair. His thoughts were interrupted by a knock on the door.

"Come in," Coleman said.

His secretary slowly entered the executive office, carefully maneuvering her body through the opening, allowing the silver platter and service to move freely without interference from the heavy, wooden door. The woman, in her fifties, was evidently intimidated by the two senior advisors. Her slight obesity was accentuated by her burgundy dress with blue, white and black flowers printed on it. Her corpulence caused her forehead to perspire as she walked.

"How would you like your tea, sir?" she asked of William Olson obeying the politics of respect reserved for individuals of high-ranking stature.

"Just milk please," he replied smilingly. He had sensed the woman's uneasiness and tried to speak as delicately as the situation would allow.

She prepared Coleman's tea in the usual fashion and placed the tray on the small, leather inlaid table in the corner of the room. Upon completion she smiled courteously at the visitor and quickly departed.

Coleman had seated himself in the matching wing chair beside Olson. He leaned forward and took a sip from his steaming cup of tea.

"I want you to come up with something that will give us an edge." He took a noisy quaff from the fine china cup. "Something that will shatter Argentinian morale."

"It's Argentine," Olson interjected casually.

"What?" Coleman looked up at his guest. "What did

you say?"

"The expression is Argentine, not Argentinian."

"Well whatever the hell it is, I want you to figure out a way of demoralizing it."

William Olson listened carefully to the senior advisor. He slowly raised his fingers, allowing their tips to come in contact with each other.

"I see," he finally said. "How much time do I have?"

"Unfortunately not very much. I would like you to put a plan together as quickly as possible."

"Are there any restrictions?"

"Only one." Coleman fixed his gaze directly at Olson's face. "None of this must ever be traced back to us or to any British Agency."

Olson nodded. He fully understood the request being made of him. "Have you any ideas of your own?" he asked.

"Yes, as a matter of fact I have several areas you may wish to pursue." The two men continued their conversation as William Olson made notes on a small sheet of white, linen paper removed from a nearby corner of the walnut desk.

TUESDAY, MAY 4, 1982 - SOUTH ATLANTIC: The Exocet missile skimmed smoothly above the choppy, white-capped water. Its guidance system was securely fixed on a target fifteen miles away. Directly before it, another air to surface missile was zeroing in on the same target.

"Good God!" a young British sailor excitedly exclaimed. "Look!" His hand shot outward trembling as he pointed toward a small, fiery bolt in the distant sky. "It's a missile, and it's heading directly for us!"

His companion, who was dressed in similar combat gear, focused his eyes on the giant black bullet racing with determination across the sky.

Captain James Salt, Commander of the Sheffield, gave the order to ready all men for battle stations. He had taken control of the destroyer only four months earlier. At that time the Sheffield was on a peaceful mission cruising the Atlantic. Now, under orders, he had directed her course, along with other British vessels in the area, to the Falklands.

A piercing whistle sounded as the French designed missile shot toward the Sheffield. The two sailors stood beside their guns. They were ready for action.

"It missed!" one of them yelled excitedly. "It's missed us!"

The missile darted with prodigious speed, barely passing the bow of the giant British war ship.

"Look, there's another one!" the second sailor yelled.

"Where in God's name are they coming from?"

His comrade did not reply. Instead, he kept his eyes trained on the second rapidly approaching projectile. This time the Sheffield was not so fortunate. The flying bomb crashed fiercely into its target. The control room in the centre of the ship was ablaze and lit up the surrounding area. Most of the combat-ready sailors rushed away from the fiery vicinity.

A violent explosion, followed directly by a second, shrilled the cold, wintry air. The Sheffield was permanently crippled. Several of the officers paced nervously back and forth on the bridge. They looked out the windows at the mounting chaos around them, constantly returning their gaze to their captain awaiting direction.

"Damage report!" Salt yelled angrily.

A nearby sailor rushed to him carrying a sheet of hurriedly scribbled figures. Salt snatched the paper from the young recruit's hand and read it quickly. He paused, allowing the paper to fall gently from his hand. He slowly raised his head and looked at his faithful officers gathered in a small circle about him.

"Tell the radio room to relay the appropriate messages." He swallowed slowly, fighting the tears from reaching his eyes.

"Gentlemen," he said softly. "The Sheffield is going down." He paused a moment. "Give the order to abandon ship."

WEDNESDAY, MAY 5, 1982 - LONDON, ENGLAND: Again the two senior officials of the British government were intruded upon. Again the unwanted interruption came from a voice sounding from the small wood-grained intercom on Coleman's desk.

"What is it?" he barked harshly as he leaned forward touching the small, metal control button.

"Sorry to interrupt you sir, but I have an urgent message."

"Alright, come in." Coleman shook his head in annoyance. The calmness he had initially displayed was being engulfed by his obvious underlying concern for the present situation.

Olson, on the other hand, had shown absolutely no emotion. He had remained stationary throughout the entire meeting, maintaining a calm exterior image. He was no stranger to stress. He had learned to keep its signs well hidden.

Once again Coleman's secretary entered. She handed her superior a letter-size, white envelope. Coleman saw fear and pain deep within her eyes. He stood up but waited for her to leave before reading the unsealed correspondence.

"Thank you Mrs. Speers," he said in a softer tone, aware of his dutiful aide's nervousness.

She left the office, closing the door securely behind her. Coleman stood erect and removed a small slip of beige stationary from the envelope, reading its contents. Slowly, as his mind grasped the meaning of each word, his mouth fell open.

"What is it?" Olson asked, still not displaying any emotion but noting that an alarming countenance had overcome his director's face.

"Good God!" Coleman exclaimed. "They've sunk the Sheffield."

For the first time since he had entered the office, William Olson's expression was that of concern. "My God," he said, "She's only seven years old."

Feeling the shock work its way through his emotional system, William Olson placed the events in priority. He forced their immediate plans to the foreground of his mind and subdued all thoughts relative to the sinking of the Sheffield.

Eric Coleman slowly raised his saddened face and looked at the short, stubby man seated beside him. Tears began to form in the corners of his eyes.

"Are there any survivors?"

"I don't know," Coleman replied slowly, shocked by the news he had just read. "John Nott will shortly be issuing a statement at the ministry office."

Olson glanced at his watch. "Let's quickly go over some of those ideas you had in mind for this plan I'm to develop." He reached for several more sheets of paper. "If anything this will lend even more urgency to the concept."

"Good idea," Coleman acknowledged, gathering his composure. "In a few minutes this place will resemble a mad house."

William Olson listened painstakingly to all that Eric Coleman had to offer. He made careful notes, detailing all relevant information, and jotted the last few words of Coleman's idea onto the white sheet of paper in his hand.

Slowly he leaned back in his chair and pondered his notes. "That certainly is a task."

"Nothing you can't handle, I'm sure." Coleman guided his fingers over each side of his eloquent moustache. "I know you'll do a superb job."

Olson smiled. "Thanks for the vote of confidence."

The two men stood up and shook hands. William

Olson walked toward the door.

"Thank you for considering me in this matter," he said. The senior official of the British Ministry of Defence departed.

1   CORDOBA

Lorne McPherson sat solemnly on a rugged rock over looking the clear, aqua-coloured ocean. It resembled a picture-perfect view taken by a studio photographer for use in a travel brochure. He was casually tossing stones into the water, watching the spherical wave patterns slowly drift away from their source, dancing freely until suddenly swallowed by the ocean which had created them. He loved the serenity of the open sea with its securing sense of peace, something he desperately longed for in these troubled times. He mentally repeated the chaotic events of the past weeks and slowly forced his mind to wander beyond the turmoil back to happier, simpler times. It was hard to imagine that only months before, everything had been perfect. Times when life had been an enjoyable escapade, a near fantasy. He had taken those moments for granted, not being attentive to the security and peace he had sublimely enjoyed. He pondered pleasurable thoughts, savouring the inner warmth they brought him; but his reflections were intruded upon by the events forever chiselled in his memory that day in May.

He recalled sitting in the kitchen of their temporary, South American home.

"What time do you think you'll be home tonight?" Rhonda McPherson asked of her husband. She poured a small amount of milk from the yellow, waxed container over his imported corn flakes. She knew he preferred them crisp instead of soggy. He smiled at her, displaying a loving affection for his wife of almost thirty years.

"I'm not sure, but it shouldn't be too late. I've got to go over some last minute inspections today. We'll be starting the new reactor soon."

"Don't forget, the Callahans are coming over for dinner."

It was obvious by the expression on his face that the scientist had forgotten the social commitment arranged by his wife.

"Do they have to come over?" he asked, frowning as he spoke. His wife mimicked his expression as she poured steaming, hot coffee into his stoneware mug. He watched the feathery, gray steam gently fade away as it rose slowly from the strong, brown coffee.

"You know better than to ask that, we hardly ever see them as it is." He did not enjoy entertaining at the best of times. Sitting around engaged in idle conversation with people was not a pleasurable event. Instead it was a waste of a good evening, an evening he would rather spend with his family or perhaps swallowed up in the thrilling adventures of an enjoyable novel. He worked long, stress-filled hours and relaxation time was precious. When it came down to reality, he disliked the Callahans but was sensitive to his wife's need for a social outlet. He loved his wife enough to succumb silently to her wishes.

Lorne dropped the subject. "Where are Kristy and Jimmy this morning?"

"James," as Rhonda preferred to call her twelve year

old son, "has left for school. Mrs. Rodrigues drove them in today." She noticed the puzzled look on her husband's face as he listened attentively to her conversation. "That's the mother of a little boy in James' class. Their family is transferring to California so they've enrolled their son in an English speaking school. Kristy should be down in a minute."

Doctor Lorne McPherson returned his gaze to the morning newspaper. His thick white hair was short and neatly combed. The deep lines on his face added a few years to his appearance. He was in his early fifties and sometimes felt it. A neat and tidy individual. Although very few of his colleagues in the hot, South American country ever wore neckties, Lorne McPherson made a point of doing so every working day. Today his brown knitted tie blended perfectly with his beige and brown, short-sleeve shirt.

"This war in the Falklands is really brewing," McPherson said as he read the headline story of the English newspaper.

His wife sat opposite him and listened to his words. She poured a cup of strong, dark Colombian coffee for herself, declining sugar and cream, vowing to trim several excess pounds from her waistline. Ever since her fiftieth birthday last year it had been extremely difficult to keep her body in shape, enjoying food as much as she did. Her personal limit however, had been exceeded and the time to act had arrived. Her short height accentuated the weight problem, making her appear heavier. She had allowed her brown, curly hair to be trimmed close to her scalp, thinking it would make her look slender.

The kitchen of the McPherson's South American house was brightly decorated. The decor was white with soft, yellow accents and the tropical sunshine added gaiety to the already pleasant atmosphere.

"Good morning, people," Kristy McPherson's cheery voice echoed as she entered the kitchen. She walked to her father and gently placed a tender kiss on his freshly shaven cheek. "Hmmm, you smell good."

"And you look gorgeous."

After kissing her mother, she took her seat around the glass topped breakfast table and poured a generous portion of breakfast cereal into her bowl, adding just the proper amount of milk to keep it crisp and palatable. Her long silky hair, though carefully brushed, loosely framed her face. The light perm gave it a coarser texture, allowing it to curl sweepingly over her shoulders. Its light brown colour had been slightly frosted to highlight the blonde strands. Her facial skin had been expertly covered with a fine layer of tan make-up, enhancing her already well-sunned complexion. Her strong cheekbones made her eyes appear narrow; they were lined with a pencil-thin stripe of navy-blue, giving her an alluring, almost mysterious appearance. Her lips had been brushed with effulgent, red, lip balm, creating a tantalizing appearance that resembled a wild bush of fresh strawberries sprinkled with a midsummer dew. The colour in her cheeks had been artificially applied, but to the untrained eye, glistened against the tanned background of her soft, wrinkle-free skin.

Her slim, yet shapely figure allowed her to wear the most fashionable clothes. The aqua coloured, cotton dress she had chosen today balanced her desirable attractiveness.

"What are your plans today?" her mother asked.

"I have some executives from a tour group coming into the travel agency today. They're making final arrangements for a large trip to Rio."

Kristy had been with a well known travel agency most of her two years in Cordoba and enjoyed her career very much. It gave her a great opportunity to utilize her outgoing personality, constantly making contact with people from different walks of life.

Lorne McPherson lifted the napkin from his lap and, after wiping his mouth, folded his newspaper and stood up. "Well it's that time again." He leaned over, gently kissed the two women in his life, and picked up his briefcase.

The hot morning sun beamed its rays onto the scientist's face. He walked briskly along the tree lined, broken, sidewalk of the quiet residential street. He halted at an intersection which linked the peaceful suburbia with the bustling downtown sector.

He saw the familiar red and white colours of the public transit bus heading toward the small cluster of people slightly ahead of him. He tried to judge the distance between the bus, himself and the bus stop and decided that he would have to quicken his pace if he was going to make it in time. He could feel perspiration moistening his shirt as he hurriedly rushed ahead. His briefcase added uncomfortable weight and became heavier with each hastened step.

He was the last one on board but managed to find an available seat. He sighed as he allowed his strained body to fall into the torn, leather simulated seat. He had been in Cordoba for just over three years. His wife and children had joined him near the end of the first year. Although he thoroughly enjoyed the South American culture, he was slowly beginning to tire of the constant heat and humidity and was pleased that his assignment was almost completed.

The Argentine Nuclear Development Corporation was a major source of employment for people in Cordoba. The Canadians had been a terrific help to the success and implementation of the nuclear reactors. Canada was known worldwide for its development of the Candu Nuclear Reactor and Argentina was one of its largest clients.

The constant bureaucratic differences between the Canadian government and that of Argentina had greatly hampered a speedy installation of the reactors and was now behind schedule. Lorne McPherson's training as a nuclear physicist had been a definite asset to the entire operation, giving a tremendous amount of credibility to Canadian business. Assuming the final checklist proved acceptable, the installation of uranium for the first reactor would be no more than two weeks away. Start-up would commence three to four weeks later, which meant he and his family could be back in Vancouver by the end of June.

The bus came to an abrupt halt directly before the entrance to the small office building at the main gate to the nuclear power facility. His body had fully recovered from the strenuous exercise incurred during his race to the bus stop. He was thankful that he had always kept a thin, muscular body. He believed it had helped him to maintain a healthy lifestyle. An avid believer in daily exercise, he had joined a racquet club shortly after his arrival in Argentina.

The bus stopped long enough for McPherson to disembark. Several white collar and construction personnel employed by the facility also jumped from the bus and raced up the twenty-or-so steps to the entrance of the building.

McPherson entered a small office on the third floor. He was greeted by a young, dark skinned girl with long, straight, black hair. She was of Spanish origin with a trace of African ancestry.

"Hello Doctor McPherson," she said. Her association with Lorne McPherson had given her an excellent opportunity to practice English. Although she spoke with a heavy Spanish accent, McPherson had little trouble understanding her.

"Good morning, Graciela. Any messages?"

"Yes, Mr. Browning is wishing to see you soon. Shall I tell him of your presence?"

"No, not just yet," McPherson said, smiling as he listened to her speak. He admired the girl's continuous attempts to perfect her English.

"I'll call for him in a few minutes."

He stepped past Graciela, entering his office through an adjoining door. A long table, covered with endless stacks of paper was set against one wall. A wooden bookcase, filled to capacity long ago stood opposite the cluttered table. Its shelves overflowing with mounds of various shaped documents. A gray metal desk was positioned in the centre of the room. Behind it were dozens of electrical and architectural schematic diagrams rolled into tubes and tossed recklessly onto the floor.

Surprisingly, McPherson's desk was free from any debris. He had an ornate, brass-framed photograph of his wife and children smiling at him from the corner of the simulated, wood-grained desktop. A small round pencil holder was filled to capacity and was strategically placed behind a note-pad. The only other item on the desk was a black telephone.

He walked to a small glass topped table in the corner of his office and picked up one of the royal blue, porcelain cups filling it with rich, black coffee, poured from a silver urn recently filled by the efficient Graciela. He sipped the steamy coffee and lifted the receiver from his telephone.

"Ask Mr. Browning to come in please, Graciela."

"Right away, sir."

Tim Browning was McPherson's right hand man. Although he was only thirty-one years old, his competence level was extremely high. If only he could improve his people skills and business judgment. Most of his associates ignored him not appreciating his crass sense of humour and continuous negative comments. Although he was an excellent physicist, he was lacking the social ability required to progress with other people in his field. McPherson liked Tim and attempted to overlook his shortcomings.

The door to McPherson's office was partially opened before the scientist heard the knock.

"Good morning, chief." Tim Browning was about five foot seven. His round head appeared too large for his somewhat small frame. Although intellectually he was quite skilled, his physical appearance lacked flair and professionalism.

"What's up, Tim?" McPherson motioned his assistant to sit in one of the two wood-framed chairs opposite the desk.

"I got an interesting phone call a few minutes ago." McPherson raised his eyebrows and waited for Tim to continue. "Charles Taylor, from the Consulate office said he had to see you right away."

"Sounds interesting. What about?"

"He wouldn't tell me. Said he had to deliver the message in person to you."

"When is he coming?"

"I told him you'd be in around eight-thirty. He said he would drop over at nine."

McPherson looked at the white with black clock on the wall of his office. He had arrived later than normal. "That was ten minutes ago. I wonder what he wants?"

"Maybe your visa has expired."

"No, I still have three months left."

"Well I don't know what else it could be."

"Maybe he wants to invite me to a cocktail party."

Tim Browning chuckled. The telephone intercom buzzed. McPherson picked up the receiver and touched the flashing button.

"It is your daughter, sir, she is on the telephone."

"Thank you, Graciela." McPherson touched the appropriate key and spoke cheerfully into the receiver.

Tim Browning turned his attention to the view outside the window, pretending to ignore the conversation. McPherson knew he was eavesdropping and was cognizant of Browning's attempt at setting himself up with his daughter Kristy for quite some time. He had asked her for several dates but she had always managed to find an excuse to shun his advances. He appeared far too indulged in his admiration for her to absorb any negative messages she might be relaying to him.

"Okay," McPherson said. "Not to worry. I'll see you in two days." He replaced the receiver on its cradle.

"Problems at home?" Browning asked.

"No, not really. Kristy has a tour group she'll be taking to Buenos Aires. Her mother had asked her to pick up a few things for a dinner party we're having. Now I'll have to get them. Remind me before I leave, Tim."

The intercom buzzed again. "This place is worse than Grand Central Station." McPherson again lifted the telephone.

"Yes, Graciela?"

"Señor Taylor." She corrected herself. "I mean Mr. Taylor is here to meet with you."

"Thank you. Please ask him to come in." He looked at Tim Browning. "Now make certain you're on your best behaviour, Tim," he smiled as he spoke.

The wooden door opened and Graciela showed the government official into the scientist's office. McPherson stood and cheerfully greeted the overweight representative of the Canadian Government.

"Good morning, Doctor McPherson." Taylor's thick handlebar moustache quivered as he spoke. There were tiny beads of perspiration forming on his high forehead. His navy blue suit was not at all designed for the tropical climate of Argentina.

"Good morning. This is my assistant, Tim Browning." He motioned to Tim who had stood to meet the official visitor.

"Won't you have a seat?" McPherson asked, pointing to the vacant chair.

"Thank you." Taylor sat down. He appeared to be nervous and uncomfortable.

"So," McPherson began, "to what do we owe this pleasure?"

Taylor spoke. "Well Doctor an envelope arrived last evening at my office with your name printed on it."

"I see," said McPherson. He leaned forward resting his chin on his fingertips. "What is this envelope all about?"

"Well, we're not exactly sure. It was marked top

secret and had the government seal stamped all over it. We haven't opened it yet."

McPherson was taken aback by the statement. It was evident by the manner in which he spoke that Taylor's office opened most documents passing through their hands regardless of their original destinations.

"Why have I been spared scrutinization by your secretive methods?"

"No. No." Taylor replied defensively. "I didn't mean to imply that we normally open mail, I only meant we usually are made aware of the contents of any official documents.

"Do you have the envelope with you?" Tim Browning asked impatiently.

"Yes, of course I do," Taylor replied, slightly annoyed. He did not feel that he should have to deal with someone as young in appearance as Tim Browning. He was here to see Dr. McPherson. Why was Browning even in this room?

He picked up his brown, zippered attaché case and wrestled with the locking clip. He reached in and pulled out a letter sized envelope bearing the official Canadian government crest, colourfully displayed in the upper left corner. Across the front, in bright red ink, was McPherson's name, clearly readable.

Taylor placed his case on the floor and delicately laid the envelope on McPherson's desk. The scientist picked it up and held it between the thumb and forefinger of each hand. He studied the printing on the front and wondered what top secret information the contents contained. He slowly turned it over.

Both Tim's and Taylor's eyes were fixed on the envelope. On the back, in bold black letters were the words: "CONFIDENTIAL. TO BE OPENED BY ADDRESSEE ONLY."

McPherson was extremely anxious to open the document but did not want to appear that way to Taylor. There had been enough meddling from government representatives into his work. He certainly did not need any more.

He stood. "Well, thank you very much Mr. Taylor. I certainly appreciate you bringing this over today."

"You're most welcome." After a short pause. "Aren't you going to open it?"

"Eventually I will. However, the contents appear to be quite confidential. Maybe I should wait until I'm alone, wouldn't you agree?"

"Yes. Yes, of course," Taylor stammered, "I should be leaving anyway." He stood up.

"Have you been in Argentina very long?" McPherson asked.

"No, actually, this is my first week."

"Excellent. I'm sure you'll enjoy it. You may find that a lighter fabric of suit would be more comfortable."

Slightly embarrassed, Taylor replied, "I've ordered several. They'll be ready this weekend."

"Have a good day."

"Thank you." He paused, turning his view to Tim Browning. "You too, Mr. Browning."

Tim stood up and nodded to the government official. McPherson reached the door and held it open for his guest. "Thanks again," he said.

"If there's anything that we can help you with, please don't hesitate to give us a call."

"I won't."

McPherson closed the door. He looked at Tim, who had once again taken his chair.

"What a squeamish little man," Browning said.

"I suppose, but remember, he has a pretty boring job. Any excitement would probably be welcomed."

Tim Browning was lacking finesse and compassion. He had trouble perceiving situations from anyone else's point of view. That was probably the major reason he had never been accepted into the social circles of his associates.

"I wonder what's in the envelope?" Browning asked.

"I don't know, but I'm dying to find out." McPherson reached for a letter opener in the top drawer of his desk. He carefully inserted it in the fold of the seal and pulled it toward himself, tearing the envelope along its crease. He removed the contents. It was a single sheet of white, linen paper folded three times. Browning watched closely as the scientist unfolded the stationary and began to read it.

As he read the letter, McPherson's eyebrows narrowed into a frown causing the lines around his eyes to become more pronounced.

"What is it?" Tim Browning asked.

McPherson didn't reply. Browning slowly crept to the edge of his seat in anticipation of being privy to the information of the contents.

McPherson finished the letter and slowly read it a second time. He placed the white parchment on his desk and folded his hands to support his chin.

"Well, what is it?"

McPherson did not respond immediately. He stared blankly at the door opposite his desk.

"I can't believe this," he finally said. "I honestly can't believe this."

"Believe what?" Browning asked impatiently, straining his eyes in an effort to catch a glimpse of the sheet of writing paper.

McPherson gradually raised his head and looked at Tim Browning. His face had a ghostly appearance, devoid of most of its colour. He slowly began to speak. "They want me to sabotage the reactor."

"What?" Browning said, not believing what he had heard.

"The fools want me to delay the start-up of the reactor."

Tim Browning's mouth fell open as he stared in

disbelief at his superior. "What in God's name for?"

"Well," McPherson replied, "it appears that conditions between Argentina and Britain are getting worse. Apparently there could be an all-out war. If that happens it'll put Canada in an extremely difficult position in its relations with Britain and Argentina. We are, after all, closely associated with England. Basically what they want to do is delay the implementation of the reactor until this whole mess is cleared up."

Browning shook his head. He whistled a sigh. "What are you gonna do?" he asked.

McPherson mechanically picked up the sheet of paper. "I don't know. I just don't know."

"Shouldn't we check this letter out to make sure its authentic?"

McPherson leaned back in his chair. "I don't know how to find out," he said, still in a state of shock. He had spent the last three years of his life getting this program up and running. Who are these people to deny him this glory?

"Well, who signed the letter?" Browning asked.

"It's not signed. There is only a code number at the bottom. Some sort of reference number I suspect." He scanned the letter again.

"Wait a second." Tim Browning said, as he glanced at the letter. "There's a phone number at the top. It's got an area code."

"Ottawa, I think."

"Well let's call and see what's going on."

He picked up the telephone and asked Graciela to hold his calls, speaking in as normal a voice as he could muster. He dialed the operator and asked for the number typed on the mysterious letter. There were several pauses followed by a few clicks. Finally a woman's voice answered the call.

"Hello," she simply said.

McPherson waited for more conversation to follow.

"Hello," he finally said, looking at the phone number on the stationary before him. He repeated the number.

"Yes," the voice said. "You have reached that number, how can I help you?"

"My name is Lorne McPherson, I'm calling from Cordoba, Argentina. I would like to verify a letter I received today."

"One moment please?"

He waited while he was placed on hold. Several seconds later a man's voice answered. "Can I help you Dr. McPherson?"

"Yes, I received a letter just now with an interesting request."

"Yes?"

"Well I was just wondering whether or not I understood it correctly?"

"Did you read the letter carefully?"

"I believe I did."

"Then there should be no questions left unanswered."

"Well, I realize that, its just that I find the request rather difficult to comprehend."

"Sometimes we ask the most difficult tasks of our people. Believe me Doctor we would not have sent the letter if we did not feel it was absolutely necessary."

"I see. I suppose that answers all of my immediate questions. Are there any instructions as to how I should carry out the task?"

"No sir. That is strictly up to you. You will be compensated for your extra activity via a package which will arrive at your house today."

"What kind of package?"

"I'm sorry sir, I can't go into that and please sir don't call this number unless it's an absolute emergency."

"Thanks," McPherson said robotically."

"Thank you sir. Good luck."

McPherson laid the receiver back on its cradle. He

looked at Tim Browning. "Well Tim, it looks like this is for real. We seem to have quite a task ahead of us."

"Okay chief what do we do next?"

"Why don't we go and grab a coffee? I would like to talk about this outside of this place." McPherson folded the letter and placed it inside his shirt pocket.

The morning sun was forcing its hot rays on both men as they walked along the quiet street away from the office building.

"God, I'm beginning to hate this weather," McPherson said as minute perspiration droplets formed on his forehead like dew on a morning blade of grass.

"I know what you mean." Tim Browning wiped his forehead with his sleeve.

They entered a small restaurant cooled by two slow moving fans tucked into the corners. The table they chose was directly in front of one of the two fans.

"Hell of a way to catch a cold," Browning said as he tried to manoeuvre his body away from the direct draft of the fan.

The restaurant was very old and evidence of recent dust was everywhere. The marble simulated tables had been scratched beyond repair. The only decoration was the twenty year old Coca Cola sign slightly askew on one of the paint chipped walls. The painted face of the advertisement's waitress, her smile etched for eternity carrying the famous soft drink, was partially faded.

"Good morning gentlemen," the heavy set waiter said with a strong Spanish accent. "How are you today?" The perspiration was running down his face as he spoke. He wiped his hands on an apron loosely tied around his waist and covered with numerous stains from previous orders.

"We'll just have a couple of coffees," McPherson said.

"As you wish." The waiter returned to the kitchen.

McPherson removed the letter from his pocket and read it one more time.

"You're gonna have that thing memorized!"

"I still can't believe that this is happening."

"Can I see the letter?"

McPherson handed the document to Tim. He read it carefully. "Incredible," he said. "Simply incredible."

The waiter returned carrying two ceramic mugs of steaming coffee. He placed a small cup of milk on the table and picked up a napkin dispenser and sugar bowl from the lunch counter behind him.

"Thank you," Tim Browning said. The waiter retreated to the privacy of his kitchen. The restaurant was quiet. There were three aging gents chatting in a corner. Their vocal discussion centred around major political events of the day and they each offered opinions eliminating most of the global crises facing mankind.

"Well," McPherson said as he lifted the mug and sipped the strong rich coffee. "I guess all we need to do is simply rig the mechanics so the reactor won't function properly."

"Sounds simple to me." Browning said mockingly. "I guess that means we're really going through with it."

"I don't know what to think," McPherson said, "I really don't know."

The ocean breeze was picking up as Lorne McPherson snapped back into the present. He heard the sound of carefree laughter behind him and turning his head saw his daughter Kristy building a sand castle with Jimmy. Warm thoughts of the happiness provided him by his children filled his mind. He hoped this present conundrum would not create lasting problems for them. He loved his family very much and wanted desperately to keep them from any harm.

His wife was strolling along the beach toward him.

She had come from the rented beach house to be with her husband in this time of distress. He smiled as she approached.

"What are we going to do, Lorne?" she asked softly, placing her hand on his shoulder.

"I don't know." He realized her concern and made an effort to soothe her. "I'll think of something." He forced a smile but knew she could see through the pretence.

"How much money do we have left?"

"We'll be okay, don't worry." He placed his hand on her back and rubbed it lovingly. "Don't you worry," he repeated and turned his gaze back to the calm, blue ocean wondering how on earth he was going to deal with this predicament.

2   SABOTAGE

Slowly, McPherson lost track of all surrounding noise upon the beach. His gaze was fixed eternally on the waves caressing the shore. He became oblivious to the voices of his family as they enjoyed the tropical playground. The yellow-orange sun began to lose focus as his mind drifted back to that hot, summer morning in Cordoba several weeks earlier.

"What are you going to do?" Tim Browning asked.

"I don't know, I just don't know." McPherson rubbed his forehead as the waiter poured more coffee into his cup. "I can't believe they want me to blow this thing up."

"I'm not sure if blowing up is the right terminology to use," Tim Browning said. "Based on the letter I think they only want you to halt its start up."

"When is the first reactor scheduled to begin operation?" McPherson asked sipping his coffee.

"I believe it's July the fifth."

"We don't have much time."

"Do you have any idea how you're going to do it?"

McPherson shook his head. "None, whatsoever." He finished his coffee and laid an appropriate amount of money on the table. "Let's go back to the office and study this thing a little deeper."

The scientist and his assistant left the restaurant, remaining silent as they returned to their office building, routinely showing their security pass cards to the uniformed guard on duty upon their arrival.

"Excuse me Dr. McPherson," his secretary said as the two men walked into the outer office. "Your wife telephoned, asking if you could come home early because of your dinner party."

McPherson stared at her for a moment and smiled as a mental image of his wife, busily running throughout the house in preparation for the evening ahead, came to his mind. He once again focused on the evil task he had been asked to perform. He made an effort to place the situation in perspective. The depth of a problem was relative to an individual's perception of it. Directly behind his desk on the large table lay several, rolled, engineering drawings. He took one and using his other hand moved the objects on his desk to the side. Tim Browning walked around to peer over McPherson's shoulder as they studied the details of the schematic. McPherson slowly shook his head and replaced the floor-plan to the pile. He took another, and after studying the document for several minutes, pointed to an object resembling a large, thick sausage.

"The pressurizer, right beside the steam generator," he said. "That's the only area I could see us doing anything."

"The pressurizer?" Tim Browning asked.

"Yes, that has to be it."

"But won't it be full of water?"

"Yes but there are valves located along the pipe. If we fix one of the valves so that it shows a leak on the computer during the test, the only thing that would escape would be steam." McPherson paused for a moment. The reactor was continually monitored by computerized mechanisms. A final test would be administered shortly before the uranium was to be installed. If anything failed during the concluding test a major re-evaluation would be ordered, causing weeks of delay.

"We can't do anything to the calandria or the fuelling machines because it would cause a series of explosions. If we attempt entry into the power house or vacuum building the risk would be too great."

Tim Browning looked inquisitively at the scientist.

"By rights we have no clearance to go anywhere outside the reactor building. The areas are within visual range of the guards and are outside of our jurisdiction. We would have no reason to be there."

He looked again at the large diagram of pipes and circles and tapped his finger on a small, bullet-shaped item near the top.

"There is a small valve right here which we installed about a week and a half ago. It is scheduled to be tested by the end of this week. The uranium blocks won't be deposited until next week because Dr. Laos, who controls the uranium, is away until then. What they'll probably do is test the reactor with water only. The valve will show faulty and it will put a halt to the installation. We could order a new valve and lose it in the paper work, delaying the installation by at least a month. I'm sure that would give the government in Ottawa enough time to get their act together."

McPherson felt pleased with himself. His idea was relatively simple and it would take very little work to initiate.

"So no one should be around to get hurt?"

"That's right, there'll only be a few people on hand during the start-up and the only thing that will come out will be steam."

"What is your next move sir?" Tim Browning asked.

McPherson took a moment to ponder the question. "I guess I'd better telephone Ottawa first and tell them what we're doing." He unfolded the letter and reached for the telephone. He dialed the appropriate numbers and waited for a voice to answer. He gave the code listed on the letter and explained that the task would be performed in the next several days. After he hung up the receiver he stared at the black instrument for a few seconds, questioning the logic of this entire act.

"When will we do it?" Tim asked.

"I don't think you should be involved. This is something I must do by myself. One person would be less obtrusive than two."

"I'm not sure if that's a good idea sir. If I went with you I could act as a look out."

McPherson smiled. "You've been watching too many James Bond movies, Tim. There is no reason for anyone to be suspicious. I'll do it tonight around midnight."

McPherson spent the rest of the day quietly in his office going over different aspects of the task that he was about to perform. He stayed in during lunch and had his calls forwarded to his secretary. At three o'clock he phoned his wife and explained he was leaving. The last thing that he wanted to do was visit with company tonight, however, making everything appear as normal as possible was important to the success of this scheme.

Dinner with the Callahan's was exactly as McPherson expected it to be. Boring and nauseating. Bill Callahan continually talked about his job, his future, and all the golden opportunities offered him. He was in his early fifties, however dying his hair had given him a youthful appearance. It was apparent his clothes had been purchased at expensive shops and had been altered to fit him perfectly.

He had been in Cordoba for six years and worked for

an American firm which manufactured hydroelectric generators. His wife Helen was slim and in very good shape. She had spent a great deal of time at the local fitness centre or the 'Club' as she preferred to call it. Lorne McPherson noted designer labels on every item she wore. Her black hair was spiked with gel and had been recently styled.

The conversations were pointless and Lorne could not understand why his wife insisted on asking these people to their house. His mind kept drifting back to the deed he was to perform later that night. After dinner the foursome sat around the living room and covered a vast range of subjects. Rhonda McPherson had made another terrific dinner. She was an excellent cook and had a meticulous way about planning her dinner parties. Lorne smiled to himself when he thought of his wife's enthusiasm and enjoyment in preparing for these small get-togethers. Every now and then his mind drifted back into the conversation as Bill Callahan directed a comment or two at him. A wave of relief came over Lorne when Helen Callahan finally turned to her husband and expressed a desire to leave.

"Oh must you leave so soon?" Rhonda McPherson asked.

"Yes, we have to get up early tomorrow morning. Bill has to be at work and I have a tennis lesson."

"Oh that's a shame, are you sure you wouldn't have one more drink?"

Lorne was about to nudge his wife as the Callahan's stood up. He walked to the closet to retrieve Helen Callahan's designer shawl.

"You didn't seem to be in a good mood tonight," Rhonda said to her husband as they waved farewell to their guests.

"No I have a few things on my mind, and I have to go back to the office to get something."

"What, tonight?"

"I'm afraid so."

"How long will you be?"

"Not too long, it's just something that I forgot to check on and if I don't do it tonight we could have some problems tomorrow."

"Well if you must but I don't think I'll be waiting up for you."

"Why don't you leave the dishes until tomorrow and I'll give you a hand?"

"What and do them at six in the morning before you go to work?" She smiled as she kissed him on the cheek.

He grabbed his keys from the little hook beside the front door and walked toward the driveway. The night air was cool and Lorne rolled up the windows of the car.

The drive to the office took only ten minutes. There was little traffic this late at night. He checked the dashboard. It was just past eleven. He examined his wrist watch for verification but the lack of illumination in the interior of the car made it difficult to see. He was planning the continuance of his little project.

When he got to the office he drove past the guardhouse. The sentry on duty waved him in as he glanced at his face. Lorne McPherson was well-respected and easily recognized by most of the personnel in the complex.

Instead of driving to his office, he parked his car in a small, dark laneway between two buildings. He checked his rear-view mirror to be sure no one was behind him and rolled down his window to listen for any threatening sounds. When he felt assured there was no one about, he opened the car door and stepped out very quickly. He immediately shut the door, keeping the dome light on for as short a time as possible. He opened the trunk and retrieved his briefcase. Earlier that day he had placed some necessary tools inside. He walked a few paces and was confronted by a large, gray, metal door. On it, beneath a small, dimly lit lamp, a sign written in Spanish and English forbade any admittance. Because the reactor had not been started, there were no guards placed by the door. Three weeks from now the area would be buzzing with armed sentries.

Lorne used his key to gain admittance to the door. A magnetic-striped pass card mechanism had been installed but thankfully was not as yet active. At least now there would be no record of who had entered.

The interior of the building was very dark. Several exit signs were illuminated and cast small shadows across the gigantic pipes and electrical equipment that regulated the flow of nuclear energy from the reactor into the pressure system. Lorne had a good idea of the layout of the building and made his way toward a metal ladder leading to a passageway many feet above the floor. He climbed the ladder with some difficulty as his briefcase was heavy and the darkness about him made it difficult to see. The walkway led to a large pipe supported by metal beams which stretched the length of the building, exiting through an opening at the far end. The other end of the pipe went into a gigantic array of metal tanks which captured the heavy water and transformed it into steam, produced by the heat of the heavy water.

The entire unit had been filled with water, however without uranium in place the fission process had not yet started causing no danger of radiation contamination.

He made his way along a small ladder to the top of a platform beside a large valve marked 'Pressurizer'. He had thought to wear latex gloves to avoid leaving fingerprints. He did not expect anyone to suppose interference had occurred. People would merely assume a faulty valve. There was after all no reason for anyone to tamper with the system.

He stretched the gloves over his fingers and smiled as he thought about the comment made to Tim Browning about James Bond movies. Here he was, deeply involved in a clandestine operation. He felt secure about its outcome and this alone allowed him to relax during his exercise.

The small valve was green in colour and blended in with the dark gray paint around the pipe to which it was affixed. He had brought a small flashlight and laid it on the metal rail of the platform, positioning it with his knee so that the beam shone directly on the valve. He grabbed a universal wrench from his briefcase and began to unlock the nut holding the valve in place. Fortunately it was not very tight as it had been recently installed.

From the far end of the construction, a noise from an opened door suddenly permeated the entire building. The sound caused McPherson to mechanically hold his breath. The abrupt silence was startling and it seemed his heartbeat was amplified throughout the building. He felt the heavy pounding deep inside his chest and perspiration began to form on his forehead. He reached for the flashlight and, nervously fumbling with the switch, managed to turn it off. Fortunately the beam was dim and he was high above the entrance. He felt certain that he had not been seen and sat motionless, straining his ears for sounds. Below him was the faint silhouette of a man standing inside an opening at the end of the building. It was a guard performing a routine check and he merely waved his flashlight in several directions as he executed the mundane job assigned to him. Having been satisfied that everything seemed secure, he left, shutting the door behind him. The scientist breathed a sigh of relief and paused for a moment to ensure that the guard would not return. He took the flashlight and turned it on, allowing the light to fall on his watch. He made a note of the time and assumed that the sentry would return in an hour. He shifted from a kneeling position to a squat and eventually allowed his body to rest in a sitting position on the cold, iron platform. The flashlight's beam remained trained on the valve and with a small pair of needle-nose pliers he removed a clip that was holding a tiny spring in place.

What he was doing could be extremely dangerous.

The anticipated pressure test would create great strain which would force the tampered valve to blow from its housing. He expected no one to be in the vicinity as metal remnants of the valve would become miniature missiles injuring anyone in their path. He felt confident that the test would be monitored closely.

The computer's safety system would prevent any severe malfunction. He was, after all, responsible for the functionality of the system. He replaced the broken valve, returned his tools to the briefcase and, using the flashlight, ensured that no trace of his entrance had been left behind. He climbed the small ladder to the platform and quickly darted along the walkway back toward the long ladder. He exited the building the same way he came in, making sure that there was no one outside to see him.

The lights in the house had been turned off and Rhonda had gone to sleep. He walked through the front door very softly and tiptoed directly upstairs. After a quick stop in Jimmy's room, replacing the sheet his son had wildly tossed aside during his sleep, he stepped along the hallway walking past Kristy's empty room. He paused for a moment and remembered that she had gone away for several days on a travel tour with her company. He walked into his room as quietly as he could, trying not to stir his wife who was breathing heavily but slowly. He slipped into his pyjamas and gently pushed back the covers, allowing his body to fall on the soft mattress, exhaling slowly, feeling great relief at the completion of his task. He closed his eyes and although he felt tired, sleep did not come easily.

"What time did you get home last night?" Rhonda McPherson asked as her husband came down the stairs still fixing his tie.

"It was shortly after one. I'm sorry I had to go out but it was just something that couldn't wait."

"I didn't even hear you come in."

"I know. The Callahan's have that effect on people.

They tend to wear you out quickly." His wife smiled as she placed his breakfast on the table.

"I see you cleaned the dishes last night after all," Lorne said as he shook his head slowly.

"Where's Jimmy?"

"He had to leave early - some science project or something."

For an unexplained reason Lorne McPherson was rather proud of himself. He felt that he had accomplished something that was totally out of character for him. A conscientious part of him felt embarrassed, however he was pleased at introducing a side of him that he really didn't know existed.

"Well, how'd it go?" Tim Browning was standing in the door opening to McPherson's office.

McPherson motioned him to close the door ensuring privacy." It went very well. It's not something I'd like to do on a regular basis, but it went with no problems."

Browning nodded his head, expressing a satisfaction with his superior's result. "I checked with the inspection team and they're scheduled to pressure test the valve the day after tomorrow."

McPherson thought out loud. "That's Friday. That's not too far off. I doubt very much if anything will happen between now and then."

As the day progressed, McPherson slowly slid back into the routine of his regular duties. The events of the previous night were transferring to the recesses of his mind. In fact, after lunch, he completely forgot about them and was again deeply engrossed in his work.

The telephone rang shortly after three, disturbing the scientist's thoughts.

"McPherson speaking," he said, listening to an enthusiastic voice at the other end.

"Lorne? Marty. Can you make a cocktail reception

tomorrow night?"

Martin Dale was responsible for public relations with the Candu project. He had little interaction with Lorne McPherson but when their paths crossed the two worked well together.

"Sure... I guess so. What's the occasion?"

"Well, Dr. Laos is supervising the uranium installation and a few people thought it would be a nice gesture if we threw a small, pre-celebration party."

Lorne McPherson missed the last half of the sentence. "They can't do that."

"Why not? It's not like we have a lot of parties."

"No, no. The reactor hasn't been tested yet."

"Well, you know more about that than I do. Can I count on you tomorrow night?"

"What?" McPherson mumbled. "Oh yeah, sure."

He replaced the receiver on the phone and slumped in his chair. He waited a moment and picked up the telephone from its cradle. After dialling three numbers and a short ring Tim Browning answered the phone. "Tim, can you come here right away?"

Tim Browning stepped into McPherson's office and saw the scientist sitting behind his desk with his head bent and resting on his arms.

"What happened?" Browning had excitement in his voice.

McPherson looked up. He paused. "I just received a call from the energy commission. The uranium arrived this morning and Dr. Laos will be here tomorrow to supervise the installation.

"What does that mean?"

"It means that they won't be doing a pressure test on the boiler until after the uranium is installed."

"Isn't that kind of stupid? If the pressure test does not work the thing will blow up."

McPherson slowly nodded his head. "I guess they

feel pretty confident about everything working."

"Can't you halt the installation or something. Tell them to postpone it for a few days until they've done the test."

McPherson shook his head in anguish. He picked up the telephone receiver and dialed several digits. "Yes, is Allan Cerswell in?" He cupped his hand over the receiver and spoke to Browning. "I'm going to see if I can get the pressure test done this afternoon."

"Just don't raise any suspicions."

"Yes. Allan? Lorne McPherson." He paused. "I understand they're putting the uranium into the reactor this week." Again he paused waiting for the other party to acknowledge his remarks. "I think it would be wise if we did a pressure test on the boiler to make sure everything is working." His face turned white as he listened to the conversation through the receiver. He spoke rapidly. "When did this happen?" he waited a moment. "I see. Yes. I understand." He slowly replaced the telephone receiver back on its base and looked at Tim Browning who was standing awaiting a comment.

"They did a pressure test yesterday afternoon."

"What? I don't understand, I was told that they were doing it on Friday."

"Yes, well it appears that you were wrong."

"What are you gonna do?"

"I don't have any choice. I'll have to go back tonight and repair the broken valve."

"I think that might be a little risky."

"Can you imagine what would happen if they started that reactor with the broken valve?"

"I know," Tim Browning said. "I'm just afraid something will happen."

"I doubt if anyone will even notice me."

McPherson did not feel comfortable about going back into the reactor room again. If the uranium had arrived, there would be more guards, making it more difficult to slip in and out easily. The second concern was that he might not be able to repair the broken valve properly. He hoped the computer system would detect a malfunction. The thought of a radiation leak as a result of his sabotage efforts would be more than he could bear. The word 'Sabotage' repeated itself in his mind and lingered longer than he had wished.

He arrived home and again, like the previous night, explained to his wife about some last minute problems which had arisen at the office. Rhonda was very understanding and hoped he would return soon.

He parked his car in the same location and stealthily entered the building, retracing his steps from the previous night. After positioning the flashlight under his bent knee, he removed the valve unit.

Suddenly, without warning, the door to the end of the room opened and a guard entered waving a flashlight about. McPherson cursed softly at the intrusion for he had anticipated at least forty-five minutes before a security check. His hand dashed for the flashlight in an effort to extinguish its revealing beam but as he grabbed the shaft the torch slipped from his grip and rolled along the metal frame coming to a halt against a steel girder. Although the noise was not very loud it was the only audible sound in the entire room. The guard directed his flashlight toward the general area where McPherson was and yelled in Spanish. McPherson sat motionless and prayed that the guard would leave. Suddenly the beam from the sentry's lamp shone directly on his face, blinding his vision. In a moment it was over. The guard pulled a revolver and pointed in the direction of the scientist. He walked to the small switch on the wall and after flipping it, illuminated a general part of the reactor room. He laid down the flashlight but maintained a strong aim with the gun directly at McPherson. The uniformed man removed his portable intercom and, speaking rapidly in Spanish, summoned help. It was a matter of seconds before troops armed with machine guns entered the thick, brick building.

McPherson, in defeat, raised his arms. At the guard's request, he stepped from the ladder, walked along the platform and allowed authorities to take the broken valve from his hands and place metal handcuffs around his wrists.

3   ISIS

Phillip Wright slowly lowered his tired body into the soft, cushioned aircraft seat. The firm, yet comfortable neck support was a treat to his aching muscles. He closed his eyes momentarily and slowly allowed a deep breath of air to escape from his lungs. He shifted in his seat, looking for his safety belt, and was thankful that the seat next to him was unoccupied.

An attractive flight attendant opened a white plastic, overhead compartment and removed a demonstration seat belt, oxygen mask and emergency card. Phillip was fascinated by the girl's appealing appearance. Her pleasing smile, the proper application of make-up and the golden blonde hair perfectly in place were evidence that the airline took a great deal of time recruiting and training. She suited her navy blue uniform, trimmed with red stripes and complimented by a red and white kerchief fastened with a silver clip around her neck. She seemed youthful and Phillip wondered how old she was. Twenty-six, perhaps twenty-seven, he thought.

The attendant caught him staring at her and smiled appreciatively as he blushed; the embarrassment he felt was that of a schoolboy who had been caught in an outward display of personal emotions. A contrite expression formed on his lips, followed by a suppressed smile. The girl winked flirtatiously in response to his repentance, acknowledging acceptance of his unpretentious flattery.

His mind drifted into the past, back to a time in his life when he was in his mid-twenties. How carefree life had been at that age. A great deal had happened in the past twelve years.

The early stages of his marriage had been filled with pleasurable events and it had seemed as if his happiness would never end. Suddenly, as if overnight, he began to lose interest in the day-to-day occurrences that made up his waking hours. He became bored with the mundane tasks that required continuous attention. His wife had suggested he see a doctor and it was only due to her constant badgering that he reluctantly decided to make an appointment. The specialist had referred to his state as typical suburban depression. One could not expect to find continued enthusiasm in mowing the lawn every weekend; it was something he would have to learn to live with. The doctor had suggested Phillip and his wife spend more time together, attending theatres or possibly enjoying a vacation; however, with the birth of their first son, entertainment was forced to take a back seat. It was a routine which had slowly crept up and absorbed the glamorous aspects of his life. Like mindless robots, his wife and he performed daily tasks without thought or emotion. They were a young suburban family growing at a rate considered acceptable to society. He had achieved a good, although uneventful, low risk position in life which offered a substantial yet not lucrative income.

He had been employed by the government as a purchasing agent for almost five drawn out years. The position was good and sought after by many of his peers. His co-workers considered him fortunate. At least that's what everyone he worked with had told him. It was secure and the income was worthwhile. He should have been thankful to have such a fine berth even if he had to sit behind the same desk every day, continually eat lunch with the same people and constantly listen to their negative complaining. That was the price one had to pay for being a part of suburbia.

As the aircraft slowly taxied toward the runway, Phillip was shocked out of his daydream by a wrenching noise streaming from the tinny, overhead speaker. The shattering sound was irritable and made comprehension of the words insuperable. He longed for the completion of the pre-takeoff instructions.

He tilted his head to the right and leaned against the plastic window moulding, permitting the cold glass to soothe his throbbing temple. He rested his chin on the palm of his hand, seeking as much comfort as was available. He sleepily glanced out the window and watched several leafless trees skim by. A number of brown, worn out airplane hangars and other antiquated buildings popped in and out of his range of vision. In the distance he could see the main thoroughfare filled to capacity with colourful, fast moving automobiles. The sky above glared a deep, rich, cloudless blue with tiny aircraft, no larger than specks of dust, shining in the reflection of the hot, hazy, late afternoon sun.

The jet came to an abrupt halt at the foot of the active runway, jolting the passengers forward. As the thrust was increased and the plane began to move, the people inside the metal fuselage were propelled back deep into their seats. Phillip could feel his stomach quiver as the nose of the craft slowly lifted from the ground. The remainder of the vessel was quick to follow its parental lead. Enjoying its freedom from the earth's motherly grasp, the carrier dashed upward through the billowy, white clouds.

As he watched the land gradually decrease in size and eventually disappear beneath the wisps of puffy white clouds, Phillip Wright's mind again drifted back into the past; a past he had tried so desperately to forget. His mind raced back to thoughts of his estranged wife. He wondered how she fared. He hadn't seen her since the divorce eight years earlier. He had despised her that rainy December day in court. She had perjured herself without conscience.

It had all started in the spring of 1976. He had finished work surprisingly early and had decided to go home for a long overdue family evening. He would help Maureen prepare a detailed dinner, perhaps barbecue some succulent steaks. He enjoyed cooking on an outdoor grill, even during the chilly, New York springtime. He had contemplated calling his wife from the office but decided that a surprise would enliven her routine day. He had stopped and purchased a colourful bouquet of cut flowers from an ambitious street vendor. He had often intended to buy flowers for Maureen but somehow always forgot and thought of it at the most inopportune times. He pictured the warm, smiling glow of felicitous surprise on his wife's face as he walked through the front door of their small suburban home in Queens. He glanced at his watch and realized that he would arrive home an hour or so before their kids did. Excitement surged through his mind at the prospect of rekindling emotions rarely allowed to surface.

He remembered walking along the sidewalk in front of his house attempting to conceal the flowers, just in case Maureen was standing by the window. As he stepped to the door he found the handle locked and wondered if perhaps she had gone out. He used his key and was relieved when he saw her shoes neatly tucked in a corner of the entrance-way. He was about to call out when he heard low, almost inaudible sounds coming from the top of the stairs. He paused slowly and strained his ears, attempting to capture the source of the frightening noise. As he tiptoed along the thickly carpeted stairs the sounds became louder. Phillip froze in his tracks as he heard his wife scream.

The moans that followed were full of pleasure and ecstasy. He heard a man's voice echoing from the master bedroom. Thoughts of anger and desperation danced wildly through his senses. His vision was blurred by the imaginings created in his mind.

He softly turned the corner at the top of the stairway and walked toward the bedroom. The door was wide open and he could hear the shouts of pleasure; sounds he had thought were for his ears only. Sounds made by his wife during their most intimate moments together. Now the sounds had betrayed him as they were shared by a stranger to his life.

Fire burned within Phillip's body. The pain made his temples feel as if they were about to burst. He stood inertly in the doorway to the bedroom. He was mesmerized by the scene before him. His wife lay naked on their bed. A man Phillip had never seen before was rhythmically thrusting into her with great determination and passion. They were both unaware of Phillip's intrusion as the interloper continued to caress her lustfully.

Phillip dropped the flowers and stared blankly at the love-makers before him. He stood in a trance, unable to speak. The man saw him first and screamed. His wife slowly snapped her mind from lascivious passion into shattering reality.

"Phillip!" she cried.

"Look," the man spoke, "I can explain." He scrambled to the side of the bed.

Phillip felt a wave of vomit building in the pit of his stomach. He swung his head away from the agonizing, shameful scene upon which he had inadvertently stumbled.

He ran from the scene and left his house, staggering along the sidewalk, crying openly. As he reached the nearest intersection, he raised his hand and hailed the first cab that came into view. He rode for miles, ignoring the idle conversation made by the cab driver. Eventually he paid the man, and left the warmth of the enclosed vehicle. His wits were not about him, and he had no idea where he was or where he was going. He could feel icy cold raindrops trickling from his hair down his forehead, running into his eyes and mixing with the salty, recurring tears. Years later, he was still unable to recall where he had gone that afternoon.

He vaguely remembered walking aimlessly through the streets of the city. He had stopped and purchased a bottle of gin at a corner store but could not recollect having finished it. He recalled nothing but the sound of nearby crowds which had caused him to waken from the deep trance which had engulfed him. He must have fallen asleep and realized by the scenery around him that he was in a park. He saw the sun slowly rising between the trees, bringing with it a new, unexplored day.

As he lay on the moist soft grass, the vision of the previous day flashed images of hatred and anger through his mind. He could feel the blood rush to his head as contempt filled his thoughts. He walked in a stupor along a crowded street, ignoring all passers-by, and entered a greasy diner.

A waitress was pouring coffee and greeted Phillip as he let his aching body fall under its own weight onto the small, vinyl covered barstool. Her grayish-white apron was smeared with grease and food stains. She smiled at Phillip and noticed his unkempt appearance.

"What'll it be?" she asked, chewing gum as she spoke.

"Just coffee and toast." She scribbled the order on a note pad, turned, and walked away. Her undersized uniform created tight ripples in areas where fat had developed in recent years. Her breasts had been forced upwards and were undulating near the top of the vestment where one too many buttons had been left undone.

Phillip, in an effort to ignore her appearance, began to feel pity for the woman. He felt a strange presentiment of peace within himself. He had been robbed of every meaningful entity in his life and yet he no longer felt the anger and hatred of the previous day. He pondered the thought a moment and was horrified by the realization that he felt no emotions at all.

Phillip finished eating and left two dollars on the table. Outside, the cold wind was blusterously whipping through the dawn-filled New York streets. He turned up the collar of his wrinkled suit jacket and stood on the sidewalk, searching the street for the first available cab.

"Where to, buddy?" the driver asked. Phillip gave him directions and the cab raced through the streets of the downtown core. Phillip was oblivious to the noise and haste of the morning sights surging past him.

He paid the driver and stepped out of the yellow, mud-splashed taxi. His eyes slowly gazed at the monstrous steel and glass structure before him. He had worked there every weekday for the past five years. All around him people were busily hastening in different directions. The dampness of the early spring air caused Phillip to shiver. Perhaps from cold, perhaps from fear.

He entered through the revolving glass doors into the spotless, white marbled lobby and walked along a shiny, tiled floor of black and white checked squares leading to a bank of elevators. As the door opened, Phillip stepped into the small compartment and was crushed into a corner by a crowd of employees beginning the unvaried routine of a new working day. Several of the passengers gave him inauspicious glances, making him aware of his frightening appearance. He reached up in an effort to adjust the collar of his deeply creased suit. The dampness of the overnight, spring dew on the wet grass had removed any indication of a previously pressed image. He brushed his hand over his bushy blonde hair and felt a film of grease on his palm. His face turned red. He was embarrassed.

He quickly stepped past the receptionist seated behind an old, wooden desk. The girl was speaking on the telephone and paused momentarily when she saw Phillip pass. Her eyes left a trail as her stare remained fixed on the man who had always taken care of his guise. She blinked twice and somehow managed to smile as she continued to fix her gaze on Phillip, outrightly ignoring the party on the other end of the telephone. Phillip neglected the girl completely. His thoughts were immersed in the shattered surroundings of his crumbling life.

He walked hurriedly through a maze of tan coloured, cloth covered partitions and stopped when he reached the desk at which he had sat for several years. The beige steel bureau had a disorganized appearance. Papers were scattered in sloppy piles and several pens and pencils had been discarded where they were last used. Two styrofoam coffee cups had been abandoned and seepage from them had left small, brown stains on the metal surface.

"Kinda' late, ain't ya, Phil?" Phillip ignored the comment. He had always disliked the pretentious attitude of Dave Black, who had sat next to Phillip for two years. "What the hell happened to you?" Black continued, noticing Phillip's unkempt appearance.

"Shut up," Phillip said softly. There was a stern tone in his voice. Black chuckled inaudibly, insinuating Phillip had partied just a little more than he should have.

Phillip removed some papers from a small cardboard box on the floor. He threw them in the garbage and replaced them with several books taken from a drawer. As he scanned the remaining belongings on his desk, he suddenly froze when he came face to face with a photograph of his wife and two children.

Guilt overcame him as he thought of the children. He felt his heart sink as he looked into the eyes of his two small sons. Their eyes seemed sad and were filling with hatred as they watched their father abandon them.

Quentin, the eldest, was developing quite a personality which in many ways resembled that of his mother. He
had unending patience and was forming attractive facial
features. Phillip felt teardrops gather in the corners of his
eyes as the memories burst into the foreground of his mind.
He silently condemned his wife for her betrayal; however,
in the same instant he missed their love dearly.

His younger son was a miniature replica of himself
including the wavy, thick, blonde hair. He had recently
discovered the art of speech and had become quite a noisy
conversationalist.

Phillip wanted so desperately to hug his children,
kiss their cheeks and tell them how much he loved them.

Then he thought of Saturday and his promise to take
them fishing. He remembered his personal joys when his
father would teach him the laborious techniques involved
in catching 'The Big One'. He wished so desperately to
duplicate those precious memories with his own boys. The
tears flowed freely from his cheeks as he thought of the
permanent destruction of those cherished hopes.

He fought hard to suppress his outward display of
emotions as he felt Dave Black staring at him from his desk
just a few feet away. He despised his wife for the agony and
turmoil she was putting him through. His feelings of anger
and hatred were rapidly replacing any longing he had for
her.

His body foundered deep into his chair and he dropped
his tear-stained face into shaking, cupped hands. He felt
relief at Black's abstinence of personal questions or remarks.

The co-worker was seated at his desk and although
he realized something was desperately wrong with Phillip,
he did not speak.

Phillip slowly raised his head and lifted the photograph from the metal desk. As he opened the frame and

removed the picture, he violently tore the portrait in half, taking a final gaze at the torn section of his wife's smiling face staring back at him.

How could he have been so naive to take his relationship so much for granted? So many questions bombarding him all at once. Thousands of small hammers inflicted short, sharp thrusts of unbearable pain to his head. He felt nauseous and tried breathing deeper in an effort to relax with each exhalation.

Slowly he regained control of his body and threw half of the torn photo in the waste basket. He placed the remaining section in the cardboard container and wiped his eyes. He decided to wash his face and clean up a little before meeting with his superior. Placing both hands on the desk, he forced his body into a standing position and paused for a moment. He rubbed his hands across his face and walked to the washroom.

Upon seeing his reflection in the mirror, a vicious wave of shock pierced his senses. He was relieved that no one else was in the small, beige tiled washroom. His blonde hair, oily and scattered messily on his head, and the bristles of his day old beard made him feel dirty. He fumbled in his pocket for a comb and tried as best he could to manage his greasy hair into a presentable format. He brushed his jacket with his hand and endeavoured to straighten his soiled tie.

He ran the cold water and, using the pink, liquid-soap from the silver wall-mounted dispenser, washed his hands vigorously. The ice cold tap water stung the grimy skin of his sully, tear stained face. The stinging was replaced by a soothing coolness, a reawakening to an over-tired body and mind. He splashed the chilling water onto his face for several seconds, enjoying the immense relief it brought.

As he tore several sheets of paper towel from the roll and rubbed his face and hands, small pieces of moistened paper caught on the day-old stubble of his beard. He was pleased some of the reddish flesh colour was returning to his corpse-like face.

Phillip walked hastily along a gray-panelled corridor and mentally prayed for time to pass quickly. He wanted so much to have the proceeding task behind him, fearing the necessity of having to explain the events of the past twenty-four hours to his supervisor. They were personal thoughts which he did not wish to share with anyone at this time for they were a compilation of his life breaking apart. A painful destruction that he could not bear to form into vocal sounds. He hoped that Don Griffith would be as understanding as he usually was.

He stopped at an office securely guarded by an efficient secretary with short, black hair. The girl was visibly shocked by his appearance and forced a nervous smile. Phillip had always liked her and enjoyed her company during business meetings. He was grateful for her sensitivity and her lack of desire to question him on his appearance.

"Hi Patti, is Don in?"

"Yes he is, Phillip." Phillip could not help notice her stare as she tried to maintain a false pretence. "I'm sure it's okay for you to go right in," she added.

"My God Phil! What happened to you?" Don Griffith had worked with the government for eighteen years. He was the head of Phillip's department. His messy desk reflected a disorderly appearance. The landscapes on the wall were crooked and the soiled green curtains which covered greasy windows were slightly torn.

"I'm leaving, Don." The words rolled much easier from his lips than he had anticipated. He had expected the brief encounter to be a stammering, word searching experience.

Don Griffith removed his glasses and placed them on his desk. Putting both hands flat on the wooden top, he raised himself to an upright position.

"What?" His mouth stayed open. A look of astonishment was evident on his face. "What do you mean you're leaving? What happened? You've got five years of your life tied up in this place. Where are you going?"

Phillip gazed blankly at his superior. There was a sincere lack of answers to the line of questions being fired at him.

"Don," he began slowly, "Maureen and I are finished." Don Griffith didn't speak. He slowly sat down in his chair and motioned for Phillip to do the same. A sudden knock on the opened door to Don Griffith's office startled both men.

"Are you free for our meeting, Don?"

The voice was that of a co-worker who, upon seeing the state of Phillip's attire, immediately recognized the importance of their situation.

"I can come back later if you want?" he asked.

"Yeah," Griffith said slowly. "Do you mind?" He paused momentarily. "Close the door will ya?" He waited an instant and looked at the scruffy, dishevelled man before him. The man who in his opinion had so much potential. What on earth had happened?

"I'm just very fed up with everything right now."

"That's no reason to throw away five years of your life."

"It's not just the marriage, I suppose that's the final straw." Phillip sat down. "I just have to get away from everything. I need time to think things out."

"Why don't you take a few weeks off? There's no problem here, we'll cover for you."

"Thanks, but no thanks. I really want to get out."

Phillip looked down and focused on a small, dried coffee stain embedded in the dirty gray carpet. "Please don't make this any more difficult for me than it already is," he asked compassionately.

Don Griffith folded his hands and sighed slowly. He could not remember the last occasion when he was stuck for words. He would remember this one.

"It's your life, your career. If you need to go then I guess all I can do is wish you the best of luck."

Phillip thanked his superior and embarrassedly left the office. He walked to his desk and gathered the small box containing the remnants of his short career. Without speaking to anyone, he quietly departed the office, knowing it would be for the last time.

There was a sudden sinking feeling in his stomach as the aircraft dipped through severe turbulence. The pilot had warned the passengers by illuminating the seat belt indicator. Phillip looked at his watch. Had he fallen asleep, or had he merely been daydreaming? He glanced through the small, plastic window at the deep blue sky extending into infinity. The airplane was hovering between two layers of white, puffy clouds.

Above, Phillip could see several white wisps of thin strands, floating graciously, freely, dominating the heavens. Below was a thick, velvety cushion of cumulus. The sun was slowly inching its way to the horizon as if magnetically bound to the edge of the earth. Evening was approaching and the sky was beginning to glow a bright, flaming orange.

Phillip's thoughts, once again, drifted back into his past. He remembered his children and wondered how they had matured. They must be quite grown by now. He thought about his wife and wondered where she was living. There had been no contact with her since the divorce eight years ago. The courts, in their infinite justice had granted custody of their children to his wife. He felt a surge of hatred pulsate throughout his tired body as he remembered the ugliness of the entire tribulation. Shortly after the ordeal she and his sons had disappeared. Phillip had tried to find their whereabouts but had been unsuccessful. She had completely vanished and in so doing had broken his heart.

In an effort to find her and his sons he had travelled to Europe. It was while he was on an escorted tour of Austria that he had first made contact with Peter Alexander. Phillip recalled the day. The sun was shining brightly overhead and the sweet fragrance of the chilled, Austrian mountain-sides was in the air.

The Bavarian cold permeated Phillip's body and seemed to penetrate deep into his bones. He had checked into a hotel and was heading for the coffee shop to satisfy a nagging hunger which had slowly developed in the bottom reaches of his stomach.

A well dressed man in his late thirties was walking ahead of him. His cream coloured suit, trimmed with a navy silk tie and puff, gave him an executive distinction. His wavy, blonde hair was thick and covered the top of his ears. The wrinkles on his face added a flair of elegance to his appearance as did the slight tufts of grayish, white hair covering his temples. Ordinarily, Phillip would not have given the man a second thought, however there was a touch of excitement about him.

Phillip, from the corner of his eye, saw two very muscular men, dressed in dark-blue business-suits, walking to the side and slightly behind the man in beige. Phillip directed his attention to the two men as they continued to shadow the blonde haired man. Phillip's mind began creating tales of daring espionage as he surveyed the threesome. He smiled secretly as he brought his wandering mind back to the reality of an obvious business situation. He was about to turn into the entrance of the coffee shop when he noticed one of the two men nod to his companion who suddenly, without warning, reached inside his jacket and removed a small, black revolver. He pointed it at the unsuspecting man in the cream coloured suit walking nonchalantly before them.

Thoughts flashed rapidly through Phillip's mind. His fictitious imaginings of espionage were not so far from the truth after all. He was about to witness an event carrying all the likelihood of a murder. The spontaneous actions which followed happened with such immense speed that if there had been time to think about his possible performance he would have surely fled from the terrifying scene. Instead, without warning, his body hurtled into motion with such speed and agility that it surprised even him. He flung his out-of-shape physique in the direction of the gunman. As he leaped through the air Phillip screamed with severe intensity. The unsuspecting victim protracted around in time to witness Phillip crash into the man with the gun, sending him toppling fiercely against a concrete pillar framing the elegant entrance lobby of the hotel.

Several people stopped and turned their attention to the clangourous incident taking place before them. The hotel lobby was crowded and everyone stood mesmerized as they watched Phillip crash against the cold, marble floor. The other man grabbed Phillip's lapels and raised his torso far enough from the ground to triumphantly smash his clenched fist into the soft, untrained stomach muscles of the ill-prepared tourist. The severe pain shattered throughout Phillip's body and caused him to cradle his arms around his aching abdomen. He could not maintain his balance as the pain engulfed his body. He slumped as anguish overcame him and stumbled to the black and tan coloured marble floor. He felt the coolness of the stone penetrate his body and feared the gunshot directed at him would soon echo through the stillness of his mind.

The dreaded sound did not surface but instead , a sharp, piercing pain riveted his back like that of an automatic drill rotating harshly into a piece of wood. There was still no sound as Phillip lay helplessly on the bare lobby floor. Several seconds passed and he began to feel an easing of painful pressure within his body. He realized that the jolt dealt him had not come from a gun but instead had been a thrust delivered by one of the two gunmen's feet. Perhaps they had fled and he would not die as he had surely imagined he would. Why had he flung himself at the assailants? Violence had never been a part of his make-up.

The gunman had regained his balance and both men ran through a nearby doorway with the man in beige racing after them.

Phillip had repossessed most of his senses and slowly began to rise from the cold, marble floor. Onlookers had gathered and were staring oddly at the injured man struggling to stand under his own support. None had offered aid and Phillip agonizingly glanced around at the gathering of heartless faces. Several seconds later he felt a powerful grip sensitively take him by the arm and offer assistance. Phillip eased his head in the direction of the supporter and stood face to face with the mysterious, blonde-haired stranger in the meticulously-pressed, cream-coloured suit.

"That was a very brave thing you just did." His proper, upper-crust, British accent matched his debonair style of clothes and well trained manner. He helped Phillip to his feet and after feeling certain that he was able to stand under his own support slowly released his helpful grip.

"Do you speak English?" he asked. His voice upheld a friendly, thankful tone.

Phillip nodded slowly. The spectators began to disperse as the excitement was nearing an end. The gladiators had entertained them but now the tournament was over.

"I'm American," Phillip said slowly, rubbing his painful stomach.

"You saved my life," the stranger said. "Can I buy you a drink?"

"I could sure use one."

The two men walked through the lobby, bypassing the restaurant and making their way to the small, comfortable lounge. The man in beige led the way but was careful to keep his step at a pace Phillip, in his agony, could maintain. It was evident by his familiarity of the surroundings that the stranger had frequented the establishment many times before.

"By the way," he began as he slid into a nearby chair, "my name is Peter Alexander."

"Phillip Wright," Phillip said as the two men shook hands. "I can't believe I actually did that."

"Well I most certainly appreciate it. Are you positive you're not injured?"

"No I'm alright." The pain had eased and was quite manageable.

"I chased after the two men but to no avail." He was about to continue when the waiter interrupted his conversation. Peter Alexander looked at the uniformed man and motioned Phillip to order.

"I'll have a gin martini with ice... no olive." Phillip said softly, still somewhat shaken after his near death experience.

The waiter nodded his head. Peter Alexander asked for a Rusty Nail and the waiter departed silently.

The cream-coloured suit complimented Peter Alexander's blonde hair and bronzed, tropic tan. He had a very straight nose giving him a slightly arrogant look. The small lines by the corners of his eyes added distinction to his well-groomed appearance.

"Why was that guy about to shoot you?" Phillip asked.

"I can't tell you that," Alexander said coldly.

"What do you mean you can't tell me?" Phillip raised his voice in annoyance.

"I'm sorry but I can't."

"Some guy pulls a gun, I get punched out and you can't tell me why? How do I know those guys weren't cops chasing you?"

Peter Alexander spoke calmly. "If they really were police, they wouldn't follow me into a crowded hotel lobby, pull their gun and run off now, would they?"

Phillip thought about the logic of the statement. It made sense.

"Perhaps this will set your mind at ease." Peter Alexander slipped his hand into his inner jacket pocket and slowly removed a passport. He opened it and held it for Phillip to see. The United Nations' seal and a government identification card bearing Alexander's picture was enough to convince Phillip that the stranger across from him was legitimate.

"I hope that satisfies you, Mr. Wright?" He replaced the passport, brushing the jacket to remove any dust or wrinkles that had gathered.

"Tell me, Phillip," he paused, "may I call you Phillip?" Alexander waited for Phillip to nod his approval before continuing. "What line of work are you in?"

Phillip looked up. He had not been asked that question since he had left his job almost two months earlier.

"Actually," he said slowly, "I'm not employed at the moment." Alexander waited, half expecting Phillip to continue. When he realized there would be no further comment he decided to probe. He understood immediately that Phillip was undergoing a stressful transition. Something shocking must have taken place for he appeared quiet and depressed, an apparent contradiction to what seemed to be an enthusiastic personality.

"Are you travelling?" he asked.

"Yes, I'm on a vacation of sorts," Phillip answered. "It's kind of a long story, but basically I needed to get away."

"Are you married?"

"Not any more." He desperately wanted to avoid any conversation on the subject. Peter Alexander seemed to sense Phillip's wish.

"I'm sorry," he said. "I didn't mean to pry."

"That's okay. It's just something I really don't want to get into."

To Phillip's relief the waiter brought their drinks and placed them on a coaster on the table. Phillip reached into his pocket but was interrupted by his new acquaintance.

"No, no, this one's on me. That's the least I can do." Alexander took a credit card from the billfold inside his jacket and handed it to the waiter. The uniformed steward placed the small plastic card on his silver tray and departed. "Tell me something, Phillip, have you any career plans?"

"Not really." Phillip thought for a moment. He actually had not planned the remainder of his life. He had spent most of his time thinking about events that had happened. "I'm more or less trying to put my life in some sort of order. I haven't put a great deal of thought into the future."

Peter Alexander continued. "I work for an international government agency that could probably use someone like yourself. If you're interested, could you call this number and ask for this person?" He removed a pen from his jacket and jotted some information on the paper napkin before him. He passed it to Phillip. "Tell the person who answers that you were speaking to me. Ask him to call me if he wishes verification."

Phillip studied the writing and folded the napkin more out of courtesy than anything else. He smiled appreciatively and directed his attention around the dimly lit bar. There were two other tables occupied by couples engaged in intimate conversation. All the tables were black marble and the chairs had been covered in a complimentary dark leather-type material. A bartender dressed in a satin shirt complete with bow tie was wiping the vinyl top of the long, dimly lit bar counter.

Hundreds of high polished crystal goblets and tumblers were stacked symmetrically on glass shelves secured by brass brackets and affixed to a smoked glass mirror.

An efficient flight attendant brought a tray and placed it on

Phillip's table. The sudden movement snapped him back to reality. He found it difficult to accept that eight years had passed since that late afternoon in Vienna. Again his mind drifted. He remembered pondering the thoughts about the number scribbled on the napkin handed him by Peter Alexander. His curiosity had been aroused and visions of glamorous espionage and intrigue danced wildly in his mind. He had let the moment pass, however after several days found that the thought still haunted him. He was surprised the entire episode had taken his mind away from his recent marital problems. It was not until the last day of his vacation that he decided to take the plunge and make the telephone call. He was sitting in his room finishing a martini which he hoped would steady his nerves and smiled when he thought of the agitation created by the potential conversation. He lifted the receiver slowly and dialed the number from the napkin held in his trembling hand.

A woman answered and Phillip politely asked for the name of the person Peter Alexander had written.

"Just a moment sir," the receptionist replied cordially in a British accent.

Phillip wondered where the call had been placed. He was unfamiliar with the country code.

Another woman answered the transferred call. Again Phillip asked for the man whose name was written on the napkin.

"There is no one here by that name sir, who referred you to us?" the voice asked efficiently.

"What do you mean who referred me?"

"From whom did you get this name?"

"A friend of mine gave it to me." Phillip said suspiciously.

"Who was that friend?" The voice asked calmly.

"Why do you need to know that?" Phillip was getting annoyed at the woman's bureaucratic response. He had spent many years of his life dealing with a bureaucratic system and knew how frustrating it could be.

"It will help me to transfer your call." Her voice had grown softer and more polite, having recognized Phillip's disagreeable tone.

"Peter Alexander," he said.

"Thank you." She put Phillip on hold for several minutes until finally a familiar click re-engaged the line and a man's voice sounded in the receiver.

Phillip was astonished when the man, after apologizing for delaying him, explained that the name written on the napkin was a code name used by senior individuals who wished to possibly recruit new members into their organization. The man asked Phillip several questions about his past and asked if he would be able to travel to London.

"I guess I could, when were you thinking?"

"Tomorrow or the next day would be fine."

Phillip was amazed at the sudden turn of events. An airline ticket was left for him the next day at his hotel. After a short flight and a luxurious limo ride through downtown London, Phillip found himself face to face with a blue-suited, straight-faced individual. After a gruelling interrogation, the man explained it would take up to three months for a thorough investigation of Phillip's background to be completed. Unfortunately these were the rules and could not be adjusted.

At the conclusion of the meeting, the man told Phillip to accompany him to Peter Alexander's office. A short walk and a four level elevator ride ended on a floor which, in Phillip's mind, could have been in a different building. The gloomy decor of the initial surroundings of his first interview had been replaced by a luxurious interior of the upper level hallway.

"Come in, come in." Peter Alexander greeted his acquaintance enthusiastically as he walked around the desk to welcome Phillip. He extended his hand which Phillip appreciatively took returning the reception.

Peter explained how pleased he had been at the news of Phillip's phone call. The two men chatted for twenty minutes.

"Stay in London for a few days... as our guest of course." Peter had insisted.

"That would be great."

"I'll make the arrangements."

The two men departed and Phillip was ushered from the building by a well-mannered security guard.

After two months of careful investigation Phillip was notified in person of his acceptance into the security division of the United Nations. He was ecstatic at the prospect and relished the thought of commencing his education.

The next two years were spent in rigorous training. Phillip had never imagined that so much knowledge in areas of self-defence and criminal investigation was available.

He was assigned to the International Security Investigations Sector of the United Nations and reported directly to Peter Alexander. Most of his assignments were in the area of illegal immigration practices. Phillip would locate people and then inform local authorities. It was a "low action" position, although danger did surface from time to time. He enjoyed working for ISIS and had grown accustomed to the risk factor in his career; one had to be prepared, for every turn had a different and surprising challenge.

As with all things enjoyable, there were always negative factors. Phillip regretted he had very little authority. He had done absolutely no future planning of any kind. His home was his suitcase and his loves had always been short affairs in different cities.

He had thought many times of leaving the agency. Each time he had forced the thought from his mind. What could he do? Where would he go? It would be impossible to return to an ordinary lifestyle.

He finished his meal and tried to get some sleep. His last assignment had been more difficult than expected. He had spent three fast-paced weeks combing through Europe in search of a man who allegedly headed a counterfeit passport operation. Phillip's combat training had come in handy. He had confronted the man and was subjected to several brutal blows before subduing him. He had walked away shaken and bruised but thankfully with no major injuries.

His chase had ended successfully in Rome. He had planned a little rest and relaxation and was surprised when he received his new directives so soon after completion of this assignment. However, he never questioned the company's requests, no matter how demanding.

Normal practice was to contact the agency to submit a report. He would then be given his next assignment. During those times when the workload was extremely heavy, the report writing would have to be delayed. This was one of those times. Phillip wished there would have been a few days of leisure to soothe his aching, tired body. As always though, he would do his utmost to succeed in this new operation and it appeared to be a more typical, low action assignment. A telegram had been hand delivered to his hotel room in Rome outlining his next directive. Only Peter Alexander knew his whereabouts as security was the vital factor in their line of work.

He was to travel to Cartagena and meet with a representative of the U.S. Government. His name was Sullivan and he would brief Phillip on the details of the task ahead.

He had read the telegram, checked the security clearance codes and followed the instructions.

Phillip had been to South America before. He enjoyed the constant warmth of the sun and tropical climate. His last trip had taken him to Bogota. Today he was headed for Cartagena, a picturesque, seaside resort. Perhaps at the completion of this assignment he would find a few days rest in the ancient Spanish-built town.

The aircraft began to descend through the clouds and Phillip was startled when he realized the time. He must have slept for several hours for the last thing he recalled was eating a soggy chicken dinner complete with rice and under-cooked carrots. It was seldom that Phillip slept on airplanes. The noise of the engines and the constant activity of the other passengers usually kept him awake.

Beneath he saw the carved shoreline of Colombia. The deep blue ocean caressed the white border of sand surrounding the green topped countryside. He saw the populous city of Cartagena in the distance. As the plane circled, the voice of the purser echoed screechingly over the worn-out speakers; first in Spanish followed by a difficult to understand English. Phillip was able to follow as his instructors had discovered early in his career that he had a flair for languages and put him through several intensive programs at an accelerated pace. Although not fluent he had a good conversational knowledge of five major languages. Asian and Slavic seemed to be his downfall. No matter how hard he tried he couldn't master their words and sounds. While this had restricted his travels to Europe and South America, he enjoyed both continents as they afforded him opportunities to experience fine foods and cultures.

Had it not been for his ability to understand Spanish he would have missed most of the aircraft announcements as the purser's competency in English was poor.

"Ladies and gentlemen, we are arriving soon to Cartagena. Please do up your seat belts."

There was an increase in passenger activity as everyone prepared for landing. Phillip adjusted his seat forward to conform with airline regulations. He wondered if Lana would be meeting him at the airport.

Lana Winters had been a courier with ISIS for almost three years. She was the attractive daughter of a senior
attaché at the U.S. Embassy in Bogota. She had worked out
of the Cartagena office for about a year. Phillip had grown
quite fond of her during their dealings fourteen months
earlier. He hoped there would be a little free time this trip to
perhaps pursue a more personal relationship.

The drag of the aircraft was noticeable as the flaps
were mechanically lowered. The rolling hills, blanketed
with thick, green forests, sped rapidly beneath them. The
roadways resembled gray pencil lines carelessly drawn on a
green sheet of paper. As the plane descended, Phillip could
see that most of the houses were old and deteriorating.
Their neglect was evident. In the distance stood a church.
Its black-with-white steeple reaching upwards as if attempting to make contact with the Creator.

The engine noise decreased as the aircraft hovered
over the runway. The nose gently lifted and with a sudden
bounce the wheels clutched the ground. A blue cloud of
smoke erupted as the rubber tires made contact with the
hot, sticky pavement.

Thick, black, streaky remnants of previous landings
were visible on the tarmac. The reverse thrust of the engines was increased and a forward motion was felt throughout the fuselage. The aircraft came to a rolling stop, turned
as if guided by an unseen force, and made its way to the
gate.

The plane came to its final halt before the terminal
building. The ladders were brought to the doors by uniformed workers diligently hustling to accommodate their
employer's demands. With great speed, the tourists and
home-comers began to descend on to the tarmac, heading
toward the main building. The sun was slowly setting but a
wave of tropical heat was still very much apparent.

4   CARTAGENA

Phillip Wright stood patiently in the crowded Customs line, tapping his foot anxiously on the gray tiled floor. He studied the fifteen or so passengers ahead of him individually noting certain features and peculiarities. Some were tourists sporting typical tropical travel-wear. Seasonal travellers enjoying their golden years had the latest technology in camera gear draped around their necks. Floral hats were popular as were bright-coloured golf shirts and white laced sneakers for the ladies. A tour escort was pacing back and forth assessing and comforting the needs of the elderly passengers. The affluent tourists were a direct contrast to the less fortunate natives visible on the opposite side of a metal barrier restraining well-wishers and relatives greeting Colombian travellers arriving on the same flight. The majority of onlookers were clad in loose fitting, floral patterned shirts and dresses. The people waved frantically as they recognized relatives and friends.

Phillip glanced behind him and saw native people waving back, attempting unsuccessfully to be heard over the thunderous roar of the crowd. It wasn't long before Phillip felt the extreme humidity of the hot, evening tropics. His dark red, striped shirt felt as if it was a part of his skin. His blue denim jeans began to cling to him in a clammy manner. Even his feet, comforted by his richly tanned, western boots, which had always been a solace were beginning to demand attention.

Phillip had not had time to purchase new clothes or have his current attire cleaned since his last assignment. Normally he was allowed enough time to reorganize before the next task. But this time it was all he could do to book a flight from Rome to New York and then, after a short but tedious layover, manage to find transport to Cartagena. He was tired, unkempt and short-tempered and was due some time-off which he desperately required. Sometimes his organization had a callous attitude toward its employees.

He placed his blue duffel bag and his briefcase, both containing his worldly belongings, on the grimy floor, and pushed them along with his feet. He brushed his fingers through his sandy hair and realized how greasy it was. Airplane travel, no matter how comfortable, always took its toll on passengers. As often as one attempted grooming, several hours compressed in a small aircraft seat would undeniably ruin one's appearance. Phillip rubbed his chin and felt his uncomfortable, day old beard. His thoughts drifted dreamily to a large, ceramic bathtub filled with steaming water and soapy bubbles. There was comfort in his imaginings.

The line was progressing very slowly and the Customs officials seemed to take an infinite amount of pleasure in delaying the weary passengers. The elderly tourists ahead of Phillip were feeling the effect of the tropical, evening heat. People were using newspapers, magazines or any articles they could acquire to fan themselves. Tediously the line between Phillip and the Customs officer began to shorten.

Once decorated with a taste of elegance during a more prosperous era, the faded, pure white painted walls of the airport building were now showing signs of fatigue. The paint had peeled in many areas allowing the raw stucco to show its grayish tones. Smudges and scrapes had become permanent components of the decor. A few lonely, neglected plants dotted the corners of the room with brown, dirty leaves scattered randomly at their base. Only two of the four large ceiling fans were operating.

Phillip looked at his watch. It was nine-thirty. The line was increasing in length as more passengers received their luggage from the brown leather conveyer belt and headed toward the Customs area. Phillip was thankful he never had to check his baggage. He had always hated waiting and today was no exception. It was one of those times he wished he had used his authority and bypassed the queue.

The U.N. agent scanned the crowd of tanned Colombians standing patiently behind the metal barrier designed to keep family and well-wishers away from the incoming passengers. At last his eyes focused on the vision he had been seeking. An extremely attractive young woman in her late twenties was standing amid the crowd. Her shoulder length blonde hair had been pulled back into a pony tail and fastened with a yellow scarf. The pale, pink dress she wore complimented her delicate yet striking features. She had meticulously applied just the right amount of lipstick and blush. It gently accentuated the soft curvature of her cheeks. She was a woman who took pride in her appearance and constantly reassured herself that every detail had been catered to. There was no fat on her well proportioned body. It was obvious that she was accustomed to the finer things in life.

When the woman saw Phillip she waved enthusiastically. She was glad of his arrival, sparking fond memories of their last assignment. He returned the greeting, smiling as he waved.

Lana Winters had been raised just outside of Washington D.C.. Her father had been attached to the foreign office for most of her life. Fortunately, although there had been occasions when she had wished otherwise, she had not been uprooted and moved to strange cities as so many of her friends had.

She had always enjoyed the pleasures derived from wealth yet had somehow managed to elude selfishness and self-importance. It was only several years earlier when an opportunity in Bogota, Colombia created a substantial promotion for her father. She had been offered living accommodations in the U.S. by her parents but a sincere wish to join them had also been expressed. She was single and unattached and travel opportunities seemed exciting. Deciding to join her family, she was awarded a clerical position with ISIS through her father's connections.

The extremely high rate of crime in the Colombian capital of Bogota had made the city an unsafe area for young, pretty, unattached American girls. A position for Lana had been secured at the U.S. Consulate office in Cartagena. Although she was performing the duties of a clerk, her connection with ISIS was nonetheless a significant one. The excitement of continuously meeting and working with different field agents gave her job an unequalled importance.

Like every employee of ISIS, she had undergone intense and in-depth security investigations. No stone had been left unturned. ISIS was thorough and its members had little knowledge of anyone beyond their immediate superior.

The size of the entire organization was known only to a select few. Its headquarters and central communications sector were located in London, while many substations located at strategic points around the globe were linked by satellite networks.

Although ISIS was not an espionage organization, it dealt in matters of international security and worked closely with other intelligence networks. There were direct links with the CIA, the KGB and Interpol as well as most national police departments and governments of United Nations member countries.

ISIS was an extremely powerful yet secretive organization. Its sole reason for existence was to ensure the balance of criminal power would be managed and controlled by the United Nations. It was not a war machine nor was it a destructive force. Instead it was a calm, well-planned mechanism that functioned discreetly in all sectors of the civilized world. All of its field agents had been issued special, international visas guaranteeing entrance into any country without the normal Customs clearance. Agents who worked continually on assignments had been issued luggage containing undetectable compartments designed to aid them in their globe trotting travels.

Phillip Wright was such a proxy and had been for the past few years. Although he was assigned to one of ISIS' minor divisions, his performance record had been excellent. He continually obeyed all the rules, an attribute greatly appreciated and admired by his superiors. He was in the habit of completing his assignments successfully. He had worked with numerous personnel and had developed excellent rapport with the majority of them. His quick wit and positive, good-natured attitude was enjoyed by most of his co-workers. It had always been unfortunate that, after a friendship had been developed, agents were sent on to different areas, seldom seeing each other again.

Lana and Phillip had gotten on well during their last encounter. She was looking forward to rekindling past memories. Although she had met several field agents, she had absolutely no idea of their assignments. Such information was considered to be of the highest security.

Phillip had met Lana once before. It was in Bogota

fourteen months earlier. He had been on an assignment searching for the leader of a passport forgery ring.

A well-organized criminal network, operating out of South America, was transporting illegal aliens to the U.S. The man Phillip had been trailing was responsible for setting up the forgeries. His work quality was superior and detection was impossible to the untrained eye. Even the most knowledgeable professionals had difficulty in distinguishing the counterfeit documents from genuine ones. Phillip had found the man and had spent many hours building a case. There had been problems. The man had covered his tracks well. Too well. There was no question in Phillip's mind of this man's guilt. Unfortunately, there was not enough evidence to make a charge stick.

Phillip had developed a plan. He had requested the assistance of a young, attractive woman. He had guaranteed his superiors there would be no danger. Lana Winters had been assigned to him. She was in Bogota and had been working with ISIS for eighteen months. Her task was simple. She was to accompany Phillip into a restaurant where the forger was dining. All that was expected of her was to accidentally upset the man's water glass. Phillip would do the rest.

The interior of the restaurant was dimly lit. The expensive, elegant decor gave the establishment an aristocratic flavour. The small candle lit tables were draped with cloths of burgundy and white. The cutlery and place settings sparkled with each flicker of the candles. The restaurant was crowded with a distinguished clientele.

Phillip and Lana entered through the artistically decorated lobby. Phillip had asked for a particular table and, with the passing of enough pesos, had secured his wish. To the unsuspecting, they appeared as two tourists dressed in semiformal attire preparing to enjoy some excellent South American cuisine.

The maitre d' ushered the two guests directly past

the table where the forger was sitting. Engaged in light conversation with two accomplices seated at his table, the man was unaware of Phillip and Lana's entrance.

He was sitting upright in his velvet chair. A white napkin, draped neatly over his lap, was a contrast to his dark suit and jet black hair. He appeared to be in his mid forties and carried an elegant manner. He gently raised his crisp, white napkin after each bite of his meal and gracefully wiped around his mouth. He cut his food with artistic flair and tasted his wine sensitively. He had an ambient glow and spoke with enthusiasm to his attentive acquaintances.

Phillip and Lana, directly behind the maitre d', were within feet of the targeted table. She had prepared herself well, as Phillip had gone over every minute detail with her many times. She had mentally rehearsed her part over and over. Lana was thankful for Phillip's meticulous attention to even the smallest aspect of her role. She had grown fond of Phillip in the past twelve hours and enjoyed his boyish ardour as he explained the intricate details of the operation to her. She hoped that after the assignment they might spend some time together. Perhaps an intimate dinner in a romantic restaurant or possibly an arm in arm stroll through the gardens of Phillip's hotel. Lana desperately hoped that he had similar feelings toward her. She sensed he enjoyed her company by his positive actions and words.

They walked within inches of their prey. At precisely the predetermined moment, Lana went into action. As she walked past the table seating their target, she turned to glance at the entrance behind her. As she did, her purse fell from her hand and made unswerving contact with the water glass placed directly before the forger. The man had little time to react. He vigorously swung to the side to avoid being soaked. Jumping from his chair, his eyes turned to Lana in anger. In the midst of the confusion, Phillip's opportunity came. His hand carefully reached to the man's jacket pocket. Delicately he placed the small, plastic sack containing white powder into it. He had completed his task without detection. The attention of the forger and his two dinner guests was focused on Lana.

"I'm terribly sorry," she said innocently. "I'm so clumsy. I hope none was spilled on you." The man's aggravated face broke into a warm smile as Lana continued to fidget.

"No harm was done, señora." He gallantly took her hand, gently raised it to his lips, and softly placed a kiss upon it.

"Dreadfully sorry," Phillip said. "She's always bumping into things."

"Not to worry." It was the first time the man had noticed Phillip. He tipped his head in a gesture of greeting. Phillip took the motion as a cue and grabbed Lana's arm waiting long enough for her to pick up her purse.

"Come along, dear." She obeyed. They followed the maitre d' to their table. The onlookers gradually returned to their dining. Phillip and Lana ordered dinner as if nothing had happened.

They ate in silence and watched the forger and his companions, after paying their bill, depart the restaurant.

"Let's go," Phillip said, wiping his mouth with his napkin.

"But," Lana stuttered, "I haven't finished."

"Sorry." Phillip threw enough money on the table to cover the bill and a sizable tip.

Outside the restaurant a scene had developed. Four police vehicles had been recklessly abandoned on the street. Lights were flashing brightly causing confusion amid the crowd which had quickly gathered to watch the ongoing activity. Phillip and Lana turned away from the action and left the area. The forger had been handcuffed and thrown rudely into the rear seat of one of the police cruisers.

"What happened?" Lana asked. Phillip was holding

her arm as they paced quickly down the street.

"It'll be quite a while before he gets out of prison. I understand drug pushing is not looked on favourably down here." Phillip smiled as he spoke.

"I don't get it. What has he done?" Lana had not been taken into Phillip's confidence and knew nothing of the intricate details of his scheme. As she thought for a moment, she realized what had occurred.

"You set him up, didn't you?" she asked, looking into Phillip's blue eyes.

"No, my dear," he relayed calmly, "we set him up."

She looked nervously at the scene behind them. She couldn't believe how easy it had all been.

Although Phillip could use his official status to clear Customs more expediently, he usually made an effort not to exert his power. Unless he was in a rush he would not infringe upon the normal procedure of a nation's policies. He was second in line for the Customs inspection. He eyed the man and woman before him who appeared prepared for a fun-filled holiday. Typical tourists, Phillip thought. The man was wearing a straw hat and a coloured shirt and his oversized stomach was a sign of too much rich food. His wife was carrying a make-up case. Three large suitcases accompanied them. Probably only staying for a week, Phillip thought. He was amused.

Phillip remained behind the fading, red line painted on the floor and awaited his turn. He glanced behind him and noticed the increase in the length of the queue. Typically, the two other counters were without attendants. Phillip balanced his suitcase on one knee and removed his passport, holding it securely in his hand as he returned the leather-covered case to the floor.

The uniformed guard's dark moustache was unproportionately placed on his emaciated, amber-toned face. His dark brown eyes were set deep within their sockets, making his nose appear larger than it actually was. The navy blue uniform was slightly larger than the man's petite frame. He was, however, a definite figure of authority. Phillip had been through enough Customs lines to know that pushiness only caused unnecessary delays.

The guard focused his attention on the next person in the lengthy line of tourists. Phillip picked up his brief-case and simultaneously advanced his duffel bag with his foot.

"Buenos Noches, señor. Your passport please." There were tones of authority in the guard's voice. Phillip leaned forward and passed the man his passport.

The guard turned to the second page and carefully scrutinized the photograph. His eyes slowly lifted from the passport to study the resemblance between the photo and Phillip.

"Are you a citizen of the United States?"

"Yes I am." Phillip replied courteously.

"What is your purpose for visiting Colombia?"

"Strictly business." Phillip said. There was anxiety in his voice. The guard looked up. His small brown eyes, fixed on Phillip.

"What is the nature of your business?"

"I am on an assignment for my organization."

"What type of assignment?"

"I'm not sure. I have to report to the U.S. consulate office to meet with someone."

"What company are you with?"

"I work for the United Nations." Phillip had never hidden his identity or nature of his business from govern-ment officials unless it might interfere with a specific as-signment.

"What do you do for them?"

Phillip's patience was near its end. The lengthy plane trip, coupled with the difference in time and layover in New York, had changed his usually pleasant nature into one of irritability.

"If you'll turn to the next page, you'll find the answers to your questions."

The guard raised his eyebrows. He was not accustomed to anyone addressing him with such arrogance. He slowly, deliberately, flipped the page of the passport and took a moment to read the official United Nations visa.

"You are with the United Nations?" the guard asked after a lengthy pause.

"Yes I am," Phillip replied. "I have already told you that."

The Customs official turned the page and stamped the date of entry into the document. He handed it back to Phillip.

"Enjoy your stay in Cartagena." Phillip ignored the guard's statement. He walked past him into the crowded reception area.

"Well it's about time you made your way through that line," Lana said with a smile. She extended her hand. Phillip gently placed it in his and leaned forward softly to kiss her cheek.

"It's good to see you again," Phillip said as he watched Lana's beaming smile.

"How was your flight?" she asked, reaching over to pick up Phillip's briefcase.

"I'll get that," he said quickly, grabbing the briefcase before she had a chance to reach it.

"The flight was uneventful," he paused, "slow and uneventful."

"You must be exhausted."

Phillip smiled as he nodded.

"I have a car waiting out front."

"Good," Phillip said, "I don't have any other luggage."

They quickly brushed past the onlookers toward the main door of the airport. Once outside, the sudden silence seemed to overtake Phillip. The air was sullen and thick. Fortunately, there was a gusty breeze blowing, adding a bit of comfort to an otherwise unbearable situation.

Lana led Phillip to a dark blue government staff car. She opened the back door, allowing him to place his luggage on the rear seat. She unlocked the passenger door and walked around to the driver's side. Phillip got in, leaned over and flipped the latch releasing her door. As she stepped into the car, he caught himself staring at her shapely legs, exposed more than usual by the movement of her entry into the vehicle.

"Did you get a chance to relax a little after your last assignment?" she asked, invading his private thoughts.

"No," he said shaking his head.

"Was it tough?"

"It certainly was a challenge."

"How long did it take?"

"About three weeks."

"Wow! That must've been quite a caper?"

"There were seventeen arrests in all," Phillip replied. "The last guy was caught yesterday morning."

Lana's hair swayed as she turned her head to smile at Phillip. He returned her warm grin. Three weeks under cover had deprived him of casual conversation. He did not feel like speaking but did not wish to be impolite. Fortunately she was not an overbearing person and gave him enough peace to relax slightly.

"Your hotel is just up the street," she said, swerving her car around a corner. "I don't know how long you intend to stay, but if you have time, there's a casino about a block from here. It's a local hang-out and can be a lot of fun."

Phillip was staring at the rundown buildings lining each side of the street. People were slowly strolling along, couples were walking arm in arm, stopping every so often to chat with acquaintances. There were numerous panhandlers and souvenir merchants along the sidewalk. At the end of the street, lit up in the evening darkness, were large, iron gates which led to the exclusive tourist hotel where Phillip was booked.

Armed guards were positioned at each side of the entrance standing in front of small, wooden sheds. Lana manoeuvred the car past the gatehouse and allowed it to roll to a stop underneath the ornate, concrete canopy which sheltered the main entrance.

"Listen," she said, turning toward Phillip, "it's almost ten-thirty. Would you care for a bite to eat before you retire?" As tired as he was, the thought of a thick, juicy hamburger accompanied by greasy french fries and a cold beer was very appealing.

"As long as it's casual, I don't feel like sitting in a fancy dining room."

"There's a small coffee shop in the hotel," she replied. "Why don't you go and check in while I park the car."

The doorman opened the automobile door as Phillip removed his belongings. He entered the spacious, air conditioned lobby and found the refreshing atmosphere a welcome shock to his hot, tired system. He walked along a row of rattan chairs and giant palm trees and approached the check-in counter. Although there were several people in the lobby, it's immense grandeur gave a uniquely spacious ambiance to the area.

A young, neatly uniformed clerk behind the counter smiled as Phillip approached.

"Good evening, sir, and welcome to the Cartagena Hilton. How can we be of service to you?" The boy spoke politely. His blonde hair and command of the English language revealed his North American background to Phillip.

"I have a reservation. My name is Wright, Phillip Wright."

"Certainly, Mr. Wright." The boy leafed through a

small stack of white cards stopping when he reached the appropriate one. He carefully removed it from the assortment and placed it on the counter facing Phillip.

"Could you please check to see that the information is correct, sir."

Phillip scanned the typed account on the card. He was impressed with Lana's acute sense of organization for she had omitted nothing, including his passport number.

"Have you any luggage, sir?"

"No, thank you." Phillip replied. "I can handle this quite easily." He motioned to his duffel bag.

The boy smiled courteously and wrote a room number on the card, handing Phillip the key.

"How will you be settling your account?"

Phillip withdrew a credit card and handed it to the boy, watching as he carefully inserted it into the small, electronic imprinter.

"Everything under control?"

Phillip turned to see Lana approaching the front desk. He nodded.

"Have a pleasant stay, sir." The boy smiled returning Phillip's card at the same time he handed him a pen to sign the credit card receipt.

"Thank you," Phillip said. He turned and grabbed his belongings. "Let me throw this in my room and I'll meet you in the restaurant," he said to Lana.

"Sounds good," she replied. "The restaurant is down this corridor, first door on your right." She pointed in a direction before her to a small opening framed by potted palm trees and large baskets of blooming red plants.

The elevator stopped at the seventh floor. Phillip stepped out and walked to his room, glancing at the brass plated door numbers to ensure he had taken the proper direction. He found the spacious suite decorated in typical hotel tradition accented with a Spanish flavour. The two beds, separated by a night table, were draped with flowered, cotton spreads. The bamboo headboards matched the twin chairs and small table in front of the beige curtains which covered the sliding door leading to a private balcony.

Phillip threw his duffel bag on the bed and placed his attaché case gently in the top drawer of the dresser. He pulled back the curtains and opened the sliding door. The evening view from the balcony was magnificent. Minutes earlier he had been surrounded by dilapidated buildings and overwhelming poverty. Now he stood gazing at a breath-taking tropical garden centring around an immense swimming pool. The tennis courts and ping-pong tables off to the left were artificially illuminated. Several tourists were huddled around the partially submerged bar along one side of the pool, splashing gaily in the synthetically-lit water. The concrete patio was dotted with chaise lounges, most of which were empty as tourists were beginning to retire at the end of a restful day.

The perimeter of the grounds was bordered by a sandy-white beach, gently caressed by the azure-blue waters of the moonlit Caribbean.

Phillip entered the room and closed the door, allowing the air conditioning system to re-engage. He glanced in the mirror and was shocked by the sight of his tired looking face. There were dark, sagging bags hanging loosely beneath his bloodshot eyes. The short, reddish blonde stubble of his unshaven beard was clearly visible. His bushy, blonde hair was desperately in need of a trim.

He opened his duffel bag and rummaged through it, searching for his razor. He checked the voltage to ensure it was still set at two twenty and after locating the receptacle, quickly ran the electronic shaver over his face, not paying close attention to detail. He combed his hair and sprinkled some cold water on his cheeks.

Again he looked in the mirror. "Well kid, that's the best we can do tonight." He smiled as he spoke to himself.

He walked along the posh, floral carpeted hallway

toward the elevator. While waiting, Phillip stared out the large window into the lush, green leafage of the courtyard below. He enjoyed the times between assignments as it gave him an opportunity to stay in luxurious hotels. There was no need to set traps inside his room for possible intruders or to constantly look over his shoulder for phantom demons inconspicuously tracking him. It was simply a chance for relaxation and it made him despise the uncertainty factor of his line of work. Never knowing what lay ahead or where his tired body would sleep that night. Constantly having to alter his plans in order to survive and successfully complete his commission.

Lana was seated at a small, quiet table in a corner of the restaurant. She raised her hand, catching Phillip's attention as he entered the dimly lit room.

"That's quite an improvement," she said sweetly, smiling devilishly as she spoke. "You actually look presentable."

"I'm sorry," he said. "I have to apologize for my appearance. It's not the best."

Lana looked and smiled at him. "I know," she said softly, with a hint of sarcasm.

"Thanks a lot," he said, grinning as he spoke. He allowed his worn out body to drop nonchalantly into the empty chair directly across from her.

Phillip picked up the plastic laminated menu and after studying it for a few moments, asked her what she was going to order.

"Probably the fruit plate," she said. "It's very fresh and this is one of the few hotels where you can eat fruit washed with water.

Phillip was always careful of what he ate and drank. When he first began travelling for ISIS he had developed severe stomach illnesses causing great discomfort and inhibiting his ability to successfully perform his tasks. His system was continually building immunities to all types of disorders and, aided by prescription drugs, was able to ward off most tropical and filth-related diseases. He seldom indulged in salads or fruits washed in local water or meats raised on local fertilizer. Rarely and only in clean establishments did he use ice in his drinks. Many of his peers had been stricken by unknown bacteria contracted through intake of various foods.

"Would you care for anything from the bar?" a waiter asked politely. Phillip looked up. He had not seen the man approach. Dressed in a traditional Spanish attire, the waiter resembled a bullfighter, complete with a neatly pressed red and black with white trimmed uniform.

"I'll have a Margarita," Lana said.

The waiter wrote the order on his pad and turned his attention to Phillip.

"I'll have a cold Heineken."

"Certainly, sir." The waiter's English was heavily camouflaged by a Spanish accent.

"Beautiful hotel," Phillip said after the man departed their vicinity.

"By far the nicest in the entire city," Lana answered. "Maybe even in all of Colombia."

Phillip removed a package of cigarettes from his pocket. He offered one to Lana.

"I shouldn't," she said. "But I think one would go good right now."

Phillip tapped the package on the table and took one out for himself. Lana picked the matches up from the ashtray and after removing one from the package, lit it. She offered the light to Phillip who inhaled deeply as he drew the smoke far into his lungs. He watched as Lana lit her own and was struck by the sensuousness of a woman lighting a cigarette.

The waiter returned with their drinks. "Would you care to order?" he asked.

"I'm ready if you are?" Phillip said to Lana.

"How fresh is the fruit salad?"

"It was cut only hours ago, señorita."

"Good. I'll have it then." She looked up at the waiter. "Could you please add some sherbet?"

"Of course." The waiter tipped his head. He looked at Phillip.

"Is it possible to get a hamburger and some fries?"

"But of course, señor. We have the best hamburgers in all Colombia," the servitor said proudly.

Phillip smiled. "In that case, I'll definitely have one." He waited for the waiter to depart. His face took on a more serious expression.

"Tell me, Lana, what's on the agenda?"

"Well," she began, sensing the seriousness of Phillip's tone. "My instructions are simply to pick you up at the airport and drop you off at the hotel. Then I'm to meet you at eight-thirty and drive to the U.S. State Department office for a meeting with somebody named Ed Bergan." She paused. "Do you know him?"

Phillip thought for a moment. He had heard the name before but couldn't remember where. Lana interrupted his thoughts.

"Apparently he works for a new division of the Canadian Mounted Police. He's involved in security relations between Canada and South America."

"I remember meeting him now. It was in Canada. He's a little fat man with greasy hair." Phillip smiled as he talked.

"I don't know," Lana said. "I've never met him."

"Any idea why he's here or why I'm meeting with him?"

"I'm afraid you'll have to ask him that. I have absolutely no idea."

The waiter brought their dinner. It was unequivocally the most delicious looking hamburger Phillip had seen in a long time. He picked it up and sloppily bit into it, discarding all manners. Lana picked up her napkin and placed it on her lap, chuckling as she watched Phillip ravenously attack his dinner.

"You act as if you haven't seen food in days."

"It's been a while since I've had an enjoyable meal." His mouth was full as he spoke.

They finished dinner with a Grand Marnier and a cup of rich Colombian coffee. "There's no need for you to pick me up in the morning," Phillip said as he wiped his mouth. "I can grab a cab."

"Nonsense, I drive right along here."

Phillip left enough money to cover their meal and a generous tip. He walked Lana to the lobby.

"Well, good night," she said, turning to face Phillip. He stared deeply into her eyes. His mind raced. He wanted her but knew he couldn't have her. He had never allowed himself to become attached to anyone involved in his career and it was for that reason he had never had lengthy relationships. The insecurity of his future allowed him no permanent involvement. There had been plenty of short affairs throughout the years, but never any meaningful connections. He missed that.

"Good night," he said softly, placing his hands on her shoulders, gently kissing her cheek.

"See you in the morning," she said. "I'll come early so we can have a bite to eat."

"Sounds good."

He watched Lana walk along the red, carpeted floor of the enormous, hotel lobby. Her pink dress swayed as her hips bounced freely with every step she took. She turned and waved. Phillip smiled.

He rested his head on the pillow. As tired as he was, sleep did not come. His mind raced feverishly through the events of the last few weeks. Names, faces, places,. He remembered the times when he was attacked, causing a fearful chill to caress his body. He was thankful he was usually too caught up in an event to worry about fear. He thought about the emptiness of his life. The lack of love. Slowly, as he became more and more immersed in his thoughts, a blanket of sleep at long last engulfed his mind.

5   FACTS

The loud, painful ringing in Phillip's head would not stop and he could only attribute the cursing pang to his lack of sleep. The deafening reverberation grew louder and louder and it reached a level where the only escape was to open his eyes and deliberately face the distressing demon. He wrestled with the anguish and forced his eyes open against their will. The intensity of the ringing seemed to increase as he glanced toward the dresser. On it, in a neat and unobtrusive way sat a small white telephone performing the only function for which it had been designed. It seemed to shake as it ceaselessly rang and he jumped from the bed, rushing to silence its deafening bells.

"Were you planning to sleep all day?" Lana's cheery voice asked.

"What time is it?" Phillip inquired, running his hand through his hair.

"Ten to eight."

"Wow," he said, realizing he had neglected to place a wake up call. "Why don't you go to the coffee shop and get a bite to eat. I'll meet you shortly."

"Okay, sleepy head, I'll see you soon."

Phillip quickly showered and shaved. He fumbled through his duffel bag to find a pair of light slacks and a clean shirt. After combing his hair, he tossed the previous day's dirty clothes into a plastic laundry bag, grabbed his attaché case, and rushed toward the elevator

. "I'm really sorry," he said apologetically, as he approached Lana's table. "Do I have time for a coffee?"

Lana raised her hand and studied her watch. She nodded as Phillip summoned the waiter.

"You must have had a good sleep," Lana said as she finished the remainder of her bacon and eggs. Phillip shrugged as he gulped the steaming hot coffee.

"We'd better move if we have to make it by eight-thirty."

After signing the check to his room, Phillip and Lana departed the restaurant.

"What's in the bag?"

"Oh I'm glad you reminded me. It's some laundry I have to drop off."

"Why don't you take care of it and I'll get the car." Phillip watched as Lana left the lobby. He walked to the counter and after leaving the plastic bag with the concierge joined her in the car.

"Ed Bergan called this morning. He wanted to confirm your arrival," Lana said as she skilfully manoeuvred the vehicle into the main flow of traffic.

The streets of Cartagena were saturated with people. Automobiles were approaching from all directions as the entire community madly dashed to arrive at its daily place of business on time. Some were on bicycles while others went afoot. The morning buses were crowded to capacity as the oldest city in South America came to life, responding once again to the morning call of another hot, sunny, tropical day. Phillip noticed a number of school children dressed in blue and white uniforms walking, on the verge of marching, single file along the cobble-stoned sidewalk.

The drive to the consulate office did not take long. Lana carefully coerced the vehicle along one of the narrow streets in the busy, downtown square. She slowed her speed and came to a gradual halt, slipping the car into a white-lined parking site. Next to them stood a massive, bronze statue of Simon Bolivar, proudly seated atop his gallant steed, carefully scrutinizing the happenings in this once powerful city.

The town square was lined with ancient, baroque buildings. It was decorated with ornate, wooden balconies. In its centre was a neatly manicured, tree-lined park. As they walked toward a three story office complex, Lana pointed out a white, stucco-faced, seven hundred year old building.

"That's the Palace of the Inquisition. Over fifteen hundred non-Catholics were put to death there during the two hundred year siege of terror back in the seventeen hundreds."

Phillip enjoyed hearing about the historical aspect of the city. He lit a cigarette and offered one to Lana who busily continued her explanations of various monuments around the downtown square.

Once inside the office building, they were confronted by a security guard.

"Good morning, Miss Winters," the older, uniformed guard said as he tipped his hat to Lana.

"Good morning," she replied courteously. "This gentleman is with me."

"May I see your passport, sir?"

Phillip removed his passport and handed it to the guard. After a quick glance the man placed it in a blue folder under his beige metal desk top.

"Who is it you're visiting this morning?"

"We're going to Mr. Sullivan's office," Lana replied.

"Yes ma'am. I'll telephone him to announce your arrival." He turned his attention to Phillip, "Please remember to pick up your passport when you leave."

Phillip followed Lana up a short flight of stairs to the elevator. On each side of the entrance a huge American flag gracefully draped the lobby. To one side, a framed photograph of President Reagan kept watch over the wood-trimmed entrance.

Lana and Phillip were the only people in the compact elevator during its short excursion to the third floor. They walked along a lengthy, narrow corridor and stopped at a large wooden door. The hall was carpeted with a deep, brown shag and the beige paint on the walls was new and maintained an odour of freshness. On the door before them was a brass plate with David Sullivan's name neatly engraved into it.

Sullivan was in charge of the State Department office in Cartagena. He had been chosen for his position because of his uncanny ability to handle all types of situations with a tremendous amount of diplomatic flair. He was well liked by his subordinates as well as contacts with which he had business dealings. He enjoyed his work immensely and the sunny South American location was a major factor in his pleasure. Cartagena was a transcendent place to spend his remaining years.

Lana and Phillip opened the door and were greeted by a gray haired secretary busily engaged in typing a document.

"Good morning, Miss Winters." She smiled as she spoke. "Mr. Sullivan is expecting you. Please go in." Her deep brown tan indicated that she had lived in South America for quite some time.

Phillip followed Lana through the adjacent door leading to the office of David Sullivan. He was a large man dressed in a comfortable looking pale blue seersucker suit.

His gray hair was trimmed somewhat short. He was seated behind a plain, old, wooden desk. Money had been saved during the decoration of this office as the decor was simple and inexpensive, a style that had been applied to most of the offices within the limits of the U.S. jurisdiction in Cartagena. The walls were void of paintings and photographs. Only a small credenza, cluttered with papers and used styrofoam coffee cups, stood in a corner behind a desk.

The carpet, stained with several spills, had seen many years of heavy wear. In the corner of the office were four chairs surrounding an oval coffee table. Seated at one of them was Ed Bergan.

"Good morning, Mr. Sullivan," Lana said cheerfully. "This is Phillip Wright."

Sullivan stood up and extended his hand to Phillip. "Good morning, Mr. Wright. I trust you had a good rest?" Phillip nodded. He looked at Lana who was smiling demurely.

"I have several things to do," she said. "If you have no other need of me, I'll be on my way." Phillip smiled at her.

"Thanks Lana," Sullivan said. "We'll give you a shout if we need anything."

She turned to leave, giving Phillip a warm smile. It was only as she stepped toward the door that she noticed Ed Bergan sitting quietly in a corner of the office. He smiled as she closed the door behind her.

Phillip turned his attention to the corner, seeing Ed Bergan slouched in his chair for the first time. His brown polyester jacket was creased and appeared as if it hadn't been pressed in weeks. The shoulders were sprinkled with white flakes of dandruff which gave the vista of a light snowfall on a crisp, fall morning. His dark, greasy hair was receding and had a dishevelled, windblown appearance. He was wearing a white, coffee stained shirt with a brown tie, loosened in an effort to combat the intense tropical heat. It was obvious to Phillip that Bergan had been sitting behind a desk for many years. Most of his weight had been funnelled to his stomach. He stood up when Phillip stared at him. Sullivan made the appropriate introductions.

"I believe you gentlemen have met before, haven't you?"

"Yeah, about two and a half years ago, I think," Bergan replied. "You were in Montreal trying to round up some people or something."

"That's right," Phillip said. "You're with the Mounted Police, aren't you?"

"Not any more." Bergan sat down. "I joined a new government division which links the R.C.M.P. to the United Nations Security Division."

"Have a seat, Phillip," Sullivan said, motioning to a vacant chair. "You must be wondering why you were asked to come here today."

"The thought had crossed my mind."

Sullivan sat down. He took a pack of cigarettes from his pocket and offered one to Phillip and Ed Bergan.

"I never turn down a free cigarette," Bergan said as he pulled the small, white, tobacco stick from the plastic wrapped packet. He fumbled in his pocket for a match. Phillip declined Sullivan's offer.

"Before we tell you what we have in store for you, and before Ed gets into his story, let me just backtrack a little. As you know, Cartagena is primarily a tourist town, not really caught up in very many national or international events. We are now heading into a situation which, if we're not careful, could bring us a whole lot of problems. I'll let Ed explain the rest to you."

Ed Bergan slowly exhaled the smoke from his lungs in an attempt to unsuccessfully create a dramatic mood as he began to speak. "As you may be aware, Canada has been working with Argentina to install a nuclear-powered reactor. This is an extremely profitable deal for Canada and was going along very smoothly until this damn war in the Falklands between England and Argentina started two months ago. England placed a great deal of pressure on the Canadian Government, almost to the point where they insisted Canada stop her dealings with Argentina. As you can imagine, to simply stop the transactions would cost hundreds of jobs and God knows how many millions of dollars.

"The Canadian government looked at many different alternatives. Finally it was decided that in order to keep Britain happy, yet maintain their relationship with Argentina, they would stall the implementation of the program slightly. After all, there was no way that the war could last very long.

"To shorten a long story, the government contacted a senior Canadian scientist who was working on the project in Cordoba and ordered him to delay the implementation of the reactors as discreetly as possible. No one was to know the reason for the slow-down.

"Well, the scientist gets a letter from his boss in Ottawa telling him to slow down the installation process by two or three weeks. What does he do? He sneaks into the restricted area and breaks part of the reactor."

"Excuse me," Sullivan interrupted. "Would anyone like some coffee?"

"Not for me, thanks," Bergan replied. Phillip also declined. Bergan's story was becoming interesting.

"Sorry, Ed, go ahead."

"Well, lo and behold the scientist gets caught, which was a good thing, otherwise the damn equipment would have blown up, killing God knows how many thousands of people, resulting in a major catastrophe. Luckily no one was injured.

"As you know, the war ended rather quickly and every one had forgotten about the situation. This kind of left our scientist in a real predicament. You see he had been arrested and was told not to leave his house.

"He tried to contact his superiors but after several days of trying was told that no one had issued any sabotage orders of any kind. This really left him in a spot.

"He kept insisting that he was repairing, not breaking the equipment, and after a short, and I mean short, investigation, the authorities decided he was lying.

"As I said they arrested him but because he was an official of the Canadian government they went easy on him by placing him under house arrest only. They charged him with trespassing and treason and everyone he reported to in Ottawa denied any knowledge of the incident.

"Now here we've got this poor scientist, whose name is..." Bergan fumbled through a folder in front of him. "I've got it here somewhere."

Phillip and David Sullivan exchanged glances as Ed Bergan displayed his unorganized mannerism.

"Yeah, here it is. His name is McPherson, Lorne McPherson."

"Let me ask a question," Phillip interjected. "Why is the U.S. Government involved in this anyway?"

"I'll come to that, just hang in there. So this poor scientist, who's under house arrest and is about to be charged with sabotage and treason hasn't got anyone to turn to. What does he do? He gives them the slip." Bergan looked at Phillip for a reaction. There was none.

"That's right," he continued, after he assured himself that everyone was listening. "He takes his wife and kids and gets on a plane, along with his assistant and takes off."

"How do you know all this?" Phillip asked. "Considering no one at the government admitted to knowing anything about the matter."

Sullivan answered Phillip's question. "Well that's the damnedest thing. I came in here last Saturday afternoon to do some work and on my desk was a brown envelope. I opened it and found a document outlining this information.

I read it, twice, and didn't have a clue what to do. I contacted the Canadian Embassy in Buenos Aires first thing Monday morning, and told them I had a document which threatened Canadian security. They said they would get back to me very shortly. Half an hour later I got a call from this fellow." Sullivan pointed to Ed Bergan. "He told me who he was and I explained the contents of the document. He told me to hold tight..."

Bergan interrupted Sullivan. "When I got here Sunday I read the document and immediately realized that this could really hurt Canada's rapport with Argentina. I called my boss and told him the story. He made arrangements to contact someone from your area and here you are."

Phillip nodded confirmation of his comprehension of the story.

"Well," Sullivan said, "to be very honest, I really don't want the U.S. to get any further involved. This matter has absolutely nothing to do with us or Cartagena. If you gentlemen will excuse me I'm going to get some coffee."

He placed his hands palms down on the table and slowly lifted his large frame.

"Are you sure I can't interest you in a cup?"

"Yeah, I think I can use some about now," Bergan said. "My throat is getting dry."

"How about you?" Sullivan looked at Phillip.

"Thanks. Black, no sugar."

"Just cream for me," Bergan said. "Got to keep this weight down." He patted his oversized stomach as he spoke.

Phillip noticed that a button was missing from Bergan's shirt, adding to his slobbish appearance. Phillip detested people who didn't take care of themselves. There was no excuse for not staying neat.

"Be back in a minute." Sullivan left the office and securely closed the door behind him.

"So what happened to McPherson?"

"Well as I said, he took his family and left. The

Argentines of course tried to track him down. They find out he's on a flight that lands in Bogota. As soon as he lands he gets picked up by the Colombians. They can't figure out what to do with him because the last thing they need is to get involved in this mess."

"They take custody and confiscate his passport figuring now he can't leave the country and they can wait until this whole mess is cleared up."

"Well McPherson's no dummy. He disappears again, family and all. Now nobody knows where he is. Argentina is ticked off with Colombia and Canada hasn't got a clue what's going on."

"Now this envelope arrives and I get a call, on a weekend, I might add. I get told to hustle my ass down here and meet with this guy Sullivan."

"After reading the document I call Ottawa. They say that Canada can't get involved, however, it would likely be important to all concerned to find this scientist. We must avoid any kind of a possible scandal. I get a call yesterday that someone from ISIS was gonna come down. And here you are."

Bergan leaned back in his chair. He took a cigarette from his pocket and struck a match taken from a crumpled pack of paper matches. He did not offer one to Phillip.

"From here your best bet is to go to Bogota. Here's an envelope for you." Bergan opened his briefcase and removed a brown, manila envelope, handing it to Phillip.

"This has photographs of McPherson, his family and Tim Browning, McPherson's assistant. It also has passports for them all as well as the hotel they last stayed at in Bogota. It's not much to go on, but it's all I've got. The only sure thing is that, assuming this document is authentic, they're still in Colombia."

"When you find him, call me. I'll tell you where to take him. For God's sake don't give him the passports until after you've talked with me." He fumbled in his pocket.

"Here's a number where I can be reached, day or night. It's a clean line. Call me only when absolutely necessary. Remember, it's extremely important to play this whole thing down. My instructions are simple. We have to contain this thing. You'll report only to me. If anything goes wrong, Canada, the U.N. and ISIS will deny any knowledge of this entire matter. Understood?"

Phillip nodded. "I wonder why they chose me? Surely there are lots of other field agents available?"

"Apparently you have the best reputation for tracking people."

"I'm flattered." Phillip took a cigarette from his pocket. He took Bergan's matches and slowly brought the flame in contact with the white cigarette paper.

Sullivan re-entered the office carrying a tray with three styrofoam cups, each filled to capacity with steaming hot coffee. He removed the cups from the small plastic tray and placed them on the glass-topped table.

"Hope this is alright?"

"Great stuff," Bergan said. "Nothing like good, Colombian coffee."

"Can I get a copy of the document explaining this entire caper, the one that was left in the office?" Phillip asked.

"Yeah, it's right here. I made an extra copy." Ed Bergan removed another brown envelope from his briefcase. Phillip placed them in his attaché case.

"Do either of you gentlemen have any idea who put the envelope on your desk?" Phillip asked, looking at David Sullivan.

"Not really," Bergan replied, pausing to take a sip of the strong coffee.

"Remember, your job is strictly to find him and to get him out of this country, nothing else." Phillip was not impressed by Bergan's attempt at condescension.

"Where do you want me to take him?"

"I'll let you know. We may have to do some negotiating with the Argentine government. As you get closer to
finding him I'll try and work out a meeting with Argentine
officials. I'll let you know as time goes on.

"What's going to happen to the scientist when I
catch up with him?"

"He'll probably go back to work in Canada. He
really didn't do any damage. It was mostly political. The
Falklands war ended and life went on. The reactor is now
back on schedule and everyone's happy."

"Why not let things go on without any intervention?"

"We would, except McPherson doesn't have a passport and therefore can't leave Colombia. The Argentine
government wants the matter cleaned up."

Phillip carefully scrutinized the photographs in the
envelope studying each one with interest.

"She's quite a looker." Bergan said as Phillip turned
to the photo of McPherson's daughter. She was extremely
attractive Phillip thought as he eyed the eight by ten glossy
of the pretty, sandy blonde haired girl.

Bergan interrupted his thoughts as he passed a
smaller, brown envelope to Phillip. "Here's ten thousand
dollars. This should cover all your expenses. If there are
any more just report them through the normal channels.
Don't use your credit card. I don't want to bring any more
attention to this than necessary."

Phillip nodded his comprehension. "I've already used
my credit card at the hotel."

"Damn!" Bergan said annoyed. He paused for a
moment. "Okay, I'll take care of it. Tell me where you're
staying and I'll settle your account."

Phillip thanked Bergan and told him he would do
his best.

Ed Bergan took a final sip from his styrofoam cup.
He placed the empty container on the table directly beside

the tray and stood up extending his hand to Phillip. "Good luck, Phil. I know you'll get us through this mess."

"Thank you." Phillip turned and thanked David Sullivan. The men departed from the office.

Phillip walked toward Sullivan's secretary busily chatting on the phone. As she caught a glimpse of Phillip, she curbed her conversation and quickly replaced the receiver.

"Could you please arrange an airline ticket for me for this afternoon. I'll pick it up at the airport."

"Certainly, Mr. Wright. Where would you like to go?"

"Bogota, please." She picked up the telephone and dialed the appropriate number.

"All finished?" Lana's cheery voice asked as she walked toward Phillip.

"Sure are," Ed Bergan replied. He smiled at Lana.

"What are your plans?" she asked, directing her question at Phillip.

He looked at his watch and then at Ed Bergan. "Are we all through?"

"Yep, I guess we are. What time is it?

"Twenty to eleven."

"I guess I'd better get moving, I've got a busy schedule."

"Have you got time for an early lunch?" Lana asked.

"I'll know in a second." He glanced at the secretary who was completing the call.

"The flight is at three this afternoon. You're confirmed on it."

"Thank you very much." Phillip turned to Lana. "Lunch sounds great but let me check out of my hotel first."

She smiled and looked at the other two men hoping they would not plan on joining them.

"You people go ahead," Sullivan said. "I've got lots of work to do."

"Me too," Bergan said. "Nice seeing you again, Phil. Good luck to you and keep in touch." Again he shook hands with Phillip.

"I'll be back in a little while, Mr. Sullivan," Lana said to her superior.

"Take your time. Maybe you can drive Phillip to the airport." Sullivan turned his attention to Phillip. "Good luck, young man."

Phillip picked up his passport and joined Lana, leaving the building through a back entrance to the small, tree lined parking lot. Lana had left her car in a shady spot, attempting to keep it as cool as possible in the hot, Colombian sun. She first unlocked the passenger's door then walked around the car to let herself in. Phillip was beginning to feel the midday heat and was thankful for the air-conditioning in the government automobile.

Lana drove the car expertly through the narrow, winding, building-lined streets of downtown Cartagena. It took only half the time of the earlier trip to return to Phillip's hotel. The streets were less crowded as the community had settled into its daily routine.

Upon check-out, Phillip was told that the account had been settled by a Mr. Bergan. The credit card voucher was returned and Phillip dashed upstairs to gather his belongings.

"When will my laundry be back?" Phillip asked as he returned the room key.

"I am sorry señor, not until late this afternoon."

"Damn," he cursed. "Okay, I'll make some other arrangements. Thanks a lot."

Lana was waiting in the car. "Everything okay?"

"I forgot about my cleaning."

"What time will it be ready?"

"Late afternoon."

She paused and thought for a moment. "I can pick it up for you and you can grab it next time you're through here."

"I don't want to put you to any trouble."

"Don't be silly," she smiled. "It'll give you an excuse to stop by. Write down my phone number," she ordered.

Phillip found a pen and scribbled her number on a piece of paper. "Thanks a lot. How about that lunch."

They arrived at a quiet little restaurant. Its exterior decor resembled that of an ancient Spanish sailing vessel. The entire building was painted blue and white. All around the exterior were circular windows, framed with old, brass steering wheels taken from abandoned ships. Beside the shiny, polished entrance hung a menu displaying the day's bill of fare. Phillip and Lana glanced at it.

"I hope you like seafood, Phillip?"

"I sure do."

They entered the restaurant and required a second to adjust their eyes to the dimly lit surroundings. A tall man, dressed in a beige short-sleeve shirt greeted them as they entered the dining area. "Buenos dias, señorita, señor."

"Buenos dias," Lana said, returning the greeting. "We'd like a table for two, please."

"This way, please." The maitre d' gracefully led them through a set of old-fashioned saloon doors into the main section of the restaurant. The establishment was comparatively empty with only five or six other guests seated at small round tables draped with brown and white checked cloths.

"I guess we're a bit early for lunch," Phillip remarked, noting that it was only eleven forty-five.

The maitre d' turned to Phillip. "In Cartagena, señor, one eats when they are hungry, one sleeps when they are tired." His face was showing a big, happy grin, giving his patrons a chance to see a few empty spaces where once unhealthy teeth existed. He seated them at a quiet corner table near the bar and Phillip waited as he watched the man professionally hold out Lana's chair.

"Must you carry that briefcase with you everywhere you go?" Lana asked as Phillip sat the burgundy leather case on the floor directly beside his feet.

"I'm afraid I do. Everything I need and own is in this case."

"In a way that's kind of sad." She smiled compassionately.

A man in similar attire to that of the maitre 'd walked toward their table.

"Anything from the bar, señorita?"

"Yes, I'll have a caesar."

"And for you, señor?"

"I'll have a gin martini with ice, no olive."

"Would you like some lemon?"

"Yes, please."

"It's a little early to be drinking that kind of stuff, isn't it?" Lana smiled as she spoke.

"Yes, I suppose it is."

Lana thought for a split moment she detected a remorseful look in Phillip's eyes. She cared a great deal for this handsome stranger who had re-entered her life after a fourteen month absence. Lana had enjoyed the pleasure of Phillip's brief company during their last encounter. Although there had been several men in her life, none had been able to satisfy all of her emotions. She was certainly not in a hurry to settle down, however, if the right man did appear she would have no objections to sharing her life. Until that moment arrived however, there would be fun and freedom. She deeply wished she could spend a little more time with Phillip for she longed to be intimate with this boyish man across from her, sheepishly reading his menu.

"So Mr. Wright, where are you off to from here?"

"I'm heading for Bogota."

"I take it you're heading alone?"

Phillip nodded.

"You couldn't find room for an accomplice?"

"I'm afraid not," he said smilingly.

"What kind of case are you working on, or is this another one of those deliciously top secret matters?"

Phillip smiled. "Very top secret," he said mockingly. "I don't really have many facts." He made it a point never to discuss the terms of his assignment with anyone other than his superiors. There had been times when his safety had been compromised by accidental slips from his allies.

"Tell me something," Phillip began. His conversation was interrupted by the waiter who had a tray of drinks in his hands.

"Your drinks." Phillip watched the man expertly handle the tray. He gracefully removed the glasses and placed them on the small round coasters, bearing the brand name of a local beer. "Are you ready to order lunch, señor?"

Phillip directed his attention to the menu and then glanced at Lana. "Are you ready?"

"I'll just have a salmon sandwich on rye." The waiter scribbled the information on his cream coloured note pad.

"I guess I'll have the seafood plate," Phillip said, his eyes still fixed on the menu. The waiter nodded and backed away.

"You were about to ask me something?" Lana said.

"I was wondering if you were working last weekend?"

"I was for a little while Saturday morning. Why do you ask?"

"Did you happen to notice anyone who looked a little suspicious?"

"No, not really. Why?" Lana awaited a reply. When there was none forthcoming she continued. "Does this have anything to do with that letter on David Sullivan's desk?"

Phillip was taken by surprise. "How did you know about that?"

"When someone does something out of the ordinary at this office, everyone knows about it. Is that what you're working on?"

"Indirectly," Phillip answered. "Do you have any idea who might have left it there?"

Lana thought for a moment. "None," she replied sincerely. Phillip changed the conversation.

"It sure gets warm here," he said curling his lower lip at the same time blowing cool air upward, onto his face.

He made a point of keeping the remainder of the conversation away from business related topics. They thoroughly enjoyed their meal as well as each other's company. Lana talked about her life in Washington and Phillip listened attentively. He savoured her company and hoped he would see her again soon.

They left the restaurant and Lana drove Phillip to the airport. "You still have lots of time before your flight." She swung the car through the entrance to the airport terminal.

"Do you want to grab a coffee or something?"

"No, no. You've done enough, I'm sure you've got work to do." He smiled. "Besides, I still have to get my ticket."

"Are you sure?" she asked hesitatingly.

"Yes, of course. It's silly for you to hang around."

Lana pulled the car up to the main entrance as Phillip reached over to the seat behind him and grabbed his briefcase. Holding it on his lap, he turned to Lana. "Thanks very much for all your help. I've really appreciated it." His words were sincere. Lana could tell.

"It's all part of my job," she said tantalizingly, smiling as she spoke. "I hope we'll meet again, soon."

"I'd like that." Phillip paused. "I'd like that very much." He extended his hand. As she took it, she leaned forward, placing a gentle kiss softly on his lips.

"Enjoy your flight and take care."

He closed the door and watched as she manoeuvred the car out of the circular drive, waving as she drove onto the main street. Phillip watched her slowly disappear into the flow of traffic.

6   BOGOTA

The airport was abuzz with activity as ticket agents stood before terminals busily engrossed in keypunching activity. Few were actually engaged in affairs with passengers as most seemed to be engulfed in a timeless world of their own. Phillip glanced from one end of the marbled floor area to the other end. He spotted a quiet corner from which he would be able to see most of the terminal's main floor, yet be secluded enough not to be noticed. He preferred being hidden from view whenever possible. Airports were a serious hindrance in his line of work. Travelling a great deal, he became leery of strangers lurking and often suspected them of stalking him. He had made enemies throughout his career as a field agent and never relaxed his senses enough to enable someone to penetrate his vulnerability.

He sat on a black, vinyl-covered chair and slowly scrutinized the area. He saw no one of a suspicious nature and felt foolish for being overly cautious. There was no reason for anyone to be trailing him. His last assignment had gone well and all participants were safely locked away in Italian prisons. He was overcome with fatigue and was in dire need of rest. Not the kind of relaxation one finds in a hotel while working, but a lasting, peaceful respite, somewhere in a safe location where the climate was pleasing and the air was clean. Somewhere a person could sleep without fear of intrusion. He began to construct a mental curse against Peter Alexander for sending him on this assignment without any leisure time after completion of his previous duty. His thoughts rummaged loosely through the events which took place during his meeting with Ed Bergan. He had disliked the government representative at their initial meeting several months before and maintained the same repugnance for him today. Bergan had little regard for the value of human life. His only concern was to complete a task; at any cost. He struck Phillip as the type of individual who advanced his career at the expense of others.

Phillip glanced around the departure hall once more before placing his attaché case on his lap and opening the safely guarded combination lock.

The case had been skilfully constructed by ISIS' special technical unit and contained a hidden compartment, undetectable to visual scanning. A small, concealed lever recessed within the latch, when pressed, exposed a second, even smaller lever. This was the entry path to the cryptic compartment and its surreptitious contents.

Phillip removed the light brown, manila envelope given him by Ed Bergan. Inside the envelope was a small, neatly wrapped bundle containing a stack of crisp, U.S. currency. Again he lifted his head and scanned the immediate vicinity. He counted the money twice and removed several hundred dollars, which he placed safely in the confines of his pocket. The remaining currency he returned to the envelope and restored it to the secret area of the attaché case. It appeared there would be enough cash to see him through this caper. He had always been careful with money, never spending it needlessly and whenever possible returning the unused portion, or a fragment thereof, to ISIS upon completion of his assignment.

He withdrew his passport from his jacket and mindfully situated it in the secluded compartment, removing a similar one which also bore the United States' crest. This one, however, made no mention of his U.N. status. Often when he travelled he assumed the role of an insurance claims adjuster. He had even taken this masquerade to the point of having had fictitious business cards printed. He was always careful to carry current insurance documents in the upper portion of his briefcase in the event of harassment by government authorities. The insurance deception allowed him exemplary cover, with reasonable permission to ask pointed questions of anyone he made contact with, thereby avoiding suspicion.

He returned his attention to the brown envelope. Inside were several large photographs which Phillip removed, focusing on the first. It was of a man in his mid-fifties. There were numerous creases around his mouth and soft, blue intelligent eyes. The man's face was lean and drawn and he had almost pure-white, thick and neatly combed hair.

Phillip turned the coloured print over and noted the details on the back. Lorne McPherson was born in 1931 making him only fifty-one, Phillip thought. The photo did not do him justice for he seemed to look older. He was a nuclear physicist who had been employed by the Canadian government for quite some time. He had been in Argentina for three years.

The remainder of the information on the flip side of the photograph pertained to his vital statistics. Hair: white; height: six foot, two inches; weight: one hundred and seventy-one pounds.

The second photograph was that of the scientist's wife. Studying her face, Phillip undertook drawing a mental image of her as he scanned the information on the reverse side of the eight by ten. She was five foot-three and weighed 165 pounds. Her brown-coloured hair was short and had been permed into tight curls. She, like her husband, was also fifty-one years old and had the appearance of a pleasantly plump, lively individual.

The next photograph, that of their daughter, made a distinct impression on Phillip. The beautifully featured girl had long, sandy-blonde hair gently curled, producing a wind blown effect. Her deep blue eyes were small, creating a mysterious characteristic in her face. Her lips were slightly parted and outlined perfectly with lipstick. Her features were a compliment to her soft, strikingly elegant appearance.

Phillip read the data on the back. Her name was Kristy McPherson. She was twenty-eight and single. Her stature was tall and thin. Phillip looked forward to meeting her. If she looked half as good as her photo the encounter should prove to be pleasurable.

The next picture was that of Tim Browning, assistant to Lorne McPherson. His circular face had been stretched over his head eliminating all wrinkles and lines and creating a strange, almost horrifying facade. Phillip's eyes were immediately drawn to the oversized, slightly deformed nose. Perhaps it had been broken in his younger years. His hair was shaggy and long and was desperately in need of grooming. He was thirty-one, weighed less than one hundred and forty-five pounds and was slightly shorter than Phillip. His occupation was listed as chemical engineer.

The last photograph was of a little boy displaying an enormous grin, revealing a space where a front tooth had recently been extracted. The blonde haired, twelve year old child had been christened Jimmy.

Phillip stacked the photographs neatly in order, carefully studying each one again. After being convinced that every feature of each photograph could be recalled from memory, he replaced them in the envelope, securing them in the hidden compartment of the briefcase. Once again he studied the movements of the travellers at the airport.

Phillip held the four passports which Ed Bergan had familiarized him with. He turned to the identity page and ensured that everything was in order.

He carefully placed the passports in the hidden compartment of his briefcase and closed the small, yellow latch locking away the information for only him to rediscover. He loosely placed the insurance related documents on top, giving the case a normal, non-suspicious appearance.

Phillip paused, running his fingers through his hair. He thought of the laundered clothes returned and neatly stored in Lana's closet. A sense of longing overcame him when thoughts of the attractive blonde with whom he dined only hours ago sprinted through his mind, and he wondered if he would ever see her again.

He knew that he would have to purchase some additional clothes as soon as an opportunity arose. Phillip made a point of always travelling light, leaving numerous articles of clothing in various embassies and airport lockers around the world, always with the intention of returning someday and retrieving them.

Phillip checked his watch. There was plenty of time before reporting to the gate. He picked up the second envelope, containing the manuscript left anonymously in Sullivan's office, and began to read it. He read it twice, making certain that he had remembered every detail, no matter how minor.

He left the comfort of the chair and walked casually to a nearby washroom. A foul stench permeated the small room, creating a nauseous sensation in Phillip's stomach. He scanned the cubicles for signs of people and after ensuring that no one else was present, entered one of the small compartments and removed a book of matches from his pocket. He struck a match and carefully touched it to the document. Twisting the flaming pages, he allowed their smouldering ashes to fall into the toilet bowl, creating a hiss as the hot, charred journal made contact with the cool water.

He collected his belongings and exited the soiled atmosphere of the restroom, heading for the gate of his departure.

He checked through security and slowly settled in a seat toward the posterior of the plane. It was a position he preferred, awarding him an excellent opportunity to scan the rest of the aircraft and procure a good glimpse of the other passengers. The Avianca 707 was filled to capacity, mostly with tourists.

Phillip leaned back and awkwardly attempted to find a small bit of comfort in the cramped aircraft seat. He mentally reviewed the details of the mysterious document found in Sullivan's office and he went over all the points which Ed Bergan had explained. His mind had been trained to accept only facts and was developing an uncanny ability to differentiate between truth and fiction. An ability to carefully discard all irrelevant information and to system-atically place the filtered remains in clear and logical order.

Locating Doctor McPherson was a routine task, the sort of assignment Phillip was familiar with. The type he had been trained for. Several unanswered questions contin-ued to play in his mind: how receptive would McPherson be to returning to Canada; where was it that Bergan wanted McPherson delivered; what plans did the Canadians have for the scientist once they got their hands on him.

The never-ending questions were the worst part of his job. Very seldom was he ever given the entire overview of a situation, usually only playing a minor role in the disintegration of a major international incident. The most frustrating aspect was that he rarely discovered the final conclusion. Eventually, assuming he continued to perform in an above average manner, his career would lead him to a position with greater responsibility. He would have other agents reporting to him, granting him greater control of situations. Presently he was unaware of the inner workings within his organization. All directives were supplied through security coded, specially sealed envelopes. There was always an amount of cash accompanying his orders. Receipts were not necessary and when Phillip had first been assigned to the field, he had always rendered every unused penny, however, as time progressed, he had kept more and more, filling discreet bank accounts around the world. ISIS had never questioned his credibility and, until they did, he would continue to build his nest egg.

The flight to Bogota lasted an hour and no meals were served. Lukewarm coffee was offered in stained, ceramic cups which Phillip declined, yearning only for peace to allow him to gather his thoughts and plan his next manoeuvre.

The aircraft bounced slightly as turbulence caressed the wings, causing them to flutter in rapid vibrations. The seat belt sign was illuminated as the plane continued to soar high above the Andes. Phillip continued to close his eyes in a constant effort to seek comfort in an environment that bequeathed none. At long last the purser announced the landing instructions, bringing a conclusion to an unpleasant flight.

Bogota was hotter than Cartagena. The warm humid air in the terminal was like a thick blanket of moisture and immediately wrapped itself around anyone who entered. Phillip followed the corridor to the baggage and exit area. He had his attaché case in one hand, his duffel bag in the other, and was thankful he had discarded the blue denim jeans. The pair of light, khaki rugger pants he was wearing were much more comfortable in the extreme heat.

Phillip walked to a secluded area of the terminal where a row of brightly painted lockers stood. He searched for a specific number and, upon finding it, removed a key from his attaché case and inserted it in the tiny slot. Inside,

wrapped in an oil cloth, was an automatic pistol loaded and
ready for use. He had developed an immense displeasure for
the weapon and detested carrying it unless he felt he would
embark on a life-threatening situation. He had witnessed
far too much violence in his career to promote any further,
unwarranted use of firearms.

He walked to a row of vending machines displaying
candy bars and fumbled through his pocket for some loose
change. His growling stomach had become a priority and
its craving had to be satisfied. He glanced through the
scratched glass opening of the mechanical food machine
and was about to deposit the proper amount of coins when a
shuffling sound behind him alerted his senses. From deep
within Phillip's instinctive nervous system a feeling of fear,
attempting to rise was immediately crushed by the necessity
to act. From a small corner of his eye he caught a glimpse of
a slight movement behind him. In one complete gesture,
the length of a blink, he raised his arm and swung around
in readiness to defend any assault made upon him.

Before him stood a brown-skinned man, somewhat
shorter than Phillip. His dark eyes were uniquely large and
widely spaced apart in comparison to his narrow face. The
man was smiling. Phillip relaxed his rigid expression of
readiness. A wave of embarrassment swept over him as he
realized how foolish he must look standing, arms poised,
ready to attack an innocent, old man in line to purchase a
chocolate bar. Phillip slowly moved his hand to his head
and scratched his scalp in a desperate attempt to cover up
his disconcerting action.

The man spoke to Phillip in Spanish. "Buenos dias,
señor. I see I'm not the only one who has an afternoon
craving for some chocolate."

Phillip returned the smile. Was he over reacting?
Was he becoming obsessed with a fear of constantly being
attacked at any time, from anywhere? His senses were very
seldom wrong. He had learned many times to rely on them.

His error in judgment bothered him.

Again the stranger spoke. "You are American?"

"Yes," Phillip said in Spanish.

Phillip was about to collect his chocolate bar when he saw a man leap from behind a palm type plant twenty feet away from him. The stranger made momentary eye contact, then turned and fled.

This time it was not an idle threat created in the recesses of his imagination. Phillip grabbed his attaché case and duffel bag with one hand and ran in the direction of the possible assailant. Behind he could hear the old man yelling, telling him he had forgotten his chocolate bar.

Phillip had focused his senses on the figure charging ahead of him. A figure he was certain had been spying on him. People had stopped to watch the two men racing wildly through the airport. Phillip followed the stranger around a corner and out through an exit door. He stopped on the sidewalk and glanced in both directions. He saw no one. Was his mind playing tricks? Was he reading more into this than was actually taking place? He had always put a great deal of faith in his instincts. Usually they were based on enough facts to form an opinion. Seldom was he wrong.

Outside, he could see no sign of the man he had chased only moments before. It suddenly occurred to him that no one, with the exception of the Consulate staff in Cartagena, knew he was here.

"Taxi, señor?" a uniformed porter asked as he saw Phillip on the sidewalk.

Phillip nodded. There was no point in remaining here. The attacker had fled and would certainly not be returning. The porter turned to the nearest parked taxi and yelled at the driver. The uniformed man was resting comfortably against the fender of his cab. He looked up, lifting his head ever so slowly, somewhat annoyed by the porter's disturbance. He took a final drag of his hand-rolled cigarette and expertly flicked the butt onto the pavement, slowly walking around the cab and entering through the driver's door, waiting for Phillip to step in the back before starting the engine.

"Where to?" he asked, viewing Phillip through the rear view mirror.

"Hotel, Blas de Legos."

The driver nodded and the car began to roll forward, augmenting in speed as it exited the airport area. With increasing traffic, the driver's ability appeared to decrease. Phillip had difficulty concentrating on anything aside from the reckless manner in which the cab was being driven. It seemed the man had absolutely no consideration for anyone else on the road.

"Your first trip to Bogota?" the driver asked, turning his head toward Phillip as he spoke.

"No," Phillip replied, wondering when he would turn his attention back to the road ahead.

"You are here on business, yes?"

"Yes, I am."

"Where do you come from?"

"New York."

"Ah, America," the man said, smiling as he spoke. "I thought you were but it's difficult to tell. Your Spanish is very good."

"Thank you."

The man switched from his native Spanish to a broken English. "You like our heat?"

"Not really." The conversation was not helping to take Phillip's mind off the wild driving ability of the cabby.

"It is always hot in Colombia. You will become used to it. You are staying long?"

"Not very long."

"What type of business do you do?"

"I'm in insurance," Phillip replied.

"Now that is interesting. Is it a good business?" There was enthusiasm in the man's voice.

"When someone wants money from the insurance company I'm sent out to investigate to make sure that it is legitimate."

"I see," the man said, not really being any wiser. "That is very interesting."

The cab driver slammed on his brakes, forcing the car to come to a screeching halt.

"What's the matter?"

"These stupid drivers. They know nothing of automobile safety."

The understatement of the year, Phillip thought. Through the front windscreen, Phillip saw a massive congestion of cars forming as would football players congregate to discuss strategy.

"It's always the way," the driver said, slamming his wrists on the steering wheel. "Always when you are in a rush this happens. Always."

"But I'm not in a rush," Phillip replied softly.

The cab driver turned his head around. "But you are American. You are always in a rush, no?"

Phillip smiled as the traffic started to move again.

"Your hotel, it is just around the corner," the cabby said as he changed lanes, manoeuvring the car around a corner. "If there is anything you want, señor, you give me a call, okay?" He turned and handed Phillip a card.

"Thank you." He took the card and glanced at the scribbled telephone number. "I'm actually quite tired."

"It is no problem for me. When you feel like a good time, you call me. I know many señoritas."

The driver parked the car in front of the hotel. Phillip paid the man and grabbing his belongings left the cab.

He stood on the deteriorating, cracked, concrete sidewalk and gazed up at the old stucco building before him. The seven or eight windows on the top two floors held the remains of what were once ornate balconies.

The interior of the establishment had received as little attention as the outside. The paint was peeling from the walls and the corners were filled with cobwebs. There was no carpet covering the white with black tiled floor. To each side of the door were windows, draped with soiled, torn, beige curtains.

Directly in front of Phillip stood a wooden counter, cracked in several areas from the humidity, with a board holding twenty or so keys hanging behind the closure. A book, probably a register, lay open on the frail wood. Next to it was a small bell. Phillip looked at the register and flipped the pages back searching for any trace of McPherson. Before he had got too far, a man emerged from behind a curtain.

"What do you want?"

"I'd like a room."

"That's why you are looking through the book?"

The man spoke with a cigarette hanging from his mouth. His trousers were forced downward by an oversized stomach. The man had not shaved in several days.

"Some friends of mine stayed here a few weeks ago," Phillip said. "I was only trying to find their name in the register".

"What was their name?"

"McPherson. There were five of them. Two men, two women and a small boy."

"They were not here. I would remember." The man's expression did not change.

"Perhaps they used another name," Phillip said.

"Why would they do that?"

"I think they might have been running from the police."

"Look, I don't need any trouble. You want a room, I have a room. You want questions, you go somewhere else."

Phillip decided it would be pointless attempting to get any information from this man. "I'll take the room."

The man swung the book toward Phillip. "Sign here."

He turned and grabbed a key from the rack. "How will you be settling your account."

"Do you take American money?"

"Yes, twenty dollars."

Phillip removed some bills from his pocket. He was careful not to let the hotel owner see how much he had with him. He placed two tens on the counter. The man gave him the key.

"Third floor."

Phillip walked up the old wooden staircase, along a hallway with faded carpets until he came to a brown, wooden door where number thirty-two was etched in place of a long since removed number plate. He inserted the key in the lock and opened the door, feeling ill at the sight of the rundown room. There was a single bed against one wall. A small dresser supported the only lamp on the premises. The layer of dust on the dresser was very thick and had obviously been there a long time. He debated going to another hotel but decided that if McPherson had stayed here with his family there might be several clues lying about.

Phillip's analytical mind tried to compose a mental picture of Lorne McPherson. A man who appeared to have a distinguished and prominent position, complete with family and a career of solidity. Suddenly, overnight, his entire world changed... crumbled, all because of a minor governmental decision.

He must be feeling frustration and fear, Phillip thought. Perhaps anger was a better word. No doubt a man who has had to uproot his entire family, leave his job and career in jeopardy and become a sought after fugitive by a foreign government without support from his own would feel anger.

Now Phillip had to slowly begin assuming the role of the scientist. He had to begin thinking like McPherson. Every clue, every detail, no matter how minuscule, must be studied, preserved and analyzed by the trained mind of Phillip Wright.

7   ATTACK

Phillip Wright casually threw his duffel bag on the blue, wrinkled bedspread. The rundown hotel room was dark and was embraced by an odour of mildew. Its only light came from an artificial source, a dimly lit shadow bulb suspended from a wire in the centre of the ceiling. He threw back the torn curtains allowing the evening sunset to filter its crimson rays into the room. He walked to the soil-stained sink, and after removing his jacket, washed his hands and face. The towel he used to dry himself was damp. The thick, Colombian humidity could be felt everywhere.

Phillip recapped his plans. The first item on the agenda was to establish the precise time McPherson had stayed at the hotel. He had little faith in the reliability of the hotel manager. Phillip was certain that the man's loyalty could be bought for a few pesos.

He opened his briefcase and removed a small spool of white thread from a sewing kit. After closing and locking the case, he placed it on the brown, faded dresser, the only piece of furniture aside from the bed in the lodging. He scanned the room in search of a safe locale to hide his briefcase in the event of being discovered. As there was little furniture, he once again had to rely on his ability to extemporize.

He studied every detail of the third-rate hotel room and finally decided on a concept. Reaching under the sheets of his bed he clutched his pillow and, after taking a pair of scissors from his attaché case, surgically slit a smooth tear into the seam. Cautiously he removed several handfuls of feather stuffing, being careful not to spill the unbound contents on the floor. Phillip lifted the sewing kit from his attaché case and placed it on the bed. Slowly and circumspectly he positioned the briefcase into the partially stuffed pillow insuring that the feathers engulfed it totally. Using a needle and a small spool of white thread, he adroitly restitched the cloth pillowcase, placing it under the sheets when he was finished.

He tied the string to the handle of the centre dresser drawer and allowed the other end to fall through the rear of the commode into the bottom drawer. He closed the middle drawer and opened the lower one pulling the string tight. He manoeuvred the spool around the bottom drawer and tied it to one of the legs of the antiquated bureau. The remainder of the string he led over the inside handle of the hotel door. He stepped into the hallway and looked in both directions. Seeing no one, he tied the end of the string to a small splinter in the deteriorating door frame. The use of thread was a precaution often taken while on assignment. He had learned a long time ago that someone in his profession could never be too careful. A broken thread upon his return would indicate the mark of an unwanted intruder.

Phillip walked briskly to the end of the hall and opened the door. He followed the un-carpeted stairs which led to the lobby. The foul smelling stench in the staircase brought a wave of nausea to his stomach. He forced it back deep into its pit and continued down the stairs. He was not certain of the rating this hotel had received but was convinced it was not worthy of any stars. When he arrived in the lobby, Phillip saw the fat attendant resting his upper chest and arms on the greasy counter deeply engrossed in a newspaper. He saw Phillip approach and slowly raised his head.

"Si?" he muttered.

"I wanted to ask you again about the people I spoke of earlier. Perhaps you have had a recall the last little while?"

"Look, I told you I don't remember anyone fitting the description you gave."

"Maybe I wasn't clear enough in my description."

The innkeeper interrupted Phillip. "I notice everyone who comes into this hotel. There were no group of four people. Never."

"No, no. I said five," Phillip replied. "Five people, not four." He paused. "Let me just go through their descriptions once more."

The clerk was about to interrupt again when he saw Phillip reach into his pocket and remove several pieces of U.S. currency. Phillip placed a twenty dollar bill on the counter and continued giving an accurate description of McPherson and his family.

"I am sorry señor, I honestly do not remember." The man's voice had taken on a much more sincere quality. Phillip again reached into his pocket and placed a second twenty dollars next to the first temptation. The clerk's mouth gaped open while his eyes were fixed on the green currency. He knew that he would have to work many hours to realize such high profits. He folded the newspaper and placed it under the counter, turning his full attention to Phillip's description of the McPherson clan.

"When did you say this was?"

"About two weeks ago."

"Let us look one more time at the register." He

began to flip the pages and with Phillip's help, carefully scrutinized each entry. After about fifteen minutes and three pages, the results were unsuccessful. Phillip was surprised by the number of guests who had stayed at the hotel. He noticed that the majority were single individuals. Nowhere in the last three months had a group of more than two people stayed together or checked in at the same time. How careful was this Lorne McPherson, Phillip thought.

He was beginning to have second thoughts about being in the wrong hotel. Perhaps he had been fed incorrect information or perhaps McPherson was a craftier individual than Phillip had first surmised. Could he have had enough foresight to have planned these types of details? To have his family check into a run down hotel under assumed names and at different times?

"I am sorry señor, I do not know what to tell you," the clerk replied in broken English. He had visions of the American currency escaping his possession. "You are more than welcome to look at it again if you so wish."

"Thank you." Phillip glanced at the book and leafed through the pages again, allowing his fingers to slide back and forth over each entry.

At the ringing of the telephone, the clerk walked to the end of the counter and lifted the receiver, putting a halt to the loud, deafening chime. Phillip continued to study the book, not understanding why there would be no entry. He felt certain he had the right hotel and knew there was no point in searching back more than three weeks. None of the names of the guests seemed familiar to him. He looked for any connection. Possible initials that might be the same, any reversal of names or letters etc. There was nothing. If McPherson had stayed here he had been extremely thorough in hiding the fact.

Phillip thought back to the document left in David Sullivan's office. It had said the Colombian police had escorted the McPherson family from the plane to this hotel.

They would certainly not have been registered under assumed names. Something seemed very wrong. He had no desire to get involved with the local authorities as that would lead to an international affair and create an embarrassing situation between Argentina and Canada.

Phillip was about to turn the page again when something caught his eye. A tiny piece of torn paper, no more than an eighth of an inch in size, was attached to the seam at the very bottom of the register. He opened the book as wide as he could and examined the possible minute clue closer.

A page had been carefully removed, he thought excitedly. Where once a page had been, now only a small speck of paper remained. It had been removed very neatly, perhaps with a knife. The bottom corner, however had been overlooked. They had missed a small piece of the page. Phillip's mind raced quickly. He flipped to the pages before and after his discovery checking the dates of each one. There had been no omissions. This could mean only one thing. A page had been removed and all of the proceeding entries had been re-copied; all but one. Phillip continued to glance at the surrounding pages. He was looking for possible impressions left behind. Something, anything, to show that there had been some tampering with the entries. There was nothing. He checked the date of the preceding page and closed the book as he heard the clerk hang up the phone.

"Any luck, señor?"

"I am afraid not."

"Perhaps you have the wrong hotel," the clerk said, eyeing the money on the counter.

"Do you know of any others with a similar name?"

"No señor, I'm afraid that I do not."

"Oh well," Phillip replied casually, "nothing we can do about it."

He picked up the money from the counter and looked at the clerk. If the money had been food, the obese man would have been drooling. Phillip took twenty dollars and handed it to the man.

"For your trouble." He paused. "And your silence."

"Thank you. Thank you señor. You are most kind. Do not worry about me señor. I am always discreet when it comes to my guests." The man put the money into his pocket.

"Tell me, does the restaurant next door serve good food?"

"Oh yes, the very best in the whole neighbourhood, perhaps the best American food in all Bogota "

"Good. Then I'll give it a try." Phillip turned to leave almost knocking over a small plant which sat, probably for the past ten years or so, on the end of the counter. The green foliage had been unattended for some time. The few leaves that were remaining were ready to be blown off with the slightest gust of wind from the noisy overhead fan. Phillip grabbed the pot and held it to keep it from tipping. A small ring of dust had accumulated where the plant had rested.

"Sorry señor," the clerk said. "We must move that plant."

"Or throw it in the garbage," Phillip muttered.

"Pardon señor?"

"Nothing. Have a nice day."

"Thank you señor, you also." The clerk's eyes followed Phillip as he exited from the lobby. After being certain that the inquisitive, American stranger had left, he stepped to the end of the counter and picked up the telephone. He removed a small piece of paper from his pocket, read the figures scribbled on it and dialed the number.

An extremely large sign with blue and red lettering was hung directly over the entrance to the "famous" restaurant. The glass window panes in the peeling, wooden frames were layered with grease which had accumulated since the last cleaning several months ago.

Phillip was about to enter the restaurant when a young, tourist couple almost knocked him over trying to exit through the narrow entrance.

"Gee I'm sorry mister," the boy, in his early twenties said. His arm was tightly embracing his girlfriend's shoulder. She was a cute blonde with a deep tan.

"Not at all," Phillip replied smiling as he spoke, addressing the pretty young girl.

"Oh, wow!" the boy said. "It's nice to meet someone who speaks English. Where are you from?"

"New York."

"Terrific, we're from Atlanta!"

"Tell me," Phillip said wishing to terminate the conversation quite quickly without sounding abrupt, "is the food inside any good?"

The girl answered first. "Actually, it's not all that bad. If you stick to the hamburgers you should do alright."

Phillip enjoyed listening to her southern drawl. He smiled and thanked them for their advice. "Have a nice holiday!" he said and entered the restaurant.

Phillip sat down at a red, checked-covered table in the far corner. The eating area was quite full with patrons obviously enjoying the well-prepared dishes. A man dressed in a short-sleeve, opened-collared, white shirt, walked to Phillip's table and asked if he cared for a drink.

"I'll have a gin martini with ice," Phillip said.

"Yes sir, excuse me," the owner continued, "are you American?"

Phillip nodded. He could tell from the owner's skin that the man was not native to the hot tropical climate.

"Where from?"

"New York," Phillip replied. "And you?"

"Originally from Detroit. We moved down here about twenty years ago, stayed ever since. My choices were Canada, here or Vietnam. I hate snow and I don't like war, so this is it."

"Business good?"

"Can't really complain, nobody wants to listen anyway," he smiled. "The special for the day is pastrami. That includes a bowl of clam chowder."

Phillip raised his eye brows and looked at the man. "That's quite a combination."

"Well," the owner replied, "If we get too much selection in our meals we'll have to put up the prices. That'll kill what little business we have. "

Phillip smiled. "I'll have the pastrami on rye, with a bowl of clam chowder."

The owner smiled and nodded as he walked away. Phillip's eyes expertly scanned the room, studying the clientele. He had picked up many observation habits over the last few years and had learned to expect the unexpected.

As he glanced around the room, his eyes were met by the gaze of a young Colombian boy in his early twenties. The boy held Phillip's stare for a split second and returned his attention to the array of tables before him. Phillip made a mental picture of the boy's features and stored them for future use; straight, greasy-black hair, combed back but falling down in the front wearing a blue plaid jacket with dark skin and a tattoo on his arm. Something about the youth struck Phillip as being odd, perhaps it was the second of mutual eye contact. Maybe it was the fact that most of the restaurant's guests were not Colombian.

It was a family restaurant, not the kind of place where single men would frequent. Of course it occurred to Phillip that the youth might be thinking the same of him. Nevertheless, it bothered Phillip.

The owner returned with the martini. "You did want it with ice didn't you?"

"That's right."

"There you go, one dry martini." He placed the glass in front of Phillip and was about to turn.

"Excuse me," Phillip said, "I want to pick your

memory."

The owner looked at Phillip. "Go ahead," he said, "I don't miss much."

"About two weeks ago," Phillip began, "a family of five Canadians stayed at the hotel next door. They stayed for a few days. The man was mid fifties with white hair. His wife was short and plump. They had an attractive daughter about thirty. A guy was with them, he was also in that age bracket with a face that's hard to forget," Phillip smiled. "They also had a little kid about twelve."

The waiter scratched the two-day stubble on his chin. "Yeah, I remember them. They came in for dinner a couple of times. Nice group of people, especially the girl." He rolled his tongue around the inside of his lower lip. He smiled.

Phillip returned a grin, hoping that his anxiety wouldn't show. "Any idea where they might have gone."

"You a cop of something?" the owner inquired.

"No, not at all. " Phillip said, forcing a chuckle in his voice. "I'm an insurance adjuster. We are following up a claim on some lost jewellery."

"Oh I see," he paused, "I don't really know where they went. Probably back home I guess."

"Tell me something," Phillip said, "what's the best way of getting to the airport from here?"

"Well," the owner said pondering the question, as he ran his fingers through his hair, "I guess the easiest way would be to take a cab. It's kind of tough to get a bus from here especially if you have a lot of luggage."

"Are the cabs that hang out in front of the hotel usually the same ones?"

"Yeah, it's always the same guys who hang out there," the owner replied. "Why? Do you think they'll remember your friends?"

"You did," Phillip said. "One other thing, who's that kid over there?" Phillip tipped his martini glass in the direction of the youth sitting. "Have you ever seen him here before?"

"No I haven't, why do you know him?"

"No he just looks familiar, I thought that maybe I'd run into him somewhere before."

"Oh well." He shook his head. "Can't say that I've seen him. Excuse me, I have some important customers waiting. American tourists, you know." Both men smiled as the waiter walked back to the kitchen.

After receiving his meal Phillip ate quickly. He left a healthy tip and, purposely walked past the young Colombian youth, hungrily attacking his meal. As he passed, Phillip could feel the boy's eyes burning in his back. Once outside, he decided to play a hunch. Rather than walking back in the direction of the hotel he decided to go the opposite way. He walked about a block and stopped to face a store window. In doing so, he turned in the direction from which he came and spotted the youth. The lad had maintained a surveillance during the course of the meal.

He saw Phillip staring into the window and walked in that direction. Whoever he was, he was not a professional. Only an amateur would allow himself to be noticed so easily unless he wanted to be observed. Phillip pondered the thought but ruled the idea from his mind. He had made it too easy to be seen. He was definitely an amateur.

Phillip waited patiently until the boy was a block or so behind him before he started to walk again. At an opportune moment, he darted into the street and, sidestepping several cars, made it safely to the other side. He threw a quick glance over his shoulder and saw his tracker nervously trying to cross the street in a similar fashion. He could not help smiling as he heard the car horns loudly blasting the pedestrian jetting between the moving vehicles. Although the rush hour had passed there were still numerous vehicles on the street.

Phillip came to the end of the block and turned right,

walking along the gaily decorated windows of a large department store. The mannequins were poised in a casual manner. They appeared outdated and their skin-toned, plastic faces were fading in colour. The straight hairstyles reminded Phillip of the sixties. Thin clothes with bright and colourful accents displayed the ambience of the South American culture.

Phillip walked to the edge of the dirty-white, stucco building and slid into a narrow alleyway. Quickly he hugged the wall and pressed the side of his face against the cold brick exterior, allowing his eyes to peer out onto the sidewalk. There was no sign of the youth. A garbage can was in the alley beside Phillip. He picked it up and quickly sat it on the sidewalk creating an obstruction in the path of any passers-by. Phillip crouched to fix his glance between the garbage can and the building. The youth was rapidly looking in all directions hoping he had not lost his target.

There were no pedestrians between Phillip's hiding sanctuary and the Colombian youth trailing him. Phillip squatted, placing his hands beneath him. He allowed his weight to rest on his finger tips and waited what seemed an eternity not daring to even so much as breathe.

At the split second his eyes came into contact with the youth, Phillip shifted his weight back onto his hands and forcefully pushed his feet into the garbage can, sending it hurtling into the assailant. The boy, surprised by what had happened, could not keep his balance and stumbled to the ground beside Phillip who had regained his equilibrium and was now standing.

He grabbed the youth by the collar and dragged him into the alleyway. Recklessly he propped him against the brick wall, holding him upright with his arm firmly pressed against his vulnerable throat. His knee was raised and forced into his groin. Phillip placed his weight against the boy's left arm and grabbed his right with his free hand. The youth squirmed but found it impossible to move.

"Now tell me," Phillip said, his face only an inch from the fear-filled expression of his would be assailant, "who are you, why are you following me?" Phillip spoke in Spanish.

The boy refused to answer and constricted his lips tightly together in a show of defiance. Phillip concentrated his weight onto his right arm, pressing tightly against the boy's throat. The Colombian youth coughed under the painful stress and tried in vain to wrench his head free. Phillip was much stronger and would not release his grip. Instead he forced more power against his arm. At last the boy, overcome by exhaustion and pain, began to form feeble words on his lips. His mutterings were indistinguishable. At that very moment, Phillip saw the boy's eyes shift slightly to the left. He knew he was too late. Although his reactions were fast they were not that fast.

He heard a scraping sound behind him and as he turned he lifted his knee and bolted it into the boy's groin. He dove to the ground in an effort to avoid an attack but his movement was too late. He felt a pounding pressure against his left temple and a piercing pain in his stomach. He became cold and the surroundings grew dark. He could not stop shivering and became afraid as he lost touch with reality. A thick blanket of darkness began to close in around him and he fell victim to its crushing power as he lost the effort needed to thwart off the evil environs.

Suddenly, as quickly as it appeared, the darkness began to fade. It was replaced by a bright, menacing daylight. Phillip squinted as the brightness endeavoured to penetrate his closed eyelids. The chill that moments earlier had caused him to shiver began to slowly leave his aching body. As he regained consciousness he became aware of his surroundings and attempted to shift his unwilling body into an upright position. The throbbing pain in his head overwhelmed his persistent efforts and he allowed his painful body to fall back onto the flat, cold support beneath him. He could feel moist, warm blood trickling down along the side of his head.

A wave of nausea came over him as he became aware of the terrible stinging pain in his stomach. The treacherous events of the past few moments were forming haunting images in his mind. Beginning to get up, with the aid of the solid, brick wall he remembered the events that had just happened. The slight noise behind him and thrusting his knee into the boy's groin before he was attacked. The youth must have kicked Phillip in the stomach as he had fallen to the ground. He propped himself into a sitting position, cradling his cramping stomach, and slowly allowed his eyes to glance around, not expecting to see anyone or anything.

It was mostly an instinctive reflex. Perhaps he would uncover a minute clue that would give him some assistance in revealing his attackers. The garbage can had remained where he had kicked it. The rest of the alley was filled with the same rubbish that had been there before he had been assaulted by his attackers. How many moments had it been? He forced his eyes to focus on his watch. Not long he thought, however too long to follow any thoughts of pursuit. He slowly started into the street trying to hold his beaten body as erect as possible. He hailed the first cab he saw and hurled his weary frame helplessly into the rear of the taxi.

He quickly arrived at his hotel and walked as casually as he could through the lobby, holding a handkerchief to his bleeding temple. The clerk behind the counter was still reading the newspaper. When he heard Phillip enter, he looked up and seemed very surprised.

"What has happened señor?"

Phillip lifted his head slowly and painfully tilted it into the direction of the clerk. "Nothing," he said angrily and continued to walk to the stairwell slowly climbing the never-ending steps.

The clerk gazed at Phillip's back as he staggered up the stairs out of sight. He arrived at his room and looked at the white thread. As expected, it had been cut. He opened the door and immediately walked to the bed and removed the covers. He was relieved when he felt the hardness of his briefcase, ripped the pillowcase and checked its belongings carefully. The pains in his head and stomach were now secondary. His duffel bag had been ransacked but nothing had been taken.

The thieves had left the leather trimmed bag and its contents in place. Phillip chuckled to himself as he thought of their unprofessional nature. If it were him he would have checked the bed first.

8   PURSUIT

Phillip grabbed both his bags with one hand while still holding the handkerchief to his temple. He stepped into the hallway and walked in the opposite direction, hurrying down the neglected, back stairs. The paint was peeling from the walls and graffiti colourfully stained the bare, gray stucco. A broken bannister was hanging loosely by one hook and was about to fall at the slightest vibration. Phillip stepped carefully on the worn treads wanting to avoid any loud, creaking sounds so as not to disturb the attention of the hotel clerk. It would be in his favour to keep the treacherous man from knowing he had departed, especially since he was obviously responsible for the recent attack on Phillip's life.

There was a large wooden door at the bottom of the stairwell outfitted with a shiny brass deadbolt at least twice as large as was needed. Above the door was a small window, slightly open in order to allow ventilation to circulate throughout the hot, muggy hallway.

Phillip released his carrying bags and allowed them

to fall to the ground. He presumed the door would be securely sealed but tried it in the chance that its closure had been neglected. Unfortunately the wooden structure would not budge under Phillip's pressure. He paused, stepping back slightly to analyse the situation, wondering if he would be able to squeeze through the small opening above the door, providing he could remove the window.

He hoisted himself on the door casing and pushed hard against the paint chipped frame, forcing his weight against the glass barrier. With a sigh of thankfulness he exhaled as the antiquated, rotting frame began to move. A squeaking sound preceded the loosening of the rusty screws which held the worn hinges in place. He could feel the agonizing pressure of his weight bearing down on his foot, locked against the deadbolt, enabling him to remain suspended allowing free movement of his hands. At last he managed to release the window from its loosening grip, shifting his weight from his wedged leg in an effort to allow his body to fall limply to the security of the floor. At the same time he maintained a tight grip on the window frame so as not to bang it into the wall. He carefully squatted onto his knees easing the pain which had developed in his leg as a result of the ordeal. A few moments later he again faced the door and jumped slightly, grabbing the windowless opening. He crawled upward, hoisting his body high enough to allow his head to penetrate the opening.

Fortunately no one was in sight and he allowed himself to fall back into the building letting his legs absorb the impact of the landing. Even though the bleeding had subsided, a deep, stinging ache in his head was hideously noticeable.

Phillip picked up his duffel bag and attaché case and tossed the two bags through the opening on to the gravel path below. He hoisted himself for a third and final time and carefully manoeuvred his body through the tiny opening. He grimaced as his stomach scraped along the wooden frame once again reminding him of the subsiding yet lingering pain. He tried to break his headfirst fall by pressing his calves and feet tightly against the sides of the window opening but was unable to support his weight. After a painful, jolting somersault he stumbled onto the gravel below, groaning softly as the piercing stones burrowed into his back and shoulders. He glanced carefully in both directions before getting up. He grabbed his belongings and began walking along the laneway into the main flow of pedestrian traffic.

With his instincts fully poised, Phillip saw no suspicious characters. It was almost dark as Phillip walked to the front of the hotel. He halted before reaching the entrance and hopped into the back of the first cab he came to, causing the driver to surprisingly swing around studying the sudden commotion in the rear seat of his vehicle. Phillip took a twenty dollar bill from his pocket and noticed the man's deep brown eyes light up.

"Two weeks ago, five people, Americans, left this hotel in a cab. A man and a woman in their fifties, a young man about thirty, an attractive woman in her late twenties and a little boy about twelve. Do you remember taking them anywhere?" Phillip asked in Spanish.

The cabby gazed at the crisp green currency. He thought deeply but shook his head slowly from side to side.

"Are you absolutely certain?"

"Yes, I am sorry but I did not see them." His eyes lit up again. "You'll wait a moment while I ask my friends," he said motioning to the other two cabs parked in front of him. He opened the door and stepped out from the black and white painted car. Phillip watched as the young Spaniard leaned on the driver's door of the car in front. After a short conversation he glanced at Phillip and shook his head.

Phillip's heart sank as he saw another ray of hope darkened by a cloud of disappointment. He watched the driver walk to the other cabs parked along the front of the hotel. Again the results were negative. A new taxi pulled to the curb. Phillip stepped from his cab and entered the new one.

"No. No, señor, you must take the first cab that was here," the driver said, eating a sandwich as he spoke.

"I only want a few words with you." Phillip asked the man about McPherson and his family. The cabby could not recall.

"I would remember five Americans staying at a dump like this señor, especially if there was a beautiful señorita."

Phillip thanked the man and left the cab. The other driver approached, shaking his head in dismay, realizing he was forfeiting a substantial amount of cash.

"Take me to the airport," Phillip said.

The driver jumped in the front and raced the car through the narrow streets passing signs with the familiar airport symbol. Phillip asked the cabby whether or not anyone else could have been driving a cab around that time.

"I am afraid not. You must appreciate señor, this hotel does not have many guests who can afford cabs or who go to the airport." The driver went into a detailed explanation of how unproductive it was to sit in a cab in front of these types of hotels.

"What other methods are there for someone to get to the airport from the hotel?"

"There is always the bus señor, but it would take very long with many changes." He paused for a moment. "The best way would be a rental car."

Phillip sat back in his seat and stared out the window. A rental car was definitely ruled out as McPherson had no passport. No company in its standard nature of operation would lend an expensive automobile without proper identification, especially if that individual was foreign.

Phillip slowly stroked his chin, thankful that traffic was becoming quiet as evening approached. He was totally baffled and had no idea where to continue his search. His trained mind carefully organized all relevant facts and details which had transpired over the past few hours. To find the young assailant would be next to impossible, especially now that it was almost dark. As they approached the airport Phillip thought it best to interview the bus drivers then make his way to the car rental booths. The driver advanced to the passenger loading area of the Bogota's Eldorado Airport.

"Good luck señor," he said, this time in English. "I hope you find what you are looking for."

"So do I," Phillip said slowly, "so do I." He gave the man a substantial tip and walked across the broken concrete into the building. The deafening roar of jet engines accompanied by the smell of burned fuel was irritating and forced Phillip to subconsciously quicken his pace.

Once inside he glanced at the overhead signs and headed for the one marked 'Buses'. There was only a handful of passengers at the airport as evening approached bringing with it a blanket of silence covering the normally noisy flow of people arriving from or leaving for exotic destinations. Phillip was thankful for the peace and serenity of the evening hours as the conclusion of a stressful day had left him with an unwanted, throbbing headache. Several tourists were walking with heavy suitcases dragging sluggishly behind them. A few fortunate ones had managed to locate luggage carts.

Phillip side stepped a small child playing on the ceramic floor with a recently purchased plastic toy. He smiled sadly as sentimental memories of his own two sons permeated his thought patterns. He longed dearly for their loving affection. A chance to embrace them one more time. An opportunity to explain how much he missed them. He wondered if his wife had filled the empty gap left by his disappearance. Phillip forced the thoughts from his mind. Time seemed to halt endlessly as his memories drifted back to happy moments spent as a family. His precious thoughts were interrupted as a gray haired, frail, gentleman called to the playful child before him. Phillip gazed at the hunched man carrying a tray with milk for his grandchild. Phillip's mesmerized gaze followed the cheery twosome as they sat enjoying their treat. He could feel tears welling in the corners of his eyes as a hurtful pain slowly, deliberately embraced him. He began to bite his upper lip in an effort to prevent his painful emotions from breaking down. He had to force his thoughts back to the reality of the moment. To maintain control of his senses knowing that failure to do so could result in his downfall.

He walked into a washroom, suspiciously eyeing all he came into contact with. Cold water sprinkled on his face felt refreshing and revitalized his senses. The antiquated cloth towel dispenser had not been changed in quite some time and rather than risk contamination from the surrounding filth, he chose to let the water droplets dry by themselves.

After glancing under the cubicle doors, reassuring himself that he was alone, Phillip placed his briefcase on the sink and undid the latch revealing the hidden compartment. He reached inside, removed some cash and placed it securely in his pocket. He glanced at the blue steel of the automatic weapon tucked into the compartment of his attaché case. The Baretta Eighty-four was a small, lightweight pistol capable of holding thirteen rounds.

He wished he would never have to carry a gun. He hated the potential power unleashed by such a small metal terminator. On too many occasions had he watched as human life stopped breathing, laying helpless on cold floors or in dark alleys. Precious life sucked from them by one person's instant decision to move a trigger an eighth of an inch. Several of Phillip's peers enjoyed the authority given them by a firearm creating a false feeling of strength and power. Their careers usually lasted only a short time. Phillip had learned to depend mainly on his own abilities and tools such as guns and knives were a secondary means of defence. His own skill and ability were with him at all times. A true ally whose reassurance one could constantly depend on.

One of the rules of his organization was to carry a weapon at all times. And Phillip did... in his attaché case. To constantly have it on his person would greatly increase the possibility of using it. The thought sickened him.

Airlines did not allow anyone to carry firearms while on the aircraft and entry permits into countries were a lengthy procedure. ISIS and other, similar facilities, had arranged drop-off and pick-up points for weapons around the globe.

The parking area for the buses was filled with heavy carbon-monoxide fumes as most of the drivers kept their vehicles running. The high humidity allowed for little air movement. Phillip passed along a row of lockers and searched through his pockets for loose change. Most of his coins had been used in his earlier effort at the candy bar dispenser. He thought again of the mystical figure hidden stealthily behind a plant. His mind raced through patterns of familiarity in an effort to expose the identity of the possible assailant.

He deposited a coin in the slot and after removing the key opened the locker, placing his duffel bag and attaché case inside the small steel chamber. He secured the locker door and glanced in both directions before leaving the area.

There were four buses parked in the bays, engines idling and drivers sleepily resting in between runs. He walked to the first uniformed man and explained his search, giving a description of the McPherson family and asking if he remembered them.

"No, I do not señor. About when was it?" The driver

was a short stocky man dressed in a well fitted uniform. The continuous heat had left a brown stain of sweat around the collar of his blue, short sleeve shirt.

"Two weeks ago," Phillip replied.

The driver paused and thought deeply for a moment. "No señor," he finally said. "I wish I could help you." He removed his cap and scratched his head. "Perhaps one of the other drivers saw them."

Phillip looked at three other men wearing similar uniforms huddled together. They watched suspiciously and began to approach as the man beside Phillip motioned to them.

"This gentleman, he is looking for some friends," the driver said in English. He winked at Phillip as he stressed the word "friends". He switched his conversation to Spanish and spoke in a dialect beyond Phillip's level of comprehension.

Two of the men shook their heads as the conversation continued. The third, however, rubbed his chin in thought causing Phillip to feel a surge of excitement rise from deep within him. The man spoke directly to the first driver and the two carried on a rapidly paced discussion.

Finally the driver looked at Phillip. "This is Chico, señor. He speaks no English but he thinks he remembers your friends."

Chico's cap was tilted back and perspiration droplets trickled slowly from his forehead. The man was vastly overweight and the heat of the tropics made his uniform uncomfortable.

He spoke in a dialect unfamiliar to Phillip. "What did he say?"

"He said, this girl, she travels with her family and a boy who is ugly?"

Chico interrupted the translation. The two drivers exchanged words. The translation continued "He says the boy has a big nose, he is very thin."

"Ask him about the rest of the family."

The translator laughed as Chico patted his oversized stomach. He turned to Phillip. "He says the father was thin with gray hair, the mother was fat like him." The translator smiled as he spoke.

Phillip broke into a grin. "Ask him when he dropped them off."

"No, no, señor," the translator said after a moment. "He did not drop them off here." Phillip looked puzzled. The man continued. "He picked them up here."

Phillip repeated the statement softly to himself. "Where did he take them?"

Phillip found the translation a time-wasting nuisance and tried desperately to understand the conversation.

"He said he brought them to the bus depot downtown."

"Why would they go downtown?" Phillip asked softly thinking out loud.

Chico spoke to the translator as Phillip listened "He says he thinks they were going on a trip."

"Why would he think that?"

"They asked him many questions about vacation places in Colombia they could visit."

"Did he recommend anywhere special."

The two men spoke. "He said he told them the best place was the Rosario Islands." He paused. "Islands of the Rosary you call it."

"Thank you very, very much," Phillip replied, grabbing Chico's hand and shaking it vigorously. The bus driver laughed and Phillip took several bills from his pocket passing them among the four drivers. Their faces beamed at the sight of the American currency. He hurriedly walked back to the main section of the airport building and left the drivers to talk rapidly amongst themselves as they counted the money.

Phillip raced to the area where the cabs were parked

and slipped into the back seat of the one nearest him, so caught up in the excitement that he forgot his briefcase. "Bus depot, downtown please!" he said hurriedly as the cabby looked over his shoulder.

"Si señor." The man started the engine and drove toward the exit sign directly before him.

As they passed the edge of the terminal building Phillip noticed three men busily engaged in conversation. Something struck him odd about the trio but couldn't put his finger on it. Uncertain as to the source of the nagging menace he suddenly realized the relevance. As the cab cleared the edge of the building his vision of the threesome became more defined. The smallest of the three men was the youth that had followed him from the restaurant. The same person he had attacked in the dark alley by his hotel. Were they following him or were they waiting for him? Phillip had to make a decision. To continue on or confront the men. The bus depot could wait. A chance like this might never arise again.

He leaned over the seat to the driver. "Go around this corner and pull over."

The driver turned questioningly.

"Quick!" Phillip ordered. "Turn right here."

"You want me to stop señor?"

"Yes, immediately!"

"But, I don't understand?"

Phillip handed the man some money. "You don't have to."

The driver looked at the money. He smiled and stopped the cab. "Thank you señor."

Phillip ran from the cab as the driver shook his head from side to side. He had a puzzled look. "Strange these Americanos," he mumbled to himself.

Phillip raced between the parked cars toward the entrance of the building. He crouched among the vehicles and looked in the direction of the three men. They had disappeared and Phillip cursed the cabby for not stopping sooner. He had to increase his guard for he could not risk being attacked from behind again. He now wished he had the Beretta in his pocket.

At the ticket counter Phillip saw one of the three men talking with a clerk. He looked to be in his mid forties and quite overweight. His gray, outdated suit had been purchased before all the weight had been gained and a matching felt hat was pushed back on his head. His hands were in his pocket and his stomach dangled over his belt. He turned away from the clerk and allowed his eyes to wander around the building, looking for someone who fit Phillip's description.

Phillip crouched along the wall in an effort to avoid contact at this time. His only intention was to observe. He crept around the corner out of sight, eyes continually scanning the area. He saw the Colombian youth standing beside a tall, blonde, well-built man in his late thirties. Their eyes were darting at the passers-by.

The fat man approached his companions and joined in their conversation. After a few moments the trio, led by the tall blonde, headed toward the exit. Phillip waited until they were outside and quickly stepped to the side of the door. He watched them hurry to the well-lit parking lot.

Phillip saw the young boy and the fat man step into an old, beat-up stationwagon. The blonde haired man unlocked the door of a later-model, burgundy BMW.

Phillip kept his body concealed from view for as long as he could. When the two cars were at a point of leaving he ran to the nearest cab and jumped in the back.

"Do you see that burgundy car straight ahead?" He waited for a confirming nod before continuing. "Well, here's twenty dollars if you stay far enough behind, yet close enough to see it."

Phillip pulled the money from his pocket and tossed it over the seat. The cabby stared at the money and smiled.

"For this señor I will follow him for a week."

The cab swung away from the curb and headed onto the main thoroughfare leading into the city. The sun had almost totally set and the city took on a brand new appearance. Sparkling, colourful lights could be seen everywhere. Phillip reached into his pocket and removed a packet of cigarettes. He picked one and gently placed it between his lips, inhaling deeply, feeling his lungs fill with the aroma of the tobacco filled air. As Phillip slowly exhaled blue clouds of smoke, the cabby turned to him.

"That is good American tobacco," the cab driver said as the smoke reached the front of the car.

Phillip smiled slightly so as not to distract the driver from his mission. "Would you like one?"

"Oh thank you very much." He took the cigarette and fumbled in his shirt pocket for a lighter.

As they neared the downtown core, they saw groups of kids hanging out on street corners. There was a definite absence of tourists and shoppers as the night people came from their sheltered dwellings to dominate the dark evil.

In recent years Bogota had become one of the crime centres of the world. A beautiful South American city that had been wilfully transformed from a haven for sightseers to a bustling drug centre which had attracted various forms of low life. There were thousands of stories of people being accosted while strolling along the streets; stories about kids on motorcycles attacking elderly visitors. Phillip hated the thought and hoped that his work might cause a slight dent in crime related organizations.

Phillip kept a close watch on the two cars about ninety yards in front. The cabby was doing an excellent job, maintaining an even distance behind the stationwagon and the burgundy BMW. He was pleased with the situation. The chances of being spotted by the two men in the wagon were much less than by the blonde.

Phillip thought about the key to his locker. He reached

for his pocket and confirmed that it was still in place. All of his possessions were concealed in a square foot compartment. All of his past eight years were stored in that small cubicle. He had several bank accounts around the world each containing funds acquired as gifts from governments, thank you's from private individuals, income from his job and left over expense money. He had never intended to keep the money for personal use. It was there only in the event of necessity. He wasn't even sure how much there was. He made a mental note to take care of the funds once this assignment was complete.

"The cars are pulling over señor." The cab driver interrupted Phillip's thoughts.

Both cars pulled up beside several tall buildings.

"Drive past them," Phillip said, "and keep your eyes on the road." He looked ahead. "When you get to that stop light pull over."

As they drove past the cars, Phillip saw the fat man and the boy walk from their wagon to the burgundy car. The blonde got out and the trio stepped onto the sidewalk. Phillip thanked the driver and left the cab.

"Any time señor, any time you want to follow someone, you call me."

Phillip turned the collar of his jacket up and with his hands in his windbreaker pocket stood rocking on the street corner, facing the other direction. Glimpsing behind him he saw the men walk toward a building and enter through the glass door. The white stucco-faced building was not unlike the rest in that area. The only exception was the cleanliness of this particular establishment.

Phillip glanced inside and saw many small tables covered with red linen cloths, place settings and a lit candle in the centre. The three men walked behind the maitre d' to a table at the far end of the restaurant. Phillip studied his alternatives. How the events had changed in the last four hours. He knew the McPhersons disappearance was connected to these men but why they were following him was unclear. Another thought struck him. Perhaps they weren't.

Phillip walked to the burgundy car. He slipped his hand from his pocket to the chrome handle. The door was locked. He strolled to the other side of the car and tried the driver door. He was luckier this time. He opened the door, moved the seat forward and crouched onto the floor of the rear seat. After closing the door he removed the gun from his pocket and released the safety. He tried to make himself as comfortable as possible and hoped that his assailants would not be long in the restaurant.

A thought struck him. What if the threesome did not return to the cars? Or even worse, what if they all decided to get into the burgundy car? Phillip tossed the thoughts from his mind and shifted his weight to make himself more comfortable.

9   CONFRONTATION

Phillip counted the agonizing minutes for what seemed like a painful eternity. He estimated no more than forty-five minutes had passed and his crouched position in the rear of the automobile was causing immense discomfort beyond tolerance. Yet he knew he had to remain calm and silent.

Suddenly, from the stillness of the night, he heard voices directly beside the car. He manoeuvred his body as close as he could to the floor boards, feeling the nagging ache of a cramp developing in the lower part of his right leg. He longed to massage his calf, but dared not move. If he were caught there would be no hesitation on his captor's part to eliminate him.

Phillip could not make out what the men were saying but developed an acidic feeling in the pit of his stomach when he heard the car door open. He tried to assess the situation and ever so slowly exhaled a sigh of relief when only one person entered.

"All right," a voice said, "we will meet tomorrow

morning at seven o'clock at my house." The accent was European, Austrian or German Phillip thought.

The roar of the engine started with a click of the key. Phillip had spent his waiting time developing an action plan for when his conspirators returned to their car. He had envisioned forcefully seeking information from them and escaping unhurt. Immediately he realized this plan would never work. At best he could cause an accident, bring attention to himself and be captured; assuming he survived a collision.

He made the decision to sit tight and see where the ride took him. If his hunch was correct, the lone driver, now only inches before him, would drive to his house and Phillip could wait there until morning. He had no alternatives and settled in great discomfort for the remainder of the journey. Painfully, each agonizing thud and pothole shot fiercely through his body as the car sped along the unimproved, Colombian road.

They roared along the streets for thirty minutes, which to Phillip seemed an eternity. The pain in his leg was becoming increasingly worse, almost unbearable, and was relieved only when the car suddenly came to a grinding halt. The driver stepped quickly from the vehicle and closed the door behind him. Phillip waited a minute and slowly hoisted his weight on to his arms, carefully raising his head in an attempt to look through the window unobserved. He watched the man walk to a small, stucco-finished bungalow surrounded by huge, moss covered trees. Visibility was poor as there were no lights on in the house and the nearest street lamp was fifty feet away.

The house was the only one in the area and by Colombian standards was definitely middle to upper class. As his eyes grew more accustomed to the darkness Phillip began to note details of the exterior. He could make out flower boxes beneath the windows and neatly trimmed bushes framing the concrete walk to the driveway. Several

interior lights had been switched on as the man walked
through the comfort of his house. Who were these people?
The nagging continued to play havoc with his mind. He had
no plausible solution and could only hope that in time he
would discover the answer.

Phillip waited several minutes before attempting to
leave the car. When he thought it safe he slipped into the
front seat and as he released the door, touched a small dome
light control in the opened door frame, avoiding illumination. He slithered from the car and remaining crouched,
closed the car door ever so gently. He cringed as the pain
from the cramp in his leg shot throughout his body. Resting
on the soft, moist grass he tenderly rubbed his calf feeling
the pain begin to subside and life slowly return to his leg.

He crept along the car and found a ditch running
parallel to the road. As he followed it, he never once took
his vision from the house centred before him on the grass
covered tract.

When he reached a small clump of trees he stopped.
His body was sheltered from the house as well as the road.
Luckily this was a remote part of the suburbs, far away from
downtown crowds and activity. Phillip raised his arm and
twisted his watch allowing the light from the street lamp to
reflect on its face. He assessed the situation and his immediate surroundings. There was nothing to do but wait until
morning. He walked a few paces in each direction and
decided the area near the shelter of the trees would be the
best to hide until his next move. A move to which he would
have to give careful consideration.

He huddled among the trees and feeling the moist
evening air buttoned his collar and pulled his shirt tight
around his body. Assured that nothing would happen until
the morning, he closed his eyes in an attempt to get some
sleep. It wasn't long before a thin dark layer of slumber
passed over him.

His mind continued to grasp his subconscious and tried to

force him into an awakening stage. A constant battle lasting for what seemed an eternity until at last the early morning sun projected its first rays of soft, warm light onto his face. Finally, this time for good, his mind snapped back to reality.

His instinctive training took control of his body. He was aware of being awake, however he dared not move a muscle. Slowly he opened his eyes, darted his pupils from left to right and after being assured he was alone, moved his legs, stretching his limbs. He was getting too old for sleeping on the ground.

Phillip felt a slight ache in his previously cramped leg. There was no sign of activity from the quiet, stucco bungalow. Phillip looked at his watch. He had at least an hour before the scheduled rendezvous was to take place.

He walked stealthily beneath the trees, then prowled alongside the house toward the rear. The back garden had been meticulously manicured. Phillip thought it odd that a man engaged in some form of foul activity was responsible for such care to a garden. Perhaps he had a wife; a new thought for Phillip to ponder. It was a definite possibility and probably very realistic. It would account for the neatness and attention paid to the garden, however it did not fit with the character of the individual.

In the far corner was a wooden patio deck which had been framed around an aqua coloured, kidney shaped swimming pool. A thin mist was lifting from the water as the cooler air caressed the warmth of the chlorinated water. Phillip thought of the many parties that must have taken place in the garden. He envisioned beautiful women holding tall champagne glasses and dressed in colourful attire laughing gaily as they spoke with tall, handsome men.

The house itself was coated in a slight layer of pink stucco. White shutters framed each window and red geranium filled flower boxes were suspended gently from the sills. A European touch, Phillip thought adding evidence to his suspicion that the man was involved with an international network.

He walked to the end of the bungalow and raised his head slowly to the level of the last window. Phillip shivered slightly, partially due to having spent the night on the wet grass, but also because of fear building within him caused by the anxiety of the covert situation. The sun began to cast long, distorted shadowed outlines of trees and shrubs against the exterior wall of the house. Phillip began to feel the warmth of the morning rays on his back, soothing the discomfort he refused to grow accustomed to.

He glanced through a corner of the window pane and saw the tall, blonde man who, hours ago had unknowingly acted as his chauffeur, sleeping soundlessly in his bed. He was alone and Phillip felt relieved there was no wife. He preferred to deal with his opponent in a non-personal manner. The vision of the man with wife and family haunted Phillip's mind momentarily and surrendered explicit visions of his former lifestyle. The thoughts saddened him and made him long to be anywhere far away and secluded, away from this life of insecurity into which he had stepped and now lay trapped. He shook the thoughts from his head for he knew through his training that he could only concentrate on his present surroundings. His mind had to be clear in order to deal effectively with the ongoing events.

Phillip gently stepped along the house to a window at the other end and as he looked inside the dimly lit room made it out to be a study. The window had no screen and there appeared to be no visible burglar alarm. Phillip pressed his fingers to the glass and pushed it to the side. He moaned with despair as the frame refused to yield. He looked at the pane and noticed a small flip lock holding it in place.

He reached under his pant leg and removed a Swiss army knife held in place by an elastic suspender directly below his knee. After opening the knife he inserted the blade between the glass and the window sill. Skilfully he slipped the steel edge along the small crack until the point was in line with the white, plastic lock. Firmly he pushed the knife against the latch and with the thumb of his other hand pressed on the handle causing the point to open the catch, allowing the window to come loose. Phillip removed the knife and replaced it in its original position. He pressed his fingers against the glass a second time and as he pushed the pane to the side felt relief as this time it slid with ease.

He quietly hoisted himself up and placed his knees on the window sill. He lifted his left leg followed by his right until he sat in a squat position in the opening. With his hands placed on the sill, he lifted his feet inside, sitting on the ledge. He looked in to the study to ensure that no one was there, knowing that he would be too late even if there was.

The interior of the den was as carefully looked after as the garden was. One wall was lined with brown, teak shelves filled with hundreds of colourful, leather bound, literary masterpieces.

The centre of the parquet floor was covered with the hide of a North American black bear. Directly behind it was a brown, leather tufted sofa. Two side chairs decorated in similar style graced the remainder of the room. It was a man's den. Paintings of German, Swiss and Austrian Alps were hung on the remaining walls. A telephone table sat beside the only door into the room. Matching end tables stood guarding a chesterfield from either side. On one sat two glasses and a bottle of Petrus.

Excellent taste, Phillip thought. The man who had decorated this room had savoir faire. What was his aim? What was his reason for causing this unnecessary havoc?

He looked around the room for bugging or burglar devices. After he felt assured that there were none, he slowly and quietly lowered himself to the floor. Closing the window behind him and sealing the flip lock back into position, he tried to hide any traces of his forceful intrusion.

He had not yet planned an escape or for that matter any scheme of what he was about to do. He assumed that he would wait and listen to find out as much as he could, then telephone Ed Bergan for assistance.

Phillip tiptoed to the door and quietly opened it. He faced a small, darkly wallpapered hallway which led to a brightly, sunlighted kitchen. The thought of food awakened Phillip's senses and he realized he had not eaten in some time. Later, he kept telling himself... later, when there would be time.

Suddenly Phillip's trained sense of hearing warned him of someone approaching. He retreated to the den, just in time to close the door all but half an inch. He leaned his ear against the small opening and listened to hear the kitchen tap being turned on. The sound of feet shuffling and water in the kettle beginning to boil could be heard. He listened carefully to the familiar sounds of breakfast being prepared. The sound of a chair being pulled out from the table and the rustling of newspaper gave Phillip the indication that the man was enjoying his morning meal.

Thirty minutes passed before Phillip again heard the sound of a chair being slid across the kitchen floor. It seemed like an eternity before the man left the room.

Phillip had no alternative but to remain in the den. Going into the kitchen would increase his chances of an unwanted confrontation. He waited for ten minutes not knowing where his unsuspecting host had gone. The chime of a clock in another part of the house snapped Phillip's mind back into an active mode. He hated time periods during which his intellect wandered from the present. It made him vulnerable. A second chime sounded but this time the tone was not produced by the clock. Instead it was made by a doorbell near the front of the house.

"I am coming," the man yelled from a different part of the bungalow.

Phillip listened attentively as he heard the man walk

toward the front door.

The door opened. "Good, you are here." He spoke in Spanish. "Come into the kitchen. I am making tea."

From Phillip's vantage point he could see a small section of the bright, floral wallpaper-covered kitchen. He saw a chair, occupied by the fat man. He shifted his weight to get a better view and in so doing brushed against a picture of several uniformed men standing sternly in front of Mount Jungfrau. Although the noise was faint it was amplified in Phillip's mind. His hands quickly shot forward and grasped the painting to stop it from swaying. He held his breath and listened to the sounds coming from the kitchen. After a moment of tension he was relieved when none of the trio changed their conversation to reflect his discovery.

The photograph on the wall was slightly crooked after having been shaken by Phillip's carelessness. He felt foolish and angry, knowing that such a blunder could cost him his life. He knew of agents who had died needlessly during moments of carelessness.

He saw in the photo his unsuspecting host standing before three military officials wearing high ranking Colombian army uniforms. Beneath the photograph, in small text, was the date and names of the four people. Three were in Spanish and one, which Phillip assumed was that of his tall, blonde, European host, was German.

'Willem Rolf'. The name meant nothing to Phillip as he looked at the photograph again. He recognized none of the people shown and made a mental note to inquire of Ed Bergan. The shuffling noise of chairs being moved in the kitchen brought Phillip's mind back to the reality of the present. Phillip strained his eyes to get a better view, ensuring at all times to avoid discovery. It seemed unusual for three strangers to put so much into seeking him out. Although there had not been much time to think out strategies, he felt certain that their pursuit of him was linked in some way to the scientist who had been missing for three weeks. More than likely they were representatives of the Argentine government and had been assigned to locate McPherson. The last thing they needed was a stranger interfering with their task.

"So Ricardo," Willem Rolf said with a heavy German accent, "did you drive past the hotel this morning, to see if our friend had returned.

"Yes I did," the boy replied. "I spoke with the manager and he was quite upset about being taken advantage of for a night's rate. It seemed the American gave him the slip without paying his bill."

"I see." Willem Rolf replied. "We know that Phillip Wright must still be in Bogota. I wonder," he slowed his speech, "I wonder...," he repeated, raising his hand to his chin and rubbing it slightly, "if perhaps Phillip Wright has no idea where McPherson is either."

"If that is the case," the other man, whom Phillip assumed to be the fat man at the airport, said "why are we following him?"

Phillip could hear the chair shuffling as the three men in the kitchen changed position. He leaned his face closer to the small opening in the door. He could see the fat man sitting beside the table stirring his tea. He was wearing the same gray suit as the night before. His felt fedora was resting on his knee. The young boy, Ricardo, moved within range of Phillip's eyesight and appeared tense as he sipped his tea nervously.

"That is a stupid question!" Rolf snapped back at the fat man. "It is not that we cannot find the scientist but you see we are limited to the types of information we can get. Wright on the other hand has access to far greater intelligence and would be able to find McPherson easier. We would be foolish not to take advantage of such a situation. We will simply follow him wherever he goes and, presto," he snapped his fingers triumphantly. "We will locate the missing scientist." His voice was harsh. It reminded Phillip of a school master lecturing sternly to his pupils.

"What you did yesterday was very stupid," Rolf continued. Phillip watched as the fat man lowered his head and focused on an imaginary spot near his knees. He was pinching the brim of his hat nervously between his thumb and index finger. Ricardo was staring directly at Rolf, his mouth parted slightly.

"Ricardo," Rolf continued, "I am surprised you would allow yourself to be caught so easily. I was under the impression that you were smarter than that. To be caught so easily while performing such a simple task is stupid."

The fat man saw an opportunity to bring some blessing on himself. "It was a good thing that I followed Ricardo just like you told me," he said.

So it was him, Phillip thought, it was the fat man who jumped him from behind in the alleyway, not Rolf as he had presumed.

"You are just as stupid," Rolf continued, directing his attention at the obese man dressed in the outdated, tight, gray suit. "If you had not hit him from behind and almost killed him Ricardo could have made up some excuse that was totally unrelated to us. Now he knows that we are after him."

"But, but," the boy protested, "he was going to kill me."

"No, he was not going to kill you, idiot." Rolf's voice was losing its patience. "He would never have killed you. All he wants is information." He paused. "For God's sake he is a professional. Be more careful in the future. Both of you."

"You are right Señor Rolf," the fat man agreeably nodded, thankful that most of the scolding was over.

"What are we going to do now?" Ricardo asked.

"We are going to split up. I am going back to the airport and you two are going to the bus station."

Rolf stood up and leaned over the table picking up the coffee cups from his early morning guests.

It was the first time since Phillip had been in the house that he had made visual contact with the tall, short-haired German. He heard the water running and the continuous clanging of dishes as they were being washed and neatly stacked in the cupboard. Phillip waited patiently as the three men prepared to make their exit from the house.

As soon as he heard the front door slam he swiftly left the study through the short hall and entered the kitchen at the rear of the house. He speedily stepped past the table and chairs when suddenly, the loud ringing of the telephone broke the silence. Phillip froze in his tracks, not daring to move or breathe. He wondered if the men outside could hear the loud, piercing ring reverberating throughout the house. It was only a split second between the third and fourth ring that Phillip heard a key rustling in the front door lock. His eyes focused sharply in the direction of the sound and he had a perfect view of the door latch as it was being turned. He did not wait around to see the door open. Instead he dashed into a corner of the kitchen beside the rear entrance. Phillip's heart was pounding fiercely and he felt a thickness develop in his throat. If only he had been a moment quicker, he would have escaped through the back door and been safely tucked in the security of the bushes. As it was, he was vulnerably exposed to the fierce tactics of Rolf and his two accomplices.

Willem Rolf strode quickly through the hall and into the kitchen entrance, grabbing the telephone receiver as it finished its fifth ring. His attention was focused on the caller and was oblivious to Phillip standing motionless in the corner. His eyes were poised toward the front door which placed his back in the direction of the uninvited intruder. Phillip was hoping that Ricardo and the fat man would not return to the house. He forced his breathing to be as slow as possible which in turn caused his hands to tremble. A numbness overtook him causing a great desire to move any part of his body. He suppressed it by focusing his thoughts on Rolf's conversation with someone Phillip assumed to be his superior.

"Oh, it is good to hear from you." His voice had taken on a serious tone. "Yes, I understand," a pause while he listened to the other party, "of course I will." Phillip was convinced by his tone that he was definitely talking with his superior. He heard Rolf laugh and watched the back of his head move slightly up and down. He had a certain charm about him, Phillip thought. Perhaps his commander was a woman; Phillip could not help but wonder if Rolf resented reporting to someone of the opposite sex. Phillip smiled to himself.

"No, not yet," Rolf continued. "Yes, I understand... well uh, no," he stammered, "we have temporarily lost him... yes I fully understand the consequences... do not worry we will find him very shortly and continue our pursuit."

Phillip was angered by the situation which had arisen mostly due to his own negligence. Rolf had lost his trail and Phillip was left with a perfect opportunity to get away and continue his search for the scientist. Instead he was trapped in his assailant's kitchen, not more than twelve feet away from him. He had to make a judgment call. Rolf's foot was sticking in the doorway leading from the hall. If he was to turn around, which he would surely do when hanging up the phone, he would certainly see Phillip crouching in the corner.

Quickly he glanced around the kitchen in an effort to locate an alternate hiding place. He found none and decided to make a run for it. Phillip athletically leaped from his hunched position and strode sideways toward the rear door of the kitchen. He knew that if Rolf stepped back he would immediately be seen. He reached the back door and grasped the handle firmly and was shocked at the realization of the door being locked by a dead bolt located slightly above Phillip's hand. He had lost the race and knew the moment he turned the upper lock he would be discovered. There was no alternative left to him. With his back turned he grabbed the second lock and twisted it, causing a slight, squeaky noise as it gave way. He opened the glass inlaid door and knew Rolf had heard the sharp, high-pitched noise. Phillip glanced over his shoulder at the hallway entrance to the kitchen. His eyes stopped all movement when they met the deep blue eyes of Willem Rolf. For a split second the two men stared hypnotically at each other in a fashion which resembled a mutual respect. Phillip's instincts took over and he grabbed the nearest chair, lifted it from its place and flung it at his assailant. Rolf instinctively jumped aside, however his timing was thwarted by the unsuspected motion and the chair caught his shoulder sending a grimacing pain through his upper body. It was enough to give Phillip an ever-so-slight edge.

Phillip pulled recklessly on the door handle and raced thoughtlessly through the opening, diving head first into the bushes beyond the small pathway outside the door. He could feel the piercing pain of the brittle branches scraping along his bare face. A sudden jolt accompanied by a sharp, thudding jab acknowledged the end of Phillip's soar through the shrubbery. He quickly righted himself but stayed low and from his crouched position spread the branches to get a glimpse of the back door.

Rolf stood in the opening and watched silently, nursing his injured shoulder where the chair had made its mark. Phillip remained motionless, keeping his trained eyes on Rolf who was desperately looking in all directions around the yard. He darted back inside the house. It was Phillip's cue to jump into action. He scurried through the bushes toward the side of the house, noticing the full morning sun casting a yellow haze on the pink stucco creating a haunting effect. From behind a clump of trees Phillip saw Rolf, accompanied by the fat man, reappear at the kitchen door . Both had their guns drawn and were surveying the surrounding area. Ricardo had been left out front in the event of Phillip slipping by. The twosome walked cautiously toward the bushes searching for signs of their intruder.

Phillip wondered how long his luck would last. He ran swiftly across the lawn heading to the road. Behind him he heard the fat man yelling furiously. He made it to the burgundy BMW and quickly jumped inside. He glanced over his shoulder and saw the fat man clumsily run across the green, well-manicured lawn. His hand reached for the ignition, however panic quickly raced through his senses as his fingers felt the empty slot. He acted on instinct. Time was no longer on his side. He opened the car door and jumped out. Ricardo was running from the front of the house toward the automobile. Rolf had gone to the far side and had not come within view of the chase scene. He made it to the station wagon seconds before the fat man was upon him. Phillip had his hand on the door handle and heard noisy panting as the fat man fell in place directly behind him. Without hesitation he swung around raising his leg as he turned. His foot made contact with his attacker and he felt his heel dig deeply into the softness of the fat man's stomach. The movement gave him the extra time he needed and he jumped into the car. Relief came as his hand touched the small, silver plated key. He pumped the gas pedal furiously but the engine refused to respond. Glancing over his shoulder he could see Rolf surveying the situation as he came out from behind the house.

Without warning, an all too familiar noise rang loudly throughout the car. Phillip turned his head and saw the rear window crumble into thousands of tiny pieces. Another piercing blast roared through the air and from the corner of his eye Phillip saw a large hole in the side window as well. Phillip looked at his attackers and felt a surge of despair as they were within feet of the vehicle. Rolf raised his gun, took aim and fired a riveting shot which came within inches of his ear. Phillip lowered his head in an attempt to avoid the path of the small, destructible missile. At last he heard the comforting sound of the car engine starting. Without wasting the slightest millisecond he threw the lever into drive and cranked the steering wheel as far left as it would go. As he slammed his foot on the accelerator, the rear wheels spun, spat dirt and finally grabbed the loose gravel road beneath them.

Phillip had misjudged the corners on the station-wagon and, as the car lunged forward it crashed wildly into the burgundy BMW parked in front of it. Phillip frantically manoeuvred his car into a straight position when he heard another piercing gunshot within inches of his head.

He ripped the car forward this time clearing the other vehicle. In his rear view mirror Phillip could see the threesome climbing into the burgundy car. He watched as the crumpled bumper fell to the ground. It had no effect however, on the performance of the well built, German automobile.

He kept the accelerator to the floor and watched as the speedometer climbed slightly over one hundred. The car was old and lacked performance. If he stayed on this straight road he would soon be overtaken by his pursuers.

Phillip had no idea which direction led back to the city. Luckily the gas gauge was more than half full and he felt confident about being able to travel for quite some time. Behind him the burgundy car was rapidly approaching. There was no other traffic on the road and visibility was excellent. As Phillip crossed a side road, he slammed on the brakes, forced the gear-lever into reverse and wildly spun the car around, racing onto the gravel road.

Trying to regain his bearings he could tell from the sun that he was heading in a south western direction. He felt certain the airport was south of the city however his bearings had been mistaken on the previous night as he lay trapped in the rear seat of a car. He forced the car to its limits, pushing it over hills and around treacherous curves. The constant clanging of stones against the underside of the chassis made Phillip aware of his speed. He tried to shield his eyes as best he could from oncoming insects being hurtled to their death through the large hole in the windscreen of the car. He glanced in his rear view mirror but the curvature of the road made it impossible to see more than a few feet.

Phillip cleared his mind for he knew he had to concentrate on his assailant's actions. He had to put himself in Rolf's place and endeavour to imagine what they were thinking. If he had lost them they would probably drive directly to the airport in anticipation of meeting him there. It would be the obvious place to go.

Phillip thought for a moment. His only other choice would be the bus depot. Going there however would mean leaving his attaché case behind. He couldn't do that. He needed the money, information and passports inside. He had to take the risk and head for the terminal building.

The road straightened out and far in the distance Phillip noticed a tiny red speck. As he came closer it grew in size and he strained his eyes trying to see. The wind, however was blowing fiercely through the shattered glass causing his eyes to water and blur his vision.

Perhaps it was a stop light. A major cross road. Phillip could feel his heart beating faster. The gravel road combined with the speed and reckless driving was taking its toll on the already badly beaten automobile. The temperature gauge was climbing and Phillip was not sure how long it would be until his only means of transportation crumbled.

The trees seemed to slide past him as he continually pushed the car to its limit. The red dot grew larger as he approached. It was not a stop light but some type of sign. Phillip squinted his eyes in an effort to see beyond at what seemed to be a moving vehicle. Phillip was elated at the sight of another automobile for it meant a busier road. There was also no cloud of dust visible, indicating pavement.

Phillip glanced in his mirror and although it was difficult to see anything through the cloud of dust, realized the road behind him had straightened out. When he arrived at the stop sign he carefully looked both ways in an effort to decide which direction to follow. Feeling certain he had evaded his followers, he turned right, praying it would lead him to either the downtown core or the airport. He kept his eyes on the rear view mirror hoping the burgundy BMW would not pull out of the intersection. Ahead were more signs, road indicators, the names of which were not familiar to Phillip. He saw another sign, this one on the other side of the road and he stretched to look over his shoulder as he passed it.

The automobile fiercely squealed to a stop as Phillip slammed on the brakes. The sign on the opposite side of the road had the familiar airport symbol largely painted in fluorescent white on a forest green background. He vigorously spun the steering wheel in a circular motion as far as it would go in order to retrace his steps. Phillip silently cursed himself for choosing the wrong direction. He also knew that if Rolf had taken the same route there was a chance they would meet. Phillip pushed the stolen automobile to its maximum limit. He glanced quickly at the heat gauge which had now firmly locked into the red position. He knew the car would not hold out much longer and prayed nervously that it would carry him as far as the airport. He passed over several small hills and saw the intersection from which he had previously exited. He slowed the car down and tried to shield the wind from his eyes to improve his vision. After quickly scanning the area he was convinced there were no other cars in sight.

As he crossed by the mouth of the intersection his

head turned in all directions, hoping feverishly that there were no other cars. He brought the vehicle to a slow crawl and continued to scrutinize the scenery for signs of his pursuers. Phillip slowly exhaled, allowing a long overdue sigh of relief to escape from his lungs. If the burgundy car had taken the same route it would have caught up with him by now. Suddenly it occurred to Phillip that perhaps Rolf had outsmarted him and had ventured to the airport. That would place the burgundy BMW in front of him rather than behind. Either way it allowed him the opportunity to drive in peace for several moments, giving the crippled automobile the rest it so longingly craved.

The time also gave Phillip an opportunity to gather his thoughts. He fumbled through his pockets for a pack of cigarettes, never once taking his eyes from the road. He shook the pack and lifted it to his lips, glancing at the dashboard to see if a lighter was in place. Something about a cigarette calmed the nerves, Phillip thought, as he aspired to ignite it against the fierce wind blowing into the car from all directions. He enjoyed the few minutes of brief relaxation brought on by the smoke.

Ahead Phillip saw another airport sign indicating a turn. He slowed the car as he approached the next intersection and turned the wheel to follow the new route.

As his journey neared completion he tensed all senses. His eyes darted between the rear view mirror and the road ahead as his astute mind gathered all information available, sorting it rapidly into proper categories and perspectives. The road became busier as he neared the airport. Thankfully the burgundy BMW along with Rolf, Ricardo and the fat man was not in sight.

10 Locker

Phillip rounded the corner and was forced to slow his speed. He caught up to a cab also heading for the airport. As he drove slowly behind the taxi, constantly looking in his rear view mirror, an idea came to him. He suddenly pushed his foot hard on the accelerator and swerved into the centre of the road taking the driver of the cab by surprise. Just at the moment when he passed the car, he drove off the road, onto the shoulder and jumped from the beaten automobile leaving the door open behind him. He fled into the centre of the roadway waving his arms frantically. The cab driver had to swerve his vehicle back and forth and eventually halted in the opposite lane stopping just short of hitting Phillip. The cabby cursed loudly in a Spanish dialect as Phillip raced to the side of the taxi and opened the passenger door.

"I'm sorry." Phillip said. "Very sorry, my car ran into trouble. There is something wrong with the steering. I have to get to the airport."

Until this moment Phillip had not noticed an elderly

couple quietly sitting in the rear. Their hands joined in fearful anticipation and their eyes fixed on the American stranger who had recklessly disrupted there peaceful travel plans.

"Hello." Phillip smiled as he spoke to them. Although they had not replied their harsh stare gave Phillip a feeling of discomfort.

The driver threw his arms in the air in exasperation. "Get in, I will drive you," he said in disgust. "Anything to keep you from driving on our roads and killing someone. You understand señor, it is not very profitable for me to take someone from here to the airport."

Phillip took ten dollars from his pocket and handed it to the driver. "Now it is profitable."

The driver looked at the money and then at Phillip. "You must be American."

Phillip chuckled as the cabby sped off leaving the abandoned stationwagon behind. Phillip had meant to check the glove compartment for a possible gun but in the hurriedness of the situation had forgotten.

As the cab continued Phillip saw no sign of the BMW. His mind relaxed slightly as he thought of the cab driver. A simple job in contrast to his own. Probably a family man complete with many children, lots of friends and happy, Sunday dinners. It brought back memories of the past. He thought of his children and felt moisture develop in his eyes.

The airport terminal building came into sight as the cab rounded the next turn. The couple in the rear seat had not moved nor spoken since Phillip had entered the vehicle. The driver stopped at the main entrance and Phillip spotted the burgundy car immediately. It had been abandoned recklessly beside the curb. None of the occupants were in sight, however Phillip could not afford to take any chances. He asked the driver to pull ahead and let him off at the corner. As soon as the cab came to a halt Phillip stepped out,

walking along a concrete sidewalk which led to the corner
of the gray brick building.

As the morning progressed the terminal began to fill
with incoming and outgoing passengers. Most of the people
were tourists carrying suitcases or students sporting back-
packs enjoying a vacation. There were also businessmen
with suit bags and briefcases. Uniformed porters were busy
guiding passengers in and out of the building hoping for a
substantial reward for their assistance. Phillip's eyes peered
through the crowd but were unable to mark his assailants.
He cast his vision to the side of the terminal building where
the activity was far less than in the centre area. He wondered if there was any chance of getting into the building
from a side entrance. He took a last glance at the burgundy
car parked in full view directly in front of the main gate.
What amateurs these people were, he thought to himself.
To leave a car stranded like that and then have no one
guarding the entrance. Who were these people and why
were they following him?

Phillip watched as a policeman walked to the parked
vehicle. He smiled to himself as the uniformed officer
removed a pad from his inside jacket pocket and began
writing a ticket. Phillip walked around the building until he
came to several flat, gray doors used as utility entrances. He
tried the handle of the first but it would not turn. The
second and third were also securely fastened and he continued along the side of the building until he encountered two
loading docks. Luck was at last in his favour as one of them
had been left open. He hurriedly walked toward it looking
around him at all times for his hunters.

After making certain that no one was watching,
Phillip stepped to the platform. The loading dock was
raised and the door was a good six feet from the ground.
Phillip scanned the area and decided a frontal approach
would best suit his needs.

Old, rubber tires which had been nailed into place

around the base of the landing to protect trucks from damage as they backed in, improvised as a ladder. He placed his foot on a tire and hoisted himself upward, rolling into the opening. His eyes quickly darted in all directions looking for anyone who might hamper his entry. All was quiet as he infiltrated the storage area. Once inside he quickly surmised the situation and headed for the only door visible.

He opened it slowly so as not to arouse any suspicion. The door made a grinding noise and Phillip froze momentarily in his tracks.

"Hey señor," a voice from behind him called. Phillip quickly spun around, automatically slipping his hand into his pocket to reach for his automatic when he realized the gun was locked in his briefcase. Fortunately he stood face to face with a person dressed in a baggage attendant's uniform.

"What are you doing here?" the man asked.

"I'm sorry," Phillip stuttered. "I was looking for a washroom."

"Well this is not it, get out of here!" the attendant shouted.

"Yes, of course," Phillip said obligingly, downplaying any further unwanted attention.

He opened the door and stepped through looking at the people in the immediate vicinity. He saw none of the three men and walked carefully in the direction of the lockers. The row of red lockers were directly before him and he continued to advance with caution, suspiciously eyeing everyone.

Phillip wondered where the threesome had gone as he reached into his pocket for the key to his particular locker. Without warning, his eyes, guided by instinct, were alerted in a direction beyond the row of lockers. He automatically focused on a young, Colombian youth leaning against the wall several feet away. Phillip recognized the youth as Ricardo, the youngest of the trio following him.

Intuition took control of his actions and Phillip dashed in between a row of brightly painted lockers, avoiding eye contact with the juvenile looking for him.

Beside him a child was drinking thirstily from a fountain. He held his breath, hoping Ricardo would not walk toward him, and smiled at the child who looked inquisitively at the tall stranger fearing for his life.

Slowly Phillip leaned against the cold edge of the lockers. He pushed his face tightly against them and peered around the corner. Ricardo was standing motionless with his back against the lockers. His eyes were surveying all passers-by as a hawk would carefully scan a field seeking its prey.

Phillip slipped back into the security of his hiding place. He glanced the other way. There was no sign of Rolf or the fat man. A group of people were casually walking in his direction talking feverishly amongst themselves about their vacation adventures. Amid the small crowd Phillip saw an attractive girl appearing to be in her early twenties. She had a way about her suggesting her travels had taken her through the tropical countryside for quite some time. Her long, blonde hair was snarled and hung recklessly down each side of her face. It had been bleached by the sun and had most of its golden tones removed, leaving it an attractive white. Her face had been tanned to a deep bronze colour, setting her deep blue eyes apart from her other features. Her blue and yellow flowered shirt seemed a little tight and had been hastily fastened in a knot just above the waistline, revealing more of her body than was necessary. Her blue denim cutoffs were frayed along the bottom and had shrunk over time. She wore white sandals, a contrast to her long, tanned legs. She was struggling with a backpack that she had decided to carry in her hand rather than on her back.

Phillip had a clear view of the crowd and focused his eyes on the attractive stranger walking in his direction. She caught his glance and returned it with a smile.

A plan began to form quickly in his mind. The attractive girl, now only feet away from him would be a great asset in decoying the young conspirator leaning against the row of lockers further along the hall. He somehow had to work her into the scheme.

"Excuse me," Phillip whispered as the girl neared his position.

"Hi," she said.

Phillip smiled. "I wonder if you could do me a favour?"

"Depends," she said displaying a devious smile and curling her tongue on the inside of her upper lip.

"It's really quite simple," Phillip said innocently. "This key belongs to locker number two-twelve." He held out the small, silver key for her to see. "There are some things inside that I need and I was wondering if you would open it, take the stuff out and continue walking. I'll meet you at the end of the corridor."

The girl looked at Phillip inquisitively. "Why don't you just go and get it yourself?" she asked.

"Because that guy standing in front of the locker is looking for me."

"Are you in trouble with the cops?"

"No, not really. You see I am an international jewel thief and there are forty million dollars worth of diamonds in that locker." Phillip's face broke into a sincere smile.

"Why do I have trouble believing that?" the girl said, grinning as she spoke. She felt a rush of excitement tingle her body as she continued to talk to Phillip.

"Because I'm not a good liar," Phillip smiled. "Will you do it?"

"Are there any drugs involved?" she asked, hesitantly.

"No. I swear to God." Phillip shook his head confirming his words. "It's only some personal stuff."

"Well I guess I will. I'm a sucker for cute guys, and you are kinda cute. Even if you are old." Again she smiled and took the key from him.

"What was the locker number?"

Phillip repeated the figure as he handed her the key. He experienced a long-absent sensation as her fingers pushed lightly against his and wondered if she also felt it. His eyes searched her face but the moment had passed too quickly. She placed her arm through her knapsack straps and straightened it onto her back. Phillip could not help notice her breasts heaving with the movement as they pushed tightly against her brightly coloured, floral shirt.

"See you in a minute," she said as she walked around the corner toward the locker.

Phillip's eyes carefully followed her stride. He watched as Ricardo immediately noticed the attractive blonde and smiled as the youth ignored all other persons in the vicinity. Phillip observed his eyes caress the slender, well shaped body of the blonde traveller walking in his direction. Phillip had to be careful not to prod his head out too far even though the boy was momentarily distracted.

The girl inserted the key in the locker and in so doing turned her head sideways smiling at Ricardo. He blushed slightly and returned her grin. After opening the locker she carefully removed the two bags and turned in the direction of Phillip. Ricardo took his eyes from the girl's face and followed her stare along and across the hall.

Several passengers had obstructed Phillip's vision. He was able to catch a glimpse of the girl now halfway between the locker and his position. Suddenly his eyes met the stare of the Spanish youth who had found an opening in the crowd. The boy shouted loudly in Spanish as he realized Phillip was hiding amid the row of lockers. His body became rigid and sprang into action, running along the same path the girl had recently created.

Afraid that Rolf and the fat man would soon be on

the scene, Phillip fled his hiding place and ran toward the loading dock. Behind him he heard the girl yelling as Ricardo spun her around in an effort to rush past her.

Quickly, Phillip grabbed the handle and opened the loading dock door.

"What do you want this time?" the shipper's voice yelled as he looked up momentarily abandoning his job of sweeping the area. He paused and rested on his broom as he watched Phillip burst through the door and run across the floor.

The sweeper picked up his broom and angrily swung it overhead shouting obscenities. He stopped and watched in awe as Phillip hurled himself through the loading dock opening onto the pavement below.

As he landed, Phillip could hear Ricardo crashing through the door. The youth saw Phillip fly through the entrance and raced across the loading area floor, hurling himself in the direction of the opening. Phillip took advantage of the moment and raised his leg, connecting his foot directly into Ricardo's chin. The youth flew backward with immense force and fell sharply against the cement wall surrounding the loading dock. Phillip steadied himself and as he withdrew from the scene his eyes detected a slight movement.

Ricardo had located a large, shiny knife concealed beneath his belt and took careful aim at the running figure before him. Phillip knew he was too late to escape the hurl and he attempted to anticipate its direction. He had a fraction of a second in which to move and summoned all of his force to propel his body in a circular motion. A final effort to avoid the sharp tip of the blade from coming in contact with his skin. His guess was good but his reaction was too slow and the point of Ricardo's knife caught Phillip in the upper arm.

A sharp pain penetrated Phillip's body as the edge of the knife broke the skin and embedded itself deep into the fleshy interior of his upper arm. Phillip screamed with agonizing pain as the serrated edge tore violently at the soft muscle tissue.

The pain was excruciating and caused Phillip to lose his balance he tripped and crashed to the floor with a violent thud. Ricardo, at the sight of Phillip brought down, was overcome with a wave of bravery. He ran toward the downed man now lying helplessly on his stomach comforting his wounded arm. Phillip painfully turned his head and saw with horror the fiery look in Ricardo's eyes. It had become an obsession, fuelled by the youth's anger over the embarrassing scolding received from Rolf earlier that day. Phillip knew his crippled body was no match for the young, aggressive Hispanic. He tried in vain to rise knowing he would be too late.

Phillip braced himself for the piercing thrust about to be lashed by his attacker. He imagined the anguish from a second knife riposte and wondered if consciousness would flee, permitting him avoidance of suffering.

At last it came. A thundering crash filled the air surrounding Phillip's senses and as quickly as it had approached the noise subsided, but oddly there was no pain. He felt relief at the prospect and quietly thanked whomever had penetrated his consciousness for a quick, painless end.

"Oh my God!" a voice yelled.

Phillip frowned at the sound of the high-pitched scream for he knew this was not how it was to be. He had envisioned soft music and billowy, white clouds. He heard more screaming bringing his mind from the subconscious slumber to the reality of the present. This time the sounds were in Spanish and he felt perspiration from his forehead trickling into his eyes, stinging as he slowly opened them. His vision was blurred but he distinguished the shape of Ricardo lying helplessly on the floor a few feet away. There was blood exuding slowly from a deep, sickening gash in his forehead.

The yelling continued and Phillip knew it came from the caretaker with the broom.

"Shut up!" he suddenly heard in English. He tilted his head up and saw the blonde girl hovering over him, smiling as she stared into his awakening eyes.

"Are you all right? Are you alive?" she asked with concern as she knelt beside him.

Phillip smiled. "Yes, I'm fine and no, I'm not dead." He held his gaze momentarily on the slender, tanned legs only inches from his face.

Phillip slowly raised his body feeling the pain from the knife wound in his arm. He stumbled as he inadvertently shifted his weight on it. The sudden, jerky motion caused the knife to fall from its loose implant of Phillip's fleshy arm. As it fell to the paved surface, Phillip cried out in pain.

"Oh my God!" the girl said noticing the blood-stained shirt. "You're hurt!"

"I know," Phillip said as she helped him up. Together they stood staring down at Ricardo's motionless body.

"I think I've killed him!".

"You did this?" Phillip asked in astonishment, raising his eyebrows as he spoke.

"I saw him coming at you so I threw this crate and hit him in the head." Phillip saw the small, wooden, orange crate lying beside Ricardo. "Is he dead? Did I kill him?" the girl shrieked, raising her hands to her mouth.

"No. I don't think so, but I'm sure his head will hurt for awhile."

"What are we gonna do now?"

From behind they could hear the shipper yelling. They saw him drop his broom and run for the exit. Phillip climbed the steps heading back into the loading platform.

"Where are you going?" the girl yelled.

"To get my stuff." His duffel bag and attaché case

were lying untouched where the girl had dropped them by the entrance to the loading area. He tucked the bag under his good arm and grabbed the brief case. "Let's get out of here!" he yelled as the twosome rushed through the shipping doors and made their way along the terminal building.

"Here, let me take that." The girl motioned to Phillip's attaché case.

"Thank you," he said, "take this one." He pushed the duffel bag forward.

When they neared the front of the building, Phillip cautiously glanced in both directions ensuring that Rolf and the fat man were nowhere in sight. He saw the burgundy car still parked in the awkward position in which it had been left. A bright-yellow, parking ticket, slapped on the windscreen, was flapping in the breeze.

"Where to now?" the girl asked

"We'll have to get a cab. Cops will be swarming all over this area in a few minutes. I think the shipper got a pretty good look at both of us."

"We can't go anywhere like that," the girl said pointing to the bloodstained sleeve of Phillip's shirt.

Phillip looked at the wound. The panic of the situation had made him forget the increasing pain now brought to the foreground of his mind. The bloodstain was getting larger and he leaned against the wall motioning for his duffel bag. He removed a shirt and held it between his teeth allowing him to tear a section from it.

"Here let me do that," the girl said. She took the shirt and tore a thin section of cloth which she wrapped tightly around Phillip's arm above the wound.

"There's a jacket in there too," he said.

After draping the windbreaker over his shoulder they walked out to the front of the building.

"Where to now?" the girl asked.

"It's best if we parted here. I don't think you should get involved any further."

"Forget it," she said matronly. "You would never make it on your own. Remember you'd have been dead by now if it hadn't been for me." With that she looked up and down the street, raised her arm and hailed the first available cab.

Phillip felt too weak to argue her directives and realized she was right. Although he had no right to involve her, a perfect stranger, he was thankful for the assistance in facing this agony. The cabby stared curiously at him as he slid slowly into the back.

"My husband drank a little too much on the plane," the girl said believably, aware of the driver's concern. "He hurt his arm," she continued. "Could you drive us to a hospital?"

"No!" Phillip clamoured. "No hospital. Take us to the bus depot."

The driver diverted his glance from the girl to Phillip. "The bus depot, señor?"

"To hell with that," the girl interjected, "we're not going to any bus depot. Just take us to the nearest hotel. Okay?" Phillip raised his hand in protest. "Just never mind," she said sternly. "You look terrible," she said shaking her head scoldingly.

The red flush had disappeared from Phillip's cheeks and had been replaced by a bleached complexion. The makeshift bandage seemed to ease the pain and Phillip leaned his head against the soft cushion of the seat-back, daring to close his eyes for a few moments. He felt the girl place her arm around his shoulder, comforting, as a mother would her injured child.

Phillip looked up and smiled. "Incidentally," he began, "I'm Phillip Wright. What's your name?"

"Lily," she replied.

"Thank you Lily," he said. His eyelids drooped and his head felt dizzy from the loss of blood.

It seemed most of the hotels Phillip stayed at during

assignments in Bogota were dingy and dismal and this one was no exception. The well used mattress sagged in the centre as if someone had tossed a barrel onto the soft, foam rubber. Against the wall at the foot of the bed sat a small, wooden dresser. Two metal chairs with tan-coloured, wooden seats stood neglected side by side facing the bed.

Phillip removed his shirt as Lily returned from the bathroom carrying wet towels. She wiped Phillip's wound, cleaning off most of the blood.

"Looks a lot better than it feels, that's for sure," Phillip said, staring at Lily's soft hands dabbing tenderly at the wound with the moistened towels.

"You'd better get some rest while I go out and find some food and bandages."

Phillip watched her from behind as her hips swayed from side to side. Although he was overcome with exhaustion, his mind still twinged with pleasure in watching the well rounded buttocks fill the tight, denim shorts. He wondered momentarily if she was intentionally teasing him but cast the thought immediately from his mind as he pictured the gentleness with which she had cared for him during the past several hours.

The loss of blood had caused a heaviness to overcome his sensations and it wasn't long before Phillip fell soundly asleep. He tossed wildly at first but soon settled into a deep, peaceful, long overdue slumber.

Phillip opened his eyes but did not stir. His pupils darted from side to side. It took a few moments before he recognized his surroundings. As he tilted his head to his side he saw Lily sleeping soundly beside him and allowed his eyes to travel along the outline of her sensuous body. Ever so slowly his vision caressed each delectable inch of her sleeping beauty.

He gently lifted his tender arm and tried to focus on his watch. He had been asleep five hours and the effect was incredible. Although his arm was stiff, the pain had lessened substantially and was replaced by a constant but low pulsed throbbing. The wound had been cleaned and dressed by Lily as Phillip had slept. Beside the bed on one of the chairs sat a small plate with several, assorted sandwiches. Phillip quietly leaned over and took one. He smiled as he saw a small jar with mustard. He kicked his legs over the side of the bed and slowly sat up trying not to disturb the girl who had nursed him so well. He could feel the blood rushing to his head and waited a moment before he stood straight. On the dresser stood a small, unopened bottle of scotch. The rich, golden liquid, shimmered as the late afternoon sun danced gaily, creating a prism effect through the glass.

"Where do you think you're going?"

Phillip turned and saw Lily propped up on her elbows, smiling at him.

He returned the grin. "Can I get you a drink?" he asked.

"As long as it's a double." She winked and smiled sweetly.

Phillip obeyed and poured two glasses of scotch. He decided to fill them slightly fuller before returning to the comfort of his bed.

"To your health," she said, lifting her glass and gesturing toward Phillip. He returned the greeting and allowed his glass to gently click against hers. They smiled, as the cheap, hotel glasses echoed a hollow sound. Their faces were only inches apart and Phillip stared sternly into her deep blue, angel eyes.

Thoughts of passion sprung wildly into his head. Feeling boyish excitement surge throughout his entire body he slowly, as if drawn magnetically, moved his face closer to hers. She responded willingly by closing her eyes anticipating Phillip's intent. He glanced at her moist lips and watched as she parted them slightly. A moment later he felt the soft, delicate skin of her face brush against his as their

lips met. Phillip had longed for a moment of passion and
tried to withhold the feeling of urgency building within his
groin. He was a soft and gentle lover, constantly aware of
his partner's feelings and emotions As her lips pressed
tighter against his he parted them with his tongue and was
surprised at her cooperative response. He knew he wanted
very much to enjoy the pleasure this girl was capable of
giving him. Clumsily they put their drinks on the floor not
releasing their lips from each other. Slowly, following Phillip's lead, Lily allowed him to manoeuvre his body onto
hers. He was careful to shift his weight avoiding undue
stress on his injured arm yet transferring all his passion
into her. She moaned sensuously as she felt Phillip's body
press firmly against her own. Realizing his injury was
restricting his movement, she aided him in untying the
double knot of her flowery shirt, allowing it to part and her
breasts to fall free.

Lily walked from the bathroom rubbing a towel over her
freshly-washed, blonde hair. "What time do you have to be
at the airport?"

"I don't," Phillip replied, still lying in bed. He raised
his arm and put it behind his head, inhaling deeply from a
newly lit cigarette. The smoke slowly expired from his
lungs. He was staring at the wonderful vision of Lily's
perfect, naked body covered with water droplets as she
continued to rub the rough hotel towel against her well-
tanned skin.

"I thought you had a plane to catch?"

"No, not now," he replied. "I was only picking up
my brief case."

"Oh, I didn't know that." She paused as she shook
her head in an effort to get water out of her ear. "I have a
flight at eight thirty tonight." She held a towel in front of
her, barely covering her breasts and thighs. "What time is it
now?" she asked as she walked toward the bed. She let the

towel fall as she smiled at Phillip.

"Almost six-thirty. You'd better hustle." He smiled as he looked at her standing naked beside him. She picked up the towel and spun around walking toward her clothes.

"Will I see you again?" she asked.

"I sure hope so," he said.

After putting on her cutoffs, she took a pen from her knapsack and scribbled on a piece of paper which she handed to Phillip.

"Here is my address. Do you ever get to California?"

"I'll make a point of it."

"You take good care of your arm."

Phillip ogled her as he watched her finish dressing. She gathered all her belongings and put them in her knapsack. After glancing around the dimly lit room, ensuring nothing had been left behind, she walked to the bed, leaned over Phillip's face and gently planted a moist kiss on his lips. A surge of excitement resurfaced throughout his body as he felt her soft hair dance against his cheeks.

"Call me," she said quietly.

Phillip stared at her. She picked up her knapsack, waved, and smiled. A moment later she was gone.

11   FATMAN

Phillip calmly finished a cigarette before he moved, enjoying each exhalation of smoke from his lungs. His mind felt saddened by the prospect of never seeing Lily again. He rested a few minutes longer, savouring the moment, and eventually butted the cigarette in the small, glass ashtray on the floor. Slowly he rose, favouring his arm, and ransacked his duffelbag looking for a razor and some shaving cream. A smooth shave and long, hot shower was the perfect prescription for his ailment.

The hot, steamy spray, falling like a summer rain shower on his naked flesh, relaxed the tension embedded in his aching muscles. He reminisced over the past hours engulfed in fond memories of his encounter with Lily. As the shower continued to cleanse his sweat-stained pores he allowed his mind to drift into the reality of the present. Grateful that his duffelbag and briefcase were again in his possession, he found no reason to stay in the vicinity. He decided the bus stop would be his initial point of exploration in hopes that Rolf and his men would not be there.

Lily had thoughtfully bought extra bandages which he used to carefully dress his wound. The throbbing was beginning to subside and the blood had stopped flowing. The wound was not as bad as he had first expected. He took his wrist watch from the counter and rubbed the steam from its face. A little food, he thought, would probably sit well as the now eaten sandwiches were not very filling.

He sorted his two shirts and discarded the one he had torn earlier. Phillip combed his hair and studied his aging face in the mirror. His rollicking experience with Lily had given him youthful confidence. He smiled, pleased with the situation, and regretted that he could not meet more women in his line of work. Throughout his travels he had met many girls with whom he would have liked to cultivate a relationship. Unfortunately there never seemed to be enough time. He had enjoyed several short affairs over the years but each had left him feeling empty and alone. He thought of the sex he had enjoyed with his wife during their years of marriage and missed the companionship which accompanied a relationship. Suddenly a vision of Lana Winters raced through his head. Her sweet smile directed toward him. Her flowing, blonde hair waving in the sullen breeze as she tilted her head to one side. He caught himself smiling as he watched her eyes flare devilishly in his direction. A feeling of guilt washed the happy image away and Phillip wished he had not met Lily, that instead he had been with Lana.

He walked to the lobby of the hotel and approached a dark-haired woman behind the counter. He began speaking to her in Spanish.

"I was in room ...," he paused for a moment as he fumbled for his room key. "...four-nineteen. I would like to check-out."

"Of course," the slim attendant replied. She smiled and walked to the end of the counter, locating a card in a small metal box. She read the information.

"Oh, you will not be staying overnight?" she asked, realizing that he had checked in earlier that same day.

"No, I have had a change in plans."

"I see," the lady replied. A smile came to her face as she remembered Lily leaving less than an hour before.

Phillip felt embarrassment surging through his body and felt his cheeks burn as the woman continued to smile. He settled the accounting task and was about to leave.

"Señor," the woman called after him. "Some friends of yours. They were here earlier looking for you."

Phillip returned to the counter. "Some friends you said?" Phillip asked.

"It was actually my husband who spoke with them. They felt very bad for you."

"And why was that?" Phillip asked, trying to act as casual as he could.

"Apparently you went to a party with them and had a small accident. They wanted to see how you were."

"What were their names?"

"I don't know. My husband didn't ask."

"What did he tell them?"

"That you were resting comfortably and that he remembered you because of the blood on your arm."

"Tell me, did your husband describe the men to you?"

"Not really, only that there were two of them."

"Very good of them to drop by." Phillip smiled as he regained his composure. "Any indication of when they will be returning?"

"No they did not say."

"Well, I guess I'll get a sandwich and check back in half an hour. If they come back ask them to wait."

"Certainly," the woman replied. "And thank you for staying with us."

Phillip nodded as he left the lobby. He stepped out the front door and quickly glanced in both directions, assuming one of the two men would be stationed nearby.

He stood in the doorway for several seconds. The fat man would probably be out back. That meant that Phillip would have to deal with Rolf. Physically he was no match for him. Rolf was bigger and healthier. Phillip would have to keep out of sight. He waited in the doorway until a cab pulled up in front of the hotel. Hurriedly he raised his hand and patiently waited for the cab to stop. When it did he jumped in.

"Quickly! To the bus depot!" Phillip snapped. "I'm in a hurry!"

He looked out the rear window as the cab sped off. There was no sign of the burgundy car or the two assailants. He was grateful that Ricardo had been successfully eliminated, at least temporarily. He reconstructed the scene at the airport loading dock and smiled as he thought of Lily. It was after all she who had rendered the young Latino inoperative.

He continued to glance behind him. "You're nervous, señor?" the cab driver asked in English.

"No, not at all," Phillip said trying to steady his speech. "I'm just admiring the beautiful city you have here."

"Oh have you not been here very long?"

"No only a short time. I was thinking of taking a few days and relaxing at a resort or something. Can you recommend any place?"

The cabby thought for a moment. "Well, the mountains are very nice this time of year. The tourists go there but unfortunately it is not very safe any more with all the drug dealers attacking everyone. There are many robbers who will take all you have with you." He paused and looked over his shoulder into the rear seat. "Do you have a camera señor?"

"No," Phillip replied. His mind had re-focused on the missing scientist who had no passport. Where would he have hidden his family?

"On the other hand," the cabby continued, "if you enjoy the night life you can go to Cartagena. It is only one hour by air."

Cartagena was still fresh in Phillip's mind. He instantly thought of Lana and wondered how she was. He pictured her strolling carelessly through the downtown streets of the ancient, Spanish city.

They arrived at the bus depot and Phillip paid the man.

"Gracias señor." The cabby was smiling as Phillip handed him the money.

He looked both ways for signs of his followers and after being fairly satisfied that there was no one, he stepped into the security of the bus depot. The building was much smaller inside than its outside appearance suggested.

Red, cloth-covered chairs hung in aluminium frames and had been placed along three walls of the square room. The fourth was made up of a row of glass-enclosed ticket cubicles.

Phillip walked to one of the chairs, sat down, and opened his briefcase. He found the photo of Kristy McPherson and removed it, closing the case and securing it under his arm. He walked to one of the ticket windows, leaving the duffel bag on the floor.

"Excuse me," he said. The older gentleman behind the window looked up and peaked over the rim of his bifocals at the stranger standing before him.

Phillip continued. "I'm trying to find my brother and his family. There has been a terrible accident at home and I must get in touch with him. I believe they were here on June 22 and took a bus to Cartagena or Medellin."

"I don't recall that far back," the man replied.

"I have a picture here of my brother's daughter. Perhaps you recognize her?"

The man studied the photo. He shook his head from

side to side. "I'm afraid not." He handed the photograph back to Phillip.

"Could anyone else have been working at the time?"

"There are usually only two of us on duty," the man replied. "Excuse me for a moment," he said, looking past Phillip.

A man and woman had lined up to purchase a ticket. Phillip stepped aside to allow them to complete their transaction. The woman turned her head toward Phillip and studied his face. Phillip smiled as he caught her staring. The woman decided he was not the kind of person she would associate with and abruptly turned her head back. Phillip stared at her for a moment and sadly shook his head.

After the couple departed, Phillip positioned himself before the wicket. "Excuse me, I wonder if you would mind asking your associate?" Phillip's eyes were trained at a woman sitting behind a desk. Her pencil was poised to begin writing.

"Let me look at the photograph again," the uniformed man said helpfully.

"I have another picture, one of my brother. Let me get it." Phillip opened his attaché case and removed another eight by ten glossy and handed it to the man.

He studied both prints carefully and began rubbing his chin. "There was also my brother's wife, a rather short, chubby lady as well as their twelve year old son. They might also have been travelling with my niece's boyfriend."

"I think maybe they were here. Just a minute," he said and turned to the lady behind him. She looked up and smiled softly as the man approached.

Her white blouse and brown skirt resembled her counterpart's uniform. She looked at the photos and pondered the question asked of her. Phillip felt a surge of excitement within him when she nodded positively in response.

They both stood up and walked toward the counter.

The lady self-consciously held her skirt as she walked. Her obesity caused her concern and she tried to tidy herself as she walked cupping her hand against the back of her hair to confirm it was in place. Two more people had lined up to purchase tickets. The man in uniform motioned to the next ticket window allowing Phillip the privacy he would require. The lady smiled as he approached.

"You are looking for these people?"

"Yes I am. It's my brother and his children."

"Your Spanish is very good," she said sincerely.

"Thank you. I have spent a great deal of time in your country." Phillip tried desperately not to sound anxious about the news he might receive.

"They were here a few weeks ago. Lovely people. I remember them well because we spoke of Vancouver. I have been there once myself. It is very beautiful. They were such a nice family. They wanted to go on a vacation somewhere in Colombia."

"Did they tell you where?" Phillip interjected.

"Yes they did. They wanted to go to the Rosario Islands. They were looking for a secluded place. A place they could get some rest. I suggested they take an airplane because it would be a very long journey by bus. I explained that they would first have to go to Cartagena and then arrange for boat passage.

"Did they take your advice and fly?"

"No. The small boy apparently had a problem with his sinuses. He could not fly for several weeks so they purchased bus tickets." Phillip knew the real reason for not flying was lack of passports.

"I guess I had better go to Cartagena then."

"Will you be requiring bus tickets as well?"

"No thank you. I much prefer flying to sitting in a bus for ten hours." Phillip smiled as he spoke.

"It is a twenty-four hour bus journey señor. The forest and mountains are very treacherous."

"Thank you ever so much. I would like to ask you a favour." The woman looked inquisitively at Phillip. "My brother has made several enemies in his line of work. That is why he wanted to get away for a rest. If any of them come looking for him please don't reveal his destination."

"No señor, I understand."

Phillip smiled at her and walked back to the chair where his duffel bag was left. He was thankful his make-believe story had sounded convincing. The last thing he wanted was the helpful woman second-guessing his true intentions. He sat down and replaced the photographs in the briefcase. He walked toward the exit and as he was about to open the door noticed the burgundy BMW pull up and come to an abrupt halt. The fat man was peering through the window but Phillip managed to dash back inside before being discovered. Without hesitation he ran back to the ticket counter and asked when the next bus was leaving for the airport.

"Eight thirty," the clerk answered. "If you hurry you can catch it." Phillip pulled out the appropriate amount of money and handed it to the clerk. The man passed Phillip the ticket and pointed toward the door at the end of the building. Phillip ran to the exit and jumped into the half empty bus. He found a seat toward the rear where he could be alone and view the entrance. He placed the duffel bag and briefcase beside him and looked out the window, wondering if his assailants had discovered his location and destination. Phillip realized as the bus began to move that he had only bought himself a few minutes of time. He knew the woman would tell Rolf exactly what had happened and that she would also tell him that Phillip asked about McPherson. No doubt Rolf would be aggressive in his questioning and draw the proper information from the unsuspecting woman. Suddenly it occurred to Phillip that she would also reveal his destination. They would be in a position to overtake him and lay in wait at the airport the

way a lion would wait amid the tall grass preying on its
unwary victim. Phillip shivered as the thoughts raced through
his mind and he focused his attention out the window
searching for the burgundy BMW. He made a mental note
to call Ed Bergan at the next available opportunity. Rolf
had made it clear earlier that day that once they had
McPherson there would be no need to keep Phillip around.
The thought did not sit well and Phillip became anxious to
depart the bus.

He continued to stare out the window as the bus
approached the main road, trying to work out a plan of
action. The bus, which only a few minutes ago had been a
ray of hope had instead become a prison which would allow
him no escape.

There had to be a way out and Phillip searched his
instincts for a solution. He knew there had to be one somewhere. His mind began to panic. He could find no plausible
result. Nervously he tapped his fingers on his knee matching a rhythm already started by his feet. Suddenly he saw
Rolf's car passing the bus. Phillip leaned away from the
window to avoid being seen. The bus continued on and
shortly thereafter turned into the airport parking lot. Phillip's eyes scanned the pavement for the all too familiar
burgundy vehicle. Unfortunately, without fail, he saw it
parked in the waiting area, mocking him as if it knew he
had no choice but to walk into its grasping arms. The fat
man and Rolf were leaning against the car eyeing Phillip's
prison as it approached.

Phillip opened his attaché case and removed the
automatic. He quietly slipped the gun in his pocket, glancing around to ensure he had not been seen.

When the bus stopped in the off-loading zone the
two men began walking toward it. They remained casual so
as not to attract any attention. Phillip pressed his body back
into the seat as far as he could, assaying to hide his face
from view. He watched as the other passengers left the bus.

When he was certain there was no one else on board, he slowly slipped down into his seat keeping his eyes on the rear view mirror to make certain that the bus driver had not seen him. When he felt secure he slid onto the floor, reached into his pocket, and removed his automatic. From his crouched position he levelled the killing weapon in between the legs of the seat in front of him. He pointed it directly into the aisle and waited patiently amid the silence of the bus. The engine had been shut off and the only sound present was the soft hush of Phillip's breathing.

The bus driver left the bus and closed the door behind him.

"Is that everyone?" Rolf snapped at the driver. The man looked at the large, blonde German standing before him. Rolf grabbed the Hispanic by the shoulder. He spoke to the fat man.

"Tell him!" he commanded. The fat man re-phrased the question. This time in Spanish.

"Si señor," the driver shivered as he spoke, unaccustomed to such harsh mannerisms.

"How can that be?" Rolf asked furiously. "Get on that bus and find him!" he screamed, motioning to the fat man. "I will go back to the building." He pushed the driver out of his way as he stomped back to the terminal. The uniformed man was unfamiliar with this type of treatment. Although he resented Rolf's bullying, fear kept him from voicing his opinion. The bus driver flitted from the scene and entered the lobby, deciding not to report the incident. These men were professionals and the last thing he needed was to involve himself in other people's business. From inside the bus, Phillip heard a noise. As the bus door was being pried open, he felt his heartbeat increase. He forced his body to remain calm and inhaled deeply, cleansing his mind from any thoughts which might distract him from his immediate, life-threatening situation.

A squeaking sound, followed by a loud crash signalled the opening of the doors. He heard the slow shuffling of leather soles against the metal floor. The noise stopped.

"I know you are in here," the fat man said. Phillip had no difficulty in understanding his Spanish. "Come out with your hands up and you won't get hurt." There was a long silent pause. "If you don't, you know that I will find you and kill you."

Phillip made no sound. The hot air in the enclosed bus became stifling. The footsteps continued. Again they stopped. There was silence. Phillip's finger slowly, encircled the trigger of his gun. He could feel the perspiration building on the inside of his palm and grew terrified as he lay waiting for the fat man to approach his lair. Again the feet moved. Slowly coming closer. Although he could not see any movement he knew the man was nearing the location where he lay in hiding. A scraping noise of feet brushing along the grit on the floor was the only audible sound. He waited and saw nothing. His grip tightened around the trigger of the gun and he endeavoured to steady himself as much as possible. The shuffling noise continued.

Suddenly Phillip saw the black shoes and gray trousers. The fat man was about three feet in front of him. The footsteps moved slowly. The fat man was getting cautious. Phillip knew he needed the element of surprise. His life depended on it.

The throbbing pain in Phillip's arm as it began to cramp was agonizing but he dared not move. He waited patiently. When the fat man's foot was twelve inches from his vantage point Phillip lowered the gun slightly. The man slowly raised his foot and moved it forward in line with Phillip's seat. At that precise moment Phillip squeezed the trigger engaging the firing mechanism of the destructive weapon. The echo of the burst had not yet subsided when a different noise, an ear piercing shriek reverberated throughout the enclosed, metal bus. The scream sent shivers along Phillip's spine and he re-focused his attention before continuing. The sight before him caused vomit to form deep within his throat. Blood, mingled with tiny chunks of flesh was splattered all around. A pool of thick, red liquid was forming before him on the floor.

Phillip waited for what appeared an eternity for the fat man's weight to overpower his butchered leg. He began to fall forward and at the precise moment when the fat man's eyes met Phillip's, he jumped up forcing his fist violently into the wounded man's stomach. As the injured assailant doubled over Phillip lifted his leg with incredible force thrusting his knee into the fat Hispanic's face. The man groaned and dropped silently onto the metal floor of the stationary bus.

Phillip jumped over the body and ran to the front of the vehicle. He looked out the window hoping he was faster than Rolf. When he got to the front of the bus a blanket of relief fell over him. The driver had left the keys in the ignition. Phillip jumped into the small bucket seat and rapidly twisted the key depressing the clutch and gas pedal at the same time. The massive, metal machine came to life with a furious roar as Phillip's foot pumped the accelerator.

Phillip looked through the door window and saw Rolf walking toward the bus. Suddenly Rolf became aware of the bus engine running and increased his pace. Phillip saw two uniformed policemen at his heels and wondered what fictitious tale Rolf had concocted. As the bus jumped from its stationary position, Phillip saw Rolf pointing at the moving vehicle. One of the policemen pulled his gun and shouted. Phillip, however, had already manoeuvred the bus into the flow of traffic.

From behind Phillip heard a loud, agonizing groan. The fat man was regaining consciousness. The movement of the bus had awoken his senses. Phillip kept his foot to the floor and navigated the bus toward the exit of the airport. He travelled the same route as the day before heading away from the city. He passed the area where he had previously abandoned the stationwagon and surveyed the landscape. The forsaken vehicle was nowhere to be seen. Rolf must have removed it to keep suspicion away from his questionable activities.

Phillip studied the mirrors of the bus to see if there was any trace of pursuit. Although he saw none he knew it would only be moments before Rolf, now aided by the police, would come into view.

The bus travelled rapidly along the paved road. In the distance, Phillip could see the intersection which he had passed several times the day before. There would be absolutely no room for error today.

He spun the steering wheel to the right, sending the bus into a screeching, ninety degree turn. Blue smoke steamed from the wheels as he hurled along the dirt road. His rear vision was camouflaged by a dust cloud trailing him. He glanced at the fat man who lay in a semiconscious state moaning painfully, his senses still numbed by the shock of the past events.

Ahead Phillip noticed a tiny speck of light nearing the bus. He slowed in an effort to avoid attention, illuminating his headlights as the little speck anamorphically tweened into the shape of a car. He clenched his fingers tightly around the steering wheel in preparation of unwanted events. His vision was impaired as the setting sun shone its bright, lightened rays directly into his eyes. Phillip judged the distance from the oncoming car to be two hundred feet. His concentration became intense as the distance between the two vehicles decreased.

As the predetermined moment arrived, Phillip's hands yanked the steering wheel toward the other side of the road at the same time slamming on the brakes. The bus swerved violently causing its back end to fishtail, eventually coming to an abrupt halt blocking the entire road. No traffic could pass. Pleased with the result, Phillip looked out and saw the oncoming car, engulfed by a cloud of dust.

The driver was struggling to maintain control of his vehicle while bringing the car to a safe stop. Phillip turned to look at his unconscious passenger and felt pity at the harrowing expression on the fat man's face. Although still insensible, signs of pain were evident by the man's expression. Phillip detested what he had been forced to do and wished he could explain his feelings to the motionless form on the floor of the bus. He snapped his mind back to the task ahead and in an effort to waste no further time, opened the door, grabbed his duffel bag and attaché case and jumped from the bus.

The other vehicle roosted in a field adjoining the road. Phillip rushed to the misguided auto and with one hand on his Baretta, opened the driver's door, deliberately shoving the cold shaft of the weapon into the man's face. Phillip was relieved that he was unharmed. His hands were still tightly wrapped around the steering wheel as he turned his colourless face toward Phillip. His mouth hung open from shock. Phillip spoke to him in Spanish.

"You will not be harmed. Just do as I say. Get out of the car." Phillip grabbed the man by his suit jacket and forcibly pulled him from the vehicle. He grabbed his left arm and twisted it behind his back. "Move!" he commanded pushing the man around the car to the passenger side. Phillip motioned for the man to open the door. He shoved his hostage into the car and immediately sat next to him.

"Now drive!" he yelled. The man nervously turned the key in the ignition. The car made a loud, clattering noise. "It's already running." Phillip said. His voice contained a much higher degree of patience than it did a few minutes before.

"I'm not going to harm you. All I want is for you to drive me to the airport." He motioned for the man to drive over the grass, around the bus and back onto the road. In extreme fear for his life, the captive did so obediently. Phillip had been fortunate. It was a late model car and in excellent condition. A dark brown sedan would not be easily noticed in a crowd. The driver was in his late twenties. A businessman, Phillip thought. There was a suitcase in the back seat.

"Were you planning to go to the airport anyway?" he asked.

"Yes," the man answered

"Well, good," Phillip replied calmly. "I hope I haven't made you miss your flight."

The man slowly raised his wrist and glanced at his watch. "No," he stammered.

"Excellent," Phillip said, pleased that the stranger was beginning to show signs of relaxation.

The car approached the intersection. "Turn left!"

The man did so and as the twosome cruised along the paved road, flashing lights of an oncoming police cruiser became visible in the distance.

"Pay no attention to these police cars," Phillip said showing the man his gun. "Drive as if nothing was wrong."

"Are they after you?" the man meekly asked.

"Yeah, unless you know someone else who has stolen a bus, shot a man and hijacked a car?" Phillip smiled as he spoke.

As they approached the police car, he slid down onto the seat and partially covered his face with his hands, constantly looking at his chauffeur to ensure that no secret signals would be transferred. As he watched every movement the driver made he shoved the muzzle of his Baretta into the man's flabby, midriff area.

The man emitted a small grunt as he realized what was happening. He had no intention of disobeying his attacker's commands.

The police car passed them, its siren screeching a piercing entry into a still evening. Although it was difficult for Phillip to see who was in the cruiser, he assumed it to be Rolf.

The hijacked car approached the final bend in the road before its entry into the airport area.

"Where should I go?" the captive asked.

"Just park your car where you normally would. Try to be as casual as you can."

"Do not worry señor, I will not report you."

"Do as you wish, just give me twenty minutes."

The man said nothing and watched in awe as Phillip ran from the car with his two pieces of luggage.

When he entered the building his eyes immediately darted left and right searching the surrounding area to see if Rolf had stayed behind. After being assured he had not, Phillip walked to the ticket counter. He was studying the map of Colombia and with the help of a pretty attendant found the Rosario Islands. Cartagena would definitely be the closest city. Unfortunately the next flight was not until noon the following day. He checked his watch. It was nine thirty.

He saw the former hostage walking nervously through the security gate and into the boarding area. He was glad that the man had not missed his flight and felt relatively certain that he had not contacted the police, however precautions were still necessary.

Phillip pondered his options. He dared not stay in Bogota overnight. He knew that Rolf had probably questioned the woman at the bus depot and that she had told him everything he wanted to know. Rolf would know where Phillip was heading as well as the flight he would be taking. Phillip checked the route. The flight was nonstop to Cartagena. He left the terminal and walked to a long row of cabs. The drivers were patiently awaiting a flight from the U.S. Phillip looked for one in relatively decent condition.

"Buenos dias," Phillip said to the driver. The man returned the greeting.

"You want a ride?"

"Maybe." Phillip paused, "How much would it cost

and how long would it take to get to Medellin?

The man looked at Phillip before answering.

"Madre Mia!" he said in a loud voice. "You are crazy señor, do you know how far that is?"

Phillip nodded his head. "How much?"

"Señor, you can take an airplane there and it would be cheaper."

Phillip began to move on. "I'm sure someone will take me."

"Wait, wait señor. Do not be hasty. I will take you but the roads are not very good. It goes through the rain forest. There are many banditos. Many drug dealers along the way. It will take at least twelve hours. That is nonstop. I cannot drive that long without rest."

"That's all right." Phillip said. "I can drive. I must get there. Now how much is it?"

"Are you going to pay in American dollars?"

"I can if you want," the driver smiled and nodded his head. "It would be about two hundred dollars." He paused looking for a reaction from Phillip. There was none. "One hundred in advance," he added softly.

Phillip counted the money and handed it to the driver. He stepped into the cab, threw his duffel bag and attaché case into the back seat, and checked the safety on his automatic before he replaced it in his pocket.

The car's air conditioning was a great comfort in the humid, tropical country. The automobile began to roll down the paved, uneven parking lot, bouncing with each fracture in the asphalt. Phillip exhaled slowly, allowing himself the luxury of relaxing for the first time since his arrival in Bogota. He took a cigarette from his pack and offered one to the driver. Again he exhaled slowly, allowing each muscle group within his tired body to calm itself. He closed his eyes and thought of golden meadows covered in a blanket of warm, summer sunlight flowing from an azure-blue sky. Slowly his mind cleared. He opened his eyes and saw the bustling city of Bogota disappear as the automobile traced the curvature of the mountainous terrain.

Phillip felt quite pleased with himself. He did not tell the driver his intent to spend the night just outside of Bogota. They would then get up early and take a leisurely drive to Medellin. Phillip judged it to be about seven hours without unforeseen problems. They would spend a restful night in Medellin and he would catch the flight to Cartagena the day after.

He knew that Rolf had probably surmised Phillip's intentions of going to Cartagena. With luck, Rolf would be waiting at Bogota's Eldorado airport. He was no longer needed now that Rolf had presumably discovered McPherson's hideout.

Phillip tried to picture the look of surprise on Rolf's face when he would be unable to locate him. Phillip felt certain Rolf would take the flight because his mission was the scientist, not the agent, and Rolf was a professional. He would never deviate from his primary objective.

Phillip's plan would place Rolf in Cartagena one day before him. He had to militate on Rolf's inability to locate McPherson's exact position quickly. Phillip would call Lana Winters and give her instructions to begin looking for the scientist and his family. Lana could be trusted. Again he saw her sweet face innocently smiling at him from the hidden recesses of his memory. A smile crossed his face as the image lingered in his mind.

If he telephoned Lana tonight, she could begin searching first thing in the morning. That would give her enough time to be at the airport in Cartagena and meet Rolf's flight. Should Rolf be successful and find the elusive scientist, Lana would know and be able to translate the information to Phillip. He was extremely satisfied with the arrangements and was looking forward to a good night's sleep.

In the distance Phillip saw a police car, its emergency lights flashing brightly. He wondered if it was leaving the scene of the abandoned bus.

Phillip focused his attention on the driver. "Excuse me," he said politely. "I have changed my mind." He paused. "I want to stop at a hotel for the night and continue our journey tomorrow." He waited for a reaction. The cabby looked confused and surprised. "I will pay for your room, of course."

"Well señor, you are the customer. Frankly, I much prefer to drive in the daytime. It will be easier."

"Find us a hotel, will you?"

"I know a place only five miles from here. It is very clean. A real tourist trap." He paused, realizing what he had said. "But I will get us a good price." He paused again. "Incidentally señor, my name is Pedro."

Pedro's impression of tourist class hotels left a little to be desired. Although the establishment was clean it had not been modernized for some time. He ordered two rooms and handed a key to the driver. "Breakfast at eight. No need to get up too early." The two men bade each other good night and Phillip watched Pedro walk toward the staircase.

"Hey cutie. Hope I didn't wake you?" Phillip asked as Lana answered her telephone.

"No. Not at all. I'm actually surprised to hear from you so soon."

"Well I need a favour."

"Oh sure, don't call me to say hello," she said mockingly.

"I'm sorry," he said boyishly. "How are you?"

She laughed. "What can I do for you?"

Phillip explained his situation and relayed the information about Rolf to her. He gave her enough facts to get a good start on locating the scientist's whereabouts. Lana's response was enthusiastic. She was looking forward to what she considered field work.

"I'd appreciate it if you didn't tell anyone what you were doing. This guy Rolf is really out to get me. I'd fear for your safety."

"How sweet you are Phillip Wright." There was compassion in her voice. "Don't you worry about a thing."

"Could you also contact Ed Bergan and give him Rolf's name. Ask him to find out what he can about him. Tell him I'll call him soon."

"Will do."

"I'll call you tomorrow night."

"I'll look forward to it."

Phillip felt secure knowing that Lana would give full dedication to his project. He was looking forward to a restful night in this quiet, Colombian hotel.

After an enjoyable breakfast and hearing of Pedro's tales of local folklore, the two travellers headed for the cab. Phillip sat in the passenger's seat and watched the driver start the car.

The man tilted his head back, settling in for the long journey ahead. He wiped an arm across his forehead, mixing several small droplets of sweat with his thinning black hair. His pale green shirt showed stains of coffee similar to those found on a dirty table cloth in a greasy restaurant.

Phillip slowly slid back into the seat in an effort to find the most comfortable position possible. He acknowledged the driver's trivial comments, at the same time hoping that it would not be an idle chatter-filled trip. Once en route out of Bogota, Phillip closed his eyes and attempted to find comfort in a nap.

12 MEDELLIN

Willem Rolf rose later than he normally did and after twenty minutes of sit ups and a brief shower, devoured a healthy breakfast of nearly raw eggs, brown toast and yogurt. Although he rarely had trouble sleeping, last night was a stressful experience. His two assistants had been badly beaten. Carlos would be in the hospital for several weeks. The doctors questioned whether he would ever walk again. Ricardo had taken stitches to his head and was undoubtedly suffering from a severe headache. Phillip Wright had escaped him again. There was however a blessing of having learned where McPherson was.

Rolf had been in Colombia for two years but had never had the opportunity of learning Spanish. He was born in Austria and spent most of his youth in Switzerland. He enjoyed travelling and thrived on adventure. He had spent a great deal of time mountain climbing. It had taught him discipline and determination. He was extremely aggressive and was accustomed to fulfilling his goals and was upset at losing Phillip Wright again, however it had no bearing from this point on. His job was to get McPherson not Phillip Wright who probably had slipped into hiding until the departure time for the flight to Cartagena. Rolf telephoned the airport and made arrangements for a reservation on the same trip. He gathered a few belongings, put them in a small suitcase and did a quick check of the meticulously kept house, ensuring all lights were off and windows were secured.

He made the journey to the airport, recapping in his mind the events of the previous few days. After parking his car in a lot far away from the entrance, he briskly walked between the parked cars and made his way to the ticket counter.

"I have made a reservation for the eleven fifty-five flight to Cartagena. My name is Rolf." His square jaw moved rhythmically with each word he spoke.

The girl smiled and keyed information into the terminal at her finger tips. Rolf scanned the vicinity for signs of Phillip Wright.

"Excuse me, I was supposed to meet a business associate of mine here. I wonder if he has checked in already. His name is Phillip Wright." Although his accent was heavy, his enunciation was very clear.

"I am sorry but we cannot give out any information about other passengers."

"It is very important. I do not want to miss him."

"I'm sorry sir there is nothing I can do. Once you are on the airplane I am sure you will see your associate." The girl spoke sternly. She had been well-trained in her job and took it very seriously.

She handed Rolf the boarding card and he nodded. He walked toward the exit and swiftly crossed the tarmac, his eyes continually prodding the morning, sun-filled airport for signs of Phillip Wright.

The flight was only half full. Rolf returned the greeting the flight attendant extended him. His eyes scanned

each seat in the cabin as he walked toward the rear. He
ignored the seat number on his ticket and sat in the last
row, adjusting his seat belt and placing the suitcase underneath the seat in front of him, never once taking his eyes off
the entrance to the aircraft. Five or six passengers entered
the cabin and found their seats quickly. Rolf watched everyone. There was no Phillip Wright.

His initial intention had been to request the assistance of several men and apprehend Phillip Wright at the
airport. He had decided at the last minute not to, thinking
the attention might hinder him. He had planned to eliminate Phillip somehow on the flight but had not yet devised
the method.

The absence of Phillip was very confusing and made
no sense to Rolf's logical mind. At last he realized that
Phillip had probably driven to Medellin and would catch a
flight there. Of course, he thought, that's exactly what
Wright would have done. He would have assumed Rolf, not
seeing him at the airport, would have gone back into Bogota to look for him.

It was all so perfectly analytical and a brilliant ploy.
Rolf was impressed with Phillip Wright and his methods.
He respected someone who meticulously planned his pat-
terns. The plan, however, would backfire on Mr. Phillip
Wright, Rolf thought, for while Phillip was in Medellin,
trying to evade his pursuer, he, Willem Rolf would already
be in Cartagena, finding the whereabouts of McPherson.
Rolf would have the scientist in his control while Phillip
Wright was half way across the country. It appeared that
Phillip had devised a plan which would be easily out-
smarted by Rolf. He shook his head and smiled.

The flight attendant made the standard announcements which echoed from tinny speakers throughout the
aircraft. Moments later the plane was climbing hungrily
toward the sky. The thundering roar from its engines forced
it faster and faster against the invisible air. Like a jaguar

gripping the bark of a tree, pulling itself higher and higher, the airplane soared upward. The late morning sun was pouring its rays onto the tropics below. The ground was covered in a thick, moist, green layer of velvety jungle-foliage. Small rivers sparkled like tinsel falling from a Christmas tree winding their way in amongst the trees and mountains. The sky was empty of clouds and the shadow of the airplane was visible below as if racing across the terrain dancing wildly over hills and vales. It must have been frustrating for Wright, Rolf thought, not knowing what was going on. He was pleased that he was ahead of the game now. Phillip Wright was no longer a threat. The flight attendant brought him coffee and a newspaper. He sank back in his seat, allowing himself the luxury of a short rest.

The trip to Medellin took Phillip considerably less time than first anticipated. The cabby had let Phillip drive for about two hours but showed unnecessary signs of nervous tension.

Phillip felt extremely good about the circumstances. Rolf would be in Cartagena exactly one day before him. It would take him at least that long to search out the where-abouts of McPherson.

They arrived in Medellin with plenty of daylight left. Phillip asked the driver to find a hotel. He wanted to get plenty of rest. His muscles had stiffened. Comfort was not to be found in an automobile after so many hours driving. His injured arm was paining him again.

The cab driver turned down a road which seemed to lead toward the busiest section of town. He stopped the cab in front of a large wooden house. On the lawn there was a sign which read 'Guest House'.

Both men stepped from the cab and stretched their arms and legs.

"Madre Mia" the cab driver sighed. "I will never walk straight again." He rubbed his back as he wandered to where Phillip was standing.

Phillip grabbed his briefcase and duffel bag and the twosome walked to the front door of the guest house. The entrance lobby had been fashionably decorated in pinks and grays. There were several white rattan chairs surrounded by lovingly-maintained plants. At one end of the small lobby stood a large wooden desk with an older, white-haired gentleman seated behind it. He was engrossed in the evening newspaper and his senses were not alerted to the arrival of the two strangers.

Phillip cleared his throat. The man looked up. His deep rich golden tan stood out against the white shirt and grayish hair. He had a thick white moustache which enhanced his distinguished appearance. He was definitely not of Spanish descent.

"May I be of service to you?" the man asked. Although his Spanish was perfect there was a slight hint of a British accent.

"Yes," Phillip said, "I wonder if you might have two rooms for my friend and myself for this evening?"

"But of course," the man said, folding the newspaper and standing to greet his profitable guests. "Our rooms are twenty-five dollars per night." The man held silent, staring at Phillip and the cab driver, awaiting a reaction.

The cab driver was the first to speak. "That is far too high. The rooms are not worth half that much."

"I am very sorry señor but it is extremely expensive to maintain an establishment of such high quality."

"We will give you fifteen dollars each."

The man stared at the cab driver, secretly debating whether or not to call his bluff.

The man sighed. "What can I do, señor? It is getting late and I am tired. You leave me no choice."

Phillip reached in his pocket and paid the hotel man the money. The cab driver turned to Phillip. "Well, señor, I guess this is where we say farewell. I will be leaving very early in the morning and I shall do so silently so as not to disturb you. I still don't understand your reasons for wanting to drive all this way rather than taking an airplane, however, I wish you every success in your journey."

Phillip reached into his pocket and removed a one hundred dollar bill which he had placed there earlier that day. He handed it to the cab driver, extending his hand in a farewell greeting. "It was nice meeting you and I can't thank you enough for everything you have done." Both men departed to their rooms for a well-earned rest.

Phillip's room, although small, was extremely neat and well kept. A white, lacy bedspread covered the double bed and matching curtains hung in front of the windows. He threw his duffel bag and briefcase on the floor and let his aching body fall lifeless onto the bed. His arm was still very sore but he could feel that the healing processes had started to take over. The pain was lessening but was being replaced by a constant itch. He avoided scratching it as much as possible for fear of tearing the newly formed scar tissue. After a few moments of rest he went back to the lobby.

"Do you have a telephone?"

The old man reached behind the counter and lifted a black telephone set, making the bell chime as he placed it firmly on the counter. Phillip thanked him and dialed the appropriate numbers.

"Hello?" Lana's familiar voice answered.

Phillip was relieved to hear her speak. He had secretly developed fears about Rolf discovering and somehow harming her. "Is everything okay?"

"Sure is," she said cheerfully.

"What have you got?"

"When you get to Cartagena go to the Hilton. There is a small real estate office that specializes in rental properties. I think the woman who runs it rented McPherson his island. I got the information from the secretary so don't let on that you know."

"Excellent," Phillip said. "What about Rolf?"

"Well he's really frustrated and doesn't know where to look. He tried all the boat charters and realty firms in town but missed the one at the Hilton. He finally checked into a hotel on the strip. I think he's crashed for the night."

"Do you think he saw you?"

"Not a chance. I was very careful."

"Lana," Phillip said, "you're quite a girl."

"Do you want me to meet you at the airport?"

"No, I don't think that's a good idea."

"Will you at least call me?"

"Why not wait until I'm finished and maybe we can spend a few days together."

"I would like that very much." The thought sent tingling sensations through Lana's mind.

"I would too," Phillip said. He paused a moment before he continued. "Lana, I need a favour. I can't get on the plane with my gun . Could you arrange to get one for me in Cartagena?"

"That shouldn't be a problem. I'll talk to Mr. Sullivan and see what we can do. I'll wrap it and leave it with the front desk of the Hilton."

"Thank you," he said.

Slowly he replaced the receiver on its cradle and thought for a moment of the sweet girl he had just spoken with.

Phillip had slept well and awoke feeling refreshed. After a quick shower and securing his attaché case he hurried to the guests' dining room. There was no one else there. The cab driver had left hours earlier for his return journey to Bogota. Phillip had plenty of time to spare before the flight to Cartagena and decided he would spend it by enjoying a leisurely breakfast and brisk walk. He decided on farm fresh eggs and crisp country sausages. The lady who ran the dining room seemed to enjoy cooking and prepared his meal with great patience.

After breakfast he strolled out onto the terrace of the guest house. He looked in both directions along the narrow paved road and saw no other buildings aside from a farm house half a mile away. The city proper must be quite a distance from here, he thought. He decided to walk in the direction of the farm house, inhaling the fresh tropical air. The rays of the morning sun were beginning to heat up the area. There was definitely rain in the forecast. A moist wind was blowing briskly against his face as he walked. Phillip strolled casually for twenty minutes and paused when he came to the crest of the hill. In the distance, through the haze, he could see the outline of the city. He guessed it to be about a ten minute car ride and looked at his watch as he began to walk in the direction of the hotel. After gathering his belongings he checked out, thanking the owner for a most enjoyable stay. Very seldom did he enjoy such comforts and leisure time in his job.

The gray haired man had arranged for a cab which was waiting directly in front of the small, Colombian guest house.

"To the airport please."

The driver nodded and sped off in the direction that Phillip had earlier walked.

When they arrived at the airport, Phillip paid the driver and walked into the shabby, neglected terminal building. The tile floors had been chipped in many places and were covered with grime. Several antiquated posters of far away places decorated the paint-peeled walls. The terminal building was no wider than forty feet and had a counter along one side. A man and a woman dressed in navy-blue, airline uniforms stood behind the desk tinkering with the computer printer from which they had removed the cover. There was one door exiting onto the tarmac which led to the narrow runway.

Phillip walked to the counter. "Excuse me I would like to purchase a ticket for Cartagena please."

"Of course señor," the woman replied. Her skin was smooth and well tanned. Her dark hair neatly framed her face. "We are having some difficulty with our printer but we will have it repaired in a moment."

Phillip smiled. The man mumbled something to the woman in Spanish and a look of satisfaction beamed across his face. He replaced the cover on the printer and turned the system on. The woman pressed several keys on the keyboard. "Perfect," she said. "Now, where is it that you would like to go."

"To Cartagena on the eleven-fifty flight."

"Certainly señor," the woman replied as she entered information into her computer.

"Will that be smoking or non-smoking?" She glanced up at Phillip.

"Smoking please."

"Certainly sir." Again she entered information into the computer. Once finished she looked up at Phillip and gave him the amount. "How will you be paying?"

"Cash," Phillip answered as he removed the appropriate amount of funds from his pocket. He handed them to the woman who acknowledged the transaction. Seconds later the printer began buzzing and Phillip could see his ticket eject from the slot in the top.

"There you go, señor. Have a very lovely trip." The woman handed Phillip the ticket and smiled as she did so.

"Thank you very much." Phillip studied the ticket and glanced at his watch. He still had two hours before the flight departed. He decided that he would go into town, do some shopping, and phone Ed Bergan to see if there was any news on Rolf. He felt as a tourist would, walking between stores looking at souvenirs and clothes. He picked up a pair of slacks, a shirt and some toiletries, carefully folded them and placed them in his duffel bag, and walked along the main street, stopping at a telephone booth. Just before he entered he could feel several drops of moist, warm rain. He stepped inside the sheltered telephone booth and opened his attaché case, looking for Ed Bergan's phone number.

After being transferred through several operators Phillip was finally connected with the Canadian Government official.

"Good morning Phillip," Ed Bergan replied. His voice was strong and echoed through the telephone receiver. "How are things in Bogota?"

"Good," Phillip replied. He decided not to tell Ed his exact whereabouts in the event that his superior did not agree with his tactic. "Have you heard anything more about Willem Rolf?"

"Yes I have a little bit of information. Apparently Rolf is wanted by Interpol for a series of politically organized crimes such as murder and robbery as well as several alleged terrorist attacks. It seems nobody is aware that he's in South America. No one knows what he's doing there."

"What's his background?" Phillip asked.

"His father spent most of his life in prison. He was with the S.A. during World War II and was associated with several death camps. Rolf was in the army but only served a short time. He prefers to be marked as a mercenary. He makes his home in Aachen, a small town in South-Western Germany. There's nothing that I can find that links him to McPherson.

"Why do you think he's after McPherson?" Phillip interjected.

"I really don't know. I have no idea where the connection is. I would suggest that you try and get a hold of him and force him to tell you who he's working for. That would give us some insight into this entire caper."

"That seems to be a lot more difficult than it sounds," Phillip replied.

"Of course you realize, Phil, we don't know why he's after McPherson. So far all he seems to be doing is tracking you. Where is he now? Do you know?"

"Yes, I believe he's on his way to Cartagena."

"Why's he going there?"

"Probably because I'm heading there."

"What are your immediate plans?" Ed asked.

"I've got a lead on McPherson."

Ed Bergan interjected. "You have, why didn't you say so earlier?"

"I believe McPherson's gone to some resort area and is holed up there with his family. It's somewhere off the coast of Cartagena."

"When do you expect to get there?"

"I should be in Cartagena by noon and I'll probably rent a boat and start travelling immediately."

"Well, let me know the minute you hear something, and remember we don't want McPherson to panic so be careful when you meet him." Phillip replaced the receiver and decided to head back to the airport.

The flight to Cartagena was short and uneventful. A snack was served which Phillip picked at after his large breakfast. The plane came to an abrupt halt and the passengers jerked in their seats. Phillip looked out the window but could see nothing unusual. He dismissed any thought of trouble and assumed the pilot was new.

Phillip left the airplane and walked across the pavement into the terminal. His eyes caught every passer-by as he looked for any suspicious signs. He had grown accustomed to being followed and found suspicion in not seeing anyone that he recognized. Rolf was nowhere in sight but deep down Phillip felt he was in the vicinity. Lana's reports of Rolf's frustrated failures had excited him but it also meant he would probably be on the lookout for Phillip.

He glanced around the airport building and noticed a small booth marked 'Tourist Information'. Behind it sat a pretty young girl in a colourful flowery blouse. Phillip walked up to her.

"Excuse me," he said, "where is the Hilton Hotel from here?"

The girl smiled and opened a book kept under her desk. "Yes sir," she said politely and gave Phillip directions.

"You are not Colombian are you?"

The girl looked up at Phillip. "No, actually I'm here for the summer. My father is with the State Department and he managed to get me this job. Are you American?" she asked as she handed him the piece of paper.

"Would you mind telephoning the hotel and making a reservation for me?"

"Not at all."

Phillip nodded. "Thank you very much," he said and accepted the paper with directions scribbled on it.

Phillip smiled and turned toward the main door of the terminal building. He decided to keep his luggage with him, especially after the last fiasco in Bogota. He walked back to the tourist desk.

"Excuse me," he said as the girl looked up. "Should anyone ask whether or not you have seen me I would appreciate very much if you didn't tell them where I was staying."

"Certainly," the girl said.

The street leading to the hotel was lined with run down buildings. Some had been abandoned but the majority had been abused. Poverty-stricken beggars were lined along the sidewalks selling trinkets or panhandling sympathetic tourists.

Once inside the grounds, Phillip noticed small booths with armed guards. This site resembled a military compound more so than a posh, tropical hotel. The cab drove along the circular drive which led to the front door of the hotel lobby. The palatial entrance was extremely well maintained. The furniture was brightly covered and had the appearance of being brand new. Colombian artifacts and antiquities decorated the walls. Two magnificent, red-carpeted staircases rose gradually to connect with the mezzanine floor and balcony one flight up. A large, intricately woven macramé hanging took up the majority of the wall surrounding the stair case. From the ceiling hung two enormous chandeliers with carved crystals dropping lazily from them.

Phillip asked the smartly dressed concierge if a package addressed to him had arrived. The clerk checked under the counter and removed a small, neatly wrapped cardboard container.

"Thank you," Phillip said as he walked to a secluded corner of the lobby. He opened the package and removed the fully loaded automatic pistol. He placed it in his briefcase and returned to the centre of the foyer.

He spotted the name of the company he was looking for on the marquis and asked the bell captain where their office was located. The uniformed man politely directed Phillip toward a narrow corridor.

"May I help you?" a young girl sitting behind a typewriter in a tiny office asked in flawless English.

"Yes I would like to book a trip to the Rosario Islands and I would also like to inquire about renting a condominium," Phillip replied.

"Of course," the girl replied. "Miss Weston looks after all condominium rentals. Unfortunately she is not in right now."

"When do you expect her back?"

"Actually she usually takes her lunch break by the pool. You may find her out there."

"Okay," Phillip said agreeably. "What does she look like?"

"She is blonde, in her early forties, and is wearing a red bathing suit."

"Good." He turned and walked toward the door. He glanced back at the receptionist. "Excuse me, which way is the pool?" he asked.

"Oh I am sorry," the girl said apologetically. "Turn right and walk down the corridor until you see a sign that says terrace. Turn right again there and you will see the pool. If you come to an area with pink coffee tables you have gone too far." The girl smiled as she spoke.

"Thank you very much."

13 ISLAND

Phillip's duffel bag and attaché case were becoming a heavy burden, making him decide to check into the hotel before meeting Miss Weston in the real estate office. He returned to the lobby and announced himself to the attendant on duty. The girl at the airport had been very precise in making the reservation and the room was ready for him. Phillip took the key and for a few pesos allowed the bell boy to take his duffel bag to the room.

"You have a message, señor." The clerk reached behind him and passed a small, white card to Phillip.

It was from Lana. Phillip decided not to check into his room just yet. He was eager to find McPherson's whereabouts and call Lana to get the latest on Rolf. He searched for some change and walked to the nearest telephone.

"Hi palsy."

He smiled at the familiar voice. "How's it going? Any goods on Rolf?"

"Plenty," she said enthusiastically.

"Shoot."

"Well, you were right about the flight. He got off and headed for the tourist booth. He was there for about forty-five minutes and it looked like he didn't get any worthwhile information because he left in quite a huff.

"I talked to the girl at the booth and she told me that he was looking for some relatives at a resort hotel or something. I don't think he knows where they are.

"I followed him to his hotel where he again enquired about McPherson. It was getting late and he decided to check in for the night. I found out what time his wake up call was and went home, making sure I was back in time to catch him this morning."

"Sounds great," Phillip said.

"Wait there's more. I followed him all over Cartagena until he finally found someone who could help him. He made a phone call and seemed to get pretty excited. This is where the bad news begins."

Phillip could sense hesitation in her voice.

"What happened?" he asked.

"Well, before I knew it he had left the phone booth and I had no idea where he went. I ran outside but I couldn't see him."

"How long ago was that?"

"About thirty minutes or so."

"Not to worry," Phillip said calmly. "He's probably on his way over here right now."

"I'm sorry if I blew it."

"Don't be silly. All I really care about is that he hasn't found McPherson yet."

"Well that I can confirm." In a different tone she asked, "Are you staying long?"

"I don't know. If I get a chance I'll give you a call."

"Great," she said as the phone line went dead.

He walked hurriedly in the direction of the terrace. He knew that Rolf would be here soon if he wasn't already. His eyes darted in both directions as he walked. The rear court yard of the hotel was a magnificent compliment to the landscape. Lavish tropical plants greeted him as he stepped along the cobblestone path. Walking up several steps, he saw an Olympic-size swimming pool, surrounded by rock-gardens and thick, green shrubs. Several umbrella tables were placed strategically, blocking sun rays from hindering the affluent guests. A lavish bar sat sunken in one end of the pool and a handful of fun seekers were standing in the water enjoying a midday cocktail. Other guests were lounging lazily on stretched out padded chaise longues.

He had very little trouble spotting the slender blonde in a red bathing suit. He walked toward the woman laying stretched out in a carefree manner, glistening from suntan lotion. Dark sunglasses covered her eyes and Phillip could not see if she was awake. He stepped to the other side of the chair and purposely blocked the sunlight from her face. The disturbance in light was enough to stir her and she slowly removed her glasses, squinting at Phillip.

"Is there something I can help you with?" she asked, irritated by his interruption.

"Are you Miss Weston?"

"Yes I am."

"I'm really very sorry to disturb you on your lunch break but I'm afraid I don't have much time." His eyes drifted involuntarily to the heaving fullness of the woman's breasts forced upward by the well-fitted bathing suit.

She smiled slightly, noting Phillip's flushed appearance at being caught in the act of boyish endeavours and removed her glasses, placing the stem of one side into her mouth.

"I would like to inquire about getting some transportation to the Rosario Islands and possibly renting a condominium for a few days."

"Really?" she asked.

Phillip paused for a moment. "Yes really," Phillip said, surprised at her question. "Is that an unusual request?"

"No," she said. "It just seems to be a popular spot."

Phillip could feel his heart increase rapidly in its beat. "Has someone else called about renting?"

"No, not really," the woman said hesitantly. "Someone telephoned earlier today about possibly reserving one." She paused. "Was that you per chance?"

"No it wasn't." Phillip thought for a moment. "That was probably my cousin. Did he speak with a German accent?"

"Yes, as a matter of fact he did. He wanted to stay with the other group."

"What other group?" Phillip said trying to control the excitement in his voice.

"He wanted to know if the rest of his family had arrived?"

"And have they?" Phillip asked.

"Yes, they arrived last week." She swung her legs out from her reclined position and sat up. "Actually there were five of them. They rented a condominium on one of the islands." She paused for a moment. "Were you planning on joining them.?"

"No, I'd like to stay fairly close to them but in a separate condominium." He paused. "You know what these family outings can be like."

"Certainly," she said most agreeably. "Why don't we go into the office." She stood up and placed a small, white, terry cloth towel over her shoulders. "Where are you from?"

"New York," Phillip replied, his eyes casually glancing at her golden, tanned body.

"Are you here for a reunion or something?"

"Sort of," Phillip said hesitantly, not wanting to divulge any more information than necessary.

"I'm sorry, I didn't catch your name."

Phillip was caught off guard. He paused for a moment. "Lloyd, David Lloyd." The name was that of a person he had worked with in Italy several weeks earlier. He knew Rolf would be hot on his trail and didn't want to make this too easy for him.

"Well Mr. Lloyd, is this your first visit to Cartagena?"

"Yes it is."

"And how are you enjoying it so far?"

"Very impressive, I'm just not sure if I can handle all this heat." She smiled at Phillip as they entered the small office.

"Please have a seat, Mr. Lloyd." She motioned to an office door beyond the receptionist. She turned to the dark-haired girl sitting at the desk. "Sherry, could you please hold my calls?" The girl nodded.

The office was well decorated with modern furniture and many art nouveau decorations. "Can I get you a drink?"

"No, thank you. I just ate."

"You're sure now? I'm going to have a coffee myself." She looked at Phillip.

"All right, maybe I will have a coffee."

"How do you take it?"

"Black, no sugar, please."

Miss Weston stood up, leaned out the door and instructed her receptionist to get the coffee. She returned to her desk and walked behind it, looked at Phillip and smiled.

"Do you mind if I smoke?" Phillip shook his head. "So many people are trying to quit now a-days. Please excuse my attire I usually try and get some sun during lunch. I don't normally conduct business in a bathing suit." Phillip smiled, obviously not disturbed by her appearance. "Well let's get down to business shall we?" she said as she took a photo album from the credenza behind her.

"This is a very popular spot," she said, pointing to one of the photographs. "It's located about a two minute boat ride from your family's condominium." Phillip was anxious to ask what Rolf had done but waited until the opportune moment arrived, so as not to arouse suspicion.

She continued. "The water is beautiful and almost every rental property has a boat; it's the only way to get from one house to the other."

"Do you have a photograph of my uncle's place? The one he rented last week?" Phillip asked.

"Yes, I believe I do," she said, leafing through the pages. "This is it here." She paused at a particular photo. "They have it booked until the end of the month."

Phillip scrutinized the picture carefully, studying all the details. It was a small, brown, wooden bungalow located on a tiny rock-covered island. There were several trees in the background and a small beach to the right. A floating dock with an attached boat was suspended in the crystal clear, teal-coloured water.

"It's a beautiful looking place," Phillip acknowledged.

"It certainly is. You will find most of the condominiums in the area are on individual islands because of the privacy required. The larger islands are used for small hotels or group excursions. There is one large island about an hour's ride out from the mainland which serves as a pit stop for the majority of boats. They offer lunches and refreshments."

"The one I was looking at," Phillip said "how much is it?" Although money was not a concern to Phillip he didn't want to sound over anxious.

"It is two hundred and fifty dollars a week." She eyed Phillip carefully. "How long were you thinking of staying?"

"I think a week should be sufficient."

"There is a motor boat attached which, for an additional fifty dollars per week, you can have the use of."

"That's great, when can I leave?"

"Oh, you mean you'll take it?" she smiled, some-

what surprised at Phillip's hasty decision. She quickly regained her composure. "Our normal boat leaves at ten in
the morning. However there is a special one that we could
send out if you don't mind paying a little bit extra. It could
leave any time you want."

"That would be great," Phillip said. "As I mentioned
I would like to get out there as soon as possible."

"Let me just get the appropriate paperwork filled
in." She grabbed a folder from her desk and removed a
contract form from it. After asking Phillip several questions
about his personal status and filling in most of the blank
spaces, she looked at Phillip. "How will you be paying for
this?"

"I prefer to deal in cash, if that's all right?"

"Yes, certainly, that's fine. That comes to three
hundred dollars exactly."

Phillip removed the money from his pocket and
handed it to Miss Weston. "What about the boat fare?" he
asked.

"Your ticket will be forty-five dollars."

Phillip stared at her in disbelief. "Forty-five dollars?" he repeated.

"That's right," Miss Weston replied. She noticed the
frown on Phillip's face and tried to overcome his objection.
"I know that sounds like a lot but it will guarantee you
being there when you want. It is after all a two hour boat
ride."

Phillip nodded and removed another fifty dollar bill
from his pocket. He handed it across the desk as she opened
a book of tickets tearing off the top one. "Here you are Mr.
Lloyd." She handed him the ticket. "If you'll hold on for
just a moment I'll get you the keys to the condominium and
the boat."

She walked into the other office which was still
empty as the receptionist had not yet returned with the
coffee. Phillip decided he would ask her about Rolf when

she returned.

"That particular condominium has electricity but it does not have a telephone. Will that prove to be an inconvenience?" Miss Weston asked as she sat down.

Phillip thought for a moment. "Not really." His intention was to get hold of McPherson as soon as possible and wrap this entire matter up.

The receptionist returned with a tray containing two porcelain cups and a silver cream and sugar set. She placed it on the desk.

"Could you please get the keys for Cottage three twenty-nine." Miss Weston asked. "I can't seem to find them." The girl nodded and walked to her desk.

"Help yourself Mr. Lloyd," Miss Weston said, motioning to the coffee. Phillip took his cup and had a sip. The hot coffee tasted good, even in this tropical climate. Phillip enjoyed the rich, strong flavour of Colombian coffee.

"What did my cousin decide to do? You know the one that telephoned you. We were supposed to meet but somehow got separated."

"Oh, he decided to rent something. He asked if you had shown up yet and when I told him you hadn't he thanked me and said he was on his way."

"When was that?"

"About an hour ago."

Phillip's heart skipped a beat. Rolf was somewhere in the vicinity, probably moments behind him. There was no time to lose.

The girl returned in a moment with a small plastic bag containing several keys and some paper. She handed it to Miss Weston.

"Here you are Mr. Lloyd. This key is for the condominium, and this one for the boat." She handed Phillip the two keys. "This is a sheet of paper with instructions about the electricity and anything else you may need to know in the house. The gas tank for the boat should be full but if there is a problem there is some more stored directly behind the house."

Phillip thanked her as he scanned the list of instructions. "This is a map of the area showing the island with your house on it as well as some of the others. Over here is the house your relatives are staying at." She pointed to another island, "This is the island where the boat will stop for lunch should you decide to get a bite to eat. There is some food in your condominium and I would highly recommend that you bypass the stop. The food sucks. They serve raw fish, soggy rice and yucca roots, which are only good if you're starving. The place is really crowded with tourists and bugs." Phillip smiled as she spoke. "The condominium you're staying in is available the following week as well, should you decide to lengthen your stay. A boat will be by every other day in the event of an emergency. If you need anything, or decide to stay, just let the driver know and he'll forward the information to us."

"Thanks very much," Phillip said as he took the map from her. He took another sip of his coffee and stood up. "I don't think I'll be staying any longer than the week, but it's good to know."

"Thank you very much." Miss Weston stood up and opened a drawer behind her desk. She removed a business card and handed it to Phillip. "If you have any problems there is a telephone at the main island, please give me a call." She smiled as Phillip took the card from her. Their eyes were fixed on each other for only a brief moment but longer than necessary.

"Thanks," Phillip said, nodding his head. "I'll do that." As he walked out of the office and felt her eyes staring at his back, he paused for a moment and turned his head. "One thing, where do I catch the boat?"

"I'm sorry," she said. "It anchors just by the tennis courts to the left of the pool area."

"Super," Phillip said and departed the office. He

walked alongside the swimming pool and enjoyed the sound
of children splashing carelessly in the water. Several women
glanced at him as he passed by. He felt flattered. He had
never considered himself good looking and had to always
rely on his personality to attract the opposite sex. During
the last few years he had tried to keep his body trim but it
seemed to be a losing battle. He had put a few pounds on his
midriff and decided he would do something about it after
this assignment. He blamed the fine dining establishments
around the world for his falling-out appearance. He tried to
exercise whenever possible, however he found it very boring and there never seemed enough time. He wasn't overweight and by wearing a loose shirt no one noticed. His
facial features were becoming stronger. Old age must be
making me more distinguished he thought, and chuckled to
himself. At thirty-eight he looked better than most men his
age.

He watched the tourists around the pool leisurely
enjoying a drink and bathing in the hot, Colombian sun,
hoping some day to be in a position where he could sit pool-
side and not worry about being followed or having his life
constantly threatened.

He approached the area where the boat was an-
chored. It had been shoved onto the sand and was tilted
slightly to one side. It was about twenty feet long and had
been freshly painted. The red trim shone brightly in contrast to the white body. A red and white cloth canopy
shaded a group of vinyl covered seats. In the centre was a
steering wheel with several hand controls and a swivel
chair. The front of the boat was empty and a railing had
been erected for sight-seeing tours. It was powered by two
large outboard motors. The water around the back had been
stained with rainbow-coloured oil spills. On the side of the
boat, in meticulously painted letters, stood the word 'Margaritaville'. Two men were sitting on the beach sharing a
bottle of beer, enjoying the warm noon sun as it forced its

tropic heat on the soft, silvery sand below.

"Buenos Dias," Phillip said as he approached the twosome. They both looked up, squinting against the sun, and returned Phillip's greeting. "I have a ticket," Phillip said, "to the Rosario Islands. I understand that this boat will take me there."

One of the two men stood up. His white tee-shirt was a harsh contrast to his black skin. He smiled, showing his pearly white teeth. His features were black and he was not native to South America.

He studied Phillip closely. "You are American?" he asked. Phillip nodded and the man switched from Spanish to English. "I have spent many years in America. I was in Georgia. It's too bad they don't like blacks there. I moved down here where life is peaceful."

Phillip smiled "I'm from New York, I don't hate blacks, and I'd love to be sitting here on a beach having a beer with no worries." He handed him the ticket.

The black man stared for a moment then smiled. "Okay," he said. "I will take you."

"Thank you very much." Phillip replied.

The man grinned. "My name is Jonathan." He extended his hand. Phillip shook it.

"I'm David Lloyd." He decided to keep his alias in case Rolf was close behind.

With the help of the other man, Jonathan pushed the boat back into the water.

"You can get on the boat if you like," Jonathan said as he motioned Phillip toward a small ladder hanging over the side. His partner was already on board and had the engine running. Jonathan embarked and walked toward the back. He waved the driver to back up. The engine sputtered as the boat began to move. The driver increased the throttle and the engines coughed.

"Okay," Jonathan yelled, and the craft shifted forward. He moved the throttle and the water began to spit violently behind the craft. The boat moved faster and faster with each passing wave. The nose tilted higher as the back end forced its way into the water. Once it achieved top speed the boat began to skim across the waves. A hard, bumping noise could be heard as each wave thundered against the bottom of the hull. Phillip grabbed the arm rest momentarily, not certain what was about to happen. He had little faith in the two men in charge and was thankful for a blue, cloudless sky.

Phillip glanced behind and could see the magnificent peninsula supporting the Cartagena Hilton slowly drifting away. They passed a navel academy as well as an old, military-ship graveyard. The entrance to the harbour was guarded by two historic, Spanish fortresses. A large mass of stones lay piled together, unaware that time had passed them by. The boat began to bounce more vigorously as the threesome entered the open sea. Phillip was astonished by the speed of the small craft. He looked at Jonathan as his body was beating to the rhythm of the tune he was humming. Phillip saw his lips moving and smiled. Jonathan returned the greeting, raised a bottle of beer as a toast and put it to his lips, throwing his head back and swallowing half the contents before he stopped for air. As the boat continued to bounce, Phillip became concerned. He placed a tighter grip on the arm rest to avoid being bounced from the seat. Again he looked at Jonathan, now dancing by himself. His partner was stretched out on one of the chairs. Phillip had no problem admitting he was scared. The sooner he got to the island the happier he would be. A sudden mental picture of his wife flashed through his head and caught him by surprise. He very seldom thought of her these days. He wondered where she was. He wondered about his children and how they were doing. His oldest would be fourteen now. He could feel a burning sensation in his stomach as he thought about the growing-up experiences he had missed. He wondered who taught them how to play baseball and fly a kite. He was curious if they would still remember him. What had their mother told them about their father? Where had she kidnapped them? Why could he find no trace of her anywhere in his travels? The thought of her made him bitter. The passing of time had not healed the wound. It had left a deep, painful mark.

His thoughts of the past were interrupted by Jonathan shouting and pointing his finger toward the horizon. Phillip squinted into the sunlight and saw several small dots which grew rapidly in size to form tiny masses of land. As they approached the islands, they passed fishermen in beat up, home-made canoes. Jonathan slowed the engine as they approached the largest island in the group. The boat bobbed forward as the powerful groan of the engine subsided.

"This is the island where you buy supplies." Jonathan shouted. Phillip nodded. The wind was blowing in his face. "Do you wish to stop for anything?" Jonathan asked.

"No," Phillip shouted back. "I have everything I need."

Jonathan pushed the throttle forward and again the boat lunged ahead.

"How much further?" Phillip yelled but Jonathan could not hear him over the sound of the roaring engines. Again Phillip held on to the arm rest of his chair as the boat began to thunder through the waves. There were islands all around them. Some had houses and some were too small to support any type of dwelling. They passed one island with a tiny house and a connecting bridge to the next land mass. On the right they passed an island with a two-story white stucco house trimmed with black wood. Jonathan slowed the boat and pointed at the house.

"This man made his money from selling cocaine," Jonathan yelled across at Phillip. Phillip smiled back at him. Jonathan tilted his head back and took another swallow of beer. He increased the throttle and the boat took off.

A few minutes later Jonathan again yelled at Phillip.

He pointed toward an island. "Over there, that is your island." Phillip stood up and clenched his hand around the edge of the canopy for support. He gazed into the distance and wondered how many places like this existed in the world. Places he had never heard of or had the good fortune to visit. He looked around at some of the other islands to see if he could find a house that resembled that of McPherson's.

As they approached the island his vision of 'Shangri-La' became somewhat blurred. The house was in bad need of repair. The paint was peeling and some of the shingles on the roof had shifted. The boat turned out to be no longer than fourteen feet but appeared larger because of the smallness of the dock it was moored to. The motor on the back was much smaller than he had imagined. Jonathan pulled the boat up as close as he could to the dock. Phillip reached into his pocket and removed a ten dollar bill which he handed to the black skipper. He picked up his duffel bag and briefcase and hopped from the boat onto the dock.

"Thanks very much," he said, feeling extremely relieved to be on dry land again.

"Have a good holiday," Jonathan replied. "Remember the boat leaves from the big island everyday at five. If you need anything or you need to contact the mainland make sure that you are there. If we don't hear from you we will circle by in a few days to make sure you are okay." Phillip nodded in acknowledgement. Jonathan and his partner waved as they backed the boat away from the dock. Phillip could hear the roar of the motor as the boat lunged forward. He stared at it for a moment and watched it grow smaller as it blended in with the islands and finally disappeared.

14   GUNFIRE

Phillip hopped up the ten or so steps leading to the front door of the condominium. He had trouble with the key but finally managed to make the lock click. The inside of the cottage had been neglected as badly as the outside. Phillip tossed his briefcase and duffel bag onto a nearby chesterfield. He looked out the door over the water taking a moment to appreciate the splendour of the golden rays of sun shining down on the aqua-coloured water. In spots he could see the reef through the crystal clear ocean. There were several palm trees and yucca plants surrounding the front of the cottage. He reached for a cigarette from his pocket and enjoyed the cool smoke entering his lungs. He decided he would not wait very long before starting his search for the McPherson house. When he finished his cigarette he looked for a secure place to conceal his briefcase. He placed it between the small refrigerator and the cabinet, first removing the automatic, ensuring its clip was armed and ready to fire. He left the cottage, locking the door securely behind him, and headed toward the boat.

Phillip stood with both hands on his hips and studied the motor of the small, seagoing craft. He pulled the start rope but nothing happened. Again he studied the motor and extended the choke control. He gave the rope another tug and the motor began to purr. He quickly jumped from the dock into the boat and adjusted the throttle control. He sat on the uncomfortable wooden slotted seats and pushed a lever sending the boat backward into the dock. Phillip quickly flipped the control in the other direction and the boat began to move forward. He grabbed hold of the steering arm and began to manoeuvre the boat across the tropical sea. As he headed in a new direction he could see several islands and estimated them to be about three miles away. Phillip wished for a larger craft like the one that had brought him to the island.

The water in and around the islands was fairly calm, unlike the four foot swells of the open sea. He passed by the first island but saw no signs of life. There were no buildings or boats. The second island, however, was different. Phillip could make out the roof and side of a building. As he approached, it began to take on shape. At first it looked like a normal chalet built on an island, but as Phillip rounded the corner and viewed it face on, he knew immediately it was the same house in the photograph shown him by Miss Weston.

Moored by the dock was a beautiful steel-hulled boat at least thirty feet long. Phillip wondered how McPherson would react to being discovered. He manoeuvred the boat to the other side of the dock and noticed a small speck on the horizon heading toward him. He couldn't help but wonder if it could be Rolf and estimated five minutes to its arrival. Phillip knew he had to move quickly in the event it might be his enemy.

He looped the tow rope around the peg on the dock and jumped from the boat. As he ran across the rocks toward the front door of the house a loud, crashing sound echoed through his ear. It didn't take him long to realize someone was shooting at him. His instinct forced him to fall to the ground and roll sideways, hoping he would be shielded from the sniper's view. Another crack whizzed past his head.

Phillip's keen eyes spotted a stump about ten feet from the dock. He forced his body to roll over the hard and piercing rocks to find a secure spot behind the rotted tree remains. He gathered his thoughts and removed the automatic from his pocket. He fired a shot into the air to warn his assailant that he was armed. He looked around, trying to gain his bearings. The shots were coming from within the house.

Phillip yelled "McPherson, don't shoot!" He waited for the sniper's gun to bark again. The only sound was the waves harshly snapping against the rocks. He managed to crawl into a kneeling position and slowly raise his body from behind the stump. Another shot came from the house. This one penetrated the tree remains inches from Phillip's shoulder. He immediately fell to the ground and paused motionless for a moment.

The motor from the approaching boat was now clearly audible. From his position behind the tree stump, Phillip screened the water, fixing his eyes on the craft.

As the boat approached everything fell neatly into place in Phillip's mind. He could clearly see that the man piloting the craft was McPherson. The rest of the people must be members of his family. Phillip paused. He turned his gaze to the house. That must be Rolf in there shooting at him. Somehow Rolf had managed to find the island and get there before Phillip had. Not finding anyone inside, he decided to wait until McPherson's return.

The boat slowed as it approached the mooring dock. Phillip saw a young man and two women gazing at the other boats linked up to their dock. A white-haired man was lifting a small boy from the boat onto the dock.

Phillip shouted at them in an effort to wave them off. Again a thundering clap echoed across the stoned-faced island as Rolf released another bullet from his firearm. Phillip was thankful that his aim was off. The engine of McPherson's boat was still running and the party was unable to hear the gun shot. They began walking toward the broken tree stump. Phillip waved frantically in their direction.

"What's going on?" the older lady asked.

"Get back!" Phillip yelled. Another shot was fired from the house, now highly audible as the engine had been silenced. Phillip heard the window on the large boat shatter as the bullet penetrated the cabin.

McPherson, realizing what was happening, jumped back in his boat and started the engine. His family, in a state of panic, returned to the boat.

"Wait!" Phillip yelled and left his secure position, running as fast as he could toward the dock. Two more shots were fired and echoed extremely close to Phillip's ears. His foot made contact with the wooden dock and he decided to dive into the water rather than risk being shot. He quickly swam toward the boat, just as it was beginning to back out. He grabbed the rope ladder over the side and screamed at McPherson to go as quickly as he could. He tightly grasped the ladder as the boat began to soar forward.

Phillip could feel the rope burning his fingers but held on securely until they were out of range of the gun fire.

"Slow down!" Phillip shouted. McPherson ignored him but his daughter Kristy saw the painful grimace on Phillip's face. She pulled her father's arm and pleaded with him to slow down. Finally, which seemed an eternity to Phillip, the boat began to slow until it came to a dead stop in the water. Phillip climbed on board and allowed himself to drop over the edge onto one of the soft cushioned seats. He opened his eyes and squinted against the sun standing out against the blue sky. Rhonda McPherson was the first to speak.

"Are you alright?" There was compassion in her voice.

"Yes, thank you," Phillip said. He slowly propped himself into a seating position in an effort to catch his breath.

"Jimmy," Rhonda said looking at her young son, "grab a towel, quickly." The boy darted to the front of the boat and took a towel from underneath the cushions.

"Who the hell are you?" McPherson's voice boomed as he approached the back of the boat.

"My name is Phillip Wright. I'm here on behalf of the Canadian government to get you out of this godforsaken country."

McPherson stared at Phillip for a moment. "We have had a number of people follow us during the last few weeks and I'm not exactly impressed by the Canadian government. How do I know you are who you say you are?"

"You haven't exactly made it very easy to be found," Phillip said. "Now if you would just take me to an island about three miles from here," Phillip raised his arm in the direction of the island that he had rented, "I will give you all the proof you need as to who I am and why I'm here." McPherson looked at the island and back at Phillip. "If you don't do as I say, whoever was shooting at us from your house is going to come after us and then we won't have to worry about anything."

McPherson looked in the direction of their house and decided he had very few alternatives. He increased the throttle and the boat began to move across the water in the direction Phillip was pointing. They arrived at the island in a matter of minutes. By now Phillip's hair had dried and he had regained some of his composure. Kristy McPherson was sitting on a bench across from Phillip, with her brother Jimmy close beside her. Rhonda McPherson was looking out over the ocean, while Tim Browning sat beside Lorne.

The boat was brought beside the dock and Phillip threw one of the ropes onto the wooden platform. McPherson did the same. Both men jumped up to secure the boat.

"Come with me," Phillip said to McPherson. "The rest of you wait here." The two men quickly stepped along the path to the front door of the cabin.

Once inside Phillip went for his briefcase and opened the compartment removing his passport, credentials and photographs of McPherson and his family.

McPherson seemed satisfied and extended his hand to Phillip.

"I'm Lorne McPherson," he said.

"I know," Phillip replied, shaking his hand.

McPherson resembled the photograph. His face was thin and drawn. His thick white hair was wind blown and he hadn't shaved in several days. His skin had been burnt by the hot, island sun.

"We'd better get out of here," Phillip said. "Someone else is chasing us, I don't know why, but I don't want to stick around to find out." The two men parted the small condominium and headed back to the boat.

The McPherson family was waiting patiently for the results of the meeting.

"It's okay," Lorne McPherson said. "He's on our side."

Lorne McPherson's statement seemed to bring a wave of ease over the small company. Kristy McPherson smiled at Phillip. Her features were more attractive than the photograph suggested. She resembled her father and had the strong characteristics of his face. The long, sandy-blonde hair had been blown by the wind. Her blue eyes mysteriously shielded her inner feelings. She was tall and slender and suited the blue bathing suit she was wearing. Tim Browning cleared his throat, making Phillip aware of his embarrassing stare at Kristy.

"My name is Tim Browning. I'm Dr. McPherson's

assistant." Phillip shook his extended hand.

To Phillip this seemed like a family reunion. He had been tracking these people for several days now and had grown accustomed to their actions. He felt he knew them quite well, even now as they spoke for the first time.

"Look!" Rhonda McPherson shouted, alarming everyone. She pointed to a large craft approaching in the distance.

"Let's go!" Phillip said to McPherson.

"Where to?"

"Let's try and lose them."

McPherson jumped in the boat and immediately began to back it out of the dock area. When he was assured the rest of the party was secure in the craft, he swung the wheel around and headed away from the island. McPherson's craft was definitely quicker and it didn't take long to outrun Rolf's boat. McPherson was in total command of the craft. He manoeuvred in and out of reefs and around islands. Rolf's boat was still in the distance but was rapidly losing ground. Phillip walked to the front of the boat, stumbling several times over chair cushions. When he got to where McPherson was standing he nudged his arm.

"Do you have enough fuel to make it back to Cartagena?" Phillip shouted.

"No, not even close," McPherson yelled. "Even if we did, I wouldn't have a clue how to get there."

Phillip stared out over the ocean. The waves were beginning to increase. "Let's head over to the big island where they have a fuel depot. With a little bit of luck we might be able to catch a boat there back to the mainland." Phillip looked at his watch. He had forgotten what time the boat came by to pick up the passengers, but felt that it must be around this time of day.

McPherson nodded in agreement and turned the boat toward the large island on the horizon. The distance between he and Rolf was quite substantial.

The boat hopped across the waves as it made its way out to the open sea. It was not long before they reached the island where Phillip immediately spotted Jonathan's boat. The red and white boat stood out like a candy cane on a Christmas tree.

"Pull up beside that one right there," Phillip yelled at McPherson. McPherson navigated his boat directly beside the Margaritaville. He cut the engine immediately.

"Grab all your belongings," Phillip said, "and get on that boat." He threw his attaché case into Jonathan's boat and ran up the path which led to a large, straw-roofed, dining room. The thatched roof was boarded by bamboo poles and inside were picnic tables covered with floral-patterned table clothes. Several people were leisurely enjoying an afternoon meal, engaged in exciting conversation about their day on the islands. Phillip scanned the patrons but saw no sign of Jonathan.

He halted a waiter walking toward him. "Excuse me, do you know where I might find the owner of that red and white craft down there?" Phillip pointed to Jonathan's boat. "His name is Jonathan." The waiter looked in the direction of the boat and smiled. "Ah yes, I am sure that you will find him in the kitchen," the man said slowly with a big grin on his face. He mumbled something about Jonathan flirting with one of the staff but Phillip did not wait around to hear the explanation. He ran across the dining room to a small brick building at the back. There were two doors. One was closed and had the word 'Toilet' carved on a small wooden plaque affixed to it. Phillip looked through the other door and saw Jonathan leaning against the wall talking to a woman stirring rice in a pot.

"Jonathan!" Phillip shouted, as he entered the door. Jonathan turned around, "Hey man, what are you doing here so soon?"

"I need your help quickly," Phillip said. Jonathan noticed the anxiety in Phillip's voice and gained a serious expression on his face.

"You need my help. I'm here." Jonathan smiled and walked toward Phillip. "What can I do for you?"

"I'll explain later. Now we need to get your boat back to the mainland as soon as possible."

"I can't do that," Jonathan said. "I've got to wait for the rest of the people."

"No. You don't understand," Phillip said. "We have to leave right away."

"But I can't, I will lose my job."

"You won't lose your job. Just tell people I forced you into it. Now let's go."

Jonathan shrugged his shoulders. "Okay but you better be there to cover for me when my boss starts screaming at me."

Phillip smiled and the two men walked hastily toward Jonathan's boat.

As they headed down the path, Phillip saw the McPherson family standing around the dock.

"Get in the boat," Phillip shouted. He ran to Jimmy McPherson, who was by the water's edge throwing stones at fish in a penned area. He grabbed the boy and quickly stepped into the boat.

Jonathan started the engine. As the boat began to leave the mooring area, Phillip saw Rolf's craft appearing within firing range. "Get down!" Phillip yelled to everyone, not certain whether Rolf would begin shooting at them. He looked at Jonathan and motioned him to hurry up. Jonathan grinned, not aware of what was going on, and began to ease the boat forward. It appeared to Phillip that Rolf had somehow increased the power of his engine. Jonathan had also noticed Rolf's craft heading in their direction.

He had a puzzled look on his face, and was about to question Phillip, when a gunshot fired across the bow of the ship and tore a hole in one of the chairs. Jonathan's face became strained as he pushed the throttle all the way to the front. The engines roared as the nose pushed up, sending the craft shooting forward.

Everyone's eyes were strained on Rolf's craft, rapidly approaching from the side. Jonathan's boat was not as fast as McPherson's had been and Phillip questioned whether they could out run Rolf. He removed the automatic from his pocket, pointed it in the direction of Rolf and fired. The bullets had no effect on the steel hull of the boat. Panic set in the small company as collision seemed inevitable. It was only Jonathan's skill at the last minute which avoided impact and saved their lives. He darted the boat from side to side and turned in extremely sharp circles. Rolf could obviously not keep up with this type of manoeuvring. Jonathan then positioned his craft right behind Rolf. He waited for the right moment and darted away, across the sea. It took Rolf several seconds to realize what had taken place. By the time he positioned his boat on a course of pursuit the red and white craft was far ahead.

Jonathan was smiling and singing, enjoying the adventure. Straight ahead of them were several small islands and Jonathan began to zig-zag around them. Phillip had lost all sense of direction and was relying strictly on his skipper's ability to find their way back home. He looked all around but was unable to locate Rolf's craft anywhere.

Again Phillip tried to manoeuvre his way toward Jonathan by holding onto the rails in back of seats as the craft bounced through the waves of the open choppy sea.

"The water is getting very rough," Jonathan remarked. "We will have to go back a different way or we will not be able to make it." Phillip nodded. "We will have to go inland," Jonathan continued, "to a river system that will take us back to Cartagena Bay. It will be a little bit slower but at least your friend will never find us." Phillip again nodded.

The wind was blowing strongly against his hair. He stared out over the ocean. The islands were now tiny specks in the distance and he saw no sign of Rolf. Jonathan had been right about the water. The waves were almost twice the size of the earlier trip. Phillip sat down on the bench beside Jimmy McPherson. He looked at Lorne McPherson who had cupped his arm around his wife's shoulder. She looked at Phillip and smiled. Phillip looked back at Kristy McPherson. Tim Browning immediately noticed Phillip's stare. He was very possessive of the girl he tried to court. She was not enthused by Tim Browning. His unkempt brown hair covered his ears and had no shape to it. He was thinning on the crown and his hair line was beginning to recede. His cheek bones were very high making his nose protrude more than normal.

Phillip turned in his seat, facing McPherson. "We have to talk later." McPherson nodded in agreement. He grabbed hold of his wife's hand and clasped it tightly in his. Her eyes were filled with fear.

It was not long before they saw the mainland appearing on the horizon. In a matter of seconds the water began to smooth, making the ride more comfortable. Phillip looked behind him and saw no sign of Rolf. Jonathan had been successful in his escape. By now Rolf was probably heading across the open ocean back to the mainland. He would be waiting for them at the hotel, Phillip thought. Jonathan expertly piloted the craft to a river mouth hidden amongst several clumps of trees. He cut back on the power as he guided the boat through the narrow, winding path.

"You have to be very careful here," he said to Phillip. "The river gets very shallow. There is a trench that runs down the centre of this river. If you miss it the boat will become stuck." Phillip looked at Jonathan and nodded.

Tim Browning looked over the edge of the boat. "What happens if we get stuck?"

Jonathan looked at Browning for a moment and then broke into a big grin. He laughed out loud.

"How long until we are back to the hotel?" Phillip

asked.

"About two and a half hours," Jonathan replied.

The journey through the river system was an eye-opening experience. Phillip could not have imagined the poverty that they saw. Families with several children, scantily clad, living in thatch-roofed huts. Wild dogs and chickens running amid the banana trees and palms. Dugout canoes were beached along the banks with fishing rods positioned in them. The working day had come to an end for these people and supper was now being prepared on open fires. Phillip could smell the smoke and the scent of fresh burning wood. The rest of the journey continued uneventfully and very little was said as everyone took in the surroundings.

The remainder of the trip was slow and tedious as Jonathan carefully manoeuvred through the obstacles in his path. At long last, Cartagena Bay appeared before them. It took several minutes to guide the craft through the remainder of the river mouth but once they were on the open bay Jonathan forced the throttle forward, increasing the speed of the boat. Jonathan was singing out loud again. He pointed toward the top of an escarpment. Phillip followed the motion and noticed a small white building set alone amongst the country side.

"Monastery," Jonathan yelled over the loud noise of the engine.

Phillip nodded. "Impressive." His eyes slowly glanced toward Kristy McPherson. Her head was turning toward the monastery. Their eyes met and Phillip smiled. She returned the greeting.

They rounded the corner and the Cartagena Hilton came into view. It stood sullenly on a peninsula by itself.

Jonathan slowed the boat down. He looked at Phillip. "This man, the one who was following you, does he know you are staying here?"

"Probably," Phillip replied.

"What will we do?"

"We definitely won't go back to the Hilton," Phillip said. "We have to get to the airport so perhaps if you could find us a hotel as close as possible that would be great."

Jonathan nodded. He continued past the Hilton and steered the craft deep into Cartagena Bay.

15   DEPARTURE

The boat bounced wildly through the choppy waters of the open sea en route back to Cartagena. There were several occasions when Willem Rolf was tossed about but each time he had somehow managed to maintain his grip on the steering wheel. He could not recall the last time he had been in water this rough. He wondered if he had maintained an accurate bearing and for the first time in many months felt fear grinding at his senses. Time passed slowly as the boat was tossed about the wavy water. It soon became apparent that the ocean was becoming too rough for the small craft. Reluctantly he was forced to abandon his quest and steer the boat back in the direction of the main island. The sun was descending and logic dictated that it would be pointless to continue. After a short time the now familiar land mass came into view. Anger pierced Rolf's emotions as he second-guessed his decision. An easy concept to create now that he was nearing safe haven.

The evening air was warm and Willem Rolf decided to sleep in the boat. He moored to the dock and secured the ropes. Grabbing his belongings, he slowly walked to the near-empty restaurant and ordered a meal. As he waited for his dinner, he telephoned the airport and check on flight schedules. The island phone was antiquated and it took several seconds to annex a connection. He was relieved when he heard no flights were leaving that night. Phillip Wright would also have to wait until morning.

After a tasteless meal of fish and rice he returned to his boat. It did not take long before the swaying of the waves lulled him into a soundless sleep.

The harbour itself was a beautiful, serene sight as evening began to filter the bright sunlight. Dozens of colourful boats were moored to the docks. Some were sailing crafts, their high masts stretching skyward, others were touring boats awaiting the next flock of eager passengers. Each boat was colourfully painted and gaily decorated with strands of brightly-lit lamps strung from mast to mast, illuminating the entire area against the dusk of the Caribbean night.

Jonathan pulled the Margaritaville alongside a cruise boat three or four times its size.

"You wait here," he said to Phillip as he jumped from the boat onto the dock.

Phillip scanned the area for signs of Rolf, but found none. Jonathan returned after a few minutes.

"Okay, come with me," Jonathan yelled as he neared the group. "I don't think that guy can make it through this water with that boat of his."

"What do you mean?"

"He'll probably go back to the big island and wait until morning."

Phillip felt a surge of relief at the thought but also knew Rolf was not the sort of person to be underestimated.

Tim Browning was the first to jump from the boat. As soon as his feet were firmly planted on the dock, he turned around and extended his hand to assist Kristy. Phillip lifted Jimmy over the side of the boat to Tim Browning's outstretched arms. Lorne McPherson was guiding his wife up the small steps to disembark, as Phillip grabbed his attaché case.

Jonathan led the small party along the concrete water's edge, passing by spectators and tourists who had gathered around the boats to set sail for sunset cruises.

They walked a short distance and Jonathan stopped to talk with someone with whom he seemed to be acquainted. Both arms flapped in the air frantically as the twosome spoke. The rest of the party neared and Jonathan turned to introduce his friend to Phillip.

"This is Eddy." Jonathan pointed to his friend standing beside him.

Eddy was in his early thirties and had an extremely dark complexion. A thick black moustache matched his heavy set eye brows. His dark, curly hair had been trimmed very close to his skin to allow him to cope with the tropical heat. The red, yellow and blue flowers on his shirt stood out loudly against the subdued colours of the rest of the party.

"Eddy is the main man around here," Jonathan said. "He runs a tour company and he'll take you anywhere you want to go." Jonathan raised his hand and patted Eddy on the shoulder, confirming his support. "I have to leave you now and I have to admit, it's been a lot of fun. If you ever need any help, you certainly know where to find me."

Phillip smiled and extended his hand, "Thanks for everything, I really appreciate it." Phillip reached in his pocket and handed Jonathan several bills. The boat skipper grinned as he pocketed the money.

"The pleasure was all mine. I'll go back over to the Hilton now and dock my boat. I'll keep an eye out for your friend and see if I can throw him off the trail."

"Careful," Phillip said.

"Always." Jonathan shook the hand of every member of the party and waved as he stepped along the walkway to his boat.

Phillip turned to Eddy, who had a big grin on his face. "Okay, my name is Eddy. I speak good English. You have questions, you ask, I tell."

"Do you have a car?" Phillip asked.

"I have small bus, where you want to go?"

"Do you know a small, out-of-the-way hotel?"

Eddy thought for a moment. "Yes, a little place my uncle owns. He would be enchanted to meet you all. Come with me." Eddy led them up several steps toward a white van which had been parked with two wheels on the curb. He opened the side door and slid it back, giving access to the torn, brown leatherette-covered seats. Everyone took their seats in the van, Phillip sitting beside the driver. Eddy secured the door and walked around to the driver's side. He put the key into the ignition and after several attempts the engine started.

After harshly pumping the gas pedal and accelerating the engine, Eddie seemed satisfied with the automobile's response. He shifted into gear and drove along the street, away from the harbourfront area.

Lorne McPherson had his hands crossed and was staring down between his knees to the floor of the mini bus. Beside him his wife Rhonda had her head tilted back, her eyes closed, and was resting after the recent ordeal. Little Jimmy was staring out the window, intrigued by the scenery, and Kristy was brushing her hair as Tim Browning gently raised his arm and put it on the seat back around her. Phillip caught the movement from the corner of his eye and tilted his head slightly so that he could catch a glimpse of the girl with the flowing, flaxen hair. He thought she seemed annoyed by Tim's gesture and tried to move forward slightly to avoid touching his arm.

Eddie had both hands firmly gripped on the steering wheel as he swerved in and out of traffic. When he passed a building he thought was important he would mention its

relevance, as well as several trivial statistics of the surrounding area.

The hotel was very tiny and secluded. Even if Rolf
was able to reach the mainland tonight he would be unable
to locate the fleeing group.

Eddie spoke with an older gentleman sitting at a
desk. He returned carrying room keys for everyone and
asked Phillip if he would be responsible for the financial
arrangements. Phillip confirmed that he would and walked
to the older individual who sat quietly, eyeing the small
company.

Phillip turned to the entourage and bade them good
night.

"Do you have a telephone?" he asked of Eddie's
uncle. The man reached below the escritoire and lifted a
black telephone set. The bell made a short ring as the unit
was placed on the wooden top. "Would you have the number
for the airport?"

Without repositioning his fragile frame the man
looked in a small directory and scribbled the number on a
scrap of paper. Phillip dialed the numbers and after speaking with several people made arrangements to secure six
tickets for the first available flight departing Cartagena.
Although it would only take them to Jamaica, Phillip felt
tremendous relief at the prospect of leaving Colombia as
soon as possible.

The old man at the desk was busily engaged in
conversation with his nephew and smiled at Phillip. Phillip
kindly thanked him and asked if Eddie could meet them at
five the following morning for a short trip to the airport.

Frustrated, Phillip cursed at the hall bathroom as it
was shared by everyone and was without a shower. He lay
outstretched on the bed pondering questions which continued to nag at him. He wondered if Rolf would make it to
shore before morning. Phillip desperately attempted to thwart
off the irritating questions and felt relief when drowsiness

overcame him. He woke in a frenzy when he realized he had forgotten to ask for a wake-up call. Sleep again took its time in finding him and when it did, it came with twisting interrogations and disturbing queries.

Willem Rolf did not sleep well in the discomfort of the open motor boat. He stood in order to catch a glimpse of the time in a dim glow cast by a small lamp fastened to a post along side the boat. The time for him to depart had come and after performing several stretch exercises, pointed the water craft in the same direction from which he had returned the previous evening. This time the expedition gave him more confidence as the sea took on a calmness akin to a giant mirror untouched by flaws.

After what seemed an eternity Rolf was able to breathe relief when, on the horizon, he caught a faint glimpse of coastline. Pleased with his results he was finally able to remove the plague of discouragement from his mind.

He tried to emulate Phillip Wright's mind in an effort to visualize the government agent's next manoeuvre. Staying in the Cartagena Hilton with a group of inexperienced, under-dressed individuals would have been far too risky and easily identified. He decided the only move left to Phillip was to head for the airport in an effort to catch the next available flight. Should Rolf's suspicions be incorrect there would be plenty of time to search for the troupe throughout the remainder of the day.

As the boat neared the shore, Rolf noted the entrance to Cartagena Bay. A duet of mammoth, stone fortresses were guarding the mouth to this once, great city as would two fangs guard the inner safety of a lion's mouth. Rolf had a general idea of the airport location and moored the boat as close as he could to the far end of the harbour.

Phillip jumped at the fierce sound of banging on his hollow, wooden door. There was daylight penetrating the sheer curtains and he rose slowly in an effort to stabilize his senses.

"Good morning." Eddie's chipper voice whispered though the door. "It is nine-thirty."

Phillip returned the greeting and decided to get dressed. He walked to the lobby and telephoned Ed Bergan before waking the others.

"Hello." Ed Bergan answered in his usual, mono-tone voice.

"Ed, it's Phillip Wright."

"Phil. How are you? I wondered why we hadn't heard from you sooner."

"Sorry, I've been busy."

"Did you find McPherson yet?"

"Yes. I have the whole family with me."

"Where are you?" Bergan asked enthusiastically.

"I'd rather not say over the phone but we'll be back in Toronto the day after tomorrow."

Bergan hesitated a moment before speaking. "Good thinking. Call me before you get there and I'll have people waiting."

The conversation was terminated and Phillip returned the telephone to its resting place beneath the small, wooden desk.

He walked upstairs and knocked on the scientist's door. After a moment of silence the door handle turned.

"What's wrong?" McPherson asked, wiping sleep from his eyes.

"Nothing," Phillip assured him. "We have to get up in order to catch the flight. I'll wake the others and meet you downstairs in half an hour."

Kristy was already awake and had just returned from the bathroom.

"Time to go," Phillip said.

"I'm ready," she replied as she tied her terry-cloth

robe around her waist. "It'll be great to get into some real clothes. Will we have time this morning to shop, do you think?"

"Probably not but as soon as we get to our next stop, I promise we'll make time."

"Okay," she said, smiling.

Phillip knocked on Tim Browning's door and told him to meet downstairs in twenty minutes. The young man saw Kristy standing in the hall and stepped from the room. "I'm ready now," he said, not wanting to leave Kristy alone with Phillip for too long.

"Let's do it," Phillip said as the threesome made their way to the bare-walled lobby.

"Where are we off to?" Tim asked.

"It'll be a surprise." Phillip had no intention of jeopardizing the final, crucial steps of this caper by divulging information that was irrelevant to anyone but himself. Phillip noted that Tim was annoyed at his exclusion of the arrangements and tried to ease the tension. "It'll be safer for all of us if you know as little as possible." Tim nodded, agreeing with Phillip.

Eddie arrived on the scene escorted by his uncle and after several parting words, accompanied by a warm embrace, led the group outside and into the waiting van.

After a short ride, the travellers passed a sign pointing to the airport. They could see the terminal building to the right as Eddie rounded the corner into the parking lot.

He looked toward Phillip, "Where do you want to go?"

"Just pull up to the front of the building, if you would."

Eddie manoeuvred the small mini bus to the glass doors of the building.

"We can't go in looking like this," Kristy McPherson said.

Phillip turned to her and the rest of the group. "If

you just wait here I'll go in and try to make arrangements."
He grabbed his attaché case and stepped out of the van,
knowing the risk he was taking by leaving them behind,
even if it was only for a few minutes. He had to move fast.

The airport terminal was busy with eager tourists
arriving early for their flights from the tropical paradise.
Phillip paused a moment and carefully glanced around
looking for any suspicious events. When he felt assured that
nothing was out of the ordinary, he walked toward the
small television monitors suspended by gray, metal brackets from the ceiling. He studied the departures listing on the
small screen and noted his flight was on time and would
arrive in Montego Bay by two this afternoon. From Montego he would be able to fly the entire group back to North
America.

He gained his composure and walked to the ticket
counter. "I thought for a moment I was too late," Phillip
said as he glanced at his watch. A ticket agent across from
him was awaiting further instructions. "May I please have
six tickets for the Air Jamaica flight to Montego Bay. I
reserved them last evening."

The uniformed attendant smiled at Phillip and nodded. She keyed the information into the terminal directly in
front of her and watched the screen, waiting for the data to
appear. After a moment a frown came to her face.

The girl looked at the clock on the wall "You only
have twenty minutes, sir. I don't believe that you will be
able to make it."

"You get the tickets ready, prepare the bill and I'll
be back in two minutes with the money."

"Very well sir."

Phillip dashed toward the front door of the terminal
building. He fumbled through his pockets as he reached the
van. He was relieved to see that the McPherson family was
still sitting patiently inside the bus.

He opened the door to the large compartment and

yelled. "Okay everyone. Out quickly." He ran around the van to the driver's side. "How much do I owe you, Eddie?"

"It's ten dollars per person so that would be sixty all together."

Phillip reached in his pocket and handed Eddie a wad of money. "Keep the change, I can't thank you enough for bringing us here."

Eddie looked at the money. "Thank you señor it has been an extreme pleasure to help you."

"Can you do me one more favour?" Phillip asked. Eddie looked inquisitively at the American. "Can you get rid of this for me?" Phillip reached in his pocket and carefully lifted the automatic for Eddie to see.

The tour guide smiled as he recognized the fearsome weapon. "I will take it for you, my friend." He placed the gun on the floor of the vehicle and closed the door.

Phillip stepped to the other side of the van. "Come with me, and please hurry." The party walked through the door and followed Phillip to the ticket counter.

"How are we doing?" Phillip asked.

"We are all set," the girl responded. "I believe you will make the flight providing you have no problems with immigration. You will have to leave your bags and we will put them on the next flight."

"We have no luggage. Everything we have, we'll carry on board. How much do I owe you?"

The girl gave Phillip the amount and he stared at the figure. "Could you please convert that to U.S. dollars?"

"Certainly." The girl used her calculator and re-wrote the figure for Phillip.

"Just a moment," Phillip said and turned away from the girl. He walked a few paces and rested his briefcase on the counter top. As he prepared to open it, shielding its contents from view, McPherson walked toward him.

"We don't have any passports you know," Lorne said in a whisper.

"I know, I'll take care of it. Why don't you take your family to the immigration area and I'll meet you there." McPherson nodded in agreement and returned to the group.

Phillip removed what he needed from his briefcase and closed it securely. He walked back to the girl and handed her the money.

"It is not very often that we see cash señor," she said as she counted the bills.

"Here are your tickets." She picked up the package of yellow and orange coloured envelopes and handed them to Phillip. "Enjoy your flight." The girl smiled at Phillip.

Phillip nodded and walked toward the McPherson party who had gathered at the immigration counter.

"Sorry I took so long," Phillip said. He turned his attention to the guard sitting at the small table by the entrance to the boarding area. Phillip looked at his watch and then at the sentry. The heavy-set man was stamping the passport of another passenger. His short-sleeve shirt was badly stained from the heat of the tropical humidity. Phillip saw beads of sweat trickling down his forehead from the brim of his cap. His tie was undone and hung loosely around his neck. The man looked up inquisitively as Phillip approached.

"There are six of us travelling to Montego Bay."

The guard studied Phillip's face. "Passports," he grunted.

Phillip had the passports ready and handed them to the man, giving his last. The man opened Phillip's passport first and studied the picture. He immediately saw the United Nations visa and flipped through the rest of the pages glancing at the international stamps. He looked up at Phillip.

"What is the purpose of your trip?"

"Strictly business."

"Will you be returning to Colombia?"

"Not in the near future."

"Could you please put your case on the counter."

Phillip put his attaché case on the counter and undid the clasps. The guard seemed satisfied with the papers inside. He was unaware of the concealed compartment and nodded to Phillip.

He waved to the rest of the group and studied the passports of each one individually, returning them to Lorne McPherson upon his completion.

"Come with me," Phillip said. The flutter in his voice was a signal to the rest of his party to rush. He stepped briskly to the boarding counter and handed the tickets to the attendant as he looked at the clock on the wall. Eight minutes before departure. It would be okay, he thought.

"Please go directly on board." The attendant motioned in the direction of the opening on the other side of the room, as she handed Phillip the boarding passes. Through the glass windows Phillip saw the S.A.M. 727 awaiting its passengers.

The flight attendant was standing by the staircase waiting for any last minute arrivals. They were the only ones remaining in the boarding lounge.

"Thanks very much," Phillip said to the attendant. He motioned the group toward the door.

Phillip froze in his tracks. Willem Rolf was walking briskly through the entrance. He scanned all directions in an effort to see through the crowd.

"Hurry," Phillip said as he rushed his party toward the door. He led them in a sprightly run across the tarmac to the staircase. He ran up the steps, looking behind him to ensure that everyone was following. He gave the flight attendant the boarding passes.

"Welcome aboard sir," a pretty, bronze-skinned girl dressed in bright, floral attire said. "Your seats are to the rear of the airplane. It appears they are not together and unfortunately we are quite full. It is only a short flight so perhaps it will not cause a problem."

Phillip smiled. He waited for his charges to pass. "Just grab any empty seats you can find. We're the last ones."

Lorne McPherson was the last of the five to pass Phillip. Phillip leaned down and stared out the door. He tried to catch a glimpse of the terminal building but could see no sign of Rolf. He wondered whether the German had seen them. Phillip was thankful the flight was full but knew it wouldn't take Rolf long to deduce their destination.

He walked along the corridor of the aircraft and smiled as he passed Kristy McPherson. Tim Browning was several rows behind her in a centre seat tightly squeezed between two hefty people. Phillip chuckled to himself as he watched Browning's discomfort.

Lorne and Rhonda McPherson had managed to find a block of four seats at the very rear of the cabin. Jimmy had already slid into the window seat and patted the seat beside him as he saw Phillip approach.

"I'll sit here beside Jimmy," Phillip said walking past Lorne McPherson.

He allowed his body to fall into the soft, cushioned seat and sighed a breath of relief before putting his attaché case underneath the seat in front of him.

Jimmy was unaccustomed to flying and was intrigued by the exciting new surroundings. He had already buckled up his seat-belt and motioned for Phillip to do the same.

"This is a big airplane," Jimmy said. He had to speak louder than normal because of the engine noise at the back of the plane. They were in the last row and Phillip could hear the flight attendant clanging cups in the small galley behind him.

Rhonda McPherson leaned over the seat. "What will happen to all our belongings in Buenos Aires?" she asked of Phillip.

"When we get to Jamaica, we'll have a little bit of time and I'll contact my superiors to start the ball rolling. I'm sure everything will be taken care of."

He watched the flight attendant hand a blanket to Kristy McPherson who was still dressed in her bathing suit and cover-up jacket. It was not enough to keep her warm in the air conditioned fuselage of the aircraft. She tucked the blanket around her legs and glanced to the rear of the cabin waving at the foursome. Phillip smiled at her and thought for a split second that she returned a similar facial expression directly at him. She raised her hand, brushed her hair and returned her gaze to the flight attendant advising passengers of the pre-take off instructions.

Lorne McPherson turned to Phillip. "How did you ever find us?"

"It wasn't easy," Phillip said. "I arrived in Bogota five days ago and have been tracking you ever since."

As the airplane began to move the roar of the engines became louder. "I'll explain the rest later." Phillip said loudly trying to be heard over top of the engine noise. Lorne nodded and turned back to face the front of the cabin, smiling at Jimmy in passing. His wife Rhonda rested her head on his shoulder, as he placed his hand upon hers, squeezing it gently.

Phillip looked at Jimmy who was avidly staring out the window. He felt pressure as the airplane picked up speed in its race along the uneven runway. The front end of the craft lifted from the ground, soon to be followed by the rear section. The no smoking sign was turned off and Phillip could feel a thump as the wheels were retracted into the body of the jet. He removed the cigarette pack from his shirt pocket and placed one between his lips. He fumbled for the matches and as he struck one to light the cigarette, he saw Jimmy turning his view from the window toward him. Phillip caught his eye and felt guilt sweep over him. He made a mental note to try to give up smoking the first chance he had. He smiled at Jimmy as he exhaled the cloudy substance from his lungs.

"Do you like flying?" he asked.

"I sure do. How long will this flight be?"

"About five hours, I would think. There's one stopover."

"That's great," Jimmy said grinning. He turned to the window and his eyes pierced the billowy clouds hovering above green, fertile soil trimmed by white beaches and blue with white-capped waves below.

Phillip rested his head and closed his eyes for a moment, allowing his thoughts to drift back in time to his two sons. A sadness overcame him and he forced the thoughts from his mind, returning his attention to the present situation.

Turbulence surrounded the aircraft as the plane eased its way through the first layer of cumulus clouds. The seatbelt sign went off and Phillip walked along the aisle, stopping at Tim Browning's seat, smiling at the young scientist's obvious discomfort.

"Everything okay?"

"Oh yeah, fine thanks." Tim Browning looked in exasperation at Phillip, his eyes motioning to the people beside him. "What's the plan from here?"

"When we get to Montego Bay we'll make arrangements to catch a flight out." He wanted to avoid further conversation not knowing who the other people in the row of seats were. "I'll see you when we land."

He walked up the aisle a little further and stopped beside Kristy McPherson. She smiled upon seeing him and he rested his arm on the seat-back in front of her.

"How are you feeling?" he asked tenderly.

"I'm okay," she said. "I'm starving to death. I wish they would feed us."

Phillip looked to the rear of the aircraft and saw the flight attendant preparing the cart for food service.

"I think the food is on its way."

"Who are you anyway?" Kristy asked in a serious tone of voice. "Where did you appear from out of nowhere, and who's that guy following us?"

"I'm here on behalf of the Canadian Government. I was asked to find you and return you to Canada. As for the guy following us I have absolutely no idea."

"Do you think that he saw us at the airport?"

"I'm not sure, but it doesn't really matter. It won't take him long to figure out where we've gone and I'm sure he'll be on the next flight. At least we'll have a good head start."

"What's this all about? I know my dad was in some trouble and we had to leave Argentina in a hurry. Are we in some kind of danger?"

"I would think with people shooting at us, we are." Phillip replied. "They don't tell me very much but I'm sure once you arrive back home everything will be explained to you." Kristy smiled at Phillip.

"May I have one of your cigarettes please?"

"Of course," Phillip said, as he reached in his pocket and passed her a cigarette. He struck a match and as he lit it she cupped his hand with hers.

Phillip was impressed with her beautiful, gold tan which stood out against the white, terry-cloth cover-up and parts of the blue bathing suit exposed beneath. She caught Phillip staring at her and smiled.

"I guess I'd better sit down," Phillip said as the flight attendant approached with the food tray. "I'll see you when we land."

"Okay. Thanks for the cigarette," she said as Phillip returned to his seat.

"Are we going to eat now?" Jimmy asked.

"It looks like it. Are you hungry?"

"I sure am," Jimmy said enthusiastically. Phillip smiled and reached for the tray tables on the chair-backs in front of him.

16   AWAY

The fierce, blue eyes of Willem Rolf were filled with fire and anger. He had been trailing Phillip Wright in hopes of finding Lorne McPherson for the better part of a week and had, after many hours of nervous, tense confrontations, finally located the Canadian scientist.

The muscles in his face were extremely taut as he stared out the window of the airport terminal watching the plane disappear over the horizon. He was acting alone now. The fat man was wounded and would be out of commission for several months. Ricardo was useless and his services would no longer be required. Rolf had unwillingly paid both men their money and professionally thanked them for their part. He disliked dealing with failures, however in his line of work it was difficult to find men who measured up to his expectations.

He walked to a small counter where a pretty young girl was serving coffee, tea and various cold beverages. He asked for a tea and reached in his pocket for the appropriate money. He grabbed the cardboard cup and seated himself in the first available chair, along a wall, in an out of the way section of the terminal building. It was time to gather his thoughts.

Phillip Wright had found McPherson in less than a week. Rolf respected him for his ability to perform his job. There were several instances along the way in which Rolf would have performed differently, more efficiently, but he had assumed that Phillip Wright was less experienced than himself. Instead, Phillip had managed to accomplish the task in very little time and for this Rolf had to give him credit.

Rolf's instructions were simple: locate McPherson and deliver him to the group by whom he had been commissioned, then meet his contacts and collect the money owing.

Rolf was not certain of Phillip Wright's role in this incident. He had been told of a government agent who had been trailing McPherson and to let the agent do the majority of the work with all the proper tools at his disposal. He had contacted his superior three days earlier and asked about Wright but was told that no one in his organization knew much about him. Although he had worked for the United Nations for a number of years his record was average, not outstanding. He had never set the world on fire but had performed his assignments with relative accuracy and success. In Willem Rolf's mind, being alive in this business was a measurement of success.

Rolf had been doing this type of work for many years. He enjoyed his job very much and took great pleasure in accomplishing his goals. He had developed a network of accomplices around the world for various deeds and had been responsible for many political changes around the globe. Killing someone was easily justified when it was an integral part of the overall plan. Although he had no passion for murder, he firmly believed that the end would always justify the means. He worked for a small international organization which felt it was above the laws of any country. He seldom knew the details of an entire operation and was usually only involved in a small part. All of his objectives in the past had been met. His record was spotless. He took pride in the fact that he was a perfectionist and acted accordingly. His main goal was money and this caper was no exception. He would be paid handsomely in U.S. currency at the completion of this job.

It became evident to him earlier in the week that Phillip Wright had been sent in by the Canadian Government to locate and extract McPherson. He followed Wright throughout South America until he located McPherson. His intention was to eliminate the federal agent and take over the prize himself. Now as he stared off into blue skies over Cartagena airport he knew that he had suffered a set back. He knew Phillip Wright went to Montego Bay because it was the only flight out of Cartagena at that time.

He bit his lip in anger as he thought of missing his quarry by minutes. He had to fly to Montego at the next available chance and locate the scientist. If he was too late and they had travelled to North America it would be much more difficult, if not impossible, to catch his prey. He finished his tea and placed the cup in a garbage container as he walked over to a small desk marked 'inquiry'. He put both hands on the counter and waited for the young attendant to replace the telephone back in its cradle. The petite girl, dressed in a white uniform, stared up timidly at the square-jawed, short-haired man standing directly before her.

"May I help you?" she asked speaking in Spanish.

Rolf replied in English, "Yes, where may I charter an airplane?"

She changed her voice to textbook English. "You go back out through the main door and turn left, walk about five hundred yards and you will see a small yellow building. There they will rent charters."

"Thank you, very much." Rolf turned abruptly and

walked directly toward the front door.

Once outside he glanced along the roadway in an effort to get a glimpse of the building. A vacation bus was in the process of unloading its tourists and Rolf could not see past the chattering visitors.

The McPhersons and Tim Browning followed Phillip Wright to the terminal building at Montego Bay Airport. They walked briskly to the ticket counter which handled Air Canada flights and inquired about immediate passage to Toronto.

"There is one flight per day," the attendant replied. "It flies into Mo' Bay then shuttles over to Kingston and returns to Toronto." She was a pretty girl with a bronze complexion. Her hair was combed in short, tight curls which had been neatly cut and her make-up had been applied with perfection. The navy blue uniform with white blouse and red and blue scarf was clean and well-pressed.

"The next one leaves at one-thirty tomorrow morning."

"Thank you." Phillip paused for a moment to gather his thoughts. He turned around and spoke to his entourage "Follow me," he said and he marched his procession toward the front door of the building.

The hot, subequatorial, Jamaican air was humid. A recent rain shower had left sparkling droplets of moisture on all the leaves and grass.

"What do you know about this guy following us?" Lorne McPherson asked, speaking directly to Phillip.

"I don't really know who he is or what his game is, but I'm concerned if he works for a large organization they might have agents right here in Jamaica. Our first priority is to find a place we can sleep tonight without being disturbed."

Phillip walked to the nearest cab, a white Chevrolet at least fifteen years old. The car seemed a lot larger than

Phillip had remembered the style from his youth. There were small particles of rust along the bottom but it was in generally good condition. Phillip rested his arms against the passenger door and leaned his head through the window. The driver turned to him.

"Where do you want to go?"

The man's black skin was covered with perspiration. His long black hair had been woven in ragged strands, singed with a match in keeping with a popular, Rastafarian craze. He wore no shirt and his left hand was rubbing his chest gently in a nonchalant manner.

"Can you drive us to Ocho Rios?"

"Of course." The man eyed the troupe directly behind Phillip, his gaze stopping when he looked at Kristy McPherson. Most of her long, tanned legs were exposed underneath the terry cloth cover up of her bathing suit. "You got luggage?"

"No."

Again he eyed the small group. "Ocho Rios is far away. I will want money up front."

"That's not a problem," Phillip replied. "How much?" He reached for the cash in his pocket and paid the driver.

"Okay, we go."

Lorne McPherson opened the back door of the cab and slid into the rear-seat, followed by his wife. She motioned to her son to join them. Tim Browning opened the front door and held it for Kristy to get in first. Phillip walked back to the passenger's side and quietly spoke to Tim Browning.

"I think, by the way she is dressed, that you should get in first." Browning did so and Kristy closed the door behind her as she slid into the front seat. Phillip walked around the back and opened the trunk. He threw his attaché case in and closed the lid. With great effort he forced his way into the back seat of the cab sitting snugly beside Rhonda McPherson.

"We would have taken a van but cars are a lot less conspicuous," Phillip said in antiphon to the inquisitive faces staring at him.

The cab began to roar as the driver turned the ignition key. He sped out of the airport parking lot and raced along the main streets of Montego Bay. It wasn't long before they were on a small winding road surrounded by luscious, green trees and thick, forest foliage.

Tim Browning was the first to break the silence. "Where exactly are we going?"

The driver glanced in the rear-view mirror and scanned the crammed passengers in the back seat. Phillip tried to adjust his seating position slightly and wished that he had opted for a bus ride, instead of the close quartered cab.

By now the rest of his party was looking at him, anticipating an answer to Tim Browning's question.

"The drive from Montego Bay to Ocho Rios is about an hour and a half. We'll spend the night there and get up early tomorrow morning, continuing on to Kingston."

Rhonda McPherson interjected. "How long will that take?"

"I'd guess about five hours." Phillip saw the look of discontent on her face. "I'm sorry, but it's important to take every precaution. If the plane lands in Montego Bay at eleven, it'll be in Kingston around three. We'll be there in time to catch it and head back to Toronto. Rolf will be expecting us at Montego Bay. He won't take the plane without us. This time tomorrow we'll be back in Canada."

"That'll be great," Kristy McPherson said.

"Will we be staying in a hotel tonight?" Tim Browning asked.

"Yes, definitely. I need a shower and some rest," Phillip replied.

"Will they have a swimming pool?" Jimmy asked as he looked up at Phillip.

"They sure will." Phillip smiled as he glanced at the young boy sitting beside him.

"I hope they have a couple of stores where I can buy some clothes," Kristy said eagerly.

"I don't have any money with me," Lorne McPherson said and turned his gaze toward Phillip. "Will you be able to lend us some until we get home?"

"Of course. When we get there, we'll check into the hotel and go on a shopping spree." Phillip was trying to appease the negative feelings within the group.

The car rocked from side to side as the condition of the road turned from bad to worse. Glimpses of the deep blue ocean were had at intervals between the trees along the way. Silence blanketed the group as they progressed on their journey.

Willem Rolf was strolling along the sidewalk outside of the small, yellow building, casually eating a sandwich partially wrapped in clear cellophane. The pilot, for the only plane that could make it to Jamaica, was away for half an hour. Rolf waited impatiently and looked at his watch realizing only fifteen minutes had passed. He seated himself on the bench and rested both elbows on the back, stretching his legs as far as possible. He breathed deeply and studied the surrounding area. It was quite beautiful, he thought. It was the first time in a long time he had been allowed to take his mind away from work for a few minutes and enjoy the ambiance. He made a mental note to return to Cartagena one day and relish the sun and the hot tropical atmosphere. His mind was snapped back to reality by the loud noise of a green, antiquated, army-jeep. A man dressed in army fatigues jumped out and walked toward the doors.

Rolf waited for a moment, giving the man ample time to get organized for the rest of his day's activities.

"Excuse me, are you the person who charters the flights to Jamaica?" Rolf was standing upright waiting for the man in the green uniform to turn around from a desk behind the counter.

"Sure am, where exactly do you want to go?"

Rolf was irritated by the man chewing gum as he spoke.

"Montego Bay. As quickly as we possibly can."

The man looked at his watch. He frowned before he spoke. "Should be ready to leave in about an hour. That'll put us into Montego by three." The man paused as he watched Rolf nod in agreement. "It'll cost you though."

"I understand that. If you can tell me the amount I will make the proper arrangements and meet you back here with the money in one hour's time."

Rolf returned to the airport terminal and approached a locker and fumbled the key from his pocket. Inside was a briefcase from which he removed an adequate supply of U.S. dollars, accepted anywhere. He closed the briefcase, secured the latch and shut the empty locker, leaving the key in it. He walked to the magazine stand and scanned for an appropriate selection to endure the journey to Montego Bay.

After he paid the attendant and tucked the magazine under his arm, he briskly stepped to an information counter.

"I will be with you in a moment," the attractive attendant said as Rolf approached. "May I help you?"

"Yes I wonder if you could tell me the next available flight from Montego Bay to Canada?"

The girl entered the information into her computer system and waited for the amber screen to respond.

"There is only one flight per day and it leaves Montego Bay at one thirty, landing in Toronto at six in the evening."

"Are there any flights tonight out of Montego Bay heading for New York City or anywhere along the Eastern Seaboard of the U.S?"

Again the girl entered information and studied the screen intently as publications were projected across the CRT. "No sir there are no flights whatsoever tonight. The last one left about two hours ago and it was for Montreal via New York."

"Thank you very much." Rolf was pleased. He left the attendant and casually walked from the terminal building. As he walked, his eyes squinted against the bright sunlight of the hot Colombian sun as it was beginning to set. A smile came to his lips as he thought of Phillip Wright's surprise when the government agent would learn of his arrival in Montego Bay tonight. Rolf was certain Phillip assumed there were no flights from Cartagena tonight landing anywhere in Jamaica.

He entered the yellow building through the glass doors and spoke to the pilot who was gathering his maps and placing them in a briefcase.

"We should arrive in Ocho Rios in about thirty minutes," the cabby said. Everyone in the little group sighed with thankful relief as they neared the end of their journey

"If there are no flights from Cartagena to Jamaica tonight and this guy Rolf can't get here," Lorne McPherson asked Phillip, "why didn't we just stay in Montego Bay and catch the first flight tomorrow morning?"

Tim Browning spoke before Phillip had a chance to answer. "That's true, do you have any idea what time the first flight would arrive tomorrow morning?"

"I believe there's only one flight in the morning arriving in Montego Bay." Phillip paused to light a cigarette, and rolled down the window. "We probably could have stayed there but Rolf seems to be very resourceful and I don't think we're in a position to take any chances. We've come this far and it looks like we're home free. I certainly don't want to jeopardize anything now."

The entourage of fugitives arrived in Ocho Rios

mid-afternoon. As they entered the tourist part of the village, Kristy pointed out some stucco buildings which housed the straw market. They drove along a narrow laneway and came to a halt at a large masonry pylon. The words 'Jamaican Hilton' were etched in the face of the peeling concrete. The entrance drive to the hotel was lined with banyan trees. On the left was a large putting green frequented by older tourists, clad in Lacoste apparel, working out detailed variations of already perfected golf shots.

The open-aired lobby of the hotel was decorated with white rattan chairs and chesterfields. Phillip walked to the front desk.

"Four rooms please."

"Do you have a reservation?" an extremely well-mannered boy, dressed in a white shirt with the Hilton insignia embroidered on his pocket asked.

"No, I don't." Phillip looked directly at the boy, his face turning into a casual smile. "I certainly hope it's not a problem We've been travelling for quite some time and are very tired."

"No, of course not, this is not our busy season." He reached under the counter and removed four, white cards placing them face up on the brown linoleum top. He passed Phillip a pen. "Could you fill these out please?"

After he had completed his own, Phillip took the remainder of the cards and walked to the small, carpeted area behind him where the rest of the group had seated themselves.

He placed the cards on the small glass-topped table in the centre of the seating area. He addressed his attention to Rhonda McPherson. "Do you want Jimmy to have a room of his own or get an extra cot for yours?"

Rhonda looked at her husband for a moment. "I think I'd feel better if he was in our room."

Phillip walked to the cab driver who was talking to one of the bell boys at the entrance to the lobby.

"We want to do some shopping after we check in. Would you be available to take us around?"

"Of course, Trevor is at your service." The black cab driver had been asked by a hotel bell captain to wear a shirt before entering the lobby. He clicked his heels and tipped his head as he spoke.

"Now, what time do we have to leave tomorrow morning to make it to Kingston by noon?"

"Kingston!" I don't want to go all the way to Kingston."

"I think that you should reconsider. You've come this far."

Trevor paused. He looked at Phillip, both hands rested on his hips. "I will have to work out how much it will cost. It won't be cheap."

"Tell me how much, I'm sure there won't be a problem." Phillip smiled as he spoke.

"We'll meet you back here in one hour if that's okay with you?" Trevor nodded at Phillip's request and continued his conversation with the bellboy. They spoke in an extremely fast Jamaican dialect incomprehensible to Phillip.

He returned to the quintet, seated around the glass table, and collected the cards.

"We will only be staying one night and I would like to settle the account in cash," Phillip said to the desk clerk.

"Certainly sir, we will be requiring a small deposit in advance."

"That'll be fine." Phillip made the specific arrangements with the clerk and received the keys to four of the finest hotel rooms in Jamaica.

"We'll be meeting back here in exactly an hour and Trevor will take us shopping." Both Rhonda McPherson and her daughter Kristy seemed relieved at the prospect of purchasing a change of clothes. "There are a few things that I want you to adhere to," Phillip asked. "First of all no matter who knocks on your door do not answer it. If anyone wants to visit each other telephone first. If you receive any telephone calls that appear to be the slightest bit strange call me immediately. This man Rolf is no amateur and I don't know what his motives are but I have a feeling that he'll stop at nothing to get what he wants. Don't order any room service. We will eat in the marketplace." Everyone nodded in understanding of Phillip's requests.

Phillip entered his room and threw his briefcase and duffel bag on the bed, letting his body drop directly beside it. He issued a long sigh of exhausting breath and tried to recap some of the events of the past few hours. For a few moments he sat up and rummaged through his duffel bag, removing his toiletries. He walked into the bathroom and enjoyed an extremely long, hot shower. The prospect of new clothes gave him a clean, refreshed feeling. He was getting tired of rinsing out clothes in various hotel room sinks.

17   REST

Kristy McPherson was waiting in the lobby when Phillip arrived. Her hair was still moist from the shower she had taken. Phillip's eyes seductively wandered the full length of her slender body, dressed in her bathing suit, still covered up by the small, white, terry-cloth robe. He walked to where she was sitting and smiled.

"The shower felt great. I just wish I had something else to wear besides this bathing suit." She smiled at Phillip. Most of her make-up had been removed by the shower and her face had a fresh, natural appearance. On the small table in front of them sat an ornately decorated bowl filled with coconut shavings. Phillip reached over and grabbed a handful.

"I'm afraid you'll have to excuse the way I look. Without a hair dryer or make-up this is all you get."

"I think you look fine, considering I've never seen you dressed in anything else." Phillip smiled as he spoke, staring deep into her blue eyes. She had a demure smile. A slight rouge colour came to her cheeks from a momentary mantle of embarrassment.

Kristy watched as Phillip looked around the lobby, searching for their driver. "If you're looking for Trevor, he was here a few moments ago and said he would go to the bar. We could meet him there."

Phillip sat down directly across from Kristy. "I guess we'll wait for everyone else to show up first."

"How long have you been in this type of work?"

"About four years."

"Is this all you do?"

"Basically, yes."

"Who do you work for?"

"I'm with a small, United Nations subsidiary responsible for finding missing people around the world."

"That sounds like a really interesting job."

"It is and it isn't. The first couple of years were great. Travelling to different countries in a job that seemed to be very glamorous. Lately however, it's been pretty lonely."

"Where do you live?"

"I really don't have a home. I lived in New York up until eight years ago and moved to Virginia when I got this job. When I finally got a field position I travelled all the time. Whenever I'm between assignments I usually stay in a hotel for a few days and relax. Then I'm off to another city or country. Everything I have is in my briefcase."

"You must make a lot of money?"

Phillip smiled more to himself than for her benefit. "I managed to tuck a little bit away. I just hope I'm not to old to enjoy it."

"You don't look that old to me." She leaned forward as she spoke, taking a handful of coconut chips from the colourful bowl. "I take it you're not married?"

"Not any more."

"I imagine it would be difficult for any woman to be married to someone who travelled three hundred and sixty-five days a year."

"It's not quite like that. My marriage broke up long before I was travelling." His gaze was momentarily fixed on the colourful, shag carpet covering the floor of the lobby area.

Kristy McPherson sensed that she had asked enough of his personal life and she changed the subject. "Do you have any idea why this guy has been chasing us?"

Phillip looked up at her. "I imagine he works for the Argentine government and he had been recruited to get your father back." He paused for a moment. "Do you have any idea what might have happened?"

"Not really." Kristy said. "The police just came to our house one day and had a long talk with my father. They took him away for a couple of days and, shortly after he returned, he said that we were taking a trip. Then, when we landed in Bogota, the police stopped us and took our passports. They didn't do anything else to us, so we took a bus to Cartagena. From there we went to the Rosario Islands until you came and spoiled our little vacation."

Phillip wasn't sure whether or not she was serious. "Why would you have taken a bus to Cartagena? Would it not have been faster to fly?"

"I wondered that too but both my father and Tim seemed to think that it would be safer. I knew something was wrong but I didn't want to ask. They told me you need passports to board an airplane in this country. I didn't believe them but figured they would tell me if they wanted me to know."

Their conversation was interrupted by the entrance of Rhonda McPherson, accompanied by her son Jimmy. Her husband Lorne and Tim Browning were following closely behind.

"Have you been waiting long?" Rhonda asked directing her question to Kristy.

Phillip stood as the foursome approached. "No we

both just got here," he said. "Why don't you hang on for a minute and I'll find Trevor."

The bar was dark and it took Phillip's eyes a few moments to adjust. In the centre was a great pillar supporting the sloped roof. As Phillip looked up he saw hundreds of different hats, most of them made from straw, covering the ceiling. Several people were sitting on bar stools gazing toward the far corner of the room. A dozen or so men were crouched around something that Phillip could not see. He scanned the room for Trevor. It took him a moment to find the cabby squatted between the people on the floor. They were screaming and yelling and did not hear Phillip approach. As he came within range he saw the men enjoying crab races on the floor of the bar. Trevor was shouting at one of the crabs, waving a handful of Jamaican dollars as if to entice the six-legged creature into winning. At the completion of the race Trevor cursed, having lost what he considered a substantial amount of money. He turned around to see Phillip smiling at him.

"Oh. You are ready to go?"

"I am, but I'm not sure if you are?"

"Yeah. I've done enough damage here." As the twosome returned to the lobby, the rest of the party had moved to the entrance leading to the driveway.

Trevor went ahead and brought the cab to the front entrance. As the small party walked toward the white automobile, Lorne McPherson touched Phillip's arm.

He tilted his head slightly and whispered. "Can I see you a minute?"

Phillip nodded and held up his finger. "Just a second," he said. He addressed the rest of the group. "Why don't you get into the cab. I'll be there in a second." He directed his attention back to the scientist.

"Do you remember my mentioning I don't have any money?" Lorne McPherson asked, somewhat embarrassed.

"Oh, I'm glad you reminded me, I was going to give

you some. I almost forgot." Phillip walked back to the table and chair ensemble and placed his briefcase on it. Shielding the contents from Lorne's view, he removed ten, one hundred dollar bills. He snapped the briefcase shut, automatically closing the concealed compartment where the cash was kept. He folded the bills and handed them to McPherson.

"Here's a thousand dollars. That should be enough to buy some clothes and get you around in Toronto."

"Thanks very much." McPherson took the cash and slid it into the pocket of his trousers. They rejoined the rest of the party, busily engaged in idle chatter with Trevor concerning the shopping expedition.

The cool, air-conditioned interior of the department store was a thankful relief from the hot, tropical humidity. White, metal racks lined the walls and were filled with hundreds of multicoloured shirts, blouses and slacks. Shopping was not big on Phillip's list. His eyes continually roamed the store and surrounding area looking for signs of Willem Rolf, or any extraordinary circumstances.

Phillip had selected a pair of white denim jeans, a matching blue and white short-sleeve, polo shirt, a comfortable pair of blue-laced sneakers and a new white with beige windbreaker. His clothes maintained a bland appearance to avoid standing out in crowds. He looked for another pair of pants as well as two more shirts. He had already tossed his denims into the garbage at the hotel. They were wearing thin in the knees and, because he had been carrying his gun more than usual, the pockets were starting to show signs of erosion.

Kristy McPherson emerged from the mirrored change-room wearing a pair of well-fitted, white slacks and a royal-blue, silky blouse. She wore the colours well Phillip thought.

"Well, how do I look?" she asked as she walked toward Phillip. She stopped in front of him and did a small pirouette with outstretched arms, allowing her hair to fall back behind her as she turned.

"Really nice." Phillip's forehead wrinkled slightly as he raised his eyebrows in approval of Kristy's attire. She was very attractive and he found himself infatuated by her splendour. She had applied make up to her face and accentuated the natural beauty.

"Do you think this will be enough?" she asked. "Or should I buy some more stuff?"

"I think that'll be okay. Tomorrow at this time you'll be in Toronto and away from all this mess. There you'll be able to buy what you need to take you back to Vancouver. While you're here, it's best to travel light."

"Thank you, Mr. Wright. Always planning and thinking for all of us." She smiled, turned, and stepped toward some racks of wildly coloured dresses.

"Wow, you look really nice." Tim Browning had stepped out from the change room and walked to where Kristy was looking at the dresses. He was wearing a pair of brown slacks and a blue and green plaid shirt.

Lorne McPherson was finished before everyone else and was standing outside of the store. He re-entered through the glass door and walked toward Phillip. He looked like a new man, wearing white slacks, beige shirt and a salmon-coloured, sports jacket. His richly-tanned face was framed by his silver-white hair. It was offset by the light coloured jacket.

"I'd rather you wouldn't go outside by yourself," Phillip said to Lorne McPherson.

"I'm sorry, I only stepped out front for a moment. I was just thinking how much I am going to miss this part of the world." A thin, sorrowful smile came to his lips.

Rhonda McPherson had also been transformed into a new person. The dress she had purchased suited her and hid her slight obesity. She had combed her hair, allowing the small curls to spring free.

"How do I look?" Phillip spun around and looked at Jimmy McPherson standing before him. He had a large grin on his face, pleased with his latest wardrobe selections. He was wearing yellow shorts, blue sneakers and a multicoloured shirt.

"You look very Jamaican," Phillip said. The boy grinned.

"Come over here Kristy," Rhonda McPherson said to her daughter. "There's a bunch of make up over here. We should pick something up for the trip."

"I've already got some things," Kristy said, but joined her mother at the far end of the store.

Lorne McPherson sighed and put his hands in his pocket. Phillip watched the two women walk away from him.

After what seemed an eternity to the men standing patiently by the cashier's desk, the two women returned.

"Well, that's everything then," Rhonda McPherson said. Her hands were full of small plastic containers with various makeup applicators.

"What are we going to carry this stuff in?" Kristy asked.

"I saw a small market just down the street," Lorne said. "They sell straw bags and things like that."

Lorne paid for his family's new wardrobe and was surprised at how low the total was.

Once outside, the hot wind overtook the coolness their bodies had become accustomed to. Phillip eyed the street cautiously, looking for signs of anything amiss. Everything seemed to be normal and he walked to where Trevor had parked the car, asking the black driver to meet them at the straw market down the street. Phillip returned to the others who had already started walking in the direction of the market.

The company strolled from stall to stall eyeing all the local dexterity on display. Native Jamaicans were crafting hats or embroidering handbags. Phillip's eyed darted from person to person. He was nervous being in a crowd with so many people to look after. He wished they would hurry and buy what they wanted so they could return to the sanctuary of their hotel.

Rhonda had found a purse almost immediately. She paid the lady with money her husband had given her. Kristy couldn't decide between one bag and another and asked Phillip's opinion.

"You're no help at all," she said, after Phillip remarked that both bags looked fine.

"I like the one on the left myself," Tim Browning said pointing to the small, hand-crafted bag that Kristy was holding in her left hand. She did not remove her eyes from Phillip's gaze and lifted her left hand in the air.

"I agree," she said and asked her father for some money to pay the woman squatted at the front of the booth.

After Jimmy McPherson had purchased a handmade, straw-embroidered hat the group left to meet Trevor.

The drive to the hotel was quick even though it was rush hour in Ocho Rios.

"Boy I'm hungry," Tim Browning said. "Do we have any plans for dinner?" He looked at Phillip, seated in the front next to Lorne McPherson.

"I think we'll have dinner in the dining room of the hotel and call it an early night." He paused for a moment. "If that's alright with everyone?"

The group nodded in agreement, each in turn commenting on how hungry they were. Jimmy had decided he wanted roast beef with Yorkshire pudding.

"You're welcome to join us for dinner," Phillip said to Trevor, who had remained in the cab.

"No man, thanks but I am going to join some friends in town, have a few Red Stripe and chase some ladies." He had a big smile on his face, his white teeth standing out against his black lips.

"Can I get you anything while I'm there?" Phillip shook his head. "Are you sure, maybe a little Ganjie?"

"No thanks, I'm pretty tired. I just want to get some sleep."

"Shall we say dinner in one hour?" Phillip asked of the group. Everyone nodded in agreement.

Phillip made dinner reservations before retiring to his room. He picked up the telephone and dialed the number that Ed Bergan had given him. The phone rang three times before Phillip heard Bergan's voice at the other end. "Ed, this is Phillip."

"Phil, how are ya? No, better still, where are you?"

"I'm in Jamaica. We landed a couple of hours ago."

"Jamaica!" Ed Bergan paused. "Is everyone okay?"

"Yeah, everyone's fine. We got here about two o'clock."

"What's your next move?"

"We're catching the flight tomorrow at two from Kingston to Toronto and should be arriving there around six."

"Where are you now?'

"We're in Ocho Rios."

"Ocho Rios! You sure pick the ritziest places to stay." Ed Bergan chuckled as he spoke. "Any more contact with that guy that was following you?"

"We saw him at the airport in Cartagena. We had the last flight leaving Colombia for Jamaica so I feel pretty good about having lost him. By the time he gets here tomorrow we'll be en route to Canada."

"That's great Phil. You've done a super job. I'll talk to your superior and recommend that you get a nice bonus for this."

"I much prefer a few days rest," Phillip said.

"You got it." The receiver clicked in Phillip's ear as Ed Bergan disconnected his line. Phillip opened the sliding doors and relaxed in one of the wicker chairs on the balcony. The view of the pool was breathtaking. In the distance, several large ships were crossing the Caribbean. Although the air felt humid, an evening coolness had draped the countryside. Phillip lit a cigarette and tried to relax, closing his eyes and letting his mind drift.

"Quite a view isn't it?"

Phillip was startled by the voice coming to him from the balcony next to his. He turned and saw Kristy McPherson leaning on the railing smiling at him.

"It's beautiful isn't it? I could stay here forever." Her voice was lyrical, coated with a hint of softness.

Phillip smiled. "I couldn't afford to stay here forever."

"Are you ready for dinner?

"I'm starving."

"I'll meet you downstairs."

Phillip extinguished his cigarette and went back inside his room. He secured the latches on his briefcase and took it with him to dinner. When he arrived downstairs, Kristy and Tim Browning were waiting in the lobby.

"I made reservations in the dining room."

"Mom and Dad said to go ahead, they would meet us in a little while." The threesome walked into the restaurant and were seated by the maitre d'.

The spacious eating area was dimly lit. There were no windows but white drapes had been suspended from the ceiling partially covering the beige, linen-cloth, wallpapered walls. Most of the large tables were round and covered with pink table cloths set professionally with cutlery and crystal of the finest quality. Large yucca trees and banana plants were positioned strategically around the restaurant to give optimum privacy to its patrons.

The wine steward approached Phillip's table. A small silver chain holding a tasting spoon dangled about his neck. He introduced himself and Phillip ordered a bottle of house wine, looking at Kristy and Tim for approval.

Tim Browning had seated himself directly beside Kristy McPherson and Phillip sat across from them. The conversation consisted mostly of small talk between Kristy McPherson and Tim Browning.

The scientist, his wife, and son arrived at the same time the wine steward poured a taster sample into Phillip's glass. Phillip acknowledged acceptance even though he had no expertise in distinguishing a better vintage from a crop of lesser quality.

Everyone sat as the steward poured the wine into the remaining glasses. A tuxedo-clad waiter was directly behind him distributing menus and announcing the specialities of the house, recommending the flounder.

The conversations at dinner were very low keyed as most of the people were exhausted and had little to say. Phillip kept his conversation to a minimum. The strain of the last few days was beginning to catch up to him and he was extremely tired, plagued by an uneasy feeling as to the whereabouts of Willem Rolf.

After dinner everyone left the restaurant while Phillip arranged payment of the bill. He caught up with Lorne McPherson and Tim Browning in the lobby of the hotel.

"Would you two gentlemen mind joining me for a drink in the bar for a few minutes?"

Lorne McPherson looked at Tim Browning. "Not at all."

The trio walked to the Jippa Jappa lounge as Rhonda, Kristy and Jimmy McPherson made their way toward the elevator.

"Wow, this is incredible," Tim Browning said, his gaze fixed on the hundreds of decorative, straw hats suspended from the ceiling.

In the corner of the dimly lit cafe men were still wagering their hard-earned money on crab races.

Phillip led his two companions to a table in a remote corner of the lounge. It gave them a view of the entire establishment, especially the front door. The restaurant was mostly empty and staff were preparing the amenities as the dinner hour approached. A young man in his early twenties, dressed in a blue tuxedo with a white shirt and matching white cravat, walked over to them. He smiled as he removed a small note pad and a pencil.

"What may I get you?"

Phillip looked at Lorne McPherson. "I'll have a scotch and soda."

"I'll just have a beer, thanks," Tim Browning said as he moved back in his chair.

The waiter returned his glance to Phillip. "Gin martini with ice, no olive please."

The waiter nodded and walked away from the group.

Phillip began the conversation. "I wanted to get together with you for a few minutes in an attempt to add some semblance of meaning to this adventure. I was hoping you could shed some light on the events of the last few days." Phillip shifted in his chair. "Why don't you start at the beginning, back in Argentina when this whole thing started?"

•   •   •   •   •

"And from there you decided to go to Cartagena and take a little vacation to the islands?" Phillip interjected as Lorne detailed accounts of their activities.

He nodded his head in agreement. "I was hoping I could hide long enough for them to lose interest and then somehow contact the Canadian embassy and get hold of the people who gave me the initial orders."

"And then suddenly you showed up," Tim Browning said. "Lucky for us that you did," he added.

Phillip Wright paused to ponder the entire story. He took a sip of his martini before he spoke. "That certainly is a mess. Do you have any idea who this fellow Rolf might be?"

"I would imagine he works for the Argentine government." McPherson paused. "I'm sure they wouldn't want to send anyone official because this is quite an embarrassing situation."

Phillip listened intently. "The people I work for know little about you, however they feel that it's important to get you back to Canada so the government can get to the bottom of the entire matter."

The waiter returned to the table with his order pad and asked if they wanted refills.

McPherson shook his head and raised his hands at the same time. "No, I think I'd better be getting to bed. I'm tired."

"That'll be all, thank you," Phillip said to the waiter.

The threesome left the bar without speaking. The recollection of the events of several weeks ago had been very stressful to McPherson. Phillip sensed his feelings and could not think of anything to say. They rode the elevator in silence.

"Can we meet for breakfast at eight tomorrow morning?" Phillip asked.

Browning and McPherson nodded in agreement and the three men departed for their rooms.

18   PANIC

Willem Rolf quickly cleared Customs in Montego Bay, arousing suspicion with his abrupt manner of entry. Chartered planes were not a common occurrence in the hot, island city. He stopped in the lobby of the airport and glanced at his surroundings, expecting to find nothing. It was more an instinctive precaution than anything else. The tall German walked through the doors and hailed the first cab he could find. On his way downtown, he mentally scheduled his timetable to deal with the up and coming events and to arrange a proper search for Phillip Wright and the McPhersons. He knew the troupe had to be some-where in Montego Bay and he assumed they would be taking the noon flight to Toronto. The strenuous events of the last two days gave Rolf certainty that the company he was pursuing was holed up in a comfortable hotel.

The cab driver gently came to a stop at the entrance to one of Montego Bay's most luxurious hotels. The lobby was lined with mirrored tiles and ornate wall-hangings. The atmosphere was lively and buzzing with tourists from all walks of life. Briefcase at his side, chin up high, Willem Rolf marched in a straight line through the conglomeration of people, directly to the front desk.

Once in his room he allowed himself a few moments of relaxation. He scanned the menu and ordered from the room service section. He then discarded his clothes onto a chair and headed for a hot, steamy shower. He closed his eyes and pointed his face upward to greet the misty spray of the piping hot water. Shortly after he placed the white terry cloth bathrobe over his clammy body his dinner arrived with all the elegance associated with a five star hotel.

He finished his dinner and lifted the telephone directly from the night table, scanning the yellow pages for hotels. He assumed that Phillip Wright would use fictitious names for his company and, therefore. Rolf had used an urgent family matter as an excuse to ask questions about his targets.

At ten minutes before midnight he threw the telephone book noisily onto the floor. He was exhausted from the numerous telephone calls, all without success. The group of people he was searching for were nowhere to be found. He stood up and walked to the window, parting the beige curtains and allowing his eyes to slowly sweep across the brightly lit beachfront area of Montego Bay. The cool breeze from the air-conditioning unit located directly below the window blew upward onto his face. Where had he gone wrong? Perhaps Wright had split the group up. He pondered the thought for a few moments but discounted the idea, knowing it was extremely illogical and dangerous and Wright would never have taken such a risk. Again he scanned the telephone directory in the event he had neglected a small line of print. Every hotel in the book had been checked off. Every one had been called and descriptions had been given. Only two hotels had encountered shift changes, although they both assured Rolf that the people he was looking for had definitely not checked in. He exhaled slowly and took a Grand Marnier from the mini bar. As he felt the sharp pinch of the thick, warm, orange liqueur trickle along his throat, he became engulfed by his dilemma.

Initially he had decided to search the city but discounted the idea as the group certainly would be tired and had probably gone to an early bed. On the other hand, perhaps Phillip Wright had taken his charges from Montego Bay earlier that day and would return in time to catch the flight to Canada. Rolf decided he would go to the airport first thing in the morning anticipating the arrival of the six of them.

A sudden thought occurred to him. What if Phillip Wright had somehow made his way to Kingston and was planning to board the flight there? The plane did after all stop in Kingston before its return to Toronto. Rolf would have to board in Montego Bay even if he did not see Phillip Wright or any of the McPherson clan. What if the group had decided to lay low for awhile and catch a flight in two days? He slowly rubbed his chin and thought deeply. It was time to phone his superiors. A decision had to be made, a decision that could prove vital to the success of this caper. It was a decision that he did not wish to make alone.

He opened his briefcase and removed a small black address book. His hand lifted the telephone receiver slowly and he felt perspiration building in his palm. Willem Rolf was accustomed to acting alone. He was not in the habit of looking for directions from others. This time, however, he was under contract and was being paid for a specific task. He felt a telephone call would not be viewed favourably by the people who had hired him.

The telephone rang four times before it was finally answered.

"Yes, this is Rolf." He waited for a response. There was none. He inhaled deeply and began to relay the events leading up to the present situation.

"Yes, of course, I understand." Rolf replaced the receiver back on the cradle.

The decision had been made. It was a simple one. He was to take the morning flight from Montego Bay to Kingston and de-plane. If Phillip Wright and the rest of the party was not at the airport ready to board, Rolf would wait in Kingston until the following day. If the small group did appear Rolf would do everything in his power to capture McPherson. His orders had been strict. McPherson was all that mattered. The other five members of the group were expendable.

He contacted the front desk and asked for the airport telephone number. After several moments he was in touch with the airline counter at Montego Bay Airport. He booked a flight from Montego Bay to Kingston for the next morning, noting the times and flight numbers on a small sheet of paper.

He swallowed the last drops of Grand Marnier and retired for a restful night's sleep, setting a wake up call which would allow enough time for his preparations prior to his departure in the morning.

Phillip Wright was the first one downstairs and arranged for breakfast seating in the restaurant. The waiter arrived with steaming hot coffee and a basket of cinnamon rolls.

"Good morning." Phillip greeted Kristy McPherson as she sat across from him.

"How did you sleep?"

"Quite good," Phillip replied. "Are you ready for your flight?"

"Yes I'm packed and raring to go."

The waiter returned with coffee and left a pitcher of hot milk and a large, white, sugar bowl.

"I'm going to miss the tropics," Kristy said. "But I'm really anxious to get back to Canada and see all of my friends."

"I'm looking forward to a few days off myself."

"Will you be flying back to Toronto with us?"

"Yes, I plan to."

"Why don't you stay with us. I'm sure we'll be in Toronto for three or four days until Daddy gets things sorted out."

"I'm not sure if I can, I'll have to check with my office and see what they've got planned for me."

"It would be great if you could. We could have lots of fun."

Phillip smiled as he stared into Kristy's deep blue eyes. He found her extremely attractive in a devious way. Her skin was smooth and her face was artistically framed by soft golden brown hair. Was he reading more into her statement than she had intended? A few days rest might not be a bad idea, he thought to himself. He had been to Toronto several times and enjoyed the city. The cosmopolitan way of life and the mixture of many different cultures added a flare of savoir faire to the many restaurants and nightclubs.

Tim Browning, followed directly by Lorne, Rhonda and Jimmy McPherson joined the twosome. They enjoyed a well-cooked breakfast and engaged in conversation of planned events. Lorne expected to be in Toronto for several days and considered a trip to Ottawa as well.

Trevor was waiting for them in the lobby as Phillip checked out of the hotel. The group squeezed into the automobile for the five hour journey from Ocho Rios to Kingston.

The seating arrangements in the car were extremely cramped. Even though it was a wide-bodied automobile, seven people could not sit comfortably.

Everyone dreaded the long expedition ahead. Phillip sat in the front with Tim Browning and Trevor. Kristy was snuggled in between her parents with her brother Jimmy sitting on her father's lap. It had been decided that they would stop every hour to stretch and possibly exchange seats. Phillip explained that the discomfort felt now would be well worth it. It was necessary to administer every possible precaution to ensure the safety of his charges. Phillip did not underestimate the ability of Willem Rolf. He had so far proven to be a mysterious thorn in his side. Without Rolf's persistent pursuing, Phillip's assignment would have been greatly simplified. He would now be in Canada enjoying a little rest instead of being crammed into an automobile, on the run through the hot, distant country-side. A van or minibus would have been more conspicuous. Phillip had always been taught to select a course of action, analyse it, and remove the obvious.

"What do you think the chances of us being followed this far are?" Rhonda McPherson asked.

Phillip shifted his weight to the side and turned his head slightly. "I wouldn't put it past this guy, in fact I'd put money on it."

"But there is no way that he can come into Jamaica until later this morning," Tim Browning said.

"I know," Phillip replied. "I'm probably just being over cautious. I feel, because we've come this far, I don't want to take any unnecessary risks."

"How much time do you think we'll have at the airport in Kingston?" Lorne McPherson asked.

"Probably about forty-five minutes to an hour if all goes well." Phillip looked at Trevor as if seeking confirmation.

The Jamaican cab driver was nodding his head, yawning at the same time. The whites of his eyes were bloodshot, a contrast with the dark complexion of the skin. Phillip wondered if he had enjoyed himself the night before but decided not to embarrass the man by asking.

The automobile sped along the dusty paved road of downtown Ocho Rios. The centre of town consisted of a large square surrounding an immense statue partially sub-

merged in the centre of a round fountain. The perimeter of
the quadrate was lined with Spanish-style buildings that
had stood for many years. As the early morning sunrise
shortened the shadows within the square, people were gathering in small groups to discuss the day's events. Trevor
spun the car around the fountain and headed onto the main
road leading out of Ocho Rios. The sound of the squealing
rubber meeting the hot pavement was very audible and
heads could be seen turning in the direction of the speeding
automobile.

"Take it easy," Phillip said.

"Sorry man." Trevor eased slightly on the accelerator, slowing the car to a more acceptable pace.

The main road leading from Ocho Rios began to
narrow as they left the city limits. Run down buildings were
blotted recklessly along its side. Traffic signs were a rarity
and each driver seemed to invent his own set of rules.
Although the road remained paved it became quite bumpy,
increasing the already high level of discomfort experienced
by the little company.

Willem Rolf finished a delicious breakfast of soft-boiled
eggs, fresh fruit and brown toast. He was enjoying his
coffee and reading the newspaper as the waitress brought
the bill to his table. He smiled at the pretty, brown-skinned
girl and thanked her. He had purchased new clothes in a
small store next to the hotel. Continual travel did not allow
for frequent acquisitions of a new wardrobe. This time he
had been fortunate. The light brown slacks, gray striped
shirt and tan jacket fit him to perfection. He removed an
adequate amount of money from his wallet, ensuring that
the waitress would not be disappointed with the prompt
service she had given him, and picked up his attaché case,
leaving the restaurant for the airport. The flight to Kingston would take half an hour and there would be a one hour
layover. The most difficult part would be leaving the air-

craft inconspicuously and finding a secluded corner in the terminal building so that he could scrutinize the area.

The plane was half empty and both seats in his row were unoccupied. The flight attendant brought newspapers and magazines prior to a smooth takeoff and uneventful journey. Rolf rested his head against the seat back and gently closed his eyes. He reminisced about the events of the last few days and tried to arrive at some concrete conclusions. He realized that time was quickly running out and he had one last chance to intervene with Phillip Wright's plans. If he was not successful in Kingston, the troupe would be on its way to Canada and out of his reach permanently. His superiors would be extremely upset and quite possibly not pay him the money owed. He could not allow that to happen. He must succeed.

Rolf had decided he did not want to be in Kingston alone. Although he felt that individually none of the people he was pursuing would be a match for him, he did feel as a unit they could easily overpower him. He had arranged to meet two men at the airport in Kingston.

Desmond and Seamus Guilderdale, brothers who made their home in Ireland, were heavily involved in IRA activities. Both men were giant masses of muscular flesh in the fittest of shape. Rolf had worked with them before and liked their approach to business. They asked no questions, performed their tasks to perfection and, above all, kept their mouths shut. His sources had told him they were working in Miami and he had arranged for a flight for them to Kingston earlier that day. He had also told them to be on the lookout for Phillip Wright and the McPherson family should they arrive at the airport before Rolf's plane landed.

Yes Mr. Wright, he thought, this time you will not be so lucky.

"About another twenty minutes and we will be at the airport," Trevor said as the car travelled quickly along the unassumed roads. They had stopped several times to rear-range seating and stretch their legs. Although it was cramped, it had not been as uncomfortable as first imagined.

They arrived at the airport and Trevor pulled the taxi up to the front doors of the terminal building.

"I never want to sit in a car again as long as I live," Kristy McPherson said, extending her hands in the air as far as they would reach. Tim Browning smiled but Kristy's attention was directed towards Phillip.

Everyone said goodbye to Trevor and Phillip removed a sizeable amount of cash from his briefcase, handing it to the black driver.

"I can't thank you enough. I don't think we could have done any of this without your help."

"Thank you." Trevor smiled as he looked at the cash. "Next time you are in Mo' Bay you call me."

Phillip led the group through the glass doors and formed a small circle just inside the building, shielded by an array of various tropical plants.

"If you folks will wait here I'll go and arrange for the tickets. The flight doesn't leave for another ninety minutes. Please be on the lookout for anything or anyone that looks suspicious."

"I don't see how they could have followed us here," Tim Browning said. It was more a statement than a question.

"I know it's unlikely," Phillip replied, "but this is the last possible place they could intercept us before we get back to Canada, and we still have an hour and a half to kill."

Phillip eyed all the passengers walking through the busy tourist area as he made his way to the airline counter. There were several people in front of him and he nervously scanned each of them, continually glancing around the airport for signs of Willem Rolf.

Beside him a man and woman were attempting to subdue piercing screams from a small child unhappy with her strange surroundings. Phillip smiled as the curly-haired girl's mouth opened wide, revealing two gaps where baby teeth had recently given way to new, permanent ones. She emitted a loud, ear-shattering shriek, making Phillip and two men next to him cringe in an effort to shield their senses from the deafening sounds.

At long last Phillip's turn at the wicket arrived. "Six tickets to Toronto please."

The friendly attendant complied with Phillip's request and keyed the information into the computer terminal before her.

"I guess she doesn't like flying," Phillip said, motioning to the small child who continued to shrill as her parents dragged her away. The girl behind the counter smiled and shook her head.

"What she needs is a good spanking," the girl said softly, ensuring that only Phillip heard her remark.

After paying for the tickets, Phillip returned to where he had left his party, glad to be rid of the screaming child. As he turned away from the counter, the two men behind him casually spoke to each other, motioning to the small group gathered in the corner. One of them nonchalantly walked in their direction as the other headed for the arrival section to await the Air Canada DC-8 coming in from Montego Bay.

Willem Rolf replaced his tray table into the snug cut out in the back of the seat in front of him at the request of the purser's announcement over the speakers. He glanced out the window and saw the thick, velvety-green foliage intermixed with roads and houses as they neared the populous area of Kingston, Jamaica. The coast line was very vivid. The greenish-blue waters and thick coastal forest were separated by a thin, white line of soft, sandy beach.

The plane began to descend as Rolf tightened his seat belt. Although he had no fear of flying he was always uncomfortable during ascents and landings.

He wondered if the Guilderdale brothers had arrived and would be waiting for him. More importantly he wondered if Phillip Wright and his group were at the airport.

When the plane came to a halt, Rolf stood and walked to the exit.

A sudden thought flashed panic into Phillip's mind.

"Wait here a moment," he addressed the group. "I'll be back in a few minutes." He dashed in the direction of the arrival section of the airport.

It had occurred to him that quite possibly Willem Rolf had made his way to Montego Bay and, having been unable to find Phillip's whereabouts, decided to take the flight to Kingston instead. Phillip wanted to ensure in his own mind that his thoughts were unfounded. Passengers were de-planing as Phillip arrived, most carrying tourist suitcases and complaining about the humidity of the vacation island. He looked around for signs of the man who had been relentlessly pursuing them for the past several days.

Willem Rolf stepped from the staircase to the hot, sticky pavement of the tarmac. He quickly scanned the entrance to which the other passengers were walking. To the right of the door he saw a loading dock where men were unloading luggage from small, blue, weather-beaten carts. He hastily made his way to the large opening without being seen by uniformed officials greeting passengers. Two men unloading suitcases stopped to look at the tall, blonde European walking in their direction. Ignoring them, he continued on to the wooden platform jumping up and stepping between the suitcases. He found the exit door and made his way into the terminal building. He had somehow managed to bypass Customs officials and entered the far end of the lobby. He scanned the crowd for a familiar face and felt his heart beat faster when he saw one of the Guilderdale brothers standing next to a soft drink machine.

Desmond Guilderdale was facing the opposite direction, scrutinizing the passenger gate and unaware of his superior's arrival.

"Desmond," Rolf whispered, "I am here."

The tall, husky Irishman, startled by the voice, spun around and smiled when he saw Rolf. Desmond Guilderdale motioned in Phillip's direction, alerting Rolf to the UN. agent's locus. Rolf, alarmed at the discovery, quietly led his accomplice away from the gate. Desmond explained how his brother was watching the McPhersons in a secluded corner of the terminal building. Rolf was ecstatic when he heard the news and smiled when he saw the entourage of people whom he had chased the better part of two weeks. Rolf greeted Seamus Guilderdale and congratulated both brothers on their excellent work.

Suddenly the expression of excitement changed to concern. "Where is McPherson, the tall, white-haired man?"

"Oh, he just went to the washroom," Seamus Guilderdale replied.

"Perfect," Rolf said. "Let's go to work."

Phillip scanned all of the passengers but saw no sign of Willem Rolf. Something began to nag at his subconscious. Something seemed amiss. His instincts told him a part of the puzzle was missing. Again he looked around. This time he spotted a tall, well-built, dark haired man scanning passengers as they de-planed. He looked at the man again and was certain he had seen him earlier that day. Phillip felt a shiver at the base of his spine working its way slowly upward along his back, ending with a deep piercing ache in his neck. The feeling of shock was quickly suppressed by fear. He turned and hurriedly walked amidst the people, back to the area where he had left his wards.

He froze in his tracks as he neared the group. "Where's Lorne?" he asked, afraid of what the answer might be.

"He went to the washroom," Rhonda replied.

Phillip grunted in disgust. "We don't have a lot of time. Something is not right here. I think we're being watched as well as followed. We'll be able to board the plane in a few minutes but first I'll have to make a phone call.

He addressed his attention to Tim Browning. "Can you get Lorne? I'll be back in a few minutes. Make sure no one leaves this area," he commanded.

Phillip walked to a bank of telephones and chose the one nearest him. He made the call, entering the proper codes and was instantly connected with Ed Bergan.

"I don't have a lot of time, Ed," Phillip said. "But here's what's happened." He paused a moment. "Because we've been followed by Rolf I decided to bypass Montego Bay and drive to Kingston instead. We're booked on a flight to Toronto which leaves here in half an hour. We're just going through Customs now. I have a feeling I'm being followed but I don't want to hang around to find out."

Ed Bergan praised Phillip on his excellent work. He also expressed gratitude for looking after the matter so efficiently. Ed said that he would look forward to seeing the group in Toronto on their arrival.

Phillip placed the receiver back on the wall cradle and lit a cigarette. He turned toward the group and saw Tim Browning running in his direction.

"He's not there, I can't find him!" he yelled speaking rapidly.

"What do you mean you can't find him?'

"Well he's not there," Tim replied.

Phillip ran to the washroom, followed closely by Tim Browning. He pushed both hands against the door as he entered the small beige coloured room. He stepped to a row of cubicles and slammed the door on each one. All but one were occupied. When Phillip pushed against the door it wouldn't budge. From inside came the sound of an irritated man yelling in Jamaican. Phillip apologized, at the same time hoisting himself up the door to look into the cubicle. Tim Browning was right. Lorne McPherson was not in the washroom. He stepped outside and walked back to his now concerned group.

"What's the matter?" Rhonda McPherson asked.

"Lorne is gone," Tim Browning replied.

"Isn't he in the washroom?" she asked, concern in her voice.

"No he's not," Tim said. "We checked it twice."

"Well he can't be far," Phillip said. "You check outside the airport I'll go this way." He motioned to the far end of the airport terminal.

The two men darted off in different directions. Phillip saw no sign of the men he had spotted earlier. There was certainly no indication that Rolf had arrived, however with McPherson's sudden disappearance it was evident that the tall, blonde German had made his way to Kingston.

19   VANISHED

After several minutes of unsuccessful searching, Phillip returned to the group. Tim Browning was already there but had not seen any trace of the missing scientist.

"He's vanished," Tim said.

Phillip checked his watch. "Okay, come with me," he ordered.

"You guys are going on the plane, while I stay behind and look for Lorne."

"I'm not leaving without my husband."

Phillip stared her coldly in the eyes. "Please remember we're both working for the same cause. There's absolutely nothing you can do here except become a target for anything else that may go amiss."

Reluctantly she grabbed Jimmy's hand and joined Kristy and Tim Browning. Together the foursome walked toward the Customs line.

Phillip rushed back to the ticket counter. "I would like to see your supervisor," he said to the young attendant behind the counter.

"That's him over there," the girl said, pointing in the direction of a white official seated at a desk directly behind her. The man was on the phone.

"I'll get him for you in a moment sir. Is there anything I could possibly help you with?" the girl asked politely.

"I'll wait for a moment."

Phillip removed his passport from his pocket as he sensed the man's telephone conversation coming to an end. He looked up at Phillip and then at the girl. He nodded his head and stepped from behind the desk. Phillip had opened the passport to his United Nations' clearance stamp and laid it on the counter. The man smiled at Phillip and stared slowly at the passport.

"How may I help you Mr. Wright?" the man asked. He had a heavy European accent, its origin unclear, but Phillip assumed it to be Slavic.

"When is the next flight out of here?"

"To which destination sir?"

"Any destination."

The man looked at the girl for assistance. She keyed some information onto her computer keyboard and waited for the data to appear on her screen.

"There is an Air Jamaica flight which leaves in about four minutes."

"Where is it heading?"

"It's going to Cairo."

Phillip paused for a moment. "When is the next one after that?"

"I'm afraid there are no other flights for an hour and twelve minutes. "

"How do I find out who's on board that Air Jamaica flight?"

"I'm sorry that information cannot be given out," the supervisor said.

"It must be obvious to you that this passport gives

me a certain amount of access to classified information. I
have no problem in contacting my superiors who will then
call your superiors and direct you to give me whatever
information I need. In order to save a lot of time and
embarrassment for yourself I would bypass the red tape if I
were you." The supervisor paused for a moment to ponder
the situation.

"You will have to come with me. We don't have that
information at this desk."

The man led Phillip along the counter to a small
area marked 'General Aviation'. Two computer systems
were being used by attendants who were keying information for several passengers lined up before them.

The supervisor spoke to the first attendant in Spanish. He kept his voice low so as not to attract any attention.
The man raised his finger, suggesting a moment's pause
while he completed the transaction in progress. Phillip
nervously tapped his fingers on the white countertop. The
attendant looked up and smiled at Phillip. Phillip did not
return the man's greeting. Moments later the attendant
asked a question of the supervisor. The man turned to
Phillip.

"What is the name of the person you are looking
for?"

"There are two people, Lorne McPherson or Willem
Rolf." The supervisor ordered the attendant to enter the
information. It took the system a short time to respond.

"Yes they're are both on this flight."

Phillip's heart sank. "When did they purchase tickets?"

The supervisor turned to the attendant and posed
several questions, again speaking in a low tone.

"He says they purchased the tickets from him a few
minutes ago."

"You have to stop that flight from taking off."

"I cannot, sir," the attendant said as he looked at the

screen. "The flight is already taxiing to the runway."

Phillip thought for a moment, then he looked at the supervisor. "Is this flight direct or are there any stops in between?"

The supervisor checked the screen. "There are several stops, sir. They are very tight. If you are thinking of intercepting them on route it would not be possible."

"When is the next flight to Cairo?"

"I will work that out at my desk for you señor." The supervisor thanked the attendant and began to walk back toward his desk. Phillip joined him on the opposite side of the counter. He paused for a moment.

"I'll be back in a second," Phillip said. "I just have to check on something." He walked toward the immigration desk as the supervisor returned to his area.

Phillip showed the security clerk his boarding pass and stepped through the electronic gate. The buzzer did not sound and he waited at the end of the conveyer belt for his briefcase to come out of the X-ray machine

Tim Browning, Rhonda McPherson and her two children had not yet left the waiting area. They stood up as Phillip approached.

Rhonda McPherson was first to speak. "Did you find him?"

"He's not here." Phillip's voice was drowned out by a noisy announcement coming from a nearby, shattered speaker.

"What do you mean he's not here?" Grave concern showed in her face. Small beads of perspiration were forming at the root of her hairline.

"Where is he?" Kristy asked, grabbing hold of her brother's hand, keeping her gaze fixed sternly on Phillip.

"He's on board a flight to Cairo."

"Cairo!" Rhonda McPherson exclaimed. "Cairo, Egypt?"

Phillip nodded his head. Rhonda looked at him.

"Why is he going to Cairo?" Her voice was slightly calmer as the reality of the situation sunk in.

"I don't know." Phillip replied. He avoided staring into her eyes, for he felt that he had disappointed her.

"Did he go there alone?" Tim Browning asked.

"I don't know." Phillip said softly. He did not wish to suggest foul play to these people as they were already concerned enough.

"Well you don't know very much. It was after all your job to get Dr. McPherson out of the country," Tim Browning said with a sharp fierceness.

Phillip could feel anger well up inside him. His hands began to tremble and he found it difficult to restrain his initial desire of lashing out at Tim Browning.

Kristy sensed Phillip's feelings and turned her attention to Tim Browning. "That's pretty unfair Tim, after all you were the one who let dad go into the washroom alone. If anyone is to blame it should be you."

Tim Browning was just about to reply when Phillip interjected. "I don't think it's going to do much good trying to blame each other for something that has already happened. I'm staying behind. You folks get on the plane and go back to Toronto. I'll go from here to Cairo and see if I can find him."

He could see resistance to his suggestion in the faces of the three adults standing before him. "I've got to phone my office and get some direction. I will tell them to meet you at the airport in Toronto." He raised his hand and touched Rhonda McPherson gently on the upper arm. "I'm sorry this had to happen, I'll do everything I can to find him." He took one quick glance at Kristy McPherson and turned away from the group, exiting past the security guard. He walked back to the telephones and, after inserting the coins, again dialed the number. He was in touch with Ed Bergan immediately.

"I have a problem Ed," Phillip began.

"What's up?"

"I've lost McPherson."

"What?" There was astonishment in Ed Bergan's voice. "How could you lose him? You phoned me from the airport a few minutes ago telling me everything was fine and you were about to board the flight."

"While I was on the phone to you he went to the washroom and never came back."

"Well, where did he go?"

"He's on a flight bound for Cairo."

"Cairo? Cairo, Egypt?"

"Yes," Phillip replied nodding his head

"What happened?"

"I'm not sure. When I couldn't find him anywhere I checked with the ticket agents and they said they had issued him a ticket to Cairo. Worst of it, was he is travelling with Willem Rolf."

"What!" Ed Bergan had anger in his voice. "How could that have happened?"

"I have no idea how Rolf got here so fast. But I have a feeling he had people waiting for us here at the airport. He must have come in on that flight from Montego Bay." Phillip waited for Bergan to make a comment. The line was still. "What I thought I would do was to catch the next flight to Cairo and take up the chase."

"Let me think for a moment." Again the line went silent.

"Why do you think he went to Cairo, Phil?"

"It was the next flight out of here. I don't think Rolf really cared where they were going as long as they got away from me. I'm sure he'll take the next flight out of Cairo back to South America."

"That's what I was thinking," Bergan said slowly. "It would probably make more sense for you to go to Buenos Aires and catch up with him there."

"I thought of that," Phillip replied. "I believe Rolf

would expect us to do that. It's for that reason I don't want
to wait. I'm sure they're going to be tired when they get to
Cairo and will probably spend a few hours resting. I think
we stand a better chance of catching them if I followed.
Besides we don't know where exactly in South America
they'll be heading for."

Again Bergan thought for a moment. "No," he
paused. "No, I think it's better if I arrange for someone to
meet them at the airport and intercept McPherson when
they land in Cairo. Why don't you fly back to Buenos Aires,
telephone me to let me know where you're staying. If
anything goes wrong in Cairo and they do head back I'll
call you and let you know what to do."

Phillip was not pleased. Ed Bergan was obviously
dissatisfied with the results. Not allowing Phillip to pursue
his quest to Cairo was Bergan's way of reprimanding him.
He had no choice but to obey his superior's demands.

"Can you arrange for some people to meet McPherson's wife and family at the airport in Toronto?" Phillip
asked.

Bergan could sense dissension in Phillip's tone but
he decided to leave it alone. "I'll get somebody to meet
them and take care of them. Make sure to contact me as
soon as you get to Buenos Aires." The line went dead and
Phillip slowly replaced the receiver back on the cradle. He
gazed at the wall momentarily and was startled from his
thoughts by a familiar voice behind him.

"What happened?"

Phillip was shocked to see Kristy McPherson and
Tim Browning standing there.

"What are you doing here?"

"We've decided we'll go with you," Kristy said.

"Oh no you're not," Phillip argued.

"Look," she spoke with authority. "He is my father
and if I should choose to go to Cairo then I'll go."

"I know how you feel. All I'm concerned about is

your safety."

"Well, you'll be there."

"That's just it, I'm not going."

"What do you mean you're not going?" Tim Browning asked.

"I'm going back to Buenos Aires."

"Why?"

"Because I was told to do so. They're dispatching other people in Cairo to intercept your father and Rolf when they land."

"Well that's pretty stupid. They expect us to just sit around and wait for something to happen." Kristy was upset and it showed in her voice.

"Where is your mother and Jimmy?"

"They're on the flight back to Toronto."

"At least we did something right." Phillip muttered.

"I'm going to get some coffee. Do you want one?" Tim Browning asked.

Both Kristy and Phillip nodded their head. Phillip removed a cigarette from his package, lit it and offered one to Kristy. He watched as she cupped her hands around his and lit the flame to her cigarette. Tim Browning returned with three coffees. The trio sat on a soft, cushioned bench along the wall drinking the coffee and talking about the events that had happened over the last several days.

"What will they do to Lorne?" Tim Browning asked.

"Well if Rolf is with him and has his way, they'll probably turn around and come back to Argentina."

"It doesn't make any sense for us to wait in Buenos Aires when we're not even sure if that's where he's going," Kristy said with firmness in her voice.

Phillip was quiet as Kristy and Tim went over alternate actions. Kristy addressed her attention to Phillip.

"What are you thinking about?"

"I'm going to phone my section in London. I'll try and find out who's going to meet them in Cairo. If I know the person I'll see if I can get a hold of him and maybe they can let us know what's happening."

"Do you think it's wise to do that?" Tim asked.

"Don't be idiotic," Kristy said as she frowned at Tim.

Phillip stepped to the phones and, using the codes written on the last page of his passport, made the proper connection. A familiar voice answered the telephone and asked the purpose of his call. Phillip gave her a code word to verify the authenticity of his call.

"I thought it was you," a friendly girl's voice said through the receiver. "Where are you calling from?"

"A public telephone."

"And how is your vacation Mr. Wright?"

"I wish it was a vacation," Phillip said.

"What do you mean, are you not having fun?"

"Anything but, I'm putting in overtime and this heat in South America is killing me."

"South America?" the girl seemed surprised. "Your file came up as inactive on the screen. It has you signed out in Rome on several day's leave."

"I've been lent out to do some work for another government," Phillip said.

"It should still show up on my computer," the girl said. "Oh well I guess I don't have the information yet." She paused. "How can I help you?"

"Is Peter in?"

The girl was silent for a moment. She stuttered slowly "I guess you haven't heard." She paused.

"Heard what?"

"Peter was rushed to the hospital two days ago with a heart attack. Apparently he's okay but he can't be disturbed by any business whatsoever."

"What?" Phillip asked in astonishment. He had always been fond of his superior. Ever since their first meeting in Vienna so many years ago. "What happened?"

"He was driving home from the office when suddenly he felt ill. The automobile crashed but fortunately he wasn't hurt. It wasn't until the ambulance arrived that they diagnosed the heart attack. It was probably the accident that saved his life. He received immediate medical attention and is now resting comfortably. It appears he'll be away for several months."

"Did you want to talk to Raymond?" the girl asked.

Raymond LeBlanc was second in charge directly after Peter Alexander. Unlike Peter, Raymond was extremely casual and paid very little attention to detail. He performed the job efficiently, which was the only concern the organization had.

"No, that's okay, I wonder if you could help me though. Do you have the name of our operative in Cairo?"

"The only name I have is the person who is in charge of the Mid East sector."

"That's perfect, can you give me a code number where I can reach him as well please?"

The girl paused for a moment, then relayed the information to Phillip. He scrambled for a pencil in his shirt pocket and scribbled the digits on a blank page in his passport. "Thanks very much for you help," he said and replaced the receiver.

Phillip gathered more coins from his pocket and slowly placed them into the small, chrome-plated slot of the telephone unit. He waited for several clicks and dialed the numbers given him. The phone rang twice.

"Is Amr El Hab there please?" Phillip asked when a man answered the phone.

"Speaking."

"Amr, this is Phillip Wright, can you talk?"

"Phillip, of course I can. How are you?"

"Good thanks, and you?"

"Very well, it's been a long time."

"Too long." Phillip paused momentarily. "I have a

problem and I need some help. Have you been asked to post a man or two at the airport in Cairo within the next 24 hours?"

"I have no directives whatsoever. Why, what is happening at the airport?"

"I've been trailing someone in South America on behalf of the Canadian government, however I've lost him. All I know is he's on a flight to Cairo which should arrive sometime tomorrow evening. The person I'm reporting to on this assignment said he'd arrange for someone to go to the airport and apprehend him. I was told to stay here. My reason for calling you is to see if you can keep me posted."

"What do you mean the person you are reporting to?"

"This is an assignment sponsored by the Canadian government. I'm not sure how we got into this, you know how things go. I got my orders in Rome."

"Well they must be using their own people because there has been no contact made through my office."

Phillip paused to think for a moment. "I wonder if you could do me a favour. If you have the time could you go to the airport and check on the flight?" Phillip gave Amr the flight details.

"I think I might be able to do that. Who is it I am looking for?"

"At least two people, possibly four. The key person is a man in his mid-fifties. Tall and slim with gray hair. He is accompanied by a blonde-haired man in his mid-thirties with a square face and a German accent. They may be accompanied by two other people. Both seem in their late twenties, well-built with black hair. They won't be expecting anyone, so they may travel as a group."

"What do you want me to do if I should see them?"

"If you could just keep an eye on them I'll give you a call shortly. I'm going to see if I can get a flight to Cairo."

"That is not a problem. I will look forward to hearing from you."

Phillip returned to his seat. Kristy and Tim were engaged in conversation. They both stopped talking when Phillip approached and looked inquisitively in his direction.

"I think we are going to make a few changes. Nobody from our office has been contacted for any surveillance work at Cairo airport which means the person I'm reporting to is going through different channels. I couldn't get in touch with my boss for direction so here's what we'll do. I've asked my contact from the Middle East to go to the airport and wait for the arrival of the flight. He'll report on the whereabouts of your father and Rolf. In the meantime we're going to make arrangements to catch the next flight to Cairo. I don't expect them to turn around immediately. I think they'll wait for a little while to get some rest and cool down. Hopefully we'll be there before they depart."

Phillip led the way back to the ticket counter, looking for the supervisor with whom he had dealt earlier. The man was completing a transaction with a customer. He saw Phillip approach and smiled.

"I have the information you requested sir. I will be with you in a moment."

Phillip turned his attention to Kristy and Tim, addressing their inquisitive faces. "I asked a little while ago about the quickest flight to Cairo."

The man gave a couple of passengers their boarding passes and directed them to the departure lounge.

"Unfortunately the fastest journey to Cairo is also the most tedious." He smiled as he continued. "There is a flight leaving here in approximately two hours. It will take you to New York where you will have to take a transfer on Olympic four-twelve to Athens . There you will have to transfer again, on Olympic flight three twenty-five to Cairo. The entire travelling time will be seventeen and a half hours. There is nothing faster, but there are flights that will take you into the U.S. and then direct to Cairo. These would mean less travelling time but you would not arrive their for at least twenty-six to thirty-six hours."

"I don't see any problem with a few stopovers," Phillip replied. "Can we do all the ticketing here?"

"Yes we can. Shall I arrange it?"

Phillip nodded his head. He looked at the clock and then back to the attendant. "What is the time difference between Cairo and here?"

The attendant looked at a small sheet of paper taped to the inside of the counter. He ran his finger along a series of numbers. He squinted slightly as he tried to read the near illegible text. I believe it is seven hours." Again Phillip calculated the time of travel.

"And the name?" the supervisor asked. Phillip asked Kristy to give the details to the man while he stepped back to a small secluded corner in the terminal building. He opened his briefcase and popped a small lever ejecting the compartment that contained U.S. currency. He removed what he felt would be enough for three fares and replaced the drawer, closing the briefcase and securing the latches. He walked back to Kristy and Tim.

"What are we doing about the return trip?" Tim asked in obvious response to a question posed him by the supervisor behind the ticket counter.

"It'll just be a one way fare," Phillip replied.

The ticket supervisor continued entering information onto the keyboard.

He looked in the direction of Phillip. "How will you be paying for this sir?"

"U.S. dollars."

The man nodded and seconds later they heard their tickets being printed from a small printer to the right of where he was standing.

Phillip glanced carefully around and quickly removed the currency from his pocket. He counted out an appropriate amount of bills.

"We do not often get this much cash at one time señor," the man behind the counter said as he took the money and carefully counted it in front of Phillip.

He seemed satisfied and removed the tickets from the printer, placing each of them inside a boarding pass sleeve.

"Your flight will leave in approximately two hours. Please be at the boarding gate no later than forty-five minutes prior to departure. Enjoy your journey."

"What do we do now?" Kristy asked.

"How about some lunch?"

The threesome decided that food was an excellent idea.

"I just want to make one phone call," Phillip said as he walked toward a bank of telephones hanging on the wall. Again he removed his passport and entered the codes in order to reach Amr El Hab. He explained that he had arranged for transportation and they would be arriving in Cairo at approximately nine-thirty the next evening. Amr told him he had contacted the airport and McPherson's flight was on time. It was scheduled to arrive in Cairo two hours before Phillip.

Phillip thanked his friend and hung up the phone. "Let's go eat," he said as the trio headed toward a small cafeteria at the far end of the terminal building.

20   Giza

The fatigued travellers boarded the mammoth, supersonic aircraft and secured three seats in a row. Tim had slumped in the window seat, Kristy sat in the centre and Phillip was stretched out in an aisle seat. He preferred the corridor. It gave him a chance to elongate his legs. Moments after takeoff, the flight escort approached the threesome to take their beverage requests. The attendant smiled and proceeded to the next seat. Phillip massaged his eyes with both hands, feeling tense pain and pressure from sleepless nights endured throughout the past few weeks. He declined the headset offered him without inquiring what the movie was going to be. He detested air travel which forced one to pay for drinks and other amenities. Last minute bookings, however, did not allow for any luxuries on this flight.

An announcement concerning the duration of the flight, as well as vital statistics, was made by the pilot, followed shortly by the purser's explanation of meals. There would be ample opportunity to rest before any in-flight activity took place.

As languid as Phillip felt, sleep would not arrive. He continually shifted in his seat, endeavouring to ignore the events of recent times. He unveiled his eyes and scrutinized his fellow passengers. They were fast asleep and he grimaced as he rubbed his forehead in agony at the ease with which they dozed off.

Phillip could not put his mind to rest as the tedious journey slowly continued along endless miles of sky and clouds. They stopped in New York and again in Athens with just enough time to rush to their next boarding gate. The travelling took its toll and the passengers grew weary with discomfort and concern.

"What's the matter?" Kristy asked in a soft, sheepish tone.

Phillip glanced at her. A warm feeling overcame him as he observed her snuggled deep into her seat. Her hair had loosely settled over half her face and she slowly brushed it to one side as she squinted in Phillip's direction.

"Nothing," Phillip replied. "I was just wondering what would happen when they find out I've disobeyed orders and didn't go to Buenos Aires."

"Will you get into trouble?"

"Probably, if they find out what I've done. Hopefully we'll be able to wrap this thing up in Cairo before anybody's aware of where I am".

"Don't worry," she said compassionately. "I'm sure you'll find them in Cairo." She gently placed her hand on top of his and squeezed tightly. He smiled at her.

"You'd better go back to sleep."

She smiled tenderly as she took the small cushion which had fallen onto Tim's lap and placed it against Phillip's shoulder, tilting her head against it. She closed her eyes and Phillip stroked her hair with his other hand.

Dinner was served two and a half hours before the designated time of arrival. It was typical, unappetizing, airline food. Watered-down meat was accompanied by rubbery vegetables. Even concentrated fruit juice could not dissolve the crunchy potatoes Phillip tried to spear with his plastic fork.

"How are we doing?" Tim asked as he was awakened from a sound sleep by the clanging of breakfast platters being disbursed throughout the plane.

Kristy raised her head and stretched her arms. It took Tim Browning a moment to realize she had slept with her head resting on Phillip's shoulder. His face flushed slightly and he felt a wave of anger building deep within.

"What time is it?" Kristy asked.

"It's seven p.m. We'll be landing in about two hours."

Tim's inconspicuous silence could be felt by Phillip and Kristy. The remainder of breakfast was eaten with little conversation.

The gigantic DC-10 hovered over the runway as the pilot allowed the wheels to grasp the pavement below. The runways at Cairo International Airport were extremely long and far away from the main terminal buildings. Kristy was busy applying a layer of lipstick to her moist lips. She glanced at Tim and smiled. He did not return the greeting.

As soon as the aircraft came to a halt Phillip stood up and stretched his tired legs. Throughout the airplane people were beginning to rise and remove articles from the overhead compartments. An announcement could be faintly heard asking everyone to remain in their seats as the door of the aircraft opened and a ground official boarded the plane. A motorized ladder had been brought to the door and from the window the terminal building was visible in the distance.

"What's going on?" Kristy asked.

"I'm not sure," Phillip said, "but it probably has something to do with security." The passengers were called by row number and asked to walk past the guard down the stairs and form a straight line toward a small table that had been set up with several Customs officials behind it. Phillip was glad they were not sitting too far back. When their row was called the threesome checked for belongings and walked briskly toward the exit of the plane.

"Wow! Look at that," Kristy exclaimed. Phillip's eyes followed the direction in which she was pointing. On the tarmac, about thirty feet away from where they stood, were several armoured vehicles surrounded by a dozen or so accoutred guards.

"Is this all for us?" Kristy asked.

Phillip smiled.

"What's going on?" Tim asked as he stepped through the door onto the metal platform at the top of the ladder.

The flight attendant standing next to him responded. "They always do this with Olympic Airlines. We transport a lot of people from Libya who work in Egypt. Therefore the security is very high.

The airport official motioned for Phillip, Kristy and Tim to walk down the stairs toward one of the Customs representatives seated behind the desk on the tarmac. At the bottom of the stairwell they were met by a soldier carrying a machine gun. Phillip felt uncomfortable. He had never been to Cairo and had very little experience in this part of the world. He wasn't sure how these officials would react to his position, especially if they searched him and found the hidden compartment full of cash in his briefcase.

The threesome halted when they came to a small, portable, wooden desk behind which was seated an elderly man in an open-collared, light-brown uniform. He was surrounded by several men sporting automatic weapons and poised for action.

"Your passports please," he said in a monotone voice.

The threesome readily supplied the small, blue-coloured booklets to the officials. He looked at Kristy McPherson and then stared at her picture.

"Where were you born?"

"Canada," she replied, attempting to be as business-like as possible.

"What is the purpose of your trip?"

"Just a vacation."

Phillip was impressed by the casual manner with which she handled the questions posed to her by the Customs official. The obese man sitting behind the desk eyed her face cautiously. Without the slightest facial muscle movement he stamped her passport and returned it to her. She opened her purse and, as she put the passport inside, one of the guards leaned forward and grabbed the small, black, leather bag from her hands. The tall soldier opened the purse and motioned for Kristy to walk and stand beside him. She looked at Phillip who nodded to her to comply with the guard's request. A third man carrying a metal detector approached her and, after flipping a small switch, began to scan her body with the electronic device.

"Your passport please?" the fat Customs official asked of Phillip. Phillip handed him the small, blue, official document and waited for the man to find the page with all of the personal data. "What is the purpose of your visit to Egypt?"

"Just a few days vacation." Phillip spoke calmly. He had been through this procedure many times in the past and knew what Customs officials were looking for. He had been trained to handle their questions diplomatically, without incident.

The guard stamped the passport and returned it to Phillip. The second man took his briefcase and opened it. He tried to turn the tumblers for the combination but the lock would not budge. He motioned to Phillip for assistance. Phillip opened the briefcase with ease and the guard rifled through the papers. He seemed satisfied at its contents and Phillip was relieved that he did not discover the sizable amount of currency. Phillip joined Kristy as they waited for Tim Browning to complete his turn with the guards.

The threesome walked along the pavement toward a green bus waiting to take passengers to the main terminal building. Sunset was early in Egypt and even though the temperature had cooled it was still quite warm by North American standards. Dust clouds could be seen swirling through the air against the rays of lamps lighting the area.

There was a lengthy delay on the bus as the guard scrutinized the passengers one at a time. Since a recent highjacking in the Middle East, security had been increased drastically. The luggage had been piled in a remote section of the airport, far away from the airplane and the buildings. Passengers, once they had passed Customs, had to make their way to where the luggage was piled and claim their own bag. These were then loaded onto a small dolly which took the suitcases to the building. Any baggage left un-claimed would be immediately disposed of.

The bus was filled to capacity and the heat was unbearable. The crowd increased its mumbling roar slightly as the motor was started. The ride from the airport to the terminal was tedious in the sweltering heat of the Egyptian evening.

As soon as the bus came to a halt, everyone rushed into the building and made their way to the passport control desk. Phillip was eyeing the crowd looking for his friend Amr. They were tenth from the wicket in what seemed to be the slowest moving line in the area.

"Why must we line up again?" Kristy asked.

"I think the people by the airplane were immigra-tion. This area looks like Customs. The security seems to be really high. I guess they're not taking any chances."

Phillip saw his friend Amr waving vigorously from the other side of the Customs barrier. He returned the greeting. Amr El Hab was about six foot two and in his mid-thirties. Although his head was almost bald, his features maintained a youthful appearance. He was dressed casually and unlike most other Egyptians, was wearing European clothes. He stood extremely straight and had a dignified, almost regal appearance. What little hair was remaining had been cut very short and had a reddish tint matching the colour of his thick moustache. Although his skin was a darker colour then most Europeans, it was not near as tanned as that of his fellow countrymen. Amr had been born in Egypt but was educated in Britain. He had been recruited by Peter Alexander about the same time Phillip had.

The trio of travellers had finally managed to pass the Egyptian Customs area. Under Egyptian law, all foreign currency had to be converted to Egyptian pounds. Because of the short duration of their stay, Phillip had argued against the conversion and at long last the guards had allowed them to keep their U.S. funds. The passport officials appeared to be immune to any rules set by their government. They had given Tim and Kristy a hard time about purchasing a visa for entrance into Egypt, however after the transfer of several U.S. dollars into their hands the visa was issued immediately.

Phillip walked to Amr and the two men warmly embraced each other. As is the custom in Egypt, Amr planted a kiss on each of Phillip's cheeks.

"It's good to see you my friend," Amr said, smiling as he spoke. Phillip returned the greeting and introduced his two travelling acquaintances. Amr took Kristy's hand and, as he raised it, bowed his head slightly, planting a kiss softly on the smooth skin.

"Enchanted to make your acquaintance," he said. "I should have realized that only Phillip Wright would bring such a beautiful person into our country. Kristy blushed slightly and turned her head away from Amr to face Phillip. She smiled sweetly.

Amr directed his attention to Tim Browning who

was not at all impressed by the Egyptian's manners.

"Very pleased to meet you," Amr said as he extended his hand. Tim Browning returned the handshake but said nothing.

The crowd at the airport was immense and people were wandering everywhere.

"You have no luggage?" Amr asked.

"None at all," Phillip replied. He was anxious to get down to business. "Have you found out anything?"

"Yes, let us get a taxi and I will fill you in as we ride to your hotel."

Amr led the group through the main doors, passing the luggage control section. They walked to the first available cab they could find.

"Mena House Hotel," Amr said to the cab driver standing beside the black Mercedes. The cabby began to shout in Arabic to Amr. The tall Egyptian returned with his own variation of guttural sounds, waving his arms as if to add more emphasis to his story. The three foreigners looked on inquisitively as the two Egyptians conversed back and forth. Finally the cab driver stepped back into his car and threw the door shut in disgust. Amr shook his head and motioned for Phillip and his compatriots to step into the auto. He walked around to the passenger's side and entered.

"What was that all about?" Phillip asked as he, Kristy and Tim stepped into the rear of the car.

"The hotel at which you are staying is about forty-five minutes from the airport and the driver doesn't want to drive that far because he is giving up a lot of fares."

The Mercedes sped recklessly from the parking lot onto the main street. Never before had Phillip experienced such treacherous driving. The speedometer was constantly between fifty and sixty miles per hour on streets not designed for more than forty. Even though the road had been painted with three white lines, cars were driving at five abreast. Once they neared the centre section of Cairo traffic began to slow down. Kristy and Tim were amazed at the amount of activity so late at night. The red traffic signals had absolutely no meaning. Cars were negotiating corners with other cars and every now and then a donkey, laden with heavy bundles of straw or dry goods, carefully ma-noeuvred its way in between the speeding traffic. A few uniformed policeman were spread along the streets and had no effect on the congested traffic. The taxicab darted from lane to lane and at one point manoeuvred over the curb. The passengers in the back seat began to fear for their lives.

"So what have you got for us?" Phillip asked of Amr.

Amr turned around and rested his arm on the back of his seat. "I saw your man McPherson get off the air-plane."

"Were there two people?" Phillip asked.

Amr shook his head. "No, there were four of them all together. A tall blonde man and two heavy set men. The blonde man seemed to take charge and they cleared Cus-toms with little difficulty."

"Do you know where they went?"

"Yes. I followed them to the Mena House Hotel, the same one that you are staying at." Arm shifted around in his seat in an effort to gain more comfort.

"All four of them checked into adjoining rooms and the last time I saw them they walked across the court yard into the main building of the hotel." Amr changed his tone to that of inquisition. "Who is this McPherson fellow?"

Phillip's thoughts were elsewhere and missed the question. He excused himself and after Amr repeated it answered as best he could. He went over the facts of the previous few weeks, finding great relief in being able to convey the occurrences to one of his peers. He explained the roles Kristy and Tim had played during the last few days as he concluded his summary of recent events.

"Did you arrange for rooms for us?" Phillip asked.

"Yes. You are registered under Smith."

"That's original," Phillip chuckled.

"Maybe in your country, but here Smith is an uncommon name."

"I am so happy that daddy is alright," Kristy said, a big grin on her face.

"Let's not rush up to him as soon as we get there." Phillip said rather softly.

"What?" Kristy asked in an astonishment. "Why not?"

"I think it would be wise if we followed your father and Rolf to see what their next move is."

"Why, what would that accomplish?"

"Rolf seemed quite anxious to take your father somewhere and if we were to grab him now, there would be little reason for this entire chase not to start over again. I think it would be wiser if we sat tight and followed them to see where they went."

Amr nodded in agreement with Phillip. "I think that Phillip is right. Judging from the size of the two thugs with your father we wouldn't stand a chance if they did catch us."

Kristy was visibly unhappy, however she thought it wise not to dispute the suggestions of the two operatives.

Tim Browning looked at her and gently squeezed her hand. "If he is in some kind of trouble it would be better if we saw it through rather than make things worse."

She did not withdraw her hand from his grasp. Out of the corner of his eye Phillip could see Tim's hand gently rubbing hers.

"When was the last time you contacted London?" Amr asked Phillip.

"About two weeks ago," Phillip said. "I did call briefly yesterday and heard about Peter's heart attack."

"I was curious if they were aware of your involvement in this caper?"

"Oh. Yes they are. I was given directives to meet

with an official of the Canadian government, and take my orders from him." A thought occurred to Phillip. "Which reminds me I must contact him as soon as I get to the hotel."

"We will be there in a few minutes."

"I'm glad," Kristy said. "The thought of a nice hot bath is really enticing."

"I can't get over the number of people here," Tim Browning said. He had released his grip of Kristy's hand at her request.

Amr smiled. "Egypt is probably one of the most prosperous third world countries. We have a population of forty-three million, thirteen of which live in Cairo itself. The average income is about $380 U.S. per year."

"That's incredible." Tim shook his head in disbelief.

The driver suddenly slammed the brakes, jolting the passengers forward. The irate cabby leaned on the horn. Through the front window they could see a donkey and cart crossing the road. The owner, dressed in typical Egyptian attire had jumped from the wagon and was head to head with the mule trying to keep him from walking into traffic. The floppy-eared animal had no intention of stopping and wandered into the intersection to be met by screeching tires and loud, blaring car horns.

"Is traffic always this heavy?" Tim Browning asked.

"It is," Amr replied. "They are attempting to build a subway system to alleviate some of the congestion. Until it is finished, however, I'm afraid we are stuck with this constant mess."

They crossed the main branch of the Nile as Amr pointed to certain land marks.

"What's that over there?" Kristy asked, pointing to a large mosque with its minaret reaching skyward.

"That is one of our most famous mosques. In fact the Shah of Iran is buried there."

"Are people generally friendly?" she asked.

"Very much so. The family element is very strong in Egypt. There is no welfare or unemployment insurance as you have. It is up to each member of the family to provide for his or her relatives. Although you may be harassed by beggars or vendors attempting to sell their wares, crime in our country is very low. The punishment is very severe and in most cases deters people from pursuing a life of felony."

Kristy was impressed by Amr's knowledge of his country and the colourful way in which he described it. "Do you live in Cairo?" Kristy asked.

Before Amr had a chance to answer Phillip interjected. "Amr heads up the Middle East sector of the organization we work for." He addressed his next question to Amr. "How many people do you have reporting to you now?"

"Twelve all together." He paused. "Sometimes I wish it was just myself back in the field. I thought there would be less stress in this type of job but let me tell you Phillip, you don't know how good you have it." Phillip smiled. "When are you going to settle down and get yourself a desk job?"

"Not me, in fact I'm thinking about leaving this business all together."

"You know you can't do that, they would never leave you alone."

"I take it that both you gentlemen have known each other for a long time?" Kristy asked.

"Oh yes," Amr said. "I finished my basic training when I met Phillip. He was a clerk in the office."

"I remember seeing Amr," Phillip said. "He had that James Bond appearance, of course he was much younger then." Everyone smiled.

"Because of my Egyptian background I was sent to the Middle East, and it was about five years after we met, that we actually worked together wasn't it?"

"Yes it was," Phillip said. "I just finished basic training and they send me on an assignment in Europe."

"Don't be so modest." Amr said. He then turned to Kristy. "Did you know that Phillip saved my life on that case?" Kristy looked at Phillip. He was blushing slightly.

"I must remember to collect that favour one of these days."

"Look over there!" Everyone one looked at Tim Browning who was pointing to the side of the road. Standing along side the pavement several hundred feet back, doused in moonlight, stood a massive conglomeration of rocks built by ancient Egyptians as a monument to one of their most celebrated rulers. The great pyramids of Giza dwarfed the tiny vehicle and the people in it. All three passengers were mesmerised and could not take their eyes off the wondrous sight.

"Your hotel is just up here on the right," Amr said as the car turned into a driveway, framed by a large wooden gate. Entering the grounds of the hotel was like entering a new dimension. The building was a magnificent structure completed in the late eighteen hundreds as a hunting lodge for one of the last kings of Egypt. The grass was a luscious green carpet and had been meticulously cared for. A large swimming pool was surrounded by bushes and the moonbeams bounced from its azure-blue water.

The Mercedes pulled up under the concrete canopy and came to a halt. Amr gave the driver some money and the four passengers exited the vehicle. They walked up the steps and opened the door into the lobby.

Kristy stood with her mouth gaping open as she took in the sights of the magnificent entrance to one of the world's finest hotels.

Phillip looked at her and smiled. "Close your mouth will you?" he said jokingly.

"This is unbelievable," she said. The lobby was finished in gold coloured paint, accented with white marble. Whenever someone spoke, a slight echo could be heard in the immense vestibule. Off to one side was a lounge and a bell captain's desk.

"Let me go and get your room keys," Amr said as he walked toward the front desk.

"This is incredible," Tim said. "What a difference between here and the other side of the road."

Amr returned promptly with three room keys. "I have to take your passports. They need them to report your presence to the police." He was met with disapproving glances from the three newcomers to his country. "It is standard procedure in Egypt."

They complied with his request and handed their small identification booklets to him. He dropped them off at the lobby desk as he led the threesome to the elevators. "Are you hungry at all?"

"Not me," Kristy said. "I'm more tired than anything else."

"Shall I join you for breakfast then tomorrow morning?" Amr asked.

"That would be fine," Phillip said. He extended his hand and Amr clasped it. Phillip smiled. "It's good to see you again Amr."

The Egyptian bade the threesome good night as they entered the elevator to retire for the evening after a strenuous day.

21 · DECEIVED

Phillip said good night as Tim Browning walked quietly along the carpeted hallway toward his room. He was extremely quiet and Phillip could barely hear him return the greeting. He entered his room without saying a word to Kristy.

"I wonder what's wrong with Tim?" Phillip asked.

"He's either tired or feeling neglected. You have to understand he's been trying to go out with me for the last two years and until you came along there wasn't any competition."

Phillip was surprised at her statement as he had never considered himself competition to Tim Browning. He was pleased with the prospect of Kristy considering him so.

"Well, good night," he said.

"Good night." She leaned forward kissing him gently on the cheek. "I'll see you at breakfast."

Phillip walked into his room and automatically checked behind the shower curtain and inside the closets. He was about to call Ed Bergan when he realized that the phone number had been written inside his passport and was now with the attendant at the front desk. He picked up his attaché case and exited the room, heading for the lobby.

Phillip was writing the number on a small piece of paper and was just about to leave the lobby when, from the corner of his eye, he spotted a tall man in a salmon-coloured jacket. Although he did not turn his body he arched his head slightly to get a clearer view of the man he hoped was Lorne McPherson. His heart pounded loudly when he made eye contact with the scientist. McPherson had not seen him. Where was Rolf? Why had they left him alone? McPherson walked toward the end of the lobby and climbed the staircase, gliding his hands along the bannister. Phillip waited a moment and surveyed the rest of the lobby to see if McPherson was being followed. Neither the two Irishmen nor Willem Rolf were in sight and Phillip felt confused. Why had McPherson been left on his own? He took his attaché case and carefully followed the scientist, engaging extra caution to avoid being spotted.

Along with several boutiques, the coffee shop was situated on the mezzanine floor. Phillip's eyes darted in all directions. He read the sign for the coffee shop and assumed his target had entered. He inched his way toward the entrance, being careful to maintain surveillance for any passers-by. No one he saw looked familiar or showed any sign of interest in him.

The entire hotel had been decorated in an Arabian Nights fantasy. The walls were covered with dark wood while thick Persian rugs covered the floors.

Phillip stopped as he entered the dining area. His heart raced with anticipation and his mind was filled with hundreds of questions by a sight several feet before him. Lorne McPherson sat at a table and was sipping a glass of white wine. He was wearing a salmon-coloured jacket with white slacks and was engaged in conversation with two men directly across from him. Phillip could not believe his eyes and he jumped back to ensure his secrecy. Willem Rolf was enjoying a beer and casually conversing with a short, overweight man sitting across from Lorne McPherson.

It was Ed Bergan!

Phillip saw the men smile several times as they spoke. He darted past the maitre d' approaching the table and headed back into the hallway outside the restaurant. He raced to the elevator and tapped his foot, nervously eyeing the entrance to the coffee shop, hoping that he had not been spotted. When the elevator finally arrived he rushed inside and closed the doors immediately.

Phillip sank in his chair and rested for a moment, attempting to gather his thoughts. He telephoned Amr at home but the Egyptian had not yet arrived. He left a message on the answering machine asking him to call as soon as possible. He expressed urgency in his voice.

Phillip decided to have a shower and turned up the volume on the bathroom telephone in fear of missing Amr's call. He had just stepped from the tub when the telephone rang.

"You called. Is anything wrong?"

"Yes, I just ran into Lorne McPherson in the coffee shop. He is having dinner with Ed Bergan."

"Who is Ed Bergan?"

"He's the man I was assigned to report to. He's the person I met in South America who told me of the entire situation. The man who represents the Canadian government and was adamant about finding McPherson. He is also the person who is supposed to be in Canada right now awaiting my telephone call."

"Slow down my friend. Obviously something has gone wrong." Amr paused for a moment. "What did they say when they saw you?"

"They didn't see me."

"Well that is good, Why don't I come over and we will try and talk this thing through and figure out what is going on?"

"If you don't mind. I'd really appreciate the help."

Phillip replaced the receiver and towel dried his body. His clothes were clammy so he decided to wear the bathrobe until they had dried.

Amr arrived within twenty minutes as Phillip was finishing dressing.

"I took the liberty of getting you this," Amr said as he removed an automatic Beretta from his pocket. "I'm certain you will find it a comfort during your stay in Cairo."

"Thank you very much," Phillip replied. "I wondered how I was going to get one of these." He rubbed his hand along the shaft of the automatic pistol, ejecting the magazine to check the clip ensuring it was filled to capacity.

"What would you like to drink?" Phillip asked as he walked toward the mini bar.

"Scotch with water would be just fine thank you." Amr sat down in a soft, comfortable chair by the window.

After the drinks were mixed Phillip seated himself and began, for the second time, to explain the events of the past few weeks. Amr listened intently, jotting notes on a piece of stationary left by the hotel on the small table beside his chair.

Phillip recounted how he had met Ed Bergan in Cartagena at the U.S. Consulate office. He talked in great detail about Rolf's intervention and Phillip being followed. He explained how he finally found the McPhersons and how they outran Rolf to Jamaica. Amr had almost finished his Scotch and water when Phillip concluded his tale. He reread the notes he had made and slumped in his chair, sighing a breath of air as he did so.

"Of course you contacted Bergan throughout your travels and updated him on your locations?"

Phillip nodded. "Yes, of course I did."

"And the fact that Rolf is sitting at a table with

Bergan proves that he is also working for Bergan."

"But that doesn't make any sense? Why bother hiring me?" Phillip paused to sip his drink. "And who is this guy Rolf anyway?"

"That is something we have to find out."

"If Rolf did work for Bergan that would explain why he had so little trouble finding out our whereabouts."

"What I don't understand," Amr said rubbing his chin as he spoke, "is why they were trying to kill you when you first arrived in Bogota?"

Phillip thought about the question. "Quite possibly they weren't trying to kill me, perhaps they were only following me. Things got rougher when I knew they were tracking me. Perhaps I just assumed they were trying to kill me."

Amr finished the rest of his drink and sat for a moment. "I think we should determine whether or not Bergan is legitimate."

"The directive I received from Ottawa was legit. It had the proper coding."

"That doesn't necessarily mean it was legitimate. There is always a chance there are leaks within the organization. A code, after all, is not the most difficult thing in the world to get a hold of."

Phillip thought back to the day he received the coded letter. All steps had been taken to ensure its authenticity. Then a thought struck him. "One thing, which probably doesn't mean anything, but when I called yesterday to London and found out about Peter's accident, the girl on the telephone said my number came up as being temporarily inactive. She said my file showed as being on vacation. We both just assumed that things were a little hectic at head office. If Bergan is not who he said he is then all of the things that have happened could be false." Phillip spoke more to himself than to Amr.

The Egyptian nodded in response to Phillip's statement.

"I wonder why Bergan wants McPherson?" Phillip asked.

"I don't know," Amr replied. "But I think we had better do some digging, and do it fast."

Phillip looked at his watch and walked to the night table to make a telephone call. After dialling the appropriate digits he was put in touch with his head office in London. He asked for Peter Alexander and the receptionist asked for his clearance code before she transferred the call. After several clicks the phone was put on hold, then rang and was answered by a stern military-voiced man. Phillip asked for Raymond LeBlanc. There was a click as his call was being transferred.

"Hello Phillip, how are you?" LeBlanc's voice was casual. He spoke with dignity and flair, sounding as if he was reading from a book. There were no stammers and no pauses.

"I was sorry to hear about Peter, how is he doing?"

"He's fine, but certainly you didn't call me at night just to find that out," Raymond LeBlanc said in a business-like tone. "Incidentally where have you been? Your file shows inactive for two weeks."

Phillip was not used to the harsh directness offered by the voice at the other end. He began to relay the events of the past few weeks and was surprised that he was not interrupted once.

At the completion of the story there was a sigh from the other end of the line. Neither man spoke and Phillip became uneasy.

"Well Phillip, it appears that we have been had. There was no coded message sent from here to you since your last assignment in Italy. Whoever these people are, they seem to have a good inside knowledge of our operation." He paused before continuing. "You know Phillip, this will not have a good reflection on your record."

Phillip was dumbfounded by the comment. There was absolutely no way he could have prevented this from happening. His initial reaction was anger toward the man who was replacing his superior. He immediately collected his emotions and suppressed them, knowing he would have to deal with that problem at a different time.

"I am going to do some digging to see if I can discover anything. In the meantime work with Amr and keep a close eye on Bergan and McPherson. I will contact you in thirty minutes."

Phillip gave LeBlanc the number of the hotel and replaced the receiver.

He turned his attention to Amr who was half way through his second scotch. "Well," the Egyptian said as he looked up, "what did he say?"

Phillip was thinking of his conversation with Raymond LeBlanc and missed part of Amr's question. He looked up grasping the gist of it. "Sorry. He said he's going to do some digging to see if he can find out anything. He'll call back in half an hour. He wants us to work together and keep Bergan and McPherson under surveillance."

"What is the matter?" Amr asked knowing that something was troubling Phillip.

"Nothing," Phillip said.

"He is probably blaming you for this, isn't he?"

Phillip nodded his head.

"Don't worry about that. It is a typical procedure. There is no way possible you could have prevented these events from happening. LeBlanc is only covering his butt because someone had to have access to some very sensitive information in order to transmit a coded message to you in the first place."

"That doesn't mean I like being a scapegoat."

"Have a drink," Amr said as he opened another bottle from the mini bar and poured its contents into the glass that Phillip was drinking from.

Phillip picked up the receiver and phoned the front desk. He asked if Ed Bergan was staying in the hotel. The concierge took a few minutes to look up the information but the reply was negative.

"You don't really think he would be using his own name do you?" Amr asked.

"There is always a chance he would. After all he didn't expect me to be following McPherson out here." Phillip paused to gather his thoughts. "Why don't you wait here for LeBlanc to phone. I'm going down to the restaurant to make sure the people are still there."

"What if they leave and split up?" Amr asked.

"I doubt very much if McPherson and Bergan will split up. Bergan spent a lot of time and effort trying to find McPherson. I don't really think he'll want to lose him now."

Phillip took the elevator to the mezzanine floor and looked in both directions to ensure that no one he knew was in sight before he stepped out into the carpeted hallway. He arrived at the entrance to the coffee shop and carefully stepped inside. He scanned the area very quickly and saw that most of the people had left. There were only a few patrons still enjoying the remnants of their meal. McPherson, Bergan and Rolf were not to be seen. Phillip looked carefully at all the occupied tables to ensure they hadn't changed seats.

The decor of the restaurant was magnificent. Long, thin, wooden spirals were suspended from the ceiling by gold coloured sashes which lined the perimeter of the restaurant. The ceiling was finished in dark brown walnut accentuated by a burgundy carpeted floor. The waitresses and waiters were dressed in bright orange jackets and were extremely well groomed.

The maitre d', his arm full of menus, approached Phillip. "A table for one sir?" he asked, tilting head slightly as he spoke.

"No, actually I would just like some information please."

The maitre d' looked inquisitively at the guest.

"There were three men seated at that table." Phillip pointed in the direction where only a short time ago he had been mystified by a change in events. "I wonder if you might know whether they had left the restaurant?"

The maitre d' looked in the direction that Phillip was pointing. "Yes I believe that they left about fifteen minutes ago."

"Would you have any idea of their names?"

"No sir, actually I do not." The maitre d' shook his head as he spoke.

Phillip reached in his pocket and removed some money. He discreetly handed twenty U.S. dollars to the maitre d'. "Would you have any idea where they might have gone?"

The maitre d' took the money and put it in his pocket before any of the staff could see him. "It is customary for our guests to pay their bill by check and sign it to the room. I will see if this happened." The maitre d' walked to the small corner where the cash register sat atop a brown, wooden pedestal. He picked up a number of tabs and scanned through them, removing two bills and stepping back to Phillip.

"These are the only two receipts which would apply." He leaned toward Phillip showing him the two bills.

Although the bills had been signed to the rooms, Phillip felt that they did not apply. "But these are only for two people. The table that I was referring to had three guests," Phillip said.

"Actually the table with three people only had two patrons that dined. The third gentleman who did not have anything to eat left about ten minutes before the others."

"Would you have any idea which person left early?"

"Yes, it was the youngest man. He was tall with

blonde hair."

That explains why the bill had been signed to their rooms, Phillip thought. Rolf would never had been that stupid. "Is there no time on the receipt?" Phillip asked.

"I'm sorry, this is embarrassing, but our register clock stopped working last week and has not yet been repaired."

Phillip made a note of the room numbers and thanked the maitre d' for his trouble.

"Not at all sir, perhaps you would like a coffee or something to eat?"

"No, thank you," Phillip said, wishing he had the time to enjoy some of the local cuisine. Although he felt hungry, he knew the excitement built up within him would not allow him to properly digest or enjoy his food at this time.

Phillip returned to his room in time to see Amr replace the telephone receiver back in its cradle.

"How did you make out?" the Egyptian asked.

"They had left the restaurant by the time I got there however the maitre d' was quite cooperative." Phillip paused for a moment. "Who was on the phone?" he asked.

"That was Raymond LeBlanc. Ed Bergan worked for the Canadian Mounted Police, or some division thereof, for a number of years He resigned about four and a half months ago. Apparently forced by his superiors. LeBlanc didn't know the reason but the man has absolutely no contact or dealings with the Canadian government. He is obviously acting either on his own or for someone else."

Phillip shook his head in disbelief. "I can't believe I was taken in so completely by this guy."

"Willem Rolf works on his own doing everything from assassinations to major political upheavals. He has been credited with at least three contract killings in the last four years."

"What about McPherson?"

"He seems to be on the level. LeBlanc doesn't know what the connection is between McPherson and Bergan. However McPherson is a scientist who was installing a nuclear reactor in Argentina and was placed under arrest for sabotage. The last communication showed he had escaped to Bogota where he was picked up by the police and was mysteriously lost."

"What is our next move?"

"LeBlanc wants us to continue with what we are doing. There is obviously something going on here and he wants us to see it through and report back anything we find out." Amr paused. "You mentioned that the maitre 'd was cooperative. What did he tell you?"

Phillip fumbled through his pockets and removed the piece of paper on which he had written the room numbers. He walked to the telephone and dialed the first one.

"Hello?" a man's voice said. Phillip could not distinguish the origin of the voice, but he did seem to think that it was not North American.

Phillip thought up a likely excuse to use in order to conceal his reason for calling. "This is room service," he said, disguising his voice. "I was inquiring how you wished your steak cooked?"

"Room service? We didn't order any room service," the telephone voice said annoyingly.

"I am sorry I must have the wrong room." Phillip replaced the receiver back in its cradle. It was definitely not the voice of any one of the people he was looking for.

"Well that's not it. Let's go up and check out the other room."

Amr forced himself up from the soft cushioned chair, slightly feeling the effect of the two Scotches, and followed Phillip through the hotel room door.

They walked toward the elevator and, once inside, Phillip withdrew the automatic placed inside his shirt, tucked between his belt and skin. He checked the clip on it as Amr carefully withdrew his.

"Are you expecting trouble if we confront these people?" Amr asked.

"It depends on whether or not Rolf or his two accomplices are with them. If it's just Bergan and McPherson there probably won't be a lot of problems."

The room they were looking for was at the end of the corridor. They walked along the soft, cushioned rug quietly contemplating how to handle the events that were about to take place.

Phillip knocked on the door and immediately stepped to the side. Amr was already standing on the other side of the entrance waiting for someone to open it from within. Phillip waited a moment and, after not hearing any noise, knocked again. There was no sound from inside the room and Phillip patiently waited several more seconds before knocking a third time.

"I wonder if they have adjoining rooms?" Amr asked as he looked at the door on either side of the one they were poised beside.

"It's worth a try," Phillip said as he motioned to the door closest to where he was standing.

Both men stealthily walked along the hall to the last door on the floor. Phillip squeezed himself between the end wall and the door opening. There was just enough room for him to stand on his tiptoes with his gun poised beside his temple. Amr knocked on the door.

"Who is it?" a woman's voice said.

"Hotel security," Amr responded immediately in his most British accent.

After a few seconds the door opened slightly, held by a safety chain. A small woman in her mid-fifties, wearing a pale blue housecoat, her face whitened by a youthening facial cream, poked her long, thin, pointed nose through the opening.

From her vantage point she could only see Amr who immediately spoke to her. "Sorry to bother you this late at night madam but there seems to be concern about someone prowling this hallway. We would ask that you ensure your door is locked and it stays that way all night long."

"Thank you very much for taking the trouble to tell me young man," she said in a heavy Portuguese or Spanish accent.

Amr tipped his head slightly and thanked her for her cooperation. The woman closed the door and Phillip exhaled a sigh of relief. He lowered the gun and both men started walking toward the second door.

Although the hallway was dimly lit, their eyes had grown accustomed to the subdued lights. The sides of the corridor were panelled with brown wooden wainscot and the top half had been elegantly wallpapered in a plush, velvety material. There were mirrors across every door framed by two candle-style lamps flickering rapidly, creating an eerie effect. The brown wooden doors had small peepholes in the centres and brass plaques with bold room numbers were hung directly beside the door jams. Once again both men stood on either side of the door as Phillip knocked.

After a few moments of silence Amr emitted a sigh of despair. "I guess we will just go back and hang around the lobby waiting for someone who looks familiar to come along."

The two men turned to leave when Amr noticed a drop of deep red liquid on the door step. He stooped down and touched it with his forefinger.

"It's blood," he said.

Both men paused as they assessed the situation. Phillip grasped the door handle forcefully but it would not turn. With his hand on the brass handle he leaned his body back as far as he could reach and threw himself sideways against the door. He rubbed his shoulder as pain filled the upper half of his body. The door was solid wood and would not budge.

"Let me try," Amr said as he stepped back several feet. He raced into the door and experienced a similar result.

"You wait here," Phillip said to Amr. "I'll go down and get the manager."

The Egyptian nodded, rubbing his arm to relieve some of the ache that was pounding after contacting the hardwood door.

Phillip raced along the hallway, avoiding the elevator and opting instead for the stairs. He was panting when he arrived in the lobby and touched the elevator control before he raced to the front desk. The bell captain was noting information on a small pad and looked up as Phillip rushed in.

"Can you come with me?" he said rapidly. The uniformed man saw the urgency in his face and nodded in agreeable concern. He spoke briefly to the front desk clerk and hurriedly followed Phillip who was already standing next to the waiting elevator. It was only a few moments before Phillip, accompanied by the short, overweight man dressed in a black and white bell captain's uniform, arrived.

"That was quick," Amr said, concealing his automatic behind him.

"This is the room you wish to enter?" the Bell Captain asked in broken English.

Amr replied in Arabic. The man knocked hesitatingly on the door.

"There is no one inside, use your key," Phillip directed.

The man turned to face Phillip. "We have rules in this hotel, sir," he said in an efficient manner. He knocked again and waited a few moments. Finally he removed a small ring, fastened securely to his belt with a brown, leather strap, and inserted a key into the lock. He opened the door several inches but could push it no further.

"What's the matter?" Phillip asked.

The man spoke in Arabic and Phillip looked to Amr for translation. "He said it is stuck."

Phillip pushed his hands against the door. "Something is blocking it," he said. With Amr's assistance the two men managed to open the door enough to enable Phillip to squeeze through.

The sight beyond the door was unbelievable. The furniture had been recklessly tossed around the room indicating signs of a definite struggle. Phillip entered the room first followed directly by Amr. Because of the Bell Captain's obese size he could only manage to squeeze the top part of his shoulders through the opening.

"What has happened?" he asked.

"Nothing," Phillip answered as he cleared the debris from the area directly in front of the door.

As the manager entered Phillip and Amr ran out. They hurried to the lobby and surveyed all the guests.

"Let's go back to your room and make certain all your friends are alright."

In the midst of the excitement, Phillip had embarrassingly forgotten about Kristy and Tim.

Kristy's room was two doors down from Phillip's. He walked as quickly as he could and immediately banged his fist on her door. There was no answer. He impatiently tapped his foot as he knocked again. He was contemplating his next move and walked to Tim Browning's door. There was no answer and Phillip became extremely concerned.

He returned to his room and telephoned. Again no answer. He had to assume there was no one in the room. Disturbing the already suspicious bell captain was not an option. He turned to Amr.

"Where do you think they might've gone?"

"I have no idea. This hotel is quite large and there

are probably a hundred places. Whatever happened could not have been very long ago because the blood on the doorstep is still fresh."

"The struggle must have been as a result of McPherson trying to get away."

"From what you told me, they seemed quite friendly at dinner."

"I don't know," Phillip said in exasperation. "I can't figure it out."

"Well, if I was trying to run away," the Egyptian began, "I would certainly take the stairwell instead of the elevators."

"I agree," Phillip said. "Let's give it a try." The two men secured the door and walked briskly along the hallway heading for the staircase.

"Why don't we continue on to the basement? I doubt they would simply walk through the lobby after the serious scuffle they appeared to have."

They walked through a set of double, steel doors and found themselves outside. The brightness of the moon lit the otherwise dark, desert night. Several paces before them was a driveway leading to a major road.

"Where does this go?" Phillip asked pointing to the pavement.

"This is the main road in this area. It leads from here to downtown Cairo. It is the road we came in on. If you go the other way it curves up a hill and takes you to the foot of the pyramids. It is only a five minute walk."

Phillip's eyes followed the curve of the road and paused when he noticed a shallow, brown walled area.

Amr noticed his partner's inquisitiveness. "That is a yard where they keep camels for tourists to ride to the pyramids." There were several men leaning lazily against a wall across from where the two agents stood.

Phillip, without hesitation, headed in the direction Amr was pointing. The men standing at the entrance ceased their conversation as the two strangers approached. They were dressed in light coloured, cotton robes, each with a turban or small, white cap.

Phillip and Amr continued cautiously, not letting the men from their sight. As they approached, one of the men stepped forward and greeted them.

"It is perhaps too late for a camel ride?" The man showed an abundance of gaps where teeth had once been, as he grinned at his attempt at humour.

"I'm afraid we're not here for the camels." Phillip tried to remain calm as he spoke in an effort to gain the man's friendship. "We are looking for several men that may have come in this direction. I wondered if you might have seen them?"

The man stared at Phillip but said nothing. He spoke to his friends and they all began to laugh. Amr took a step forward and spoke sternly in Arabic. Suddenly the group fell silent, shocked that Amr was Egyptian.

Phillip understood nothing of what was being spoken, however he knew when Amr removed money from his pocket that things were progressing positively. Phillip observed curiously as the men continued to chatter back and forth.

At last Amr turned to Phillip with a smile on his face. "One of them is here."

"Where?" Phillip asked in astonishment, a hint of impatience in his voice.

Amr spoke to the man in Arabic and offered more money. The man grinned and motioned for the twosome to follow him into the compound.

The stench inside the large, brick-lined corral was unbearable. Lit only by moonlight and a small lamp over the stable, Phillip saw at least a dozen camels kneeling on the floor. Each of the beasts of burden uttered guttural sounds as they passed. Phillip's eyes could not get enough of the sight. He had been caught up in this caper and had not had an opportunity to take in the local aspects of this strange land. He made a mental note to return someday as a tourist and view the scenes with care and admiration.

The camels had been covered with burlap blankets. Colourful saddles lay beside each beast. Occasionally their heads shook from side to side, irritated by bright pompoms fastened to the reins.

The Egyptian led the two along a short corridor to an opening in the brick-walled stable. A light was affixed by a cord, creating a minimal amount of luminance which rendered the inside almost invisible. Phillip was growing accustomed to the stench and found by breathing through his mouth, it enabled him to tolerate the hideous odour.

Once inside it became evident they were not alone. Camel herders were resting quietly next to their animals.

"The man you are looking for is in the corner." The Egyptian pointed to a remote area of the chamber. "He is hurt."

Phillip removed his automatic and poised himself for action. Most of the camel herders were now fully awake and began to shuffle nervously at the sight of the gun. The guide backed away and spoke to the herders. They exited quickly and suddenly Amr and Phillip felt very much alone. The small light strung from the ceiling was not enough to lighten the corner.

Amr also drew his automatic and the two agents began creeping toward the corner. The silence was broken by heavy, staggered breathing emanating from a darkened section of the mud-brick building. Phillip crouched and crept closer to the body. He was about six paces away when he noticed the salmon-coloured jacket. "McPherson!" he said as he rushed toward the wounded being.

"Is he alive?" Amr asked as he neared Phillip.

A small pool of deep red blood stained the straw beneath McPherson's shoulder. Phillip tried to shift the scientist's weight to inspect the wound. As he grabbed the injured man's shoulder he felt a wet, sticky mass of torn flesh. A wave of nausea overcame him and he immediately released his grip of the body. The scientist groaned in agony as pain enveloped him.

"What happened?" Phillip asked.

McPherson tried to open his eyes and slowly parted his parched lips. No sounds came as he gasped desperately for air. Phillip's eyes penetrated the white face as lines of pain became visible with each muscle movement. Phillip felt pity for the injured man only inches from his face.

McPherson whispered. "Bergan shot me." He gasped for air at the end of the last syllable.

"Shot. Why?"

"Money." McPherson's eyes closed and his face seemed to relax.

"What money?" Phillip asked. He placed his hand around that of the scientist grasping it tightly. Again lines of pain traced their way throughout the pale skin of McPherson. The muscles in his neck tensed as he made another effort to speak.

"Candu." His voice was so soft Phillip could barely make out the word. He felt McPherson's hand tighten around his in an effort to cling to life.

"Kristy," McPherson whispered. Phillip could hear him swallowing and noticed a small trickle of blood forming in the corner of his mouth. Again he made a sound. "Bergan... took her."

Shock and fury penetrated Phillip's senses. The small droplet of blood had formed into a trickle along a crease on McPherson's chin.

"Where did he take her?" Phillip asked impatiently but there was no answer. McPherson tilted his head back causing his eyes to roll upward in their sockets. "Hold on!" Phillip yelled.

Lorne McPherson's lips quivered in an effort to inhale a single, precious breath of life. He exhaled and attempted to form words from the thin wisps of air. Phillip leaned forward and lowered his ear to McPherson's mouth.

"Browning... involved with... Bergan." The words were followed by a lengthy gust of air. The lines of pain again relaxed and Phillip thought for an instant that a smile crossed the parched lips before him. Phillip stared a moment longer. The only link he had to finding Kristy McPherson was laying lifeless before him.

"Is he dead?" Amr asked.

"No, but he's not doing well."

"We have to get him to a hospital."

Amr ran outside and spoke to one of the men in the compound. He cursed the camel herder for allowing McPherson to remain in agony. The man shouted back in his defence. Amr again spoke, this time in a softer more compassionate tone. Together the two Egyptians searched for a piece of wood to construct a makeshift stretcher. A few moments later the man found two pieces of wood. Amr motioned him to enter the dwelling. The man followed, anticipating a sizeable reward in return for his helpful assistance.

"How is he?" Amr asked.

"Holding his own," Phillip replied. "I don't think the bullet penetrated any major organs."

"I wonder how he got here?"

"You should ask your friend," Phillip said as he motioned at the astonished guide several feet behind.

McPherson had staggered into the compound twenty minutes before they did. The men suggested he see a doctor but he only wanted to rest. He gave them money in return for a quiet place to lie down.

"He said Tim Browning was involved."

Amr looked surprised.

"He also said they had Kristy."

Amr was astounded. "We had better return to the hotel and see if we can figure out what the hell is happening."

"I'm always amazed at what people will do for money."

The two agents lifted the body and gently placed it on the makeshift stretcher. They walked onto the street and surveyed the traffic. Almost immediately, Amr spotted a police cruiser heading in their direction. Amr spoke to the camel herder, telling him to hail the police vehicle. The Arab dashed into the centre of the road and waved his arms frantically.

The constable stopped the vehicle and surmised the situation. Accompanied by his partner, they stepped from the automobile and walked cautiously to the scene. Upon noticing McPherson, limp on the stretcher he began to shout, demanding an explanation. Amr spoke to the uniformed men and asked their assistance. One of the policemen opened the rear door, permitting the two agents to lift the body onto the soft, cushioned seat.

Amr removed his identification papers and showed them to the officer, explaining the recent events. The man in charge noted key points on a pad of writing paper and returned to their car. He explained they would rush to a nearby hospital, take care of McPherson, and then check out Amr's story.

Phillip watched as the automobile, carrying the only link to Kristy's disappearance, sped off in the distance. Amr reached in his pocket and paid the camel herder for his trouble. The two agents hurried across the street, entering the hotel through the lobby.

22   CONSPIRACY

Kristy McPherson attempted to struggle but the grip on her arms was too tight. The man holding her was tall and had hands of steel.

"What do you want?" she said nervously.

Willem Rolf sat in the large wing chair beside the television stand at the far end of the hotel room. He stared at Kristy and smiled leeringly. "What I want is for you to be quiet," he commanded.

One of the two Irishmen was sitting on the bed and reading a magazine while his brother held Kristy McPherson.

"Who are you?" she asked hopelessly, trying to shake herself free.

"My name is Willem Rolf," Rolf said, tilting his head slightly in the form of a greeting. "These are my friends." He motioned to the two dark-haired Irishmen. "If you promise to be good I will let you sit freely."

Kristy released some of the tension in her body and allowed herself to stand relaxed. Rolf nodded to Seamus Guilderdale, suggesting that he release his grip on her.

At the moment he did, Kristy's foot lashed out behind her, as she shifted her weight slightly to allow her heel to make contact with her captor's shin. The tall muscular man screamed in agony and bent forward to soothe his aching leg by rubbing it with his hand. Kristy jumped in front of Rolf and made a run for the door. She took two strides but Dermott Guilderdale, seated comfortably on the bed, lashed out his leg to make contact with Kristy's foot. The girl went plummeting face down onto the carpet. The Irish muscleman jumped from the bed and grabbed her by the hair, pulling her upright and holding her arms. Tears were streaming from her eyes but seemed to have an unemotional effect on her three captors.

"I see that you are not very reliable," Rolf said mockingly.

He stepped up to pour himself a drink and walked directly before Kristy. As he came face to face with her he lifted his finger and waved it at her nose as if scolding a child. Kristy quickly puckered up her mouth and forced several droplets of spit to shoot into the German's face. Rolf's sarcastic grin turned to anger and he lashed out his hand, catching Kristy directly in the chin sending her head backward into Dermott's shoulder.

The incident was interrupted by a solid knock on the wooden hotel door. Seamus looked to Rolf for direction before unlocking the handle. Rolf nodded his approval and the big Irishman opened the door.

Ed Bergan walked in, followed closely by Tim Browning. Kristy McPherson could not believe what she saw.

"What are you doing here?" she asked in disbelief.

Ed Bergan smiled wickedly. "What do you think he's doing here? He works for me." He laughed out loud as he stepped over to Rolf. He was dressed in a tan coloured jacket with a white, open-collared shirt. His pants were baggy and suspended below his overweight stomach. His greasy hair kept falling forward and he continually had to brush it back to keep it off his forehead.

"Is everything going okay?" Bergan asked addressing Rolf.

Rolf nodded. "Do we know where McPherson is yet?" he asked. At the mention of her father's name, Kristy turned her attention away from Tim Browning to Bergan and Rolf.

"He couldn't have gone far. I'm sure he's hurt badly," Bergan said.

"What do you mean he's hurt badly?" Kristy asked. There were signs of fear in her eyes.

"Tim was watching over him but your father, in a stupid manoeuvre overpowered him and tried to escape. He tried to get away from our friend Mr. Browning here." Bergan motioned to Tim as he spoke. "It was lucky I came along when I did and managed to get one shot fired as you father ran through the door. I know I hit him so he couldn't have gone far."

"If he's hurt I'll kill you!" She turned her attention back to Tim Browning. "How could you do this after all he's done for you?" Tim Browning's stare dropped to his feet in embarrassment.

"That's enough out of you," Ed Bergan commanded. "If your father doesn't come up with the money that he owes me he won't be in a position to touch anyone." He grabbed Kristy's chin and, squeezing tightly, shook her head from side to side.

"Leave her alone," Tim Browning said in a meek voice.

Bergan turned around. "You, shut up!"

Rolf snickered as he took a sip of his drink.

"I want you to hide the girl somewhere so that no one can find her, then take your two thugs and go find McPherson. He can't be very far." He directed his attention to Tim Browning. "You," he said sternly. "I want you to go back to the girl's room and leave a note visible enough for anyone to see. Make sure it says we have the girl and we won't exchange her until we get the money from McPherson."

Tim left Bergan's room and looked in both directions before he proceeded to the elevator.

"Where are we going now?" Amr asked.

"I guess we'll go back to McPherson's room to see if there is any indication of what might've happened. Somehow McPherson got away from whoever was watching him, not without a gun shot mind you."

"His room was on the fifth floor wasn't it?" Amr asked as Phillip pressed the seventh floor button on the elevator panel.

"I just wanted to check Kristy's room again to see if by chance she has returned."

They walked softly along the hallway, keeping their eyes poised in all directions to ensure they would not be interrupted by intruders. When they arrived at Kristy's door Phillip tried the handle but it would not turn. Amr gently touched Phillip on his shoulder and with his finger pushed against his mouth summoned Phillip to be silent. He pointed to the opened door beside Kristy's room, the room occupied by Tim Browning. Both men jumped to the door and had their guns ready for action. They were about to step inside the room when they heard a shuffling sound on the other side of the opening.

Amr nodded to Phillip and suddenly the door flung open. Tim Browning was taken by surprise as Phillip lunged at him and grabbed his shirt with one hand, pinning him against the wooden door of the hotel room. Amr jumped past the twosome into the hotel room, his knee slightly bent, both hands on his gun, ready for anyone who might be waiting. The room was empty.

"Let's take him back to your room," the Egyptian said to Phillip.

They grabbed Browning by the arms and dragged him. Amr held Tim's wrists securely behind his back as Phillip fumbled with the key to open the door. Once sheltered by the security of the hotel room, Phillip locked the door and flipped the dead bolt. Amr had frisked Tim Browning and found a small hand pistol tucked into his belt.

"Well, what is this?" the Egyptian asked, dangling the pistol in front of him.

"I'm surprised that you know how to hold one of these let alone fire it," Phillip said as he walked to Tim. "Where is Kristy?"

"I don't know," Tim Browning said.

"That's bullshit, and you know it," Phillip said angrily.

"I swear to God I don't know. Bergan told Rolf to take her somewhere, but I don't know where." He saw anger in Phillip's eyes and began to fear for his safety. "She's all right though, they'd never hurt her," he added.

Phillip picked up the upright chair from the desk placed it backwards straddled it, resting his arms and chin on its back. Amr had disassembled Tim's revolver to inspect its operational capacity and after being convinced that it was in good working order, pointed the weapon at the young, scruffy-haired scientist.

"Suppose you tell us everything that happened, right from the beginning," Phillip said, feeling relieved that at long last he was going to get answers to questions that had been plaguing him for the last several weeks.

"I can't, there is nothing to tell." Tim Browning began to tremble as he spoke.

Amr pulled back the hammer on the small revolver. The click was very audible in the confines of the hotel room and Tim turned his head in the direction of the sound.

His eyes trailed along the shaft of the cold blue steel and stopped when they met Amr's deep blue eyes staring back at him. Tim's swallow was blocked by a thick lump building in his throat. He turned back to face Phillip, paused in thought for a moment and allowed his body to slump as his resistance dropped. He knew that if Bergan discovered he had talked to Phillip, his life would be worthless. His present option, however was not any different.

Phillip continued his conversation. "How long have you been working for Bergan?"

"I received a phone call from Bergan," Tim began his story, "about two and a half months ago. He told me he was with the Canadian government on a very secretive mission. He wanted to meet with me and asked me not to tell anyone about his telephone call. I complied and kept the information to myself. Two days later Bergan flew to Cordoba and called me at my home." Tim shifted in his seat to gain more comfort.

"Bergan explained that the British wanted to stop the start-up of the nuclear reactors. I assumed at the time that Bergan was part of the Canadian government but as it turns out he wasn't. Apparently the British couldn't openly ask Canada to stop implementation of the reactors, so they hired Bergan, off the record, to get the job done. The day before meeting with me he met with Lorne and they worked out the details for the sabotage of the reactors. Lorne accepted five hundred thousand dollars, half of which was paid up front to sabotage the reactor that was about to start up. I was paid a very small amount in comparison to keep an eye on Lorne unbeknownst to him, and report back to Bergan any events that might be questionable."

"I know I can count on you Tim." Bergan said as he stood in the dimly lit corner of the South American restaurant where he had arranged to meet Tim Browning.

Tim returned the handshake. "You can Mr. Bergan, I know that this is important to Canada's security." Tim did not want to sound overly enthusiastic about the ten thousand dollars that Bergan had offered him for his role in this caper. His concern was really not for Canada's security. The money was the motivating factor for his participation. He thought it might help his relationship with Bergan if he showed sincerity.

The twosome left the restaurant and went their separate ways. Tim Browning returned to his apartment and retraced the upcoming events in his mind.

It had been decided that a letter would mysteriously appear at the Canadian Embassy at Buenos Aires and be hand delivered to McPherson.

Bergan had spent many hours with Lorne McPherson the day before and the two had, after great deliberation, reached a monetary agreement which would ensure a delay in the reactor start-up time. McPherson had insisted it be done in a way void of any potential injuries. Bergan agreed to the condition although possible loss of lives was not a concern to him. He was adamant about the completion of the job.

Bergan had insisted McPherson use Tim Browning's help. At first the scientist was opposed to third party involvement but eventually agreed, realizing he would be unable to keep such actions from his associate.

"Don't tell Browning we met," Bergan had said. "We'll send you a letter from a mysterious government office outlining your task. Open it with Tim there and don't let on you know about it."

McPherson looked puzzled. Bergan noticed the concern in his eyes.

"I don't think we would benefit from Tim knowing any of the background. Treat it as a surprise and it'll work out just fine." He nodded as he spoke. "Call me when you get the letter. Make sure Browning is with you. It'll add credibility."

Bergan did not tell Tim Browning of his meeting with McPherson. He explained about the letter being delivered from an anonymous government source but insisted that Tim not tell McPherson of his involvement. He was to report to Bergan only events which would deter from completion of the job. Bergan went on to carefully explain that McPherson must never know of this meeting or Tim's acquaintance with Bergan.

Browning had trouble sleeping that night, as enthusiasm and guilt battled continually, keeping him awake.

Although he had poorly slept, haunted by continuous dreams of events from that evening, he was surprisingly not very tired when he awoke the next morning. As he showered, shaved and dressed, he planned his deception. He had always been pleased with his ability to act and was convinced that McPherson would never detect his involvement.

The office telephone rang loudly. McPherson requested he join him immediately. Tim smiled to himself, knowing the fearful game was afoot. He was nervous and fidgeted with his collar as he walked towards his superior's office.

At last McPherson read the letter and Tim called on all of his acting ability to perform. He rearranged his facial muscles the way he had rehearsed, creating a believable look of surprise. McPherson was playing the part very well, Tim thought. He had a great deal of grief and disbelief in his voice as he read the contents of the letter.

McPherson suggested they go for a coffee down the street and discuss the ramifications of this strange request. Tim felt his knowledge of both sides of the operation was a great advantage and his self-esteem heightened as he drew analogies to famous spy heroes retrieved from movies and books. He debated contacting Bergan to say all was going well but decided against the action, remembering Bergan's comment to call only if anything was amiss.

The twosome left the restaurant and returned to McPherson's office. They scanned the detailed drawings of the reactor and decided McPherson would sabotage a small pressure valve which would cause a leak in the boiler tank designed to hold the heavy water. It would be done in such a way that there would not be any harm to people, as the reactor was not yet functional and a test was to take place prior to start-up. The plan was extremely simple yet brilliant. The pressure test would be done, discovery of the faulty valve would be made, and the entire schedule would be placed on hold. It should delay the reactor start up by several weeks.

The pressure test was scheduled for Friday and McPherson had decided to go into the reactor that night. Tim had desperately attempted to join McPherson in the sabotage operation but the senior scientist had totally rejected the idea. He felt it would be far too dangerous for both of them.

Tim had trouble concentrating on his work for the remainder of the day and mentally re-checked the plan in his mind, looking for anything that may go wrong. He called McPherson to see if he might allow him to leave early as he wasn't accomplishing anything anyway. He was surprised when McPherson's secretary told him the scientist had left half an hour earlier and was not expected to return that day. Tim decided he must have had a lot on his mind and did not want to appear troubled at the office. He was cleaning the top of his desk when the telephone rang.

"Tim, this is Eric Hodge. I have a small problem." There was a pause. "I can't reach Dr. McPherson. Maybe you could give him a message for me."

"Shoot," Tim said.

"The uranium is being installed in the reactor on Friday. We had to bump it up a week because of Dr. Laos' schedule. There won't be any problems but I think McPherson should know."

Tim paused for a moment to collect his thoughts. "What about the pressure test on the boiler?" Tim asked. "I don't think we should go ahead with the uranium until that has been done."

"Where have you guys been? That test was done yesterday. It went off without a hitch."

"Yesterday?" Tim asked, surprised. "Why weren't we told?"

"Well," Eric stuttered slightly, "the test was routine and it was executed perfectly so I didn't see any need to make an issue of it."

"I see," Tim said, not wishing to sound suspicious. "I'll make sure that Lorne gets the message."

Browning sat in his chair and retraced the events in his mind. The boiler would still be empty so McPherson would not be in any danger. Once the uranium was inserted on Friday, however, and the pressure began to build, the valve would blow, possibly causing heavy water to seep out. It would of course be minor and noticed immediately by the gauges; however, there could still be a dozen or so people killed before the reactor was shut down. Browning contemplated calling McPherson and telling him, however he wondered how Ed Bergan would view that. By now Bergan would know what McPherson's intentions were and would probably have approved them. Perhaps he should call Ed Bergan first? Yes, that definitely sounded like the best plan.

He picked up the telephone and dialed the appropriate digits.

"Hello?"

"Ed, this is Tim Browning."

"Hi Tim, what can I do for you?"

"Have you spoken with Lorne?"

"Yeah, I spoke to him earlier, It's a great plan he's put together." He hesitated for a moment. "You don't see any problems do you?"

"Well, one complication has arisen. The pressure test which would detect the faulty valve was done yesterday instead of this coming Friday. The reactor is scheduled to be loaded with uranium this week. As the pressure begins to build the valve will blow, causing a uranium leak."

"What does that mean in real life?" Bergan asked.

"That means that a number of people will be killed."

Bergan was silent as he ran the events through his mind. "About how many people?"

"About twelve, maybe sixteen."

Again Bergan was silent for a moment. "You're right, Tim," he said. "I'll call Lorne right away."

Tim was relieved by Bergan's statement.

The line went dead as he slowly replaced the receiver. Murdering twelve people would not have been something he could condone. He experienced sickening feelings of fear as the reality of the magnitude of this caper plagued his mind.

"That was quite a feat last night. I don't think I could ever do that again," McPherson said, with a smile on his face. He continued his explanation of how the security guards entered the boiler room and how he had to remain crouched, ever so still for several seconds. He spoke with excitement for the task had been an enjoyable change from his daily routine.

Tim Browning stood frozen in his tracks. Ed Bergan had never made the phone call to McPherson last night. Lorne had actually completed the undertaking. He had tampered with the reactor and now it was ready to explode. He contemplated telling Lorne of the tests which recently took place but decided not to for the first question would be why had he not said anything last evening. He couldn't believe that Bergan would lie to him and jeopardize all those lives.

McPherson's face grew solemn as he stared at Tim. He spoke slowly. "Can I count on you Tim, not to tell anyone about this? Ever?" He spoke as a father would explain a grave, family secret to his child.

"Of course you can. You know you can trust me." Tim felt a wave of guilt rise within him. He knew Lorne had done what he thought best to aid his country. He, on the other hand, had compromised his morals strictly for selfish, financial reasons. He had to get out of the office, away from the man who had offered him so many opportunities, the man whom he had just betrayed.

He returned to his office when the intercom buzzed. Lorne McPherson was at the other end. Panic echoed throughout every syllable he spoke and Tim knew something had gone wrong.

Lorne began to speak as Tim once again entered the scientist's office. "Tim, the pressure test on the boiler was done two days ago."

"What, how can that be?" Tim asked, again displaying an actor's version of surprise.

"To make matters worse the uranium is being installed tomorrow. Do you have any idea how many people will be killed?" McPherson did not wait for Tim to answer. "There will be at least twenty-five people, maybe even thirty in that boiler room, when that thing goes off."

Browning was silent. He had not realized that the death toll could be that high. This was much more than he had bargained for. "Well, there's nothing you can do Lorne."

"The hell there isn't. I've got to get back in there tonight and fix that valve."

Tim Browning was momentarily stunned. "You can't do that Lorne, it will be far too dangerous."

"I have to Tim, those peoples' lives are more important than anything," he said with conviction in his voice.

"Why don't you phone the guy who sent you the letter and see what he has to say?" Browning was grasping at straws, attempting not to reveal his knowledge of the events.

"There won't be any point, you saw what happened the last time I called."

Tim Browning left McPherson's office and returned to his own. His mind was in a daze as he desperately retraced the events that just took place. He left the office under the pretence of feeling ill and returned immediately to his flat.

"Ed Bergan speaking," a raspy voice said over the telephone receiver.

"Ed, this is Tim Browning. We have a real problem here." Tim waited for Bergan to reply; after a second or so of silence he continued. "I can't believe you didn't call Lorne last night. Do you know how many people can die?"

"That's none of your concern."

"Well, Lorne just found out that the test was already done and he's going back in there tonight to undo what he did last night."

There was silence at the other end of the line. Bergan was gathering his thoughts before he spoke. "That son of a bitch." It was the first time Tim had heard Bergan's voice show ruthless anger. "You stop him from doing that!" Bergan commanded.

"How can I do that?" Tim asked meekly.

"I don't care how. Just do it or you won't see any of that money." The line went dead and Tim Browning felt waves of fear exploding throughout his body. He knew he was getting in over his head. He checked his watch and decided to head to the reactor site.

He crouched behind a metal container around the corner from the boiler room entrance when McPherson's car pulled up. Although it was a dark night, the area was washed in a bright blue haze reflected from nearby artificial lamps.

He watched McPherson remove the briefcase, quickly close the car door, and walked hastily toward the entrance of the building. Tim ran back to his office and slipped inside without being seen by anyone. He immediately picked up the telephone and dialed security. He gave a fictitious name and said he saw someone entering the boiler room. He replaced the receiver, waited for a moment, and casually walked downstairs to his car.

Tim continued his story. "I talked to Bergan to explain what had happened. That's when he told me about the money he had paid Lorne. Two hundred and fifty thousand dollars. I couldn't believe it. All along I assumed Lorne was doing this for the good of the country. Bergan was livid. He knew that they would check the reactor after discovering McPherson, and repair it immediately." Amr and Phillip listened intently as Tim carried on with his story.

"I didn't realize that McPherson would be arrested, I thought they would simply prevent him from entering the boiler room. Bergan had already paid McPherson the money."

"What happened then?" Phillip asked.

"Kristy managed to get us some airline tickets through her company and we flew to Buenos Aires. We were on a flight to the U.S. but there was an unscheduled stop in Bogota. As soon as we landed there were officials waiting to arrest us. They were nice enough about it, but they confiscated our passports and escorted us to a hotel."

"That's when I got involved," Phillip said to Amr.

"Bergan wanted his money back," Tim continued. "Apparently he'd been advanced a small sum of money from the British Government to initiate this caper." Tim shifted in his seat before he continued his tale. "When the British found out that the sabotage venture hadn't taken place, the war in the Falklands had already ended and the entire incident became hypothetical. The British apparently stopped all contact as well as the flow of cash to Bergan. Most of the excess funds had been used by Bergan for his own expenses, including Rolf's fee. The money that McPherson received is all that's left, and Bergan wants it for himself."

"And that's why he's chasing McPherson. For the cash," Phillip said more to himself than anyone else.

"So who is this guy Rolf?" Amr asked.

Tim Browning continued. "Well, before I got a chance to phone Bergan to tell him that we were in Bogota, McPherson came up with this wild idea to take us to Cartagena by bus. He had decided to go to some islands just off the coast of Colombia and hide out for a little while. When things calmed down we would return to Cartagena and go to the Canadian Consulate office and apply for Canadian passports. It was a good idea and I'm sure it would have worked had you and Rolf not shown up when you did. That kind of spoiled everything.

"I couldn't telephone Bergan from Bogota because I wasn't separated from McPherson long enough. Bergan got very nervous and somehow arranged for you," he pointed at Phillip, "to come down and start looking for us. I still don't know how he pulled that one off. As soon as we got to Cartagena, I telephoned Bergan and told him what had happened. He seemed relieved to hear from me and told me not to worry. He said he would take care of everything, and to just stay with the McPherson family. I didn't know it at the time of course but that is when he decided to hire Rolf. I guess he panicked, not knowing where McPherson, or more important, his money was. When I called he was pretty pissed at me for not contacting him earlier.

"He now had no more use for you so Rolf was to get you out of the picture any way he could. Apparently they tried scaring you but that didn't work so I guess they thought they should kill you. Rolf was then to continue on, find McPherson and bring him back to Bergan, hopefully along with the money."

"How did you know all this?" Phillip asked, standing up and stretching his legs.

"When you were booking the tickets in Kingston I telephoned Bergan and told him we were on our way to Cairo. He explained that Rolf had telephoned him as well. He gave me the name of the hotel and told me to call him as soon as I got here."

"Where is McPherson now?" Amr asked probing to

determine how much more information Tim knew.

"I don't know, I was with him in his room and we were talking about all the things that had happened. He seemed upset but handled it quite calmly. Suddenly, when I went to get a beer from the mini-bar, he slugged me from behind and that's all I remember. I heard a gunshot but it seemed very faint. I found out afterward that Bergan, who was in the adjoining room, had heard a noise and came racing through the double doors. He saw McPherson run out the door and managed to get off a shot. McPherson ran into the hall and was at the end of the corridor when Bergan tried to get a second shot but there were several people stepping from the elevator. Somehow in the confusion McPherson got away."

"And that is when you decided to take Kristy in-stead?" Phillip interjected angrily.

"No! That was strictly Bergan's idea. I was opposed to it."

"I guess you don't carry a lot of weight with Ber-gan," Amr said. He turned his attention to Phillip. "What should we do with him now?"

Phillip motioned Amr to join him in a small corner by the front door of the hotel room. "You stay where you are," Phillip commanded to Tim Browning as he pointed his finger toward him.

"I have absolutely no idea where to begin, how about you?"

"Do you think Browning might know where Bergan is?"

"I don't know." Phillip rubbed his chin as if deep in thought.

"What are you thinking?"

"I'm wondering why Bergan would risk shooting McPherson in the hallway of a crowded hotel?"

Amr finished the statement for Phillip. "Unless he did not have the money yet."

"If that's the case, I wonder where it is? There's no

way McPherson would have left it in Colombia."

The two agents decided to tie up Tim Browning but leave enough slack so that he could escape. Hopefully he would lead them to Bergan.

They looked around the room for something to secure Tim Browning's hands with. The only functional thing was the draw string for the curtains. Phillip stood on a chair and proceeded to undo the white nylon cord. Amr finished the last of the sandwiches and washed it down with a lengthy swallow of cold beer.

They seated Tim on the upright, wooden desk chair and began to wrap the nylon twine around him. Amr removed the hand towel from the bathroom and, after soaking it in water, wrapped it around Tim's mouth, tying it at the back of his head.

"That will shut you up," he said as he smiled. "Don't try anything."

The two agents exited the room, closing the door tightly behind them.

"Why don't you go down to Bergan's room and see if there's any activity," Phillip said. "I'll wait in the stairwell to see where Browning goes."

Amr nodded his head in agreement. "If I don't find anything in Bergan's room I will go down to the lobby to see if anyone saw anything that might fit the description of these people."

The men walked toward the elevator and Amr touched the small, illuminated dial on the wall.

"I hope he doesn't take too long to free himself," Phillip said.

The elevator arrived and Amr stepped inside. Phillip walked the few steps toward the end of the corridor and exited through the thick metal door. He waited patiently with the door slightly ajar, allowing a full view of the corridor.

23   THE PLAN

Amr spoke to the bell captain in Arabic and described Bergan, Rolf and Kristy McPherson as best as he
could. The bell captain had been on duty for quite a while
and did not recall anyone fitting that particular description.
He also mentioned that there had been very little activity in
the hotel this late at night. The tall Egyptian walked to the
front desk and asked similar questions. No one had seen or
heard anything suspicious. It was obvious to Amr that the
people he was looking for had used an alternate exit.

It occurred to him that quite possibly Bergan had
also thought McPherson had left the hotel and wandered
across the street. He decided to retrace his earlier steps and
headed to the camel compound. Upon seeing him, the
Egyptian who had helped him before greeted him in a
friendly manner. Amr asked him if anyone else had enquired about McPherson. The man explained that no one
had come along. Amr sincerely thanked him for his assistance and returned to the hotel, walking freely into the
lobby, knowing that neither Bergan nor any of his accom-

plices would recognize him. Everything around him appeared calm as he walked toward the elevator heading to Phillip's floor.

En route he decided to stop once more on the floor occupied by Ed Bergan. He walked to Bergan's door and heard no sounds coming from within. He knocked lightly and waited for an answer. When none came he decided to go up to Phillip's room.

"How did you make out?" Phillip asked as Amr entered the room.

"Nothing. Nothing at all." Amr explained how he had gone across the street and checked the camel compound again. "How come you are here?" he asked and noticed the nylon ropes tossed in the corner beside a chair. "I see our friend got away okay. You didn't lose him did you?"

"No, he went to Bergan's room and banged on the door, but found no answer. He walked back to his room and went inside. I'm sure he'll call Bergan, providing he has an idea where to look. I tried listening through the door but they're just too thick to hear anything."

"What do you think will happen?" Amr asked.

"I'm sure Browning will somehow get a hold of Bergan and explain that we've got McPherson. I have a feeling Bergan will contact us before the night is through."

Amr smiled and wandered to the mini-bar, looking for something to satisfy a sweet craving developing in his stomach. He walked to the television and flipped the stations. Individually they were concentrating on the events that had led them to this point. Phillip was concerned about Kristy. Images from the past several weeks ran through his mind. He was helpless sitting in a room waiting for something to happen and felt partially responsible for what had happened to her. Had he not allowed her to come on this trip she would be perfectly safe at home in Canada right now. He very much longed to share his feelings with her again.

Amr was the first to wake up at the sound of the telephone ringing loudly from the dresser. He immediately looked at Phillip who was awakening from a deep sleep. Both were slightly disoriented and neither of them knew where the telephone was. It was on the third ring that Phillip lunged across the bed and grabbed the receiver, dropping the base onto the floor.

"Hello," he said.

"Phillip, this is Ed Bergan."

"Bergan, where's Kristy, if you've done anything to her I'll kill you." Phillip could see Amr shaking his head. The Arab saw he was allowing his emotions to run away with the conversation.

"Calm down, she's perfectly fine and nobody's gonna hurt her. As long as you do what I say."

Phillip waited patiently.

"Do you have McPherson?"

"What if I do?"

"Cut the crap Phil," Bergan said in a stern voice. "I've invested a lot of time and money into finding McPherson and I mean to have him." He was losing control of his emotions as he spoke and paused for a moment to collect his thoughts.

"Look Phil," Bergan continued, calmer than before. "You have McPherson, I have the girl. A simple trade off, what could be easier?"

"Let me talk to her, I want to make sure she's all right."

"I can't do that Phil,"

"Why not, where is she?" Phillip interjected with anxiety.

"Relax, she's quite all right. We took her away to a safe place. She is, after all my insurance policy."

"Before we make any deal I want to make sure she's okay."

"Of course, not a problem." Bergan paused for a moment. Phillip could hear paper rustling in the background. "Okay, here's the deal. Around eleven you and McPherson take the main road in front of the hotel and head south. Drive for about forty minutes until you come to a temple complex called Saqqara. You can't miss the turnoff. Follow the winding road past several tombs for about two miles and you'll come to a large temple which has a parking lot in front of it. We'll be waiting there for you with further instructions."

"We already have men stationed there now so don't try to send police or anything out in advance. If anything goes wrong the girl will be killed immediately."

"I'm not leaving the hotel until I get a phone call from Kristy. I want to be sure she's all right."

"Not to worry. We'll call around nine-thirty." Bergan paused. "Now let me talk to McPherson."

Phillip waited for a moment before he spoke. "McPherson is sound asleep, I don't want to wake him. He's hurt badly." Again Phillip paused for a moment. "It'll be enough for him just to make this trip tomorrow."

Bergan thought for a moment before he spoke. "Make sure you tell him to bring the money." Again Bergan paused before he continued. "All the money," he said emphatically. Phillip placed the receiver back on the cradle still laying on the floor.

He recounted the conversation to Amr and the two men began to develop a plan.

"What do you expect to do about McPherson?" Amr asked.

"Well," Phillip said slowly, "you're about the same size as he is, if you could get his jacket, and with a white wig you'd fit the part perfectly." Phillip smiled as he told Amr of his intentions.

The Egyptian sat staring wildly at Phillip. "I'll be a sitting target."

"No, not necessarily. They'll think you have the money and they're not going to hurt you until they're sure of that. Remember, there's no reason for them to be suspicious. They don't know that McPherson is in the hospital. They think he only has a small wound."

Amr recalled Phillip's explanation of the phone conversation. "What are we going to do about the money?"

"We'll have to fudge that one, I'll get a briefcase. You keep it with you and if you have time maybe you can work something out."

Amr's eyes lit up as an idea struck him. "Did you say there were several tombs leading up to the temple?" he asked. Phillip nodded his head. "Why don't we go to one of those and put the briefcase inside. When they stop us and ask us where the money is, we can tell them we hid it."

"What'll that accomplish?"

"Well, for one thing it will stall for time. For another it will give us a chance to see the girl, as well as assess the situation." Amr paused. "Remember they outnumber us drastically."

Phillip slowly nodded his head in agreement with Amr's plan. "I guess we really don't have any choice. They'll probably have those two thugs with them as well as Rolf, and Tim Browning."

"What will we do if they recognize me before we get a chance to do anything?"

"Well my friend, I guess it will be spontaneous action." Phillip smiled. "I doubt very much if that'll happen. They're going to be so excited about all that's going on, the last thing they'll think of is an impostor. Remember, Browning is the only one who has seen you and I doubt very much, after the way he's performed, Bergan will keep him in the foreground."

Amr nodded and looked at his watch. "We still have a couple of hours before the stores open. I will then go and find a jacket that matches the one McPherson was wearing."

"One more thing my friend," Phillip said. Amr raised his eyebrows in anticipation. "You'll have to shave off your moustache."

Amr ran his thumb and forefinger along the bristles of his bright red, thick moustache. "No, please don't ask that of me."

"I'm afraid that you'll have to." Phillip smiled. "Anyway, you'll probably look better without it."

Amr was stretched out in the wing chair by the window. His head was tucked into his chest and his arms hung over the sides of the chair. He stirred slightly as the morning Egyptian sun penetrated the opening in the curtains shining directly into his eyes. He raised one arm and with the back of his hand briskly rubbed the end of his nose. He suddenly stopped all motion and his eyes popped open. He stiffened in his chair and shot a glance at his watch; it was ten to nine. Phillip was sleeping soundly on the bed. Amr slowly rejuvenated his arms and legs and felt a little light-headed when he stood up.

He walked to Phillip and shook his shoulder in an attempt to wake him. Phillip jumped at the gesture, shooting his hand outward and grabbing Amr's wrist. Phillip was about to roll off the bed onto the floor when he realized where he was. He relaxed his body as he saw Amr staring down at him, a big grin on the Egyptian's face.

"What time is it?" he asked, now fully awake.

"Ten to nine." Amr walked to the telephone. "I'm going to order breakfast. Do you want some?"

He waited for Phillip to nod his head and briefly discussed with him the choices for breakfast from the room service menu.

"I'm gonna take a shower. Why don't you pop down to Bergan's room and see if there's any activity. "

Amr nodded in agreement and, after ordering breakfast, left the room. Phillip made his way to the shower and shaved as the steaming hot water covered his face and body. He stood facing the nozzle with eyes closed and allowed the steamy, hot water to spray directly onto his face. While he was dressing he wished he had purchased some new clothes. He decided to take a long vacation if he ever got out of this present situation. He needed a rest, with or without the approval of his superiors. He looked at the bed and envisioned Kristy McPherson lying there. He hoped that she would be all right, and felt anger inside him at the thought of anyone hurting her. He was just finishing dressing as Amr entered the room.

"Anything?" Phillip asked.

"Not a thing. I checked with the maid cleaning the room occupied by Bergan. I think they have all left. Tim Browning's room is also empty."

A soft tap on the door signified the arrival of breakfast. The waiter, clad in the standard orange hotel tunic, pushed the silver legged dolly, covered with a white cloth, into the room. He motioned to the small table by the window and asked if it would be all right to place the dishes on it. After Amr nodded approval, the boy removed silver covered platters and placed them expertly on the table. He laid the cutlery and napkins in the proper position and wished them an enjoyable meal. Amr paid the bill and did not wait for the lad to leave before he began to uncover the dishes. He poured coffee and separated the toast as Phillip was counting the cash in his briefcase.

The men had just begun eating when the telephone rang. Phillip jumped up and reached for it.

"Bergan!"

"Everything all right?" Bergan asked joyfully.

"Let me speak to Kristy," Phillip ordered.

"Just a minute." The phone went dead. A moment later her familiar voice sounded in the receiver.

"Hello."

Phillip returned the greeting with anticipation. "Are you alright?"

"Yes I'm fine." She paused for a moment.

The call was interrupted by a shuffling noise and Bergan's voice came back on the phone.

"Are you happy now? I'll see you at noon at Saqqara," the phone went dead.

"Wait!" Phillip yelled into the receiver. Bergan had already disconnected the line.

"Is she all right?" Amr asked. There was sincerity in his voice.

Phillip nodded. "She seems okay. I just hope we can pull this off."

24 DENOUEMENT

Kristy McPherson sat solemnly on a small wooden chair in the corner of a hotel room somewhere in the Egyptian capital of Cairo. Her golden brown hair was matted and tangled and had lost its lustre as it had been swept back recklessly, exposing her face. Her makeup was smeared and worn. The sockets of her eyes were framed by dark circles from a lack of sleep. Before her, on a small, round wooden table, was an untouched plate of sandwiches.

"You have to eat something," Tim Browning said.

Kristy closed her eyes deliberately, swung her head toward him and slowly opened them, focusing her attention on Tim. She gave him a pathetic look and flung her head side ways, staring out the window, refusing to answer his request.

"Fine. Suit yourself," he said as he walked toward the other end of the room.

Ed Bergan laid stretched out on the bed reading a magazine. His shoes had been kicked from his feet and left scattered on the floor. He raised his eyes and glanced at

Tim as he nervously paced back and forth near the front door of the hotel room.

"Relax," Bergan said. "It'll be over soon."

Tim ignored him. He was beginning to realize how deeply he had got himself into trouble. He never dreamed how all of this could have evolved from a simple phone call and a short meeting a few weeks ago in the hot confines of a Cordoban restaurant.

"What's bugging you?" Bergan asked.

"Nothing," Tim said softly. "It's just getting messier than I thought."

"Don't worry so much. It'll be over in a little while and everything will be fine."

Tim focused his attention toward Kristy and caught her eyes staring back directly at his. "I don't think it'll ever be fine," he said.

"Don't go funny on me now. It's your fault we're in this mess." Bergan sat up as he spoke, laying the magazine down on the bed beside him.

"My fault!" Tim shouted, staring wildly at Bergan. "What do you mean it's my fault?"

"You're the one who was supposed to stop McPherson from going back into the reactor room. Had you done your job McPherson wouldn't have been caught tampering with that valve and none of this would be happening. As far as I'm concerned you got paid for a job you didn't complete and that mistake is costing me a lot of money." Bergan stared at Tim for a moment, looked at his watch, laid back on the bed and continued to read his magazine.

Tim stared at him in astonishment and shook his head as he walked toward Kristy. He looked out the window for a few moments, then directed his gaze at the girl for whom he had cared so much. It was the first time that he had noticed how tired she looked. "I'm really sorry for all this," he said softly.

She slowly turned her face toward him and paused

for a moment. Her lips parted slightly and Tim noticed that dry sores had formed small crusts on the pink skin. "You're pathetic," she said, wishing her hands were untied so that she could slap him. "Besides, what makes you think my father will bring the money?"

Ed Bergan perked up when he heard Kristy's comment. "Don't you worry little lady, your daddy'll show up with the money. He wouldn't do anything to jeopardize your life. Besides, even if he did Phillip Wright wouldn't let him." Bergan chuckled to himself. He flung his feet over the side of the bed and stood up, making his way to the washroom.

The mention of Phillip's name put a vision of happiness into Kristy's mind. She thought of his sincerity and softness during the moments they had been close to one another. She wondered if she would ever see him again and hoped that he had similar thoughts about her. She returned to the reality of the moment. "Tim, why don't you untie me so that we can both get out of here?"

Tim Browning knew her thoughts were with Phillip. His face became flushed with anger. "I don't know if you realize it but I did all of this because of you."

Kristy looked up at Tim genuinely surprised. "Because of me?" she asked, not believing what she had heard.

"That's right, I sort of hoped that this would have given me enough money so that you and I could go away somewhere and start a life together."

She shook her head from side to side in astonishment. Words could not describe her anger.

She was about to again ask Tim to release her when Ed Bergan came from the washroom. He stared at the twosome for a moment and looked as if he was about to speak when the telephone interrupted. He walked to the small dressing table and lifted the receiver.

"Certainly," he said into the mouth piece. "Come on up."

"Who was that?" Tim asked.

"Our buddy Rolf."

The knock on the door echoed abruptly throughout the entire room. Bergan walked to the door and turned the handle. The athletic body of Willem Rolf was framed within the door. His short blonde hair was neatly combed and his deep blue eyes stood out sharply against his tanned skin. Rolf tipped his head as a form of greeting to the trio in the room. Tim felt intimidated by the presence of the gigantic stranger who had just entered the room.

Rolf walked to Kristy and leaned forward slightly. "I hope we are treating you to your satisfaction?" he said mockingly. His German accent was very pronounced and added a continental flare to his mannerisms. He lifted his hand slowly and reached behind Kristy's head to caress her hair, causing her to tremble. He smiled at her as she tried to ignore him.

He turned his attention back to Bergan. "I trust everything is set?"

"Yes," Bergan replied. "I spoke with Wright and he and McPherson will meet us here at eleven. I also told him to make sure they brought the money."

"Did he give you any indication of how McPherson is doing?"

Kristy looked up at the mention of her father's name.

"He seems to be fine," Bergan continued. "He was resting when I called."

His voice was interrupted by a knock on the door. "Who can that be?" Bergan asked.

"My two assistants," Rolf said as he walked toward the door.

Dermott and Seamus Guilderdale entered the hotel room. The latter had to bend his head slightly to avoid hitting the frame. Both men had discarded their suits for more comfortable, short-sleeve shirts and light coloured slacks. The resemblance to each other was uncanny and if it wasn't for a slight difference in height, one would think they were twins. In reality there was an age difference of four years. Seamus, the taller one, was older and much more muscular. Both men spent an average of two hours a day in a gym pushing individual muscle groups to the maximum.

"I have some food here," Bergan said. "If anybody wants anything just grab it."

Rolf shook his head. "No thank you, I have eaten." He looked at his two associates who had just entered the room. Both of them shook their heads.

"I guess you're really into health food?" Bergan said jokingly. He was dwarfed by the presence of the three men he had hired to assist him. Rolf, with a serious expression on his face, had directed his attention to Kristy. Her eye caught his stare and she turned her glance away from him.

"Are we ready?" Bergan asked.

Rolf took Kristy by the arm. She shook her elbows to free herself from his grip and with her head upright, marched by herself into the corridor behind the two body guards.

When they arrived downstairs, they walked nonchalantly through the lobby, to the parking lot. Rolf, accompanied by Seamus, walked directly behind Kristy to avoid anyone noticing her bound wrists.

Bergan decided it would take approximately forty-five minutes to get to the Temple of Saqqara. He checked his watch to confirm he would be there half an hour before Phillip Wright.

"You come with me," Bergan said, directing his attention to Tim Browning. He looked at Rolf. "Take the girl and your two friends and follow us."

"Any questions?" Bergan paused for a moment, looking at each member of his company. No one spoke but everyone nodded in agreement. "All right then, let's go." Everyone got into their respective cars and left the parking lot heading south to Memphis, the ancient, Egyptian capital and its aged temple at Saqqara.

Bergan glanced at his watch as the car pulled into the sandy parking area near the Stepped Pyramid of Zoser. The traffic had been worse than anticipated and they only had twenty minutes before Phillip Wright was due to show up. He pulled the car to the side of the road and looked in his rear-view mirror, waiting for Rolf to park his vehicle beside his. The near noonday sun was directly overhead, blanketing the area with extreme heat reflecting from the crystal sand.

The massive entrance to the steps of the pyramid, one hundred feet of which lay buried below ground, stood directly before them. Off to the left was a small, wooden structure which housed the facilities.

The area was devoid of souvenir vendors during the hottest time of the day. Bergan stepped from the car, followed by Tim, and walked to the second car to greet its passengers. One of the Guilderdales stepped from the auto, leaving the other brother in the rear with Kristy McPherson. Rolf removed his sunglasses and squinted as he wiped newly-formed perspiration from his brow with his thumb and forefinger. Everyone complained of the extreme heat, intensified by the tension of the situation. Seamus was wiping the sweat from his forehead, his massive weight causing him to perspire more than the others.

Bergan looked at his watch. "Okay, here's the plan. Both the Guilderdales will go into the washroom and I'll wait here by the car. Wright will no doubt come out and talk to me. He'll probably want to see the girl before he hands over any of the money. " Bergan sounded as if he was developing the plan as he spoke. He pointed at Rolf. "You stay crouched down in the car. Browning can stay with the girl in the other car.

"When Wright and McPherson arrive, I'll tell Wright the girl is in the washroom. When McPherson gives me the money, Wright can go and get the girl."

Rolf shook his head in exasperation.

"What's the problem?" Bergan asked somewhat annoyed.

"The plan is ridiculous."

Bergan was about to oppose Rolf's opinion but decided to listen to what he had to say.

Willem Rolf squatted down and traced his finger in a circular motion through the sand. "There are far to many unpredictables in your plan," he said. "We must always take the easiest method for it is usually the most effective."

"You," he said looking at Bergan, "you hide in the washroom with Dermott." He pointed to the small, wooden structure near the edge of the parking lot. "Seamus and Browning will wait in the car while I wait for Wright to arrive. When he gets here I will take him and the money into the washroom under the pretence that the girl is there."

Ed Bergan's lack of experience in these matters gave him no alternative but to accede to Rolf's plan.

"Look over there!" Tim Browning yelled as he pointed to a dust cloud about a half a mile from the entrance of the temple compound.

"It's them," Bergan said.

"Any questions?" Rolf asked. He paused for a moment. No one spoke. "All right, let's get to work." Rolf returned to the automobile and explained the plan to Seamus, who was still guarding Kristy. Tim Browning stepped into the front of the car and drove a short distance until it was just out of sight.

Ed Bergan and the other Guilderdale walked toward the washroom at a slightly quickened pace. Willem Rolf stepped to his car and casually leaned against it, squinting slightly at the cloud of dust approaching and the reflection of the sun shining on the windscreen of Phillip Wright's car.

Phillip pulled the car up slowly, seeing Rolf standing beside his vehicle. Amr had obtained a duplicate of

McPherson's jacket and had tied bandages around his arm and upper shoulder. His head had been fitted with a white wig that was combed in a similar fashion to the injured scientist. He was slouched down as if in grave agony. His skin was slightly white underneath his nose where his moustache had been and he had applied a small bit of make up to cover it. The two men had joked about the way Amr was dressed and privately enjoyed the idea of having a lot of hair.

"Are you ready?" Phillip asked.

Amr nodded, as he applied a little bit more of the red, inky liquid to the bandages from the bottle that he had carried with him.

"I don't see anyone else, do you?" Phillip asked as they looked around. Amr shook his head.

"No. We had better be careful. I am certain they are up to something."

Rolf's arms were folded and one leg was crossed over the other as he casually watched the approaching car. When Phillip stopped the vehicle, Rolf removed the sunglasses and very casually, deliberately, walked toward the two men. He leaned over the driver's window and tilted his head slightly downwards. Phillip had to squint as the sun was in a direct line with Rolf's head.

"Good morning Mr. Wright. We meet again." He had a mischievous grin on his face which broadened into a smile when he saw that Phillip was annoyed. "Place your gun in the back seat of the car and get out please."

Phillip reached into his pocket and removed his automatic. It made a soft thump as it fell on the back seat of the automobile. Rolf grasped the handle of the car door and opened it so that Phillip could step out. He quickly glanced at McPherson. "Good morning Doctor. I trust you are not too uncomfortable?" He noticed the blood on the wound and turned to Phillip. "How is he?"

"What do you care?" Phillip said. "He's coherent,

that's all you need to know." Amr was slouched in his seat covering his face with his hands.

"Nasty, nasty. Mr. Wright you must get used to being defeated. One can't always be the victor."

"I guess you would know."

Rolf leaned into the window and removed the keys from the ignition. He stood up and faced Phillip. "Where is the money?" he asked.

"My arrangements were with Ed Bergan, not with you," Phillip said.

Rolf paused for a moment. "Come with me," he ordered and led Phillip toward the small wooden structure which housed Ed Bergan and Dermott Guilderdale.

Sitting on a small wooden platform beside the entrance to the washroom were three Egyptians engaged in casual conversation. Beside them on the floor was a bag with a small supply of Arab headdresses and paper fans left over from their souvenir sales earlier in the day. The threesome stopped talking when Rolf and Phillip arrived. Suddenly one of them saw the gun in Rolf's hand. He began yelling in Arabic to his two compatriots. The other two glanced at Rolf's weapon and the trio instantaneously ran toward the security of the temple. Rolf smiled as he watched the men scurry off.

Phillip pushed the green door of the white, stucco building and was impressed by the cleanliness of this remote outpost facility. Ed Bergan and Dermott Guilderdale were cramped inside the small room. Phillip entered but Rolf waited outside.

"Hello Phillip, nice to see you again," Ed Bergan said mockingly.

"I wish that I could say the same," Phillip said as he looked at Dermott Guilderdale. "Where's the girl?"

"Patience my friend, you will see her in due time."

Dermott Guilderdale stepped around so that he was between Phillip and the door, trapping the ISIS agent inside.

"Did you bring the money?" Bergan asked.

"It's hidden very close to here. When I get the girl I'll give you the money."

"No, no, no! That's not how it works, when I get the money you'll have the girl!" Bergan said emphatically.

"I want to see her," Phillip said.

Bergan stared deep into Phillip's eyes and waited for a moment. "Very well." He nodded to Dermott to move aside and opened the door as bright rays of hot sunlight shone in. As he stepped onto the small platform he removed his gun from the shoulder holster and waited for Phillip to come out.

Once everyone was outside, Bergan gave instructions to Dermott to search Phillip for any possible weapons that might be concealed. The Irishman waited for Rolf to aim his gun at Phillip before proceeding with the search.

Dermott nodded and stepped to where Rolf was standing. The German whispered in his ear and the large Irishman walked along the path toward Phillip's car.

"Let's go," he said as he ushered Phillip in the same direction. When they arrived at Phillip's car, Bergan leaned over and looked in the window. Amr was doing a superb job of acting his part. Phillip gazed around for the bodyguard but could not see him. Suddenly he heard a car door slam from an area that was shielded by a small hill of sand somewhere near the entrance of the temple. It took Phillip a moment to realize there were people standing beside a large pillar next to the entrance way. The distance was about seventy-five feet but the hot sun reflecting off the sand made it difficult to see. Suddenly he realized that Kristy McPherson was one of the people standing there. Next to her was Tim Browning. Both of them were framed by the two Irish bodyguards.

"You see Mr. Wright?" Rolf mocked. "Your precious girlfriend is all right."

Bergan nodded for Rolf to join him in consultation. The two men spoke as Phillip looked on. Kristy seemed to be all right, he was thankful for that. She was standing of her own free will.

"All right, you two better get going," Bergan said as the twosome returned to where Phillip was standing. "Rolf is going to go with you to get the money. Once he has it you'll drive back here and then we'll let the girl go."

Rolf vigorously waved his arm and one of the two Guilderdale brothers began running toward him. A small cloud of dust was forming behind the heels of the large Irishman as he ran in the direction of Willem Rolf.

"Get in the back," Rolf ordered as he pointed toward the back seat of his automobile. Phillip obeyed reverently as Dermott Guilderdale sat next to him.

Phillip knew Amr had heard them and it would be up to his Egyptian colleague to free Kristy while he was gone. He stole a glance at Amr, looking for a response, but there was none. The agent was playing his part perfectly while secretly developing a plan for Kristy's release.

Rolf started the engine and circled around Phillip's car exiting the entrance to the pyramid the same way they had come in. Phillip and Amr had hurriedly cut up small pieces of paper in the shape of U.S. currency. These were put into stacks and secured with elastic bands. An actual ten dollar American bill had been placed on top of each stack and the briefcase had been filled to capacity. At a quick glance it certainly looked like a lot of money and would fool anyone until they began to flip through the paper packages. Phillip and Amr had left the briefcase in a small, deserted tomb on their way in.

The three rode in silence, aside from the occasional explanation of direction by Phillip.

Ed Bergan watched a cloud of dust trail behind the car as it sped off in the distance. He waved to the threesome standing beside a large sand dune near the entrance to the temple of Zoser. He began to walk slowly toward them as they in turn started to approach him. The heavy-set Irishman led Kristy by the arm in forceful fashion. Her hair had been blown wildly by the wind and her lack of sleep was evident by her bleached complexion and the dark circles around her eyes. Her slacks were covered in a thin layer of sandy dust.

"It appears Phillip is once again good at obeying orders," Ed Bergan said. He had a satirical smile on his face as he spoke. "Of course you know we can't let any of you live after we get the money."

Kristy ignored Bergan and stared beyond him at the car with the slumped figure of Amr dressed in her father's clothes sitting in the passenger's seat. She tried desperately to conceal her emotions as she felt tears welling up in her eyes. Her face flushed and she bit her lip to divert the pain showing on her face. Her mind was filled with hatred for the short overweight man standing across from her.

"You never said anything about killing them," Tim Browning said. It was the first time that he had spoken since they had seen Phillip Wright.

"Don't worry about it," Bergan said. "We don't really have any other choice. You should realize that."

Kristy could feel Seamus' grip lessening as he listened to Ed Bergan's conversation. She flung her arms wildly and caught the guard by surprise. He released his grip and Kristy sprung forward, raising her hands toward the level of Ed Bergan's face. She formed her fingers into a claw and could feel the flesh rip as she dug her sharp fingernails deep into the soft skin of his cheeks. The stocky little man screamed with agony. Seamus immediately went into action and grabbed both her arms, pulling her away from Ed Bergan.

Bergan stared at her in amazement and slowly raised his hand to tend his wounds. The blood was flowing freely and sent a shock through his system. He reached in his pocket for a handkerchief and began to dab at the wounds. He felt his cheeks beginning to sting as he touched the raw skin with the cloth kerchief. He directed his other hand toward Kristy and let his knuckles and fingertips make contact with her face. The blow caught her unexpectedly and she slumped into the strong grip of Seamus Guilderdale.

Tim Browning took a step forward in protest but thought it better not to speak as he watched Ed Bergan nurture the fresh wounds on his face.

Bergan looked at the bodyguard. "There is no point in keeping her around. We got what we want. Get rid of her," he ordered.

A look of panic filled Kristy's eyes. All the activity had made her forget her own safety, but it was now coming into the foreground of the situation. She twisted and squirmed but Seamus' grip was very tight. He would not fall for her little trick again.

Tim Browning spoke up. "Why don't you let her go? We don't really need her once we have the money."

"Why don't you shut up!" Bergan said, feeling the torturous pain in his face as he spoke.

Amr, who had been watching the entire escapade from the car felt helpless. To expose himself now would mean immediate death for himself and Kristy and it would not help Phillip at all. He watched as Seamus raised his gun and pointed it at Kristy's head. He pressed his hand on the horn of the car and did not release it.

The company of four reverted their attention to the auto. "My father!" Kristy yelled. She had forgotten he was in the car. "Can I go and see him for a minute?"

Bergan thought for a moment. "Go ahead," he said. He looked at Seamus Guilderdale. "Go with her."

The large Irishman replaced the gun in his holster and took Kristy by the arm, pulling her toward the passenger side of the car. Amr was still slumped down in the seat and it was not until Seamus opened the car door that he sprang into action. He raised his gun and pointed it directly into the stomach of the large, Irish bodyguard. Without hesitation the trained Egyptian agent pulled the trigger and a loud explosion took the Irishman by surprise. His mouth fell open and his face showed signs of disbelief. His grip on Kristy was immediately released and both his arms cradled his stomach. He fell backward onto the sand and groaned slightly as his body went limp. Blood trickled from the gunshot wound. Kristy McPherson shrieked as the figure of her captor crumpled beside her.

She raised her gaze from the slumped body lying at her feet to the man in the automobile. She immediately realized that it wasn't her father and a puzzled look came over her face.

"Get in!" Amr ordered as he slipped behind the steering wheel. He had removed a spare ignition key from his jacket pocket while speaking to Kristy. She couldn't move. Her body stood frozen as shock penetrated every inch of it. Her mouth was wide open and tears were streaming down her cheeks.

Both Ed Bergan and Tim Browning, upon hearing the gun shot, flung their heads in the direction of the automobile. When they saw the body of the large Irishman sprawled in the sand they ran toward the safety of the other car. Bergan stopped, raised his pistol and fired a shot in the direction of Amr. The Egyptian leaned over and grabbed Kristy by the arm, pulling her into the car.

He forced his foot down on the accelerator, causing the rear wheels to spin and creating an enormous dust cloud behind them. They left the parking lot as fast as the car would take them and headed in the direction of the tomb where Phillip had led Rolf, hoping they wouldn't be too late.

Both Bergan and Browning began shooting at the car. "Get down!" Amr yelled as he placed his hand on the back of her neck, pushing her onto the seat. The car sped along the sandy road, exiting the temple complex heading for the main street that would take him to the small, hidden tomb.

Ed Bergan fired several shots in vain and was left staring at the dust behind by Amr's speedy getaway. The pain in his face was secondary to the latest turn in events and was now only a numb sensation, recessed in the far reaches of his mind. Tim Browning had dropped to the ground and lay face down in the sand, trembling with fear.

"Get up!" Ed Bergan ordered as he started toward the entrance of the temple behind him. Tim Browning raised his eyes and after realizing they were alone, was quick to jump up. Bergan, already at the hidden automobile, was relieved when he saw the keys in the ignition.

"I wouldn't worry too much," Tim Browning said as the car began to exit the parking lot. "I'm sure that Rolf can handle the situation. Lorne is pretty badly injured and won't be a menace to anyone."

"That's good, I'll tell Seamus Guilderdale's mother that when I write her about her son's death," Bergan said with sarcasm. "We obviously have no idea how badly injured McPherson is. He's well enough to shoot someone and well enough to drive off in a car. I'd say he's appears to be quite healthy." Small beads of perspiration were forming on Ed Bergan's forehead. His knuckles became white as he applied extra strength to the steering wheel. He squinted, trying to shield his eyes from the bright, glowing sun, almost running off the road several times. Let's hope this entire thing wasn't a setup," he said.

"What do you mean?" Tim asked curiously.

"McPherson's no idiot. If somehow he tricked Wright and ended up with the money we may never hear from him or his daughter again."

"But Wright said he had the money hidden in the tomb."

"That's exactly it. '*Wright said*'!" Bergan bit his upper lip as he finished speaking. "All I know is that we have to catch up with them as fast as we possibly can."

Once the car's tires made contact with the pavement of the main road, Bergan's foot forced the accelerator lower and pushed the car to its limit.

Bergan's jacket had been torn and he wished that he had removed it to relieve some of the agony from the extreme heat. His hair kept falling in his face and he pushed it back with his hand. It became mangled with sweat, pasting it against his scalp.

"How far is it?" Kristy asked. It was the first time that she had spoken since Amr had pulled her into the car. She wasn't exactly sure what was happening but one thing was certain, the man beside her was not her father.

Amr pointed in the distance and Kristy had to strain her eyes to see a small dot which grew slowly, taking on the shape of a parked car. The dull gray of the coarse, desert sand dunes, covered with small particles of broken rock, was all that could be seen for miles around. A break in the mundane scenery was caused by a tiny, cubed building approximately ten feet high which was the entrance to the tomb. Rolf's car was parked approximately thirty feet from the entrance.

Amr parked his car as far away as he could and removed the wig and bandage that had been tied around his arm.

"Where is my father?" Kristy asked.

"He's fine," Amr said. "Once Rolf finds out there is no money Phillip's life won't be worth a damn."

"What do you mean there's no money?" Kristy asked astonished.

"Your father never told us where the money was."

"Well then what does Phillip have in the tomb?"

"Last night's edition of the Cairo Gazette." He stared at her for a moment as she reacted to the incredible situation. "Come with me," he said as they exited the car.

"Don't slam the door," Amr whispered over the roof of the car. They softly pressed against the metal doors and allowed only a small click to be heard as the door lock made contact with the latch.

Stealthily they walked toward the entrance of the small tomb. The entire wall had been covered with hieroglyphics. Faint remnants of four thousand year old, colourful paint was still visible.

They stood beside the door opening. Amr removed the gun from his holster. He checked the safety, which had not been locked since the gun had been fired several moments earlier at point blank range, into the stomach of Seamus Guilderdale.

"I want you to walk behind this temple and don't make a sound." Amr said to Kristy in a soft voice. "I'm certain Bergan and your friend Browning will be pulling up shortly. I don't want them to see you."

"What about you?" Kristy asked.

"I'm going inside to help Phillip."

"I want to come too."

"No, I think it will be more helpful if Phillip knew you were safe outside."

Kristy could hear impatience in his voice and decided not to challenge his request. She nodded in agreement and began to walk around the cube building to ensure she was out of sight.

Amr entered the temple through a small opening and stood surrounded by total darkness in what he believed to be a corridor. He stumbled his way into a larger room and saw a dim light coming from an opening at the far end. He sensed he had been walking downward and was probably underground by now. The light was coming from a torch in a connecting hallway leading into a second chamber. He carefully stepped in, allowing his gun to lead the way, and was relieved when he saw no signs of life. Again lit torches were suspended against the walls. Their flickering flames danced wildly, creating shadowy movements on the colour-ful wall paintings inside the room. He followed another hallway, leading to a third chamber which was smaller inside than the first two, and again found it to be empty. As he entered the passageway leading further underground, he began to hear faint voices. He crept slowly, forward his gun poised as he tried to make sense of the sounds that became more aural with every step.

"It is unfortunate Mr. Wright, but now that I have the money I have no more use for you," Rolf said with intimi-dation.

"Funny, that doesn't surprise me," Phillip replied. He was thankful that Rolf had not checked the briefcase more closely. He hoped that Amr had done something to free Kristy and that the two of them were away from her captors.

"I don't understand, Mr. Wright. If you expected us to kill you, why did you show us where the money was?"

Phillip paused for a moment. "I guess I was appeal-ing to your more humane side."

Rolf sneered. He turned his attention to Dermott Guilderdale. His gun was aimed at Phillip's temple. "How should we dispose of him?" Rolf asked mockingly.

Amr was surprised by the calmness in Phillip's voice and wondered how he would react in similar circumstances. He realized the opportunity for him to act was now. A moment later Phillip would be dead.

With sudden fury he leaped forward and jumped into the next chamber, clasping his gun with both hands and pointing it directly in front of him. He was about to yell when he realized that the chamber he was standing in was totally empty. He was stunned as he looked around in despair. Again he heard voices.

"Well Mr. Wright, your time has come."

The echo of Rolf's voice bounced throughout the chamber Amr was standing in. Amr quickly stepped through the vault into a hallway leading to another small room. Before he entered he saw shadows of people inside. The echoes in the tomb were deceiving but he felt certain that he had located the people holding Phillip Wright hostage.

Again he braced his body and jumped through the small opening, entering the burial chamber of one of Egypt's ancient heroes.

"Freeze!" he yelled as he came upon Willem Rolf. He caught the tall German unexpectedly as Rolf swung his face in the direction of Amr.

Although he was taken back he remained calm and slowly addressed Amr. "And who might you be?"

Dermott Guilderdale was not as professional as his superior. For an instant he lowered his aim and turned his face to greet the intruder. It was the opportunity Phillip required. His hand shot forward and he braced his palm making contact with the fist of the tall Irishman. The blow caught Dermott by surprise and the gun flew from his hand.

"Move and you're dead," Amr said to Rolf as Phillip bent over to pick up the fallen weapon.

"Most interesting," Rolf said, noticing Amr dressed in McPherson's jacket.

"How's Kristy?" Phillip asked desperately as he stood pointing the gun at the bodyguard.

"She is fine," Amr said.

Kristy McPherson waited impatiently behind the temple as the noonday sun pounded its hot rays on her. Anxiety would not allow her to stand uninvolved any longer. She slowly stepped to the side of the cubed building to see if she could spot any movement. There was no car in sight and she wondered what had happened to Ed Bergan and Tim Browning. She was nervous about Amr and Phillip and knew that she had to go inside the small building to satisfy her concerns. She paused for a moment to consider defying Amr's instructions and decided it was more important for her to be involved. She was, after all, a major force in this entire operation. As she approached the chamber hosting the foursome, she heard the voice of Amr.

"We had better get out of here, Bergan was directly behind us," Amr said to Phillip as they ushered the two captives from the chamber. Suddenly and without warning the soft, rustling sound of Kristy's approach came from behind them. The disturbance lasted only a second but it was enough to throw Amr off guard.

Rolf sprung into action. While Amr's head tilted to the side, Rolf's hand shot forward and caught the Egyptian square in the face. Phillip was about to direct his attention back to Dermott Guilderdale but the Irish body-builder was quicker. He raised his leg and his foot caught the bottom of Phillip's hand, knocking the gun upward and landing with a thud on the floor. Amr was flying into the solid stone wall and Rolf poised his body ready for combat. Dermott Guilderdale lunged forward and attacked Phillip, forcing him to fall to the ground and throwing his weight on top. Amr regained his senses and braced himself for another attack by Rolf. As expected the German pushed his fist forward, directing it at Amr's face. The Egyptian agent had nowhere to turn and took the punch directly in the jaw. As pain raced through Amr's face he instinctively threw his leg up and could feel his shin making contact with Rolf's groin. The German bent forward in agony and Amr raised his knee, hitting Rolf directly under his nose. He prayed that the contact he made would be enough as his own his eyes were filled with blood and he had no idea in which direction he was striking. Amr was terrified in the darkness but each second that passed without retaliation brought relief.

Phillip was squirming under the weight of the massive Irish body-builder. He managed to make a connection with his fist and caught Dermott in the temple. The big Irishman shifted his weight and punched Phillip directly in the side of his torso.

"Stop or I'll shoot!" Kristy shouted.

Dermott looked up and saw Kristy McPherson standing in the opening. She had taken Amr's gun from the sand and was pointing it at the head of his superior. Willem Rolf was still unconscious and bright red blood was flowing freely from his nostrils, turning a deep brown as it mixed with the sandy floor of the tomb.

"If he's not dead I'll kill him!" Kristy screamed.

Dermott saw her eyes become fiery as they filled with hatred. He decided not to test the credibility of her intentions. He began to relax the tension in his muscles and slowly slipped his body onto its side, resting on his knee and elbow. Phillip felt relieved as the burden of the weight was removed from him. The pain in his side was throbbing, causing difficulty in breathing. He managed to glance up at Amr, who was rubbing both his eyes with the palms of his hands.

"Are you all right?" he asked as he limped toward his Egyptian friend.

"Yes..., I believe so," Amr said, stammering as he spoke. His vision was returning. Both men gazed at Kristy, who continued to fix the gun's barrel at the temple of Willem Rolf, lying lifeless on the floor.

Kristy watched the terrifying scene as if it were a stage play and saw Phillip looking at the other gun as he reached to pick it up. While he pointed it at Dermott Guilderdale, she failed to notice Rolf regaining consciousness and slowly extracting a knife hidden somewhere on his person. Rolf waited for the opportune moment when Kristy's attention was away from him and flew upward in a sudden movement reversing roles, pointing the tip of the knife directly at the throat of Kristy McPherson.

"Drop it Wright," Rolf shouted.

Phillip paused momentarily but as Rolf slowly moved the point of the knife back and forth against the soft, tanned skin of the girl Phillip had grown so fond of, decided to let the revolver fall on the sandy floor.

25 Despair

Amr was barely able to see but knew enough not to move from his position against the rocky wall.

"Rolf!" Bergan's voice echoed from somewhere deep within the dimly lit series of man-made caverns. Everyone grew silent as they strained to hear the faint sounds coming from somewhere near the entrance of the tomb. The shout was repeated, this time louder, as the source of the noise was coming closer.

"In here!" Rolf yelled, not allowing his attention to be taken away from his captives.

It was a matter of seconds before Ed Bergan and Tim Browning had found their way to the chamber.

"Ah," Ed Bergan said softly, "I see you've all found each other." He drew his gun from the security of its holster and held it at Phillip. "Tim, give me the bag," he said, motioning to the suitcase believed to contain the money.

Tim walked to the black, vinyl briefcase laying in the corner of the small chamber. "Open it," Bergan directed. Tim slowly released the latches on the case and lifted the lid, allowing the contents to be viewed by everyone in the room.

"Bring it here," Bergan commanded. Once the briefcase was secure in his hand he slowly changed the position of the gun and pointed it toward Willem Rolf. A sneer came to his face as he focused the gun at Rolf's forehead. "Thank you very much Mr. Rolf. I appreciate everything you've done. Now please line up with the others."

Rolf's face spun around in disbelief as he stared at Bergan. "What are you doing, you idiot?" he asked as he glared into the barrel of Bergan's revolver.

"You know exactly what I'm doing," Bergan answered. "Now get over with the others, you too Browning," he said as he motioned Tim Browning to join the rest of the group. "I have no use for any of you."

"You can't do this," Tim stammered.

"Shut up and get over there."

Amr began to chuckle at the events unfolding around him.

Willem Rolf slackened the grip on the knife still pointed at Kristy's throat and began to move back, knowing Bergan would not hesitate to use his gun. Kristy stepped forward into the waiting arms of Phillip Wright. Tears flowed from her face as she felt the warm security of his body near hers.

Bergan set the briefcase on the floor between his feet, not removing his eyes from his captives. He directed his hand into the outside-jacket pocket and removed a small, forest-green hand grenade. He slowly lifted the pear-shaped object to his lips and with the strength of his teeth grasped the small metal ring, pulling the grenade away from his mouth and securing the small detonation lever with his thumb. He stood forward and spat the silver ring onto the sand.

"What are you doing? You'll kill us all!" Tim Browning cried as perspiration flowed from his forehead.

"Just a little insurance," Bergan said smiling.

"You know you'll never get away with this," Phillip said still holding Kristy.

"I don't really believe that you will do this," Rolf said as he stood straight and tall facing Ed Bergan.

"Rolf," Bergan replied, "this isn't a movie." He paused for a moment, smiled, and steadying his hand as best he could, slowly and deliberately squeezed his forefinger against the small metal trigger of the weapon in his hand. The gun jolted slightly as the deafening echo shot throughout the chamber of the ancient, Egyptian tomb.

Everyone was taken by surprise but no one dared move. Willem Rolf stood silent with his eyes wide open. He could not understand what was happening. Ever so slowly his lower lip began to tremble and he desperately attempted to keep his mouth closed. Against his will his lip began to fall and he could feel a thick warm liquid filling his mouth. He slowly tilted his head down and allowed his lifeless eyes to focus on a large red wound in the centre of his chest. His shirt was rapidly soaking up the blood spurting from the centre of his upper body. He could feel no pain and his vision became blurred as small dancing lights jumped wildly from all directions. Far in the distance he saw Ed Bergan staring at him. The image was clouded and fading rapidly. He tried to wave a sign of recognition but was not able to control his movements. Suddenly the image faded totally and was replaced by a black blanket of night.

Ed Bergan watched as Rolf's body crumpled to the floor. The diversion gave him just enough time to accomplish what he had planned. While the others were still stunned from the shock of watching Willem Rolf die before their eyes, Bergan grabbed the briefcase, and with his gun still fixed securely in his hand, ran from the chamber into the small hallway connecting the next room. He no sooner left the group when he heard the shuffling of feet from the five remaining captives. He released the hand grenade and dashed with all the speed he could muster into the hallway leading toward the exit of the tomb. Once outside he continued running to his car which he had left parked on the road. He hid behind the security of the auto and waited for the loud explosion to take place.

"The grenade!" Kristy yelled as Phillip and Amr dashed from the small chamber into the corridor. Kristy, Tim Browning and Dermott Guilderdale stayed behind.

"There it is!" Amr yelled as both men saw the small, oval-shaped, metal object laying several feet behind them.

It was the last sound that Phillip remembered hearing. If there had been a loud blast from the grenade's explosion, it had been totally erased from his memory. All he could feel was uncomfortable heat beating down on his tiresome body.

"Are you all right?"

Phillip could hear the words, softly at first, but then growing louder inside his head. Reality was coming back into focus. He opened his eyes and squinted tightly against the overhead sun shining directly on him. He moved his head to the side and saw Amr's body crouched over his.

"Phillip, can you hear me?"

As reality began to overcome the dullness of his senses he felt coherency return. There was no pain and his legs and arms were moveable. "What happened?" he asked, still stunned from the shock.

"The corridor wall we were standing against must have been extremely thick. It seems to have forced the blast back into the chamber behind us." Phillip slowly lifted his weight onto his elbows and looked in front of him. The tomb had been reduced to a gigantic pile of rubble. As his senses were focusing a void was filling his memory.

"Kristy!" he shouted and tried to jump up.

Amr restrained him and spoke softly. "There is nothing you can do for them now," he said solemnly.

"No!" Phillip shouted in a long draw out scream. He

released himself from Amr's grip and ran toward the heap before him. He desperately grasped at the stones, flinging them wildly about. Realizing most of the stones were heavier than he could lift, he slowly ceased his action and remained on his knees, lowering his head. Tears began to flow freely from his eyes as grief overcame him. The build up of tension over the last few weeks had taken its effect. Kristy had filled an eight year gap in his life. He had desperately spent the last two days in an effort to get her away from her captors, only to now lose her forever. He raised his hands to his face and continued to sob.

Amr walked slowly to his friend and grabbed him by the upper arms. Phillip, not conscious of Amr's presence remained stationary. As the moments passed, he slowly became aware of Amr's embrace and realized that he must get up. His Egyptian friend stared at him but said nothing. The two men quietly walked to what only moments before was the entrance to a tomb celebrating an ancient era.

Amr's car seemed untouched by the explosion and surrounding rubble.

"Let's go," Amr said as he got into the driver's side of the car.

"I think Bergan has about ten minutes on us," Amr said, judging his watch as he spoke. The tires squealed and the dust clouds rose as Amr recklessly spun the car around, heading back to the main road. He drove wildly in desperate pursuit.

As the rental auto left the scene of the hideous enactment, Ed Bergan slowly released his tightening grip on the steering wheel. His vision nervously darted between the endless road ahead and the dusty trail of windblown sand visible in the rear-view mirror. With each passing moment of time, a minute particle of fear left his senses and was replaced by the comforting ally of relief. The reality of the evil deed assured him no one would have been able to escape such a brutal blast at close range in the confined quarters of the aged, Egyptian tomb.

A haunting image appeared in his mind as he vividly imagined the facial expressions of the shocked casualties as they came to grip with the immensity of their final moment. Bergan wiped his eyes, subconsciously warding off evil spirits dancing recklessly in his mind, toying with his senses.

As the seconds became minutes, he gathered his thoughts and returned to the reality of his present situation. He smiled openly and allowed an audible chuckle to beat the deafening silence surrounding him. Even the gentle hum of the automobile engine had sifted into an indistinguishable background noise. He was pleased with his results and the reward on the seat next to him had justified the means.

Combined with a little money he had managed to save over the years, the immense fortune he had now inherited would be quite sufficient to commence a new existence in a remote region of the world. After careful consideration and months of tedious planning, he had decided on a small, Caribbean island lost in a gigantic sea of azure-blue ocean. A vision of serenity engulfed him and brought tranquil peace to his tense and tired body. Palm trees swayed gently in the breeze as dancers might sway to and fro in each others arms. Beaches were sensually caressed by soft, foamy-white water smoothing a sandy field in their wake.

Ed Bergan felt deserving of this mentally fulfilling image. He had paid a dear toll for a luxury he was about to relish. His life had never been rewarding and he had always fallen victim to greed. He recalled his previous visit to Cairo as a representative of the very government he was now creating havoc with. He had been accused of falsifying transportation documents for personal gain. They had labelled him an embarrassment to his nation and had recalled his post. He smiled as he reminisced and thought of the money securely locked in a local Cairo bank. So what if he aided criminals for self-improvement? Who were these self-righteous superiors who had condemned him into a stagnant career? He knew they too had been guilty of similar crimes throughout their professional lives. He pounded the steering wheel with his fist as the anger from bygone days resurfaced, stirring the embers of a hidden but not extinguished fire.

He sped along the road and came to a slight turn which caused the sun to shine directly into his face. He squinted tightly and fumbled through his inner pockets for his sunglasses, cursing the desert climate as he drove.

His thoughts turned to Lorne McPherson and he wondered where the estranged scientist lay awaiting his fate. How badly had he been wounded? Perhaps he had died and Phillip Wright had not been able to recover the body. He wished time would reverse itself back to that night in Cordoba when McPherson had returned to the dangerous confines of the reactor room in an effort to undo the potential damage orchestrated the prior night. If the valve had remained in its corrupt state the overall plan would have been successfully implemented. The reactor would have detonated, the British would have honoured their promissory note, and Ed Bergan would already be living a life of luxurious splendour.

He had not counted on McPherson's conscience to play an integral part in such an otherwise foolproof plan. If only events had proceeded properly from their initiation. McPherson could have kept his share of the money and Bergan would have had a much greater bounty. He would have saved tremendous expense and heartaches.

He was thankful Rolf was no longer a threat to his existence. The German assassin would have swallowed a major share of the new-found wealth now calmly resting on the cushioned seat of the automobile. He was equally joyous that Phillip Wright and his accomplice had fallen victims to his attack. Although he could not have found McPherson without Phillip's help, the agent had become a thorn in his side ever since Rolf had failed to eliminate him in Cartagena.

He felt that everything had worked out perfectly. He was extremely thankful he had the foresight to bring the hand grenade. He had purchased it the previous day from an army depot, using some of his old connections.

He mentally calculated his expenses and with great relief determined they would not exceed his expectations. He scanned his rear view mirror and, certain he was not being followed, slowed the car slightly as the sun penetrated the front windscreen, impairing his vision. His hand reached for the briefcase laying flat on the seat next to him and he caressed the vinyl coating before fumbling with the two flip locks. He raised the lid and smiled broadly as he glanced from the road before him to the stacks of ten dollar bills. McPherson had even taken the courtesy to supply him with U.S. funds. He was stunned at the thought of the vast sum of money bundled together for the sole purpose of pleasing him. Casually and with great pride he flipped his thumb through one of the piles, deriving great pleasure from the touch of the currency that would soon fulfil his earthly desires.

His eyes were trained on the road before him and he granted himself the luxury of thumbing through the stack once more. Somehow the paper had a different texture from what he had imagined. He glanced at the currency and lifted one of the stacks from the security of its safe haven. As he carefully fondled the legal tender, he noticed the sides of several bills had different markings. He raised the stack to eye level and, without deviating from his driving, turned it upside down. A sudden wave of shock riveted throughout his mind and settled insecurely, deep in the pit of his stomach. He disbelieved the vision his eyes were relaying to his brain and nearly lost control of the thundering automobile which obediently desired to follow his directions.

All but the top bill was nothing more than neatly trimmed newspaper. He flipped through the stack again as if by some wizard's magic it would change. He could not contain his anger and began shouting obscenities at Phillip Wright and all he stood for. The key with which a prosperous future was to have been unlocked was now a figment of imagination. Outraged, he threw the counterfeit paper on the floor of the front seat and grabbed a second. It, like the first, was also an illusion.

Ed Bergan wept openly and cursed at what moments before he believed to be his financial security. He failed to notice an abandoned automobile along the road. It had been discarded in such a manner that the tail end obstructed the flow of traffic. The blinding sun, coupled by tears of pain in his eyes, was enough to render the vehicle invisible to Ed Bergan's preoccupied mind.

With only one hand on the steering wheel he swerved sharply to the centre of the road in a last second effort to avoid contact with the obstructive auto. In so doing he lost control of his own vehicle, which spun wildly across the road and bolted upright as the front wheels came in contact with the thick desert sand.

Bergan lost his sense of direction with the sudden and erratic movement of the auto, as it demonically claimed control of its destiny. The car was spinning out of control and a rapid mix of sky and sand blended into a blur, followed by a strange darkness.

A tiny opening void of colour and objectivity began to grow as Bergan forced his anaesthetised body toward it. Moments later he entered the deep dark chamber of blackness as it completely engulfed him. There was no pain and he felt no motion, only a sensation of fear and loneliness as he was devoured by the darkness of these strange surroundings.

Amr was the first to spot a funnel of dust rising uncontrollably from the desert sand several yards ahead.

Neither man had spoken since their rapid exit from the scene of death and destruction. Phillip could not free his mind from the terrifying visions of the recent events. Amr was sensitive to his comrade's feelings and said nothing, realizing there were no words to console the loss Phillip felt. He continued to push the car at high speeds in the direction of the rising smoke. Immediately he recognized the crumpled vehicle and stopped directly behind it. Bergan's car had flipped on its side with two wheels spinning furiously as if they had not been made aware of the auto's inability to continue on its quest. Steam was rising from under the hood, accompanied by a hissing sound as the hot water pressure sought a route of escape from within its containment. Bergan had been flung onto his back and was laying motionless with his eyes closed. Phillip jumped on top of the car in an effort to open the passenger door. Gravity worked against him and he could not dislocate the heavy piece of metal. Amr tried to assist but found it to be a futile attempt.

The Egyptian jumped from the car and greeted several bystanders who had curiously wandered from nearby homes to the sight of the dust and noise. He spoke in Arabic followed by a shout at Phillip.

"Get down," he ordered, taking charge of the situation. Phillip looked around and saw the men who had gathered, walking in his direction. He stepped from the metal frame and stood idly by as several men pushed the car into an upright position.

Amr slowly opened the passenger door and Ed Bergan's body slumped lifelessly from the collapsed vehicle. With the help of two other men Amr lifted Bergan's limp frame onto the desert sand. He leaned forward in an effort to locate a heart pulse.

"He is still alive."

Amr's words caused Phillip to focus on the vision of Bergan's face and he instantly lunged forward, shooting his hands directly into the throat of the motionless form which had caused him so much grief. It took all of Amr's strength, assisted by one of the onlookers, to keep Phillip from mutilating the body of Ed Bergan. Amr braced himself against Phillip, forcing his forearm against his chest in an attempt to restrain his mindless provocation.

"Snap out of it!" he yelled. "This will not bring her back."

Amr felt Phillip slowly relax and he carefully exhaled loosening the tension in his arm. The reality of Amr's words were forming a truthful statement. Nothing Phillip could do or say could bring Kristy back.

"Are you all right?" Amr asked, waiting for Phillip to nod and respond. The Egyptian agent walked toward one of the onlookers and spoke to him, resulting in the man scampering to a nearby building.

"I asked him to call the police and get an ambulance."

EPILOGUE

"More wine?" the soft voice of the dark-haired Egyptian beauty asked as she held the bottle of deep, red nectar over Phillip's glass.

"No, thank you," he said softly, solemnly.

"Is there anything else I can get you? Perhaps some more food?"

"No, really. You've been far too kind already." Phillip smiled as he spoke. Amr's wife was extremely understanding and hospitable. She had prepared a delicious dinner for the two tired agents upon their arrival. Amr had briefly told her of Phillip's loss and she was sincerely sympathetic. She seemed to sense when to speak and when to act. Stepping back from the balcony, she watched Phillip playing with the stem of his crystal glass as he stared into the Egyptian sunset. In the distance the Nile was flowing freely, bringing water gathered from Lake Victoria. It brought with it debris collected along its tiresome tour of the jungle. Soon it would end its weary journey, making its way into the warm waters of the Mediterranean, only to begin anew for the remainder of eternity. A warm evening breeze was gently caressing Phillip's face as his eyes stared lifelessly forward, reminiscing about the girl he had hoped to spend a great deal of time with. Again he felt tears welling in the corners of his eyes and he fought hard to keep them from forming into droplets.

"That was Peter Alexander. I explained the situation to him and he expressed his sympathy," Amr said, entering the balcony and taking the chair next to Phillip.

"How is he?"

"He seems to be doing much better. He sounds quite normal. He is recovering in the hospital and was recently updated of our situation. McPherson is en route to Canada where his share of the money is secured in a local bank." Amr chuckled. "It seems no one has any legal claim to it so I guess he will be enjoying it."

"That's good," Phillip said quietly.

"Look Phillip," Amr said sympathetically, "you don't have to leave tonight, you are more than welcome to stay here a few more days."

"No my friend. I think I'd better go tonight. I want to get this over with as quickly as possible."

"You know they are not going to let you resign just like that."

"I know. What time do we have to leave?" Phillip said, wishing to change the subject.

"Your flight is at nine-thirty." Amr looked at his watch. "That gives us about two hours. We should leave for the airport soon."

Phillip nodded and sipped the remainder of his wine. He picked up his attaché case and thanked Amr's wife for her wonderful hospitality, kissing both her cheeks with gratitude. She had a soft warm look in her eyes and cupped his hand with both of hers as she wished him well. She kissed her husband and the two men departed for the airport.

Amr carried Phillip's case and assisted him through Customs. Phillip removed his passport in readiness for the agent awaiting his next passenger.

"Incidentally," Amr began speaking. "Bergan will be okay. Once he is released from hospital he will be taken to prison in Cairo to stand trial for murder. The Egyptians are not as easy on their convicts as North Americans are. I think that he will spend the rest of his life behind bars, should he manage to avoid the death penalty."

Phillip no longer felt the uncontrollable anger shown earlier toward Ed Bergan. The deep loss of Kristy McPherson had diminished his angered emotions and transformed them into sorrow.

He bade his friend farewell and thanked him for all his help.

"Why don't you consider working in the Mid East for a while? We would make a good team, you and I." Amr spoke with genuine sincerity.

"Thanks, but I think it'll be a while before I get back into the working spirit."

"You can't quit, it's in your blood." Amr smiled. "Besides what makes you think they will just let you walk away from it?"

"You're probably right, but I'm definitely going to take a few weeks off and think things out."

"Stay in touch." The two men embraced each other and Amr planted a kiss on each of Phillip's cheeks.

．　　．　　．　　．　　．

Phillip lit a cigarette and felt the cool, soft smoke enter deep into his lungs. He sat quietly, tracing small circles in the white powdery sand, watching a group of children building sand castles at the nearby water's edge.

The late afternoon sun shone directly overhead of the tropical, Caribbean shore. For the past three and a half weeks he had spent most of his time thinking, reading and relaxing. Rhonda McPherson had rejected him at the funeral service for her daughter. She somehow blamed Phillip for all that had happened to her family. It saddened him to think she felt that way but he accepted her remarks, knowing her grief was worse than his could ever be.

Phillip had spent a few days in London completing reports and visiting with Peter Alexander. He had just received word of his superior's progressive recovery. Peter had understood Phillip's trauma and had recognized his desire to resign before it was mentioned. It had been decided that Phillip would head up the South American sector of ISIS, working primarily out of Cartagena, with agents reporting to him. The last days of his vacation had been spent searching for a place to live and he was thankful to find a small, white stucco house with a waterfront view of the Caribbean ocean. The new-found security in his life would never compensate for the loss of the girl he had grown so fond of. He deeply treasured the moments they had spent together and locked them safely away in a secret chamber of his heart.

He exhaled the last bit of smoke from the cigarette and placed the filter deep in the sand. He decided to go for one last swim before heading back to his hotel where he had made arrangements to meet Lana Winters that evening for dinner. He knew she was not the kind of girl to be kept waiting. Phillip was thankful that Lana had been in Cartagena and had taken great interest in helping him select not only his new house but also furnishings for its interior. He enjoyed her company and it was evident that she enjoyed his. They had spent a great amount of time together in the last few days and were beginning to grow fond of each other's company. Somehow Lana had eased the pain in his heart and made him slowly realize how wonderful life could perhaps once again be. He looked forward to the future, centred around her, and felt she cared for him as well.

Phillip tiptoed along the hot sand and felt relief as the heated skin of his feet made contact with the cool, salty water. He dove head first into the ocean and swam briskly, finding sanctity in the exercise. He knew there would be happiness in this new-found life and smiled briefly. It was his first genuine smile in a very long time.